SURVEILLANCE

SURVEILLANCE

JONATHAN RABAN

Pantheon Books · New York

Pantheon Books and colophon are registered trademarks of Random House, Inc.

Originally published in Great Britain by Picador, an imprint of Pan Macmillan Ltd., London, in 2006.

Library of Congress Cataloging-in-Publication Data
Raban, Jonathan.
Surveillance / Jonathan Raban.
p. cm.
ISBN 978-0-375-42244-7
1. Seattle (Wash.)—Fiction. 2. Electronic surveillance—Fiction. I. Title.
PR6068.A22S87 2007
823'.914—dc22 2006050332

www.pantheonbooks.com
Printed in the United States of America
First American Edition
2 4 6 8 9 7 5 3 1

For Deborah Jacobs

In order that self-surveillance be fully assured, it must somehow be itself held under surveillance. Thus, there come into existence forms of *surveillance of surveillance* to which, for the sake of brevity, we shall give the exponential notation (surveillance)^2. We shall, moreover, set out the elements of a surveillance of surveillance of surveillance, in other words, of (surveillance)^3.

—Gaston Bachelard, *Applied Rationalism*
(translated by Mary McAllester Jones)

SURVEILLANCE

1

AFTER THE EXPLOSION, the driver of the overturned school bus stood beside the wreckage, his clothes in shreds. He was cupping his hands to his ears, as if to spare himself the noise of sirens, car alarms, bullhorns, whistles, and tumbling masonry. When he brought his hands away and held them in front of his face, both palms were dripping blood. His mouth opened wide in a scream that was lost in the surrounding din.

Beyond the bus, a tire dump had caught fire. Swirls and billows of black smoke, looking as thick and glossy as oil in the early morning sunshine, rose in a fast-climbing plume above the flames. The painted letters of the company sign, PACIFIC AUTO RECYCLING, swelled and popped in the heat.

A child was scrambling from a blown-out window on the bus—a towheaded boy of nine or ten, his face framing a disheveled grin. Half in, half out of the bus, he sat on the window's edge, gazing at the lurid inferno of burning tires and the screaming driver as if the catastrophic nature of the occasion quite eluded him.

Rescue workers came running—sexless toddlers in silver spacesuits— their giant feet slipping and sliding on the pulverized glass that coated the road inches deep like a freak hail-fall. Shards of glass were still dropping from the windows of buildings that had taken the full force of the blast.

The hollow *whoomph* of an exploding gas tank came from inside the auto-wrecking yard, followed by another a couple of seconds later. A spaceman with a machine gun shouted, "Keep down! Keep down!" at the rescue team, his voice muffled and distorted as he yelled through his respirator into a bullhorn. Bent low, stumbling through glass, they reached the bus, from which silvery tendrils of smoke or steam were now drifting skyward.

"Get *in* there! Get every live kid out of it, *now!*"

Silver-suited fatties clambered onto the axle casing, hoisted themselves atop the side of the yellow bus, and dropped inside through the windows. Two pairs of rescuers half carried, half hustled the grinning boy and the driver along the road, splashing through a small turbulent river that issued from a ruptured water main. The driver's head flopped against his chest, blood from his ears spattering what was left of his shirtfront.

A body in a torn tracksuit lay on its back in the path of the rescue party, her mouth and eyes open as if she'd been saying something important when sudden death interrupted. Dust, fine and pale as talcum powder, was settling on her face, as it settled on the parked cars and curbside dandelions, graying everything on which it fell.

The ground quaked to the sound of a bigger *whoomph* from the wrecking yard. The bus driver's head jerked upright from between the shoulders of his rescuers, and he let out a throaty, gargling howl. "Oh my Christ!" The word "Christ" was drawn out over several seconds, mingling in the air with the echoing rumble of the latest explosion.

"Not there! *There!* Get them on the Decon van! The Red *Cross* van, assholes. Move it! I said *move* it!"

"Go fuck yourself," said one of the rescuers from inside his hazmat hood, his voice audible only to the bus driver and, by a stretch, to his fellow rescuer. "Fucking National fucking Guard."

The stumbling trio broke into an ungainly trot, closely followed by the rescuers with the boy, like competitors in a three-legged race making the final dash for the tape.

THE TARRY CHEMICAL stink of the fire filled the Red Cross van taking them to the Decon tent at Harborview. The rear windows looked out on boiling flames and on the dense black overcast, rifted here and there by scraps of flawless blue, that now darkened the streets. In the fore-ground, a camo Humvee, spacemen with gurneys, running stick figures, splayed bodies, liberated papers seesawing in air, drifts of toxic dust, smoking heaps of bricks and torn Sheetrock.

The driver of the school bus, Tad, was trying to assign the name of a painter to the scene. Goya, maybe. Or Hieronymus Bosch. He tipped his head and jiggled his pinkie in his right ear to clear the canal of stage blood.

"How're you doing, kid?"

"Good."

"Better than school, huh?"

The boy's nose was squashed against the glass. The transfixed grin hadn't left his face since the moment when he'd first climbed out of the bus.

"You wait," Tad said. "You wait till you go through Decon. That's something else."

In Decon the boy would be stripped naked and hosed down before being admitted to the hospital. Tad had gone through it a couple of exercises ago. Never again: he'd written that into his contract. Today, as soon as the van reached Harborview, he'd be into his next part. After Bus Driver with Burst Eardrums came Psychotic Homeless Man Dis-rupting Work of Rescue Team, then Dying Amputee, Man Having Coronary, and—the one he seriously dreaded—Man Being Dug from Rubble.

Tad Zachary was one of the six professional stars of the show titled TOPOFF 27 by the Department of Homeland Security. Most victims were played by volunteers from government offices and by homeless people getting minimum wage and a free lunch. Tad and his fellow actors were scoring $1,000 of federal money apiece for their day's work. They were the ones who'd be filmed in close-up, their images beamed by satellite to the bunker in D.C. where the exercise was being monitored.

He needed the job. His last appearance on stage had been sixteen months ago, when he'd played Willy Loman in the ACT revival of *Death of a Salesman*. Since the downturn in the economy, one Seattle theater after another had gone dark, and Tad was scraping by on residuals, commercials, voiceovers, PSAs, vilely written parts in spec indie movies at $250 a throw, management-and-training films, the rare gig as MC at a corporate junket, and the interest on the proceeds of the sale of his mother's house in Portland. He had to remind himself most days that he was lucky: he had a strong local name and good connections. Even jobs in retail, the usual standby of the out-of-work actor, were in short supply now. His friend Gilda Hahn, who'd played opposite him as Linda Loman, had been on food stamps before she found her current role, working the midnight shift at a 7-Eleven on Denny Way.

For Tad the TOPOFFs were performances, but for the emergency services they were dress rehearsals: FEMA, the National Guard, the firefighters, police, ambulancemen, and civic officials were still plotting out their lines and moves, and still not getting it right. In TOPOFF 26, nearly every rescue worker had been contaminated, fatalities had vastly exceeded predictions, chains of command had broken down, hospitals overwhelmed. The reviews that came down from D.C. were so terrible, Tad had heard, that they were officially classified and never reached the press.

This one was the most realistic yet. A dirty bomb (two thousand pounds of ammonium sulfate, nitrate, and fuel oil, mixed up with fifty pounds of cesium-137 in powdered form) had gone off in a container supposedly holding "cotton apparel" from Indonesia, recently unloaded from a ship docked at Harbor Island. A fireworks expert (the same guy who directed the July Fourth display on Elliott Bay) created the terrific gunpowder explosion and the rockets laden with talc to simulate cesium. The tire fire had been set with gasoline, the broken glass supplied by volunteers standing on the roofs of neighboring buildings. At least the pictures beamed to the other Washington would look great.

A section of Route 99 had been closed for the exercise, which was happening in an area five city blocks square. Yet even in this micro version of nuclear horror, chaos was already breaking out all over, less than fifteen minutes since the bang. Judging by the fire trucks now homing in on it, and by the stream of silver suits running northward, the fire was out of control. Tad heard gunshots, which surely weren't called for in the script.

He hated working with amateurs. They never understood the fine line dividing real life from theater. They always overdid it. He hoped against hope that the exercise would be called off before he had to be dug out from the rubble.

The Red Cross driver had turned his whooping siren on. They were in regular traffic now, out of the exercise zone, speeding past a jam of diverted drivers on their way to work. This greatly excited the boy, who began to whoop in tune with the siren.

Tad hated working with children, too. "You're giving me a headache, kid. What's your name, anyway?"

"Taylor."

"Taylor, I'll give you a buck if you chill out and shut up till we get to the hospital, okay?"

"Done deal," Taylor said. He looked and spoke like one of those kids whose parents dragged them from audition to audition. Too cute by half, and then some.

Tad dug into the back pocket of his pants, removed his billfold, and peeled off a dollar that the boy took without thanks. Professional curiosity made him ask, "You getting paid for this, Taylor? Or are you a volunteer?"

"Fifty bucks," the boy said with a smirk. "I was a Munchkin in *The Wizard of Oz* at the Fifth Avenue Theatre. And I was in *The Nutcracker* at the Opera House. How 'bout you?"

"If you're getting paid, kiddo, if you think you're an actor, you better learn to wipe that stupid grin off your face. This is a pro speaking. You're a casualty. You're probably going to be dead of radiation sickness in a week. Think of your parents. Think of the funeral. You're one unlucky kid, Taylor. You in Little League?"

"Yes."

"Well, think about this. You're never, ever going to play another game. You understand that? You're history."

The grin was at last beginning to come unstuck.

"If you're going to act, act good. Act real. Let me tell you something about the way you played that kid climbing out of my bus: it stank. Every other kid was dead, and you looked like it was Christmas and Santa had just popped out of the chimney. Next time you've got to *be* the character, right?"

"Right." A chastened mumble.

Tad laid his arm across Taylor's shoulder. "Just some friendly advice from an old actor. What are you next?"

"I got a dead mom. She's lying in the road, blown out of our car on the way to school."

"So you're in white shock. It's too early for grieving. You're a disoriented zombie. A shivering blank. And after Decon, you will be shivering. Think about it, Taylor. Learn to *act*."

At Harborview, the boy joined the cheerful line of people queuing at the entrance to the Decon tent: evidently no one had warned them of the intimate humiliations that lay in store. The car with City of Seattle plates and "ZACHARY" posted in the window was waiting to drive him to his next engagement. A change of shirt and trousers was on the backseat, along with a woolen balaclava helmet and his makeup-sponge bag. Before he climbed in he turned and called, "Hey, Taylor! Taylor! Break a leg, kid!"

LUCY BENGSTROM was in luck that morning. The bomb-scare shenanigans going on downtown had freed the suburbs from their usual swarm of officious security types. On the dot of 7:30, aiming to catch the 9:30 ferry from Mukilteo to Whidbey Island, she'd parked her daughter, Alida, in the Early Birds program at her school on Capitol Hill. As it turned out, the drive to Mukilteo was a breeze: no soldiers manning the checkpoint on I-5, and the search of her car at the ferry terminal was merely a command to flip the trunk and an incurious glance inside. She was waved onto the 8:30 boat with nearly ten minutes to spare.

Earliness made her feel she'd won a surprise vacation as she got coffee from the machine in the passenger lounge and took it out onto the stern deck. It was holiday weather. For the entire last week of March, the temperature had been up in the eighties, and today, April 2, they were saying on the radio that it would likely pass ninety. To be wearing a dress that she'd bought for summer in Hawaii on a spring day in the Pacific Northwest was an oddity to add to all the other oddities of life in the last year or so: they steadily accumulated, like snowfall—another thing that wasn't happening the way it used to.

Water boiled in the dock and the ferry pulled slowly away from the ramp. Sipping at the tepid espresso, Lucy felt properly afloat again, at last.

The call from *GQ* had come in the nick of time—the first assignment in many months that she could really sink her teeth into. Back in the nineties, when East Coast editors thought of the Pacific Northwest as the new big thing, Lucy was offered far more work than she could possibly take on, but since then the region had lost much of its sexiness and the dateline "*Seattle*" was beginning to look like déjà vu all over again. The old-new public library, the international toast of 2004, had long slipped into yesterday-land, though a recent string of gruesome serial murders, recalling Ted Bundy's exploits and the Green River killings, had briefly jolted Seattle back into the news. Lately, she'd been scratching a living out of travel pieces—short trips with Alida in tow, during school breaks—and wry reports from the deep sticks for "Talk of the Town" in *The New Yorker*. She called editors nowadays, and sometimes her calls were returned.

Before the *GQ* editor phoned, she hadn't known that August Vanags lived in her territory, though she knew of his book, of course. Impossible to miss its long bestsellerdom, or the bidding war between DreamWorks/Paramount and Miramax for movie rights; Spielberg had won, if that was the word, and paid gazillions. She'd gone straight out to buy *Boy 381,* the title superimposed on a creased and grainy black-and-white snapshot of a starveling boy standing against a forbidding barbed-wire fence. Leery of its blockbuster success, she'd begun to read, expecting to find it not half as good as it was cracked up to be.

But she was swept away, almost from the first page. It was amazing that this memoir of an orphaned child caught up in the worst barbarities of World War II could be so light, sweet-tempered, brave, and funny. From his terrible boyhood spent among the displaced and terrorized people of Central Europe, overrun now by Hitler's armies, now by Stalin's, Vanags had somehow conjured a magical, inspiring book. It was as if Huck Finn had been set adrift in this refugee world of trains, and labor camps, and trudging columns of shocked, exhausted men and women trying to escape. Like Huck's, the boy's voice was clear and true. He was all eyes and ears. Faced with atrocity, he described what he saw in terms that were heartbreakingly simple and exact. Only a child could have such resilience—could have made for himself out of such wretched material a life of boyish mischief and boyish happiness. At the end, when the young Vanags was rescued in Germany by the gruff American sergeant Philip Cahan, Lucy, who never wept over books, found her eyes prickling with tears.

The guy from *GQ* had said that Vanags was as obstinately reclusive as Salinger: since the book first started showing up on the bestseller lists, he'd declined all interviews and refused to budge from his island. "It's a unicorn hunt," he'd concluded, but he somehow had got hold of Vanags' phone number. He offered $4,000 for preliminary research, and $25,000 if Lucy could talk this reticent hermit into an in-depth interview-profile. "You're good at that stuff. Like you got Bill Gates . . . that was a great piece. I don't know what's with Vanags. It could be he's just shy, but he was a history prof before this book happened, so a ton of people at the University of Washington must see him. Maybe it's an academic thing: you know, this *disdain* for journalists."

Biding her time, Lucy had set about researching Vanags in the public library. She read his only other published book, a dry study of the Yalta treaty with the misleadingly catchpenny title of *The Treacherous Pact*. She tracked down articles he'd written for history journals—more dry stuff, with titles like "The Sovietization of Higher Education in Poland, 1951–1963." In the 1970s, he wrote, rather less dryly, about the

II

Cold War for *Foreign Policy* and *Foreign Affairs*, but she could make no connection at all between the footnote-happy historian and the author of *Boy 381*. August Vanags—associate professor of history, University of Washington, as he was billed at the foot of even his most recent articles, published in the mid-1990s, so apparently they never made him a full professor—seemed no more likely to pen this dazzling memoir than he was to sprout wings and fly.

She tried to hunt him down in books—about the war on the eastern front, the camps, the postwar refugees. She Googled "Lebensborn," for at age six Vanags had been plucked from a Polish transit camp on the strength of his blue eyes and fair hair and taken to a castle in Bavaria to be Nazified. Since the boy didn't know whether he was German, Lithuanian, Latvian, Polish, Estonian, Ukranian, or even, possibly, Jewish, he was glad of any nationality he could get. "I thought that being German meant that I'd be given a uniform with silver buttons and as much *bratwurst* as I could eat," Vanags wrote. The German family to whom he was given for adoption sent him back after a month because, the boy thought, "I ate too much sausage"—the sausages in question being stolen from the butcher's next door. Soon he was back on another train, bound for Poland and the children's camp at Dzierzazna. Being six, he thought that being on a train, any train, was ample compensation for having lost yet another set of parents.

He knew he was called August and had taken the Latvian name Vanags as a flag of convenience. It authenticated him as a gentile and gave him a native land. A lucky choice, for Latvian-American voluntary organizations took care of him when the war at last came to an end.

Tad, who lived across the hall from Lucy and Alida, was at supper one evening when he saw the library copy of *The Treacherous Pact* and said, "I took a class with him at U Dub." He remembered Vanags, dimly, as a "little guy" and a "tightass." The one thing that set him apart from the rest of the faculty crowd was that he'd been a hawk on Vietnam, and Tad's class of '69 had written him off as a stooge for LBJ and McNamara. All Tad said on hearing that Lucy hoped to seduce Vanags into being interviewed was "Sooner you than me."

Lucy loved to lose herself in other people's worlds. It was what she

did best, being a chameleon, taking on the color of new and strange surroundings until she could write about them as if they were her natural
home. The more alien the world, the happier she was, feeling her way
around inside it as a novice and a nobody. Just as she'd plunged into the
Seattle rock scene for the profile of Kurt Cobain (last speaking to him
three days before his death), into the Microsoft campus, into Colonel
"Bo" Gritz's white-supremacist compound in Idaho, into Jeff Bezos'
online bookselling empire, so now she became an enthralled tourist in
the exotic foreign country of World War II, where wild children
roamed over the landscape like packs of rats.

Their faces were pale green with malnutrition. They ate acorns.
They robbed dead bodies. They preyed on old people, snatching food
from fingers too weak to hold on to the precious mildewed crust. They
held make-believe executions. They pelted through the streets on rick-
ety legs, arms outstretched, pretending to be low-flying bombers. They
were adept and fantastic liars. Telling lies was their best hope of staying
alive, and they lied to everybody, about everything. As Vanags wrote, "I
knew that if ever I were caught telling the truth, I'd be sent to the
camps."

Lucy followed these small, wizened-featured survivors across the
map of Europe, tracing their wanderings in the old school atlas that
used to be hers and was now Alida's, running her finger from Tallinn to
Riga, Vilnius, Grodno, Bialystok, Warsaw, Lodz, Poznan. From history
books she pieced together the tidal surges of the Soviet and Nazi
armies as they swept east and west across the continent, leaving cities
in shock and ruin. She could rattle off the names of the generals—
Falkenhorst and Timoshenko, Manstein and Vatutin, Schoerner and
Zhukov. She wanted to see the big picture, but the foreground details
kept intruding: Hitler and Stalin, wrecking nations, paled beside the
image of a boy and two girls hiding in the shell of a bombed-out house,
gratefully feeding on the remains of a cat.

At last she was ready to make the call. She took a diazepam so that
she wouldn't stutter on the phone, waited for half an hour for the pill to
kick in, and rang Vanags at the unlisted number *GQ* had given her. The
answering voice sounded too young and accentless to be him. His son

perhaps, or his partner. She asked whether Professor August Vanags was there.

"Speaking."

Surprised, Lucy momentarily stumbled on the "c" in "inconvenient," then recovered and rushed into her pitch. *Talk history!* was the note she'd scribbled to herself and ringed with a braided doodle on the top of a fresh page of her spiral-bound notebook. She talked history, not mentioning the magazine, careful to say she was a "writer" (not "journalist"), and showed off her seven-day expertise on the displaced children of Europe. She had to engineer a meeting before she could own up to what she really wanted.

He took the bait. Below *Talk history!* she wrote down the instructions for getting to his island house. Putting down the phone, she felt half triumphant and half ashamed—not for deceiving Vanags, but for catching him so easily.

THE FERRY was halfway across the passage when Lucy saw smoke dirtying the sky to the far south. At first she thought it was another forest fire—they'd begun in March this year—but the slowly twisting plume looked too dark, too dense and liquid to come from burning trees. It took her a moment to figure that it must be coming from the city, twenty-five miles away at least. Instinctively she rummaged through the junk in her bag for the cell phone to call Alida's school, then stopped herself. Being a neurotic mom, she needed all her reserves of self-control not to act like a neurotic mom.

It would be part of the exercise, of course. She hated these TOP-OFF things, their brazen and officious theatricality. Only a week ago she'd seen Omaha come under attack on CNN—a crop duster had sprayed the business district with ricin and killed five thousand imaginary people. The traveling horror show paid regular visits to Seattle, where the scenario was always the same: a shipping container, a bomb, panic in the streets, and the mad orchestra of ambulance, police, and fire sirens.

Alida, home from school with flu during the last TOPOFF, had come to Lucy's desk in the big kitchen/dining/living room in her night-clothes, pale and shivery, her clammy forehead hot to the hand. "It's not real, is it?"

"No, sweetheart, it's not real. It's just an exercise."

But, of course, it was real. The administration was in the business of manufacturing fear and methodically spreading its infection from city to city. The lengths they went to—setting fires, showing make-believe corpses to the cameras—surely went far beyond what was needed to test the emergency services. How could you explain to a child that "homeland security" meant keeping the homeland in a state of contin-uous insecurity? Furious, lost for words, Lucy had packed Alida back under the covers, set her up with *Guinness World Records,* Helen Keller's *The Story of My Life,* and another dose of Tylenol, then had brought her own work to the bedroom, where she sat at the desk that was already too small for Alida, trying to rid her head of the yammering sirens.

"Measures," they called them, but incremental nuisances was how Lucy saw them—the spreading rash of concrete barriers, barbed wire, magnetometers, spycams, nondescript gray boxes that were supposed to sniff out airborne pathogens. Over the last twelve months, these measures had been multiplying at speed. Lately they'd started mount-ing roadblocks on interstates. Next up, as the result of an act rushed through Congress, was the hassle of the biometric National ID card, deadline September for Washington state. The measures had driven a wedge between Lucy and Tad. To him they meant "fascism," a word he used with a maddening carelessness; to her they were just signs of how jumpy and rattled this administration had grown since the attacks, per-haps for good reason. As far as she was concerned, the worst thing they'd done was to turn dinner with Tad into a conversational mine-field. One evening last week, they'd found themselves staring daggers at each other across the table over the remains of the wine: "You're being blind," Tad had said. "You're being obsessional," she'd answered. Their six-year friendship was in peril because of the fucking measures.

This morning, the smoke over Seattle was taking the shape of an enormous many-petaled flower, like a wilting black hydrangea growing on a stalk from behind the green hills and unruffled sea. Fascinated in spite of herself, Lucy watched it grow until the raspy male voice came over the PA system, ordering passengers down to their cars.

Waiting for her turn to drive off, she switched on the radio. The morning show on the local NPR station was about salmon recovery, with a guy who'd written the book on it—so nothing too bad could have happened in Seattle if they were deep in a discussion about preserving spawning habitat. On Classic King FM she got a discordant flurry of horns, drums, and trumpets. Stravinsky, she guessed first, then changed her bet to Mahler.

Two lanky National Guardsmen, with machine guns on shoulder straps, stood by the ramp, eyes glazed, faces limp with boredom in the gathering heat. Their armored Humvee, parked at an angle beyond them, had a livelier expression, with its pig-eyed headlights and bared-teeth radiator grille. Humvees were everywhere now, lurking in downtown alleys, snarling at drivers from the median strips on freeways; they seemed to Lucy to possess the worst possible combination of maximal testosterone and minimal IQ. She veered wide left past this one, as if it might spring to life and bite.

Her holiday mood was gone. In a bid to recapture it, she pulled over at a strip mall to drop the top of the car. Madly impractical in every other way, the Spider could still lift Lucy's spirits with its collapsing roof. Exactly nine months older than Alida, and with 123,000 miles on the clock, it was dear to her because she'd had to battle to hang on to it. There'd been two close encounters with repo men when she'd fallen behind in her payments. Her mother, seeing it for the first time, had let out the tragic shriek for which she'd been famous in Miles City. "Jesus God Almighty, Lucy, are you *totally* insane?" Then she'd begun to weep. Her mother meant the baby, of course, but it was the car that gave her the cue to reprise the role of Hedda Gabler, or was it Lady Macbeth?

In Alida's early days, a single package of disposable diapers had filled the Spider's trunk to capacity and beyond. At pick up time at school, parked in the fleet of minivans and SUVs, the green car drew meaningful looks from the parental crowd. It denoted Lucy's singleness, selfishness, and general irresponsibility. Faced with the world's disapproval, she'd grown more and more protective of the car, feeding it premium-grade gas, observing its service intervals as punctually as she did Alida's medical and dental checkups, taking it to the body shop for cosmetic surgery whenever it got a scrape or ding. Usually careless of possessions, Lucy had the superstitious conviction that if she let the car go, the rest of her precarious life would go the way of the Spider, to rust and ruin.

It was in the car that she'd had her best conversations with Alida: strapped into their red leather bucket seats, both looking ahead, not catching each other's eyes, they talked as they never did at home. On the run back from school, Alida would keep Lucy abreast of the cruel snakes-and-ladders game of sixth-grade friendships in a breathless stream of gossip, like a confiding sister. But the moment she stepped out of the Spider the talk stopped, mid-sentence, and she put on her new face, drawing the shutters and hanging out the "Closed" sign. So in the last few weeks Lucy had been taking ever more roundabout and eccentric routes through the city, trying to stay in touch with her disappearing daughter.

She loved to drive. She'd had her first lesson at eleven in her father's white Jeep with government plates, dodging clumps of sagebrush on a stretch of open rangeland. "We won't tell Mom," he said, as Lucy, rapt, heart in mouth, hardly daring to breathe, piloted the Jeep in figure eights across the sun-baked gumbo clay. Driving was the nearest she could imagine to doing magic, and being sworn to secrecy doubled its enchantment. All that summer, driving figured thrillingly in her dreams, and by fall she was doing it by instinct, rattling lickety-split over the prairie with her dad in the passenger seat, even though she needed two fat cushions to see over the hood. Thirty-eight years on, she still hadn't quite managed to entirely part company with that child, bursting with pride and excitement at being behind the wheel. Reading *The Wind in the Willows* to Alida, Lucy felt a certain rueful kinship to Mr. Toad.

So now, accelerating away from the strip mall, she went from first to fifth without putting her foot on the clutch, flipping the stick to neutral and judging the revs by ear for the moment to shift up—a silly trick, and not one she did often, but it made her smile to get it right. The music on the radio was lost to wind, tire rumble, and the growl of the exhaust. The dashboard clock said 9:14, and she wasn't due to show up at August Vanags' place until sometime after 10:30.

The road, barred with the regular shadows of plantation firs, was temptingly free of traffic. Speeding through inky greenery, the sun falling in bolts of white light between the trees, she was already on the lookout for the Useless Bay turnoff when, heeling-and-toeing around a wide bend, she nearly plowed into the backside of a silver sedan going so slowly that it barely seemed to be moving at all. As she braked, the sound of woodwind and strings came up around her in lush, bass-heavy stereo. So far as she could see, the next stretch of road was all bends. Turning on the emergency flashers to warn anyone coming up behind them, she settled behind the silver car, keeping her distance, with an anxious eye on the rearview mirror. The Spider and the sedan crept along in consort, a two-car funeral procession, winding through the woods at a stately twenty mph. Lucy craned her head to the side, looking for a chance to pass these geriatric sightseers, or whatever they were. No such luck. A short straightaway opened up ahead but was immediately occupied by an oncoming car. The music kept her guessing: now sweet, now angry, now like an old-time romantic waltz, now like all-out war, and never the same thing for more than seconds at a time. She'd heard it before but couldn't place it, though she was still betting, at longish odds, on Mahler.

They were climbing a hill, its crest a liquid mirage-shimmer in the sun, when the accident happened—or, rather, when various bits of the accident presented themselves to Lucy, out of order.

She heard the crash as a musical explosion of drums and cymbals on the radio before she saw the car ahead wander across the yellow median line into the wrong lane, and the grinning, chrome-encrusted snout of the semi rise from the brow of the hill to meet it. The silver car gave itself a preliminary shake, then leaped, salmonlike, toward the sky. Lucy was momentarily dazzled by this living miracle—framed by the spiky blackness of the fir treetops, the marvelous car sailing scot-free through the blue. It caught the sun, a blinding wink of light. And here, suddenly up close, came the semi's snout, which had lost its grin, the driver's face looming behind glass way above her, his mouth a wide, astonished "o."

Her foot did her thinking for her, stamping hard down on the gas pedal as she raced through the narrowing gap between the slab-sided trailer and the ditch. From behind her, she heard what sounded like a large chest of drawers tumbling down a flight of stone steps, the jarring *whoosh* of jake brakes, and then the pretty simpering of violins. She brought the Spider to a stop in the grass at the top of the hill. The clock on the dash said 9:21.

Walking back to where the semi was slewed diagonally across the road, she felt lacking in reality, more air than flesh. The Christmassy scent of pine needles mixed with the sinus-stinging reek of gasoline and brake dust. Squeezing around the front of the truck, she saw that its entire face had gone, exposing a welter of naked machinery. Ahead of her, a man stood in the middle of the road, open hand raised above his head, impersonating a traffic cop.

"Stop!" he called, in a voice of tiresome masculine authority. "It could go up at any moment."

A woman stood behind him, yelling into a cell phone. A man in blue-jean overalls sat on the tarmac, holding his head in his hands. Then Lucy saw the silver car, nose down in the ditch, and for a second she thought the magic trick had really worked, for it looked showroom new, the name "Infiniti" spelled out in relief lettering on the trunk. But beyond its immaculately waxed hindquarters, it stopped being a car and turned into a puzzle of scrambled components. A wheel was where a window ought to be, the engine block stuck out through the crumpled tinfoil of the roof, and a wedge-shaped flange, hanging at an odd angle from the front of the mess, resolved itself into the mutilated remains of a door. From inside the woods came the keening *fee-bee, fee-bee* of a chickadee.

A man in navy sweats jogged up the centerline of the road from one of the several cars now drawn up on the shoulder. The traffic-cop guy turned on him and shouted "Stop!"

There was a brief standoff between these two alpha take-control types, then the man in sweats, addressing Lucy, said, "I'm trained in CPR," and walked over to the ruins of the Infiniti. She saw him staring at the wreckage, trying to figure it out like a brainteaser. He got down on his knees, thrust his head inside a jagged hole, then pulled it out and vomited. He came groggily away, head slowly wagging, face squinched, smelling of puke, yellow speckles of it on his T-shirt.

Then everyone, including the man in overalls and the woman who'd been talking on her cell phone, stared at Lucy. Feeling unreasonably accused, she realized she was the only person in this impromptu circle who had no visible role: she wasn't the truck driver, hadn't dialed 911, wasn't conducting nonexistent traffic, and wasn't trained in CPR.

"I am an eye . . ." She meant to say "witness" but saw the ever-tricky "w" coming, and swerved to avoid it. "I saw it happen. I was . . ." As she spoke, she found her notebook in her hand. It had been on the passenger seat. She had no memory of picking it up when she left the car.

"Ah," the traffic-cop guy said. "You're the Dodge. Blue pickup."

"No, I'm the . . ." She pointed past the truck, but saw that the Spider was hidden behind the brow of the hill. "Green convertible."

"So where's the Dodge?"

"I didn't see a Dodge."

"There was a Dodge." There was a totally unnecessary note of exasperation in his voice. "It was making a right. The Infiniti was trying to pass."

Lucy now saw that beyond the faceless truck was a muddy, fir-enshrouded driveway or logging road that she must have walked past without noticing. Of course the accident would make more sense if—

The man who'd been sick said, "Two people. I think it's only two. First, when I looked, I thought there was a kid in there as well, but . . ."

Her memory of the crash seemed already old, like a photograph from another summer. She inspected it. There was no pickup in the picture—just a car drifting across the yellow line and the semi materializing over the crest to join it, in a moment of freakish mechanical ballet. It was a pas de deux, with no one else on stage. But that couldn't be right. Somehow, somewhere, she'd mislaid the essential third vehicle.

Her search was interrupted by the noise of whooping sirens, like the horns and trumpets of a few minutes before, and what had begun as a weirdly intimate and shameful scene suddenly became a lavish public happening, like a county fair, with two fire trucks, three squad cars, an ambulance, and two tow trucks with cranes. Men and women in uniform, many of them armed, were filling the road, and the annoying man who'd been playing cop was now taking charge of the real police.

When Lucy's turn to be spoken to arrived, the young cop suggested that she sit with him in the car, where police voices boomed importantly from the radio. Deaf to the cacophony of his job, he turned the volume down only when Lucy, shouting, begged him to. The overheated car smelled of sweat and trouble.

As soon as he had hold of her driver's license, the cop was first-naming her, in a soothing parental manner that went badly with his acne. His high-schooler's face was blotted all over with little pink crusts of dried calamine.

"You a reporter, Lucy?"

"No. I mean not exactly. I just . . ." The notebook required an explanation, but she couldn't for the life of her begin to provide one.

The cop wrote on his own pad in slow-forming irregular block capitals. Lucy saw the trouble he was having with BENGSTROM, and spelled it out for him.

"So tell me what you saw, Lucy. In your own words."

Whose else? There was little enough to tell, but she found herself skirting cautiously around the magic of the flying car as if she had something serious to hide, and wondered if the boy cop was smart enough to notice. Distracted by the sound of her own voice, coming back to her a fraction of a second out of sync, as if on a bad long-distance line, she jammed on the word "median."

"That's okay, Lucy. Take your time."

People always said that, and it always made her stutter worse. Her head jerked sideways. Chin locked against her shoulder, she fought through the block to get the word out.

The boy showed his embarrassment by gazing through the windshield as if he'd spotted a bank holdup somewhere in the middle distance. Without looking at her, he said, "Relax, Lucy."

And fuck you, she thought, *you pompous asshole.* The flare of anger released the word from its trap.

"Median," she said. "The truck was swinging right across it like a closing gate. I just floored the gas pedal and squeaked through. When I looked back, the truck was sprawled over the entire road like it is now . . . but everything sort of happened in the same instant—it was all like, simultaneous, you know?"

She'd lost him. But he continued to blacken the page with twiggy, runelike lettering, his lips moving slightly as he wrote. "Erratic," he said suddenly: "You'd say they were driving erratic?"

"No, just very slowly. Like I said, twenty to twenty-five. I was crawling behind in second gear, looking for a chance to pass. So when I put my foot down . . ." She stopped, thinking it foolish to explain how lucky she was to have had the surge of acceleration that had carried her clear of the truck, with the tachometer needle going deep into the red zone.

An older officer, who'd been with the ambulance team, came over to the squad car and the boy stepped out. The two talked in ceremoniously low voices, and when the boy came back his face looked physically bigger, enlarged by the weight of the grave news that had been entrusted to him. He looked years too young for his holstered gun.

Lucy spoke to him as she would to Alida. "I know. They couldn't possibly have been alive. There almost certainly wasn't time for them to feel anything." She nearly put her hand on his sleeve to comfort him.

"I didn't see it say nothing on your driver's license about 'doctor,' Lucy."

Oh, dear. She'd affronted his precious dignity. She felt the muscles in her cheeks spring taut at the rebuff.

"We better get back to what you seen. Like you haven't said nothing about the pickup—blue Dodge, right?"

"I didn't see it." But as soon as she spoke, memory leaped to contradict, as an image, washed out in color, not quite in focus, came to mind, of a big, mud-spattered pickup with a dented tailgate. But it wasn't blue. More a sort of rusty orange. Was that it? Why could she not remember what other people had clearly seen? "I mean, I'm not sure . . ."

"That logging road dead-ends. We'll be checking it out."

The orange pickup, surely it was parked at the strip mall where she'd put down the top. That was where she'd seen it. Yet even as she realized its untruthfulness, memory was busy again, slotting the orange truck into the vacant space in the puzzle. She seemed to see it braking to make a sudden unsignaled right, and the Infiniti swerving left to avoid it, heading straight into the path of the rising semi.

"I don't know." Orange was turning into blue as treacherous memory got all its ducks in a row. "I'm sorry, I'm blanking out. If I could think it through for a minute or two, I'm sure—"

"It don't much matter. We got other witnesses."

He meant better, more trustworthy ones, not tiresome flakes like her.

"That address on your license? It's still current?"

Grateful for a question that had a certain answer, she said, "Yes, it's current."

"Phone number?"

She gave it to him.

"We'll get back to you if we need to. Where you headed?"

"Useless Bay."

"You think you're safe to drive, Lucy?"

"Yes, I'll be fine."

"I could get an officer to run you over there, it's just a couple miles. I could drive the Alfa."

"No thanks. Honestly, I'm okay."

She was totally not okay. When the boy insisted on seeing her to the car, she found herself walking like a drunk, with laborious concentration on each clumsy step, fooling the cop into letting her go.

"What year is it?"

For a moment, she took this as a trick question, meant to test her mental state, then it registered. "Oh, the car." But when she named the date, the boy's only response was an indifferent grunt.

As she seated herself behind the wheel, the boy stood beside her, hand on the door, watching—or was he just interested in the car? Luckily, she'd left the key in the ignition. Thinking painfully hard about each move, she let in the clutch, shifted the gearstick into neutral, and turned on the engine. She flinched at the sudden sound of the DJ's voice, loud enough to scare birds from the trees, saying, in a tranquilized, affectless drawl, "We've just been listening to Symphony Number 7 by Gustav Mahler, played by the Cleveland Orchestra under the direction of Christoph—"

She switched him off, distractedly thinking that at least she'd got Mahler right.

The boy was still there, his hand a few inches from her left wrist. His fingernails could do with a trim. She tried smiling at him to show what fine shape she was in to drive, but she botched the job and felt the smile coming out as a lewd stripper's wink. The boy's face stiffened into the mask of surly toughness they must have taught him in cop school. "You better drive safe now." A threat, not a well-wishing.

But she seemed to have forgotten how. The tight steering, usually a pleasure, was her enemy, as she kept overcorrecting, making the car wobble down the road, nose twitching from side to side like a prairie dog's. Driving by eye, not instinct, she crawled past the stalled traffic that had backed up from the scene of the crash and felt the eyes of every driver on her, as if the whole character of the morning catastrophe were written on her face and in her lousy driving. She risked a glance at the rearview, half expecting to find the boy cop haring after her on foot, but saw only the red, white, and blue flashes of the emergency vehicles putting on their untimely light show against the dark firs.

Then more police, putting out signs and turning cars around. She crept past them fearfully, trying to hide her incompetence as they waved her through. She wanted to apologize for the Spider—its ridiculous air of summer fun, like a dancing clown at a funeral.

At the Useless Bay turnoff, waiting to make a left, Lucy realized with a nauseous jolt that she'd seen the people who'd been killed on the ferry, an older couple, big-city tourist types, overdressed for the casual

Pacific Northwest. She'd spotted them first in the lounge—the tall man in a cashmere blazer, the woman with a suede pigskin jacket draped over her shoulders, her hair scraped back from her face and tied behind with a pink silk scarf. Later, in the crush of people going down the stairs to the car deck, the man had held the door open for Lucy; she'd thanked him, and they smiled at her with the perfectly synchronous smile of the long married. She'd warmed to them in that moment, envying them their vacation. Their silver car was parked a few spaces behind the Spider. They must have gone past her while she was taking down the top.

The road was clear. As she crossed, a rush of details came back to her: his gray hair, rather coarse and oily, swept in breaking waves behind his ears; the links of a gold chain against the white of her blouse; a whiff of male cologne; his uxorious stoop as he bent to listen to something she was saying when they were standing by the window in the lounge; her petite boniness and cautious walk, as if she were getting used to a replacement hip. *Her voice*: on the car deck, Lucy had heard her call across the Infiniti, from the driver's side, "It's already open, hon." So she must have been driving . . .

She told herself that she was connected to these dead strangers by one random, polite smile, nothing more. It was 10:14, she had a job to do: she must evict the couple from her head, at least for now.

Two horses, a mare and a foal, stood by the barbed-wire fence of an overgrown paddock. *Think horses,* Lucy instructed herself as she stopped the car, *think Montana.* The piebald mare stared at her with an expression of vacant solemnity and lifted her tail to drop a turd. The foal, Lucy guessed, was two months old, still a little shaky on his pins— a rich chestnut, except for the white circles around his eyes and an irregular flash on his forehead like a question mark or a scythe. She inhaled the sane smell of horse and cut grass as the foal held her gaze with his comical bespectacled eyes. The bald pink skin around his mouth and nose made him look almost human in his infancy. He swung his big head to his mother's teat and suckled for a few seconds, then, refreshed, turned his attention back to Lucy, his face full of candid foalish curiosity about this new oddity in his young life.

She put the car in gear and drove off, slowly, but without the shakes, feeling more or less restored. She was fully aware of the dead couple, but had managed to put them on hold, where they'd stay until she had time to take their call. So long as she could live in the moment, she'd be okay. Later, she'd get back to them—would feel sorrow for them, if she could. But not yet, not now. Accelerating cautiously through a bend, catching the sudden seaside tang of salt, mud, and tide wrack, she was securely back in the driver's seat, in control again.

She knew the route. Years ago she'd spent a weekend at the Owens' tiny cottage on Useless Bay. Alida was still in diapers then. It had been like vacationing inside a Ralph Lauren catalog—wood furniture scraped bare, cabin trunks, cushions, antique fishing stuff hanging on the walls. Not really her thing at all, but Alida had loved it.

Turning right on Sunlight Beach Road, she was shocked by the view. What she remembered as a long row of weatherbeaten shacks, each with its narrow, sandy, crab-trap-littered lawn and scrap of beachfront, was now an architectural freak show. One or two cottages were still left, but not the Owens'—which must have stood somewhere inside the pink-brick French château that looked as if it had escaped from a wine-bottle label. Lucy remembered them telling her they'd sold the place to a Microsoft VP before moving to Denver, but he must've bought at least three other lots in order to build that pile. Beside it, a surviving cottage had lost all its funky chic and now looked like a derelict privy. Beyond the château stood a gross chromium and glass affair, partly enclosed in tubular pipes, with goggling circular windows like the eyes of a giant science-fiction beetle. Then another forlorn cottage, then an adobe Spanish mission. And so it went. The late-1990s rich had taken over Useless Bay since Lucy had last been here, and their weekend mansions made their presence look like some famous imperial conquest— but this empire was already fading, with half the buildings up for sale and finding no takers, to judge by real estate agents' signs that winter gales had blown askew and gulls were whiting out with guano.

She'd written the number of the Vanags place on a Post-It gummed to the dash—and here it was, *2041,* in huge bronze figures on a rough-cut granite boulder, as if the house were a condo block, though it was actually smaller and less pretentious than its neighbors: a white clapboard New England colonial farmhouse with green shutters flanking the windows, a spread of fresh gravel out front, and a three-car garage.

Between 2041 and the Alpine ski lodge at 2049, Lucy saw a blinding sliver of sea, or sand, or shining mud: she wasn't sure which because there was so little of it. The new houses, built out to the last inch of their lots so as to grab the widest sea view possible, were practically joined at the hip, like folk dancers in national costumes doing a sort of Franco-Italian-Hispanic-American-Swiss reel. She willed herself to keep thinking like this as she fought off the lurking image of the car balled up like aluminum foil, and the broken people inside.

Tilting the rearview down, she half expected to find a madwoman reflected in the mirror, but the face that looked back was almost indecently normal; its hair in knots from the wind, color in its cheeks, the face reflected nothing at all of what it had seen.

She set the parking brake, did what little she could with the hairbrush from her bag, and went paddling uncomfortably through Vanags' gravel, which wasn't designed to be walked on in flip-flops. She'd already rung the bell when she realized her notebook was still in the car.

2

"Don't you just love him?" Alida asked her friend Gail as they walked from Math to Spanish. "He's so-o-o *über*-cute."

They were discussing the new boyfriend of their favorite girl singer, Jessica King, who'd broken up with Dustin Kavanagh and was now going out with Steve Kunz, drummer for the goth band Deadly Nightshade. It was all over the news.

"Cute? You really think he's *cute?*"

"He's got tattoos all over his arms, and he paints his fingernails bright purple. Isn't that like the essence of cute?" Alida was still experimenting with irony. Saying the opposite of what you meant was cool when it worked, but she had to put a lot of labor into keeping it going, and often, like right now, people just didn't get it. She supposed being ironical was like learning to ski—you had to fall, clumsily and often, before you got the hang of it.

Gail squinched her face in disgust. "I think he's . . . well, like kind of gross."

"He's the grossest," Alida said, glad to get back to the plain talking. "That weirdo beard."

"The lip ring. Yuck."

"He's really old."

"His nose is way too big."

"I don't know what she sees in him. I mean, after Dustin."

"It must be something we don't know about. Maybe it's like he really loves her and wants to make her happy, you know?"

But Alida was too distracted to care much about Jessica's happiness. In Math, she'd found two new pimples welling up beneath the skin of her forehead, just below her hairline. The last Social Studies project was "The Making of Mountains," about continental plates colliding, crumpling, and erupting over hot plumes and mantles beneath the earth's surface. Something similar was happening inside Alida, with volcano-pimples like Rainier and St. Helens. For the last three nights she'd gone to sleep with her entire face slathered in Clearasil—she'd gotten halfway through the tube already, and her pillowcase was stiff with it—but the zits were back on the attack.

Too much other stuff was going on, too. Lately, she'd taken to hunting out the biggest, baggiest T-shirts she could find, to hide what was taking place on her chest. Breasts she could live with, but the fatty pudges that were starting to bulge down there were an embarrassment, and Gail's chest was still lean as a boy's. In the Adult XL Maui T-shirt that she'd borrowed from her mom, Alida, shoulders hunched, shrank from the intrusive gaze of strangers—she didn't even want her mom to see. She was growing out her bangs. Soon she'd be able to hide, mysteriously, behind a safe curtain of hair through which she could look out, but other people couldn't look in. This thought made her smile.

Gail pointed to the angled barrel of the spy camera that had just recently gone up over the double doors to the gym—one of the many that had appeared around school since the winter break. Gail gave it a cheesy grin, then stuck her tongue out at the lens. Alida tipped her head to avoid the camera's violet cyclops stare.

"Are they listening to us, too?"

"You bet they are," Alida said. "Every word. They hide microphones inside the walls, and in the lights and bathrooms and stuff. They're the Watchers."

Gail giggled and said softly, "Shit!", then, "Fuck! You think they could hear that in the office?"

"They're not in the office. They're underground, in a secret cellar somewhere downtown. Men in raincoats, with sunglasses. Any time they catch someone goofing off, they report back."

"Back where?"

"Just back. To their like headquarters."

"Finn says they're making a movie about the school. Like a documentary. He called it a 'fly on the wall.'"

"Oh, yeah, that'd be a really, really great movie, with Finn in it and all. I can't wait."

"Finn weirds me out."

"Me, too. Did you get the muffin for him?"

"'Course I did. I got three."

They stopped short of the hubbub coming from Señora Benson's room.

"You know what?" Alida said. "It could be a ploy. I mean, she could be hanging out with Steve just to make Dustin mad."

From behind them came Señora Benson, a vast, dramatic figure in her swirling red-and-black-striped poncho. "Shoo! Shoo! Shoo!" she said, brushing the girls into the classroom.

"*Buenos dias, muchachos y señoritas!*" She spoke in a deafening sing-song, upsy-downsy voice, like there were a thousand kids, not seventeen, in the class.

"*Buenos dias, Señora Benson.*"

Nobody liked her: Señora Benson was nutso.

THE WOMAN who came to the door was a graying blonde with wispy hair and a vague smile that seemed disconnected from the rest of her, and certainly had nothing to do with Lucy's arrival. Explaining her appointment, Lucy saw alarm in the woman's eyes.

Then her face cleared. "Ah, you're the one who comes to lunch."

There was a European tinge—German, or maybe Dutch?—to her accent. And was she the wife or the help?

Half turning in the doorway, she sang out, "Augie!" No reply. To Lucy she said, "He's out there somewhere. Probably busy with his birds."

Beyond the front door, colonial New England abruptly became California vacation rental: an enormous open space, awash with sunshine and overhung by cross-hatched yellow beams, in which the few sticks of furniture looked too old and small for their surroundings. Lucy took in a lonely couch covered in faded beige corduroy, mismatched rugs, a cane rocker, a rolltop secretary with dog-eared books behind glass. In another house, another time and place, these pieces might have fitted cozily, but here they had the forlorn shabbiness of enforced exile. The one concession to the lofty expanse of this unhomelike home was a very new-looking grand piano with something by Schubert on the stand.

"Are you the pianist?" Lucy asked.

"Me? No, him. He's not too good yet. Plinkety-plonkety all day long. Scales!" She pronounced "Scales!" as if saying "Men!," with a sisterly wink at Lucy, yet her voice was fond.

They passed through sliding glass doors to the brick patio, where a lumpy pea-green cardigan was draped over one of the four Adirondack chairs and an American flag drooped in thick folds from an angled pole set into the back wall of the house.

"Augie?" She called again.

So they were Republicans—or was the flag just an island, waterfront thing? It looked brand new: no breath of wind or drop of rain appeared to have disturbed the virgin stitching of the stripes on the dimpled white fabric. In the lifeless air, it was as still as a sculpted marble flag on a war memorial.

"Where's he got to? *Augie?* Company's here!"

From around the corner of the house came a small man—shorter than his wife or Lucy—carrying a large pair of binoculars. His coarse white hair and bristly mustache were flecked with saffron.

"Hey there, how's it going?" He exposed a set of teeth too gleamingly regular to be his own. His handshake, brief but fierce, was a little man's handshake, making up in power for what he lacked in height. Lucy was reminded of something, but couldn't quite place the memory.

Vanags set the binoculars on the slatted table next to a fast-disintegrating copy of Peterson's *Western Birds*. "Birding," he explained.

"My dad was a birder," Lucy said. That same title—swollen, sun-bleached, leaking pages—used to live on top of the Jeep's dash, and there was always a pair of army-surplus binocs in the pocket on the driver's side.

"Know anything about gulls? I didn't. When we first moved out here, all I saw was seagulls. Couldn't tell 'em apart. I'm still a newbie, but I'm learning. Like a couple minutes ago, I figured that the little guy flying with a flock of black-headeds must be a Bonaparte gull—only a tad smaller, but with much paler undersides to his wings. I got a kick out of that. Made my day."

"Bonaparte!" Mrs. Vanags said.

"My dad was a big sparrow man. He tried to teach me, but I could never see the differences." Still learning to talk casually about him, she stumbled on a couple of words, fending off the image of Lewis Olson the rancher in his mania, brandishing the gun that killed her dad. "Fox sparrows, B-b-b-brewer's sparrows, I tried to tell which was which but was sort of blind to them. That was in Montana."

Fazed by the birding talk, Mrs. Vanags said, "You want coffee or anything?"

"I'm fine, thanks."

"We'll holler if we need you, Minna." Minna—*would that be Wilhelmina?*—looked grateful for this dismissal and faded back into the house. "Want to stretch your legs? Let's take a walk along the beach before it gets hot as a pizza oven out there."

The memory Lucy had been looking for suddenly came to her. August Vanags was the White Rabbit in the framed Tenniel print that had hung over her narrow bed in Miles City when she was a kid. They had the same albino nattiness: the rabbit with his fob watch and tightly furled umbrella, Vanags in pressed khakis and immaculate white dress shirt, the cuffs folded back to expose a few inches of forearm, as if he'd been delivered fresh from the dry cleaner's. He wasn't at all what she'd expected, this eyewitness to atrocity, victim of Hitler and Stalin. Nothing of that experience showed on his face. He didn't even have an accent. The crafty, vulnerable little European ragamuffin in *Boy 381* had turned into a dapper little American retiree. Lucy could easily imagine him in sun hat and Bermuda shorts, swanning around the local golf course in an electric cart—but in the camps? The refugee trains? The Nazification program? She felt a surge of ambition for her *GQ* piece: to connect boy and man, European and American, she'd begin out here on the patio, with "I'm still a newbie," the bird book, the flash of false teeth, and her initial disconcerted impression of August Vanags as a sort of living conjuring trick, a work of implausible self-transformation.

She followed him across the browning remnants of the lawn, avoiding the exposed white sprinkler heads whose use had been illegal since early last year. Pulled up on a sand berm at the lawn's end were two kayaks, one red, one blue, like painted seedpods. Both looked new.

"I love to be out on the water," Vanags said, "but it scares poor Minna."

Bleached driftwood logs had piled up at the head of the beach. Stepping gingerly over them, Lucy found her elbow cupped by Vanags' helping hand. It felt as though he were gripping her by the bone.

The sea was out, leaving behind it miles of puddled sand laced with crooked little saltwater creeks. As they walked, Vanags named every bird he saw. "Herring gulls," he said. "Common murres." A heron waded fastidiously on fuse-wire legs, doubled by its own reflection. "Great blue heron."

The smoke cloud to the south over Seattle had lightened to a patchy, pearl-gray stain on the blue. "It's magical out here," she said. "I'd forgotten how beautiful it is."

"Thank you," Vanags said, as if sea, sand, sky, and wildlife were his own handiwork. "Look—more murres."

As soon as they were out of direct sight of the house, Vanags reached into his shirt pocket and fished out a slightly bent cigarette. "Please don't say anything to Minna."

Lucy laughed. "You really think she doesn't know?"

"It's like being a gay in the military—don't ask, don't tell. She doesn't ask, I don't tell." He lit up, infecting the salt air with the musty stink of blown smoke. "I must have smoked my first cigarette when I was four, I guess. At five, I was quite the tobacconist."

She knew that from the book—the boy scavenging for butts, mixing the tobacco strands ("stringy brown boogers") with dirt and sawdust, and trading his roll-ups for stuff to eat. In the perverse world of wartime, starving people would barter bread for a hit of nicotine. Near the top of Lucy's long list of hopes for Alida was that she'd never ever learn to smoke.

"Ah—black guillemot. Over there."

The wet sand was silver-bright, the bird a blobby, ducklike silhouette.

"You know Ernst Mayr the biologist, the guy who figured out the importance of geography in evolution?" It was Mayr, Vanags said, who came up with the idea that new species were formed when creatures of one species became geographically isolated from the rest of their kind, on remote islands, across oceans or mountain ranges. Separated from their cousins, they adapted themselves to their new terrain until they could no longer breed with members of their original species and became genetically distinct.

"He called it allopatric speciation." With forefinger and thumb, Vanags flipped the burning tip of his cigarette into the sand and carefully restored the half-smoked remainder to his shirt pocket. "Allopatric—in another country, another fatherland. Mayr knew something about that: he came to America from Germany in the thirties, and dreamed up his theory when he was at the Museum of Natural History in New York. Know how he spent his first day in the city? He rode the subway until he'd mastered the entire system. Talk about Darwinian adaptation."

Wanting to rid herself of a small rock that was painfully embedding itself in her left heel with each step, Lucy took off her flip-flops and went barefoot. Vanags studied her ankles, his white lashes blinking slowly over eyes of crackled china blue. The piggy, inquisitive eyes looked older than the man.

Catching her glance, Vanags said, "Hermit crab!"

A rather large whelk shell was traveling fast between her feet, propelled by tiny whiskery claws.

"Adaptation again. Clever little bugger, isn't he?" Grinning, Vanags treated Lucy to a full-frontal view of his dazzling artificial snappers. "Dollars to doughnuts he killed and ate the poor old whelk to get possession of his property."

She saw now that the sand was alive with unlovely creatures—beach hoppers hopping, clams squirting, dark squadrons of flies buzzing over stranded clumps of kelp. She trod on soft, heaped spirals of lugworm poop. Spotting a jellyfish almost underfoot—a yard-wide blob of thick diaphanous slime, wrinkling fast in the heat of the sun—she put her flip-flops back on.

"It's critter utopia out here. No surf, and every tide brings in another haul of plankton. You gotta see it when the water's up and we get the sea lions and porpoises and bald eagles. Oh, man—the bald eagles. I tell you, I've counted forty here at one time, when we've had the herring in."

Sidestepping a condom, Lucy did her best to share Vanags' pleasure in his new habitat. A familiar bird call came from quite a ways inland: *Dee! Dee-dee-dee-dee! Kill-dee-a! Kill-dee-a!* "Killdeer," she said. "That's a real Montana bird."

"Yeah," Vanags said complacently. "Those guys are like chump change around here. Hear 'em all the time." He stopped to investigate a beached sea cucumber that looked to Lucy like a pimply turd. "Out here in the boonies, it's easy to forget that we're at war, huh?"

"War?"

But Vanags didn't hear the question. "Of course, we miss the city. We don't know too many folks on the island, but it has its compensations. Like this . . ." He inhaled the sea air deep into his lungs as if it were smoke from a joint, holding it in his chest before releasing it through his nose. "Ozone."

"But everyone says you're a recluse."

"Me? No, this was CollierParnell's idea. They wanted me to be a mystery man."

"The publishers sent you here?"

"Well, kind of. First, when they got the boy book, they were going to send me on a tour. Twenty-one cities. I'd been looking forward to that—there's a whole bunch of stuff I wanted to say that I couldn't get into the book. Then we had a meeting with the big kahunas in New York, and they came up with this new plan. They put the kibosh on the tour—no interviews, no nothing. They said they wanted to let the book speak for itself and spend the tour moolah on advertising. Day it shipped, Minna and me went on a cruise—Seattle to Rio de Janeiro, thirty-six days. That was my editor's idea: he said I'd get pestered half to death if we stayed in town. Had to change our phone to an unlisted number. When we got back from the cruise, the local rep told me about this house on Whidbey, and my editor talked me into buying it. 'Better get used to it,' he said: 'You're going to be a rich man now.' You wouldn't believe the trouble they went to, looking after us. All part of the marketing strategy is what they said—I tell you, they don't do things by halves at CollierParnell."

Lucy could imagine the scene at the publishers' office. Counting on a ripely accented, gaunt, hollow-eyed Holocaust survivor, a figure of haunting telegenic pathos, they'd come face-to-face with this chipper and garrulous American know-it-all. August Vanags was unworthy of being the author of his own book. Put him on *Larry King* and he'd unsell *Boy 381* at the rate of thousands a minute. They must have wanted to strangle him when they saw what they were up against.

Ahead of them, a flock of small, long-legged birds skittered across the glassy sand flats, came to a sudden stop, then raced off on a fresh heading, like panic in strict formation.

"Sanderlings."

Far from evading journalists, Vanags had lusted to catch their ear, which was bad news for Lucy. She hated people who tempered the facts to fit the story, but the whole point of the *GQ* piece was supposed to be tracking down the famously shy and elusive historian. It was going to be tricky in the extreme to tell the truth and still have a story worth telling.

"I got to hand it to them. The CollierParnell people sure know their stuff. Six hundred thousand in hardback, jeepers! Guess how many copies my Yalta book sold in toto?" Vanags had a gruff, chirruping laugh.

Aiming diplomatically high, Lucy said, "Three thousand?"

"Five hundred and fifty. But that was the UW Press," Vanags said, as if the geniuses at CollierParnell would have sold a million. "Took me eight years to write that book. I did the boy book in a month."

"That's amazing."

"It seemed dead easy at the time. Scribble, scribble, scribble, like I was on automatic pilot or using a planchette. It pretty much wrote itself, with just the occasional shove from me. I never knew I had all that stuff in my memory. It was like whenever I sat down to write, more little doors would open inside my head. Every night I'd read what I'd written during the day to Minna, like a bedtime story, and that kept me going the next day—Minna had to have her story."

"But she must have known most of it already."

"Funny thing, she didn't. I never talked to her about those times—hardly ever thought much about them myself, to be honest. Everything was news to her. A lot of it was news to me."

"How did you—"

"Hello!" Vanags had veered suddenly off to the side. "Now *what* would you call *that*?"

The thing at his feet was the size of a football, hump shaped, the color of congealed blood. Lucy heard Vanags' knees creak as he squatted down to get a better look. Whatever it was, it was the sort of object that Lucy would've given a wide berth to, belonging to the same unpleasant category as condoms, jellyfish, worm crap. But Vanags was fascinated by his find, which he prodded experimentally, as if to find out whether it would bite.

"That," he said, "is really something else," and rolled it over on its hump, exposing a sandy reddish underside.

"It's incredibly ugly," Lucy said.

"Ugly?" He seemed genuinely surprised.

"Sort of like a giant red potato bug."

"My first thought was armadillo, I don't know why."

"Turtle?"

"Touch it."

Lucy bent down and reached out a reluctant finger. It felt—as she had known it would—fuzzy and slimy in the nastiest possible combination. Leathery flesh or hard shell? It might be either. "D'you think it's some sort of mollusk?"

"Mollusk." Vanags savored the word. "Seems on the big side for a mollusk to me." His own manikinishness made the whatever-it-was look enormous.

"You know those gourd things that people bring back from like the Seychelles?"

"Coco de mer." His bridgework grin reminded Lucy, a little late in the day, of the comic obscenity of those gourds, their cheeky likeness to enormous vulvas. *Cripes,* she thought; she certainly hadn't meant to send Vanags thinking in *that* direction.

He was weighing it in both hands. "What d'you think? Animal or vegetable? Dead or alive?"

"Animal," she said. "Definitely animal."

He stood up, still holding it.

"You're not going to take that home with you?"

"Don't you want to know what it *is?*"

Lucy laughed. "I think I could go without knowing and live."

In the presence of this thing neither of them could name, she felt suddenly easy with the man. Watching him bear it tenderly before him, this weird childish trophy, she couldn't help worrying for his immaculate shirt and pants. As they walked together on the sand, in step, on their short shadows, Lucy found herself telling him about the accident. She'd meant to say nothing—to put the whole business of the wrecked Infiniti on hold until after the interview—but now, with the sun hot on their backs and the house a mile off, it seemed natural to confide in him. She told about the couple in the lounge aboard the ferry, the flying car, the dreadful roadside aftermath, her stumbling performance with the young cop. Vanags nodded as he listened, every so often turning his face to hers: his blue eyes, which she'd thought of as piggy only minutes before, now struck her as kindly, searching, full of comprehension. But when she was through with her story, all he said was, "Yeah, that's a dangerous road. Lot of people get killed on it, I hear."

But then Vanags, at an age when he should have been in preschool, had been out on the streets robbing corpses. If such everyday horrors were hardwired into your character, of course the deaths of strangers wouldn't seem that big a deal—which made it even odder to see him holding the globby red thing so protectively, like a baby.

When they reached the house, Minna was out on the patio, wearing an apron that said "Kissin' Don't Last—Cookin' Do!" She said, "Nice hike?"

"Yeah, we had a blast," Vanags said, showing his prize.

"Does he always bring stuff like that back with him?" Lucy said.

Minna eyed it with a look of doleful recognition. "Oh, yes."

"Gotta keep it damp," Vanags said, and disappeared into the house.

"The things he finds on the beach," Minna said. "One day he found an octopus. Octopus!" She shook her head at the memory. "Been a long time dead, too. It was really stinky. Oh, Augie! That's a *new* towel!"

Swaddled in the dripping bath towel, the thing bore an uncanny likeness to a baby—a very red, very angry baby, howling for a feed.

"Where'd I put my peepers?" Vanags said, and went to look for them, still carrying his precious charge, now cradled on one arm, the folds of the towel dropping from it like a christening shawl.

Peepers. The most un-American thing about August Vanags, Lucy thought, was his addiction to American slang, some of it so out of date as to be fossilized. To Minna she said, "You guys have kids?"

"No." Minna drew the word out into a sigh, making Lucy regret the question. "Is hot!"

It felt like ninety now, and through the thin soles of her flip-flops Lucy could feel the burning bricks of the patio. "Another record. Every day now, it seems to break the record."

Minna gazed into space. Her face appeared to go out of focus, then suddenly came back. "The greenhouse gases! Augie can tell you all about the gases."

Lucy bet he could, and made a mental note to avoid the topic.

When Vanags reappeared he was wearing half-moon glasses and holding an open book. "You were right on the money—it's a mollusk! Gumboot chiton. Biggest chiton in the world. Related to the limpet. Eats red algae. *Cryptochiton stelleri.* That'd be Steller, as in Steller's jay and Steller's sea lion. German guy worked for the Russians. Know about Steller?"

"Yes, a bit," Lucy said, trying to forestall a lecture. "He was up in Alaska." That pretty much exhausted her knowledge of Mr. Steller.

Vanags gently unwrapped the towel from around the chiton to show its flat bottom. "See? That's his foot there. Feel the suction! This poor critter must've gotten washed off a rock someplace. I better take him back to where he belongs."

As Vanags marched in short neat steps across the bald lawn toward the beach, Minna called after him, apparently from long and, Lucy guessed, unsuccessful habit: "Augie! Don't be late for your lunch!"

AFTER THEIR LUNCH of incredibly disgusting chicken fajitas, Gail and Alida raced each other to the computer lab to find Finn. Weird as he was, Finn was a big figure in the lives of sixth-grade girls, who usually referred to him not by name but as "the Geek," or just "Geek." If you were building a website, sooner or later you'd find yourself armed with bribes in the shape of Jamba Juice smoothies, gum, doughnuts, dark chocolate (Finn would accept no other kind), Cheez-Its, or, like today, blueberry muffins, going in search of the Geek.

Finn wrote code. He could rattle stuff out in HTML and Java faster than the girls could write English when they were I.M.-ing. If Finn had a life, which was doubtful, it lay somewhere out in cyberspace. Even seniors consulted him, gifts in hand; you'd hear them saying in low, respectful voices, "How'd you get there, Finn?" and "Can you show me that again?" He sat through tech classes, scowl glued to his face, rolling his eyes when the teacher wasn't looking. Mr. Orlovsky, Finn said, was "crap."

Last week he'd done this really cool thing with Emma's website. Emma had always had a picture on her home page of her house in Issaquah, with her entire family posed outside, right down to the aunts and uncles and cousins. It had been taken on her grandparents' silver wedding anniversary. Finn had gone to work on it. Now the whole picture was alive with links: you'd click on a face and get taken to a biography, where you'd learn everything from their favorite color to their pet peeve. If you clicked on a window of the house, you'd find yourself inside that room—at least would be able to, when Emma finished taking photos, which was getting difficult because her parents were threatening to revoke her privileges for spending too much time on her website. This amazing interactive home page, shared in strict confidence with Gail and Alida, was so totally awesome that they had to have one for themselves.

In the computer lab, the Geek was sitting, or writhing on the stool at his usual monitor. Every kid in school recognized that spot as his personal territory at lunchtime. He had big springy hair, like an Afro, and a big ass to match. The moment the girls were in the door, he shut down the screen, like what he was doing was top secret, though the one time Alida caught him out, he was only finishing an e-mail, signing it "Love ya!!!! Finn." Maybe that was his secret: whenever he sent e-mails to his girl clients, he always signed them FREAK.

"Hey, dude," Gail said.

"So whaddaya got?" Finn didn't turn around, just kept his eyes on the blank screen. He never looked straight at people; he'd talk to ceilings, walls, or windows, anything but the person who was trying to talk to him.

"Muffins."

"Three muffins."

"Blueberry?"

"What else?"

"Okay. Whaddaya want?"

He was incredibly rude. Puzzled that the website king didn't have— or said he didn't have—a website of his own, Emma had asked him why not, and got the answer, "Because I'm not a dumb-ass girl." Hilarious. Still, you only had to see Emma's new home page to swallow your pride and go buy muffins for the odious Finn.

He now had Gail's site up on the screen, with a picture taken by her dad last weekend at her house over in Bellevue: Gail was smiling (she'd taken her retainer out for the photo) with her dog Sirius lying at her feet, his tongue hanging out like he'd just run a marathon.

"Sirius is *so* cute," Alida said.

Finn surprised them both when he said, "You want a link on that dog?" He sounded almost *interested.*

Gail said, "D'you have a dog, Finn?"

"Not anymore." A long string of code unfurled across the screen. "I'm more into horses now."

"You go horse riding?" The idea of the Geek on horseback was so totally hilarious that Alida didn't dare catch Gail's eye.

"Nah," Finn said, with his whiffling, sniggery laugh.

"Oh, horse *racing,* like Seabiscuit."

"I really liked that movie," Alida said.

"This host sucks." Finn was hammering at a key with an impatient forefinger. "It's a POS."

"What?"

"Piece Of Shit. I could move you to WebspiderZ—they're cool."

"Don't you dare!"

Finn had worked that trick on Pia—moved her site to WebspiderZ, where you couldn't do anything without knowing code. So for a week or two Pia had become a slave to Finn's peculiar moods and whims, then she'd gone back to FreeWebs, where she had to start over from scratch. Like Pia said, on WebspiderZ, Finn was the spider and you were the fly.

He heaved his shoulders in an exaggerated shrug. "Just my two cents. There's a bunch of neat stuff you can do on WebspiderZ."

Parents were generally indulgent toward him. Gail's mom called him Poor Finn, like Poor was his given name. According to the mothers, his dad was a foreigner who'd gone away to Europe and wasn't coming back, so Finn had gotten some kind of eating disorder, which was why he was always pigging out on candy and muffins. To Alida, who didn't even know who her dad was, this seemed less than a stellar reason for cutting Finn a mile of slack, but she enjoyed the grown-upness that came with thinking of the Geek as an unhappy kid whose extraordinary brattiness might not be entirely his own fault. "Going through a difficult phase" was how the parents put it, and Alida liked the ring of superior maturity in the words.

When the link to Sirius came up on the screen, she said "Good job, Finn," as if she were a teacher and Finn her student.

"Cool," Gail said.

"Oh yeah, this is like *rocket* science," Finn said, but sounded gratified in spite of himself. "That dog—if you've got video of him, I could stream it for you."

"You could?" Nobody Gail and Alida knew had streaming video on her website.

Finn talked megabytes and bandwidth, not to Gail but mumbling confidentially to the screen and keyboard. Seeing his back as he bobbed and squirmed in his seat you'd think he was wrestling with an octopus, the double roll of fat around his midriff rippling inside his black T-shirt, his tangled bush of hair jerking back and forth in hip-hop time. In class he was the motionless hulk at his all-boys table, but plugged into a computer he had this frantic, cartoonish animation.

"Finn, what happened to your dog?" Alida said. "Did he like die?"

His back froze in mid-squirm. "Nah. She just got advertised."

"Advertised?"

"There's a no-pets rule in the building, so she had to get put in the paper."

"You mean somebody bought her?"

"Nope. She was free. Some woman got her. In North Bend." He made it sound like North Bend was on Mars. More slowly than usual, he wrote on the screen, *<a href="index.html"><img src="picture.gif"> </a>*. "She was called Sugar," he said.

Gail caught Alida's eye. It was partly the way he said it, but the thought of the Geek with a dog named Sugar was kind of hilarious, and Gail's whole body was trembling with the effort of suppressing a fit of the giggles. Cheeks bulging, staring bug-eyed at Alida, she put the back of her hand to her mouth to keep the laughter from bursting out.

Covering for her friend, Alida said, a little too loudly, "That's really, *really* sad."

"Duh!" Finn said. "Who gives a shit? It was only a stupid dog."

Later, daydreaming through Social Studies while Mrs. Milliband went on about maps, Alida thought about her secret algebra project.

People were always saying *x* when what they really meant was *y*. Everybody did it, usually to be polite—like the dozen times a day you had to say, "Cool," out of politeness when something wasn't cool at all. Sometimes the words people spoke were exactly like problems in algebra. Finn talking about his lost dog, for instance. Or even Alida herself, pretending to Gail that she had a crush on Eric because Gail said she had a crush on Blake.

Math was Alida's favorite subject, and this semester she was seriously into algebra—tantalizing puzzles in which you used Elimination, Substitution, and Intersection to make unknown quantities reveal their true identities. Back in fourth grade, she'd been a whiz at story problems: John had five times as many apples as Mary, or Ben and Sara were working the snack bar at the school summer fair and selling hot dogs for \$1.35 and sodas for 85¢, and Alida always had her hand up first, rapping furiously at the air even before the solution had precisely formulated itself in her head, confident that the right answer would come to her lips in time. She feared the world of the playground, where the rules kept on changing from one day to the next, but among numbers she felt gifted and secure. Each day now she saved her math homework until last, the better to enjoy her escape into this magical place where everything fit as snugly as a well-shot basketball dropping through the hoop. Working her way down a page of equations, she was engrossed and happy, letting numbers talk to her, watching k, and x, and y, and b, and c come out from behind their teasing disguises.

$6 - 2y = 7y + 13$ made immediate and satisfying sense, but what Alida really wanted was a system of human algebra. It'd be incredibly cool if you could figure people out like that, isolating their variables on just one side of the equation, adding positives to negatives to make zeros, until the problem disentangled into one clear statement: *this* means *that*.

When Susy walked to the bus stop at 3 mph, she missed the bus by 2 minutes, but when she ran to the stop at 6 mph, she arrived with 1 minute to spare. How far is the bus stop from Susy's home? The simplest equations needed a whole bunch of hard data, like all the stopwatch and tape-measure stuff they'd managed to collect on Susy. Alida was working on that. She'd already opened a secret file on her mother, who was pretty crazy a lot of the time, and in less than two weeks had filled nearly twenty pages of a locked diary with scraps of significant info—like exactly how much wine her mom drank, and when; what she said when she got mad; when her period came; which route she took to school each day. Alida was logging every visitor to the apartment, the books her mom read, her conversations on the phone. Her mom could hardly go to the bathroom now without Alida registering the event. She was still way short of building any actual equations, but felt that with each new addition to the diary she was getting slightly closer to turning her mom into a soluble problem.

She could speak to nobody about the algebra project, for Alida knew that she was unhappily unique in finding other people's talk and behavior so weird and difficult to read. Gail was never mystified by *her* parents—or by anybody else, so far as Alida could tell. All her friends instinctively understood things that Alida had to puzzle out. She might be smart at math, but she was dumb at human beings, and much acting and pretense went into hiding her peculiar stupidity from the rest of the world. Laughing at jokes that made no sense to her, having crushes on boys she didn't even like, searching people's faces for cues as to whether she ought to say *x* or *y*, *Love it* or *Hate it*, Alida usually succeeded in passing herself off as a normal kid: she alone knew the shameful effort that went into her daily performances, and the risk she ran of being unmasked as a pathetic fake.

"*Alida?*"

Her own name reached her as a slow-spiraling echo bouncing off the walls of a long tunnel, and it took a little while to connect the voice with Mrs. Milliband, who was looking down at her with the professionally tolerant smile of someone trained to deal with the severely handicapped.

"Uh . . . Mercator?" Alida said, and waited for the class to break out in mocking laughter at her dopiness.

"Right, Mercator. Now who can tell us what Mercator's 'Greenland problem' is?"

Alida's hand went up. In class, her hand often seemed to be out of her control, like an unruly puppy who couldn't grasp the meaning of "Sit!" or "Stay!" She watched from a distance as it waved urgently at Mrs. Milliband. Everyone knew that on Mercator's projection, Greenland came out far too big and Africa far too small.

"Let's hear from one of the boys. How about . . . Finn?"

"Well," Finn said, as if that were the last word as well the first that he had to say on the subject, then smooshed his face into an expression of agonized concentration. "If you peel an orange, it comes out like distorted." Two boys sitting at his table tittered, but in a friendly way: surly, geeky Finn was popular with boys. "Well," he said again. "The way Mercator did it, Greenland got all skewed. But Robinson came along and fixed it."

A fly buzzed against the dusty pane of the tall window through which the sun streamed. The air smelled cooked and stale; the class, fidgety in the heat, heavy with lunch, limped through Mrs. Milliband's lesson. Alida tried to concentrate, obediently imagining a lightbulb inside a colored glass globe, projecting the surface of the earth onto paper cylinders and cones, but with her mind adrift, she was soon elsewhere, thinking of algebra again.

She and Gail were best friends. But $x + y = z$ was only one in a set of troubling simultaneous equations. Her mom hated Gail's mom. She never said so directly, of course, but Alida could tell, from her frozen smiles and too-bright, tinkly voice whenever she dropped Alida off at Gail's house and the two mothers spoke. So $-z = a + b$. It had started— Alida was sure of it—near the end of last semester, shortly before Mr. Quigley, the girls' Language Arts and homeroom teacher, who was incredibly funny and nice, left the school. Mysteriously, Mr. Quigley was another variable in the problem. So was the fact that Gail's family went to church a lot—they were Baptists or something. This much Alida had gleaned from observing her mom, but the puzzle was missing a bunch of essential data. Subtle questioning of Gail had added nothing new, and the one time Alida had tried to question her mom she'd met evasion and denial.

Elimination. Substitution. Intersection. As Alida watched the fly— a tiny frenzy of beating wings as it flung itself again and again at the glass—it appeared to grow, until she could almost see its bulbous red eyes and bearded, spongy mouth, like the monster flies in *Microcosmos* that had figured in her nightmares when she was a little kid. Memoryless, incapable of learning from experience, it would thrash against the window till it died.

Alida was engrossed in the fly's stupid struggles when Mrs. Milliband's voice broke through to her: "Azimuthal," she said, and wrote the word up in squeaky yellow letters on the chalkboard.

Azimuthal. Alida loved ten-dollar words, and was glad to add this one to her collection, where it nestled beside such recent treasures as "egregious" and "collateral." Even as she took in Mrs. Milliband's official definition, which involved a flat card held against the surface of a globe, she was busy in another part of her head, making sentences. *All through the long hot azimuthal afternoon.* . . . *All through the egregious azimuthal afternoon . . .*

"So how did you guys meet?"

The Vanagses' kitchen-dining area was a cool refuge from the heat outside. The posy of wildflowers in the vase on the table—poppy, iris, buttercup, dogrose—looked fresh-picked from the roadside that morning.

"In the bank." Minna was putting the finishing touches to a risotto on the countertop range.

"She was the prettiest teller in the line," Augie said—he was definitely Augie now—as he extracted a half-empty bottle of white wine from the fridge.

"I opened an account for him. He had his first check from the college and wanted me to give him bills for it. I had to explain banking to him. He knew a lot of history, but he didn't know nothing about banking, poor boy. He was such an innocent."

Or good at pick-up lines, Lucy thought. It was easy to imagine the un-innocent refugee-scholar playing the scene, and the girl clerk smitten by his artful mask of helplessness.

"I was still a greenhorn then."

"He came nearly all the way across the country on a Greyhound bus. From Ann Arbor in Michigan."

"Yep, rode the dog. Took five days before the interstates."

Lucy, still puzzled by Minna's accent, said, "But Minna, where are you from, originally?"

"West Seattle. I graduated from West Seattle High."

But she said "vest" for "west." Somehow, in the strange barter-economy of marriage, Minna had picked up her husband's old accent, while he now spoke in the voice that must have once belonged to her. But since they'd come indoors, Lucy had begun to notice a distinct foreignness in Augie's speech; not an accent so much as an academic, over-precise articulation, as if his English had been learned—rather too perfectly—from lessons on tape. In "rode the dawg" or "priddiest teller in the lahn," Lucy caught a slight, actorish false note in the down-homey pronunciations.

"Join me?" Augie waved the chardonnay bottle. "Minna doesn't like to drink at lunchtime."

"Makes me go all dizzy," Minna said.

"Sure."

But Lucy was disappointed by the meager two fingers' worth Augie tipped into her glass before putting the cork firmly back into the bottle and returning it to the fridge. A real drink was what she needed—enough to stop the dead couple from paying surprise calls whenever her attention lapsed. Just as she was sitting down at the table, she realized that Minna was saying grace.

". . . for each new morning with its light, for rest and shelter of the night," she recited in schoolroom singsong.

Lucy sneaked a covert glance at Augie, and saw he was sneaking a covert glance at her.

"For health and food, for love and friends, for everything thy goodness sends."

"Amen," Augie said, and sent a crooked, collaborative smile in Lucy's direction.

In the scuffle of chairs, Lucy said, "Looks delicious!" rather too loudly.

"Minna's an ace cook. Me, best I can do is terrorize the occasional steak."

Minna passed Lucy the salad bowl. "That's a wild salad."

"Yes, isn't it just!" Lucy said, and laughed, before she saw what Minna meant: dandelion leaves, chickweed, what looked like wilted stinging nettle.

"Minna loves to scavenge."

"You've got to scavenge now, what with the war and all."

"Sorry?"

"The war . . ." That vague look again: sometimes Minna was there, and sometimes she seemed to abruptly absent herself from her own face.

Digging into his greens, Augie said, "You rely on supermarkets for your food, you're going to go hungry any day now. Do you have any idea how incredibly fragile the infrastructure of this country is—how easily it can be paralyzed by the enemy? Suppose in the next attack they hit four cities—Chicago, say, and Boston, and Houston, and Long Beach, all in the same hour. Okay, we close our borders, close our ports, order every plane out of the air: how long d'you think it'd take to clear the shelves of your local Thriftway in Seattle? Two days? Five? But then suppose that twenty-four hours after the first wave of attacks, they come in with truck bombs in Minneapolis, Atlanta, Miami . . . You better be up early, scavenging for dandelions, because sure as hell ain't *nuthin'* going to be working when that second wave hits.

"You know what mass panic looks like? Food riots? I tell you, it's two attorneys, middle-aged guys, in ties and good suits, fighting in the street over a greasy chicken leg. It's bodies on the sidewalk, rotting garbage, fires, the stink of feces everywhere. And gunfire. You go to sleep to gunfire, you wake up to gunfire. Then it's just white noise."

"New Orleans," Lucy said.

"Yeah, New Orleans. That was a good reminder. Civilization is always just twelve, maybe fifteen hours away from barbarity. Doesn't matter where you are—could be anywhere, could be Seattle—and less than a day is all it takes to turn a great city into a hellhole. Yesterday you were living in the world's finest democracy, today's it's Mogadishu. The line's that thin. Which is why we needed New Orleans.

"Trouble is, this country is reliant on a whole series of interlocking networks, and every supply line in every network is so old and brittle and squirrelly—it's like living in a house full of the latest, most expensive stuff you can buy, but the wiring and the plumbing go back to the days of Theodore Roosevelt. Or before. Think about it: food, water, power—everything has to travel from somewhere else, and everything depends on everything else working. It's crazy. We've got the slowest trains and the most flickery electricity in the western world: someone sneezes in a coal plant in Montana and the lights go out on Whidbey Island.

"It's democracy. Joe Q. Public isn't interested in infrastructure, doesn't want to pay for infrastructure, won't vote for infrastructure. Who'd vote for a politician who went to the people saying we gotta spend all these billions and billions of federal money on backup systems for these antiquated networks of ours? Can you tell me that?"

"Nobody," Minna said. "Nobody would."

Lucy suddenly saw that this was how mealtimes must always be in the Vanags household: Augie launched on a tirade, Minna fueling his rhetorical questions with mechanical answers.

"Right. Which is why we're so vulnerable to the enemy. And don't tell me"—he fixed his blue-eyed stare on Lucy as if she were a known dissident—"that our enemy doesn't know our weakness. He does. It's what he's calculating on. He's perfectly aware that the difference between everything working and nothing working is like *that*." He snapped his middle finger against his thumb. "You really want to injure the United States—hurt us economically, socially, politically, maybe inflict a wound from which we won't be able to recover—you go for the infrastructure. You don't have to kill a lot of people. That's the beauty of it: you just have to put a crimp on one network here, another network there, another over there, and bingo! you've got civil unrest, martial law, no food, no power, no water. Plus, you've got the biggest world recession in history, because you've just brought international trade to a screaming halt. Here, help yourself to Minna's risotto."

His smile was that of the conjuror producing the fourth rabbit from his hat.

Poor Minna. Lucy had been watching her while Augie talked. In the soft interior light, seen through the corner of an eye, she was still a beauty, in the ditzy, pliant 1950s mold. A Monroe type. Lucy was always seeing them in supermarket checkout lines, those fifties women, their old girl-faces hardened over the decades into surly masks of pure resentment. They looked cheated. Mouths trained to smile and simper had long given up the effort of appearing pleasant; bodies once dedicated to the pursuit of the hourglass figure had swelled into a sort of aggressive obesity, as if they'd taken to hogging down gallons of ice cream in deliberate revenge for the impossible part they'd been forced to play in the world. But Minna had not let herself go. Her face didn't have that cheated look. Marriage to Augie must have given her ample cause to hit the Häagen-Dazs, but what should by rights have happened somehow hadn't. Age had happened, of course, but to see Minna now was to see through a gauze screen the same pretty young bank teller she must have been when August Vanags first walked in with his check forty years or so ago—she'd just gotten blurrier. Lucy wondered whether Minna's eerie girlishness should be put down to a defect in her character or a strength.

But there was no denying her skill in the kitchen. A gourmet chef might have been proud of Minna's risotto: firm, moist to just the right degree, complexly flavored and generously laced with baby white asparagus and golden chanterelles that tasted of the woods. "This is genius," Lucy said. "I wish you'd tell me the secret—whenever I try making risotto it always comes out as lumpy rice pudding."

"Oh," Minna said, with a flutter of eyelashes. "Is so simple. In this heat, I think people want only to eat light."

Viennese, Lucy thought, *her voice sounds Viennese.*

"See, you don't need big death tolls." Augie was regaining command of the table. "Death tolls are good for show and symbolism, but you don't take down a country this size by killing Americans. You gotta be cleverer than that—and we have a darn clever enemy. Look how he used our own technology against us on 9/11, turning our jetliners into his bombs. We gave him all the weaponry he needed. Only thing he had to supply was his own box cutters. Hey, we're a generous nation, and we got a whole lot more stuff where those planes came from—computer systems, chemical facilities, power grids, wide-open food-supply chains, water treatment plants, creaky old railroads, and every one of those is a potential weapon if you know how to use it right."

"He always talks like a terrorist," Minna said, as if to reassure Lucy that her husband wasn't improvising his own explosive device.

"No, I *think* like a terrorist. Somebody has to."

"It's the t-t-t-talk of terrorism that t-terrorizes me," Lucy said, trying to muster her words. "Like these stupid TOPOFF dramas. I hate how the administration plays with us. You know, be scared, be very, very scared—but that's okay, we'll keep you safe, catch that plane, do that shopping. But watch out for the bogeyman! Sure, we'll sometimes get acts of terrorism, like in Oklahoma City, but I don't buy all the smoke and mirrors stuff. It's so *Wizard of Oz.*"

"Ah, you're a Christian Scientist!" Augie bared his false teeth in an alarming grin.

"No. Why?"

"Mrs. Eddy believed all disease was an illusion. A pity Mrs. Eddy died of pneumonia."

Lucy bristled at his tone. "I don't *not* believe in terrorism. It's just that there are more threatening things—greenhouse gases, earthquakes, whatever. Like Seattle gets millions of federal dollars for mock terror attacks but can't raise a federal cent for earthquake exercises, which is what it really needs."

"Mrs. Who?" asked Minna.

"This is World War IV," Augie said.

"World War *what*?" Lucy laughed. "You lived through World War II, and you seriously compare this to that?"

"I think the situation we're in now's as bad as 1939—worse, in a way. The world has changed. People have got to wake up to the complexity, the scale, the global nature of what's happening. Unless we can win this war, I'm afraid we're going to see the end of the modern nation-state, which—since I'm not of the anarchist persuasion—I happen to believe would be a catastrophe for mankind. So no, I'm not joking. I don't think the destruction of our civilization is a laughing matter, funnily enough."

He spoke in the dry, acidic voice of the classroom, and Lucy remembered Tad's tight-assed prof who was gung-ho about Vietnam; strange that this victim of war should seem to be such an enthusiast of wars in general. Her glass was empty, and she cast a longing glance at the refrigerator door. "Really? The end of the nation-state?"

"You know how Max Weber defined the state, in terms of its monopoly on violence? We just lost the monopoly. You realize how big a deal that is? Used to be, only states had the armies and the hardware to go to war. This is the first moment in modern history when a bunch of private individuals have the power to take down a state. It's like you, me, and Minna could get together and go mano a mano with the Pentagon—and what's truly scary is we could *win*. Don't laugh: the state's set up to defend itself from other states, in the old-fashioned kind of warfare, but when it comes to fighting you, me, and Minna, the state's clueless. Clueless!

"First off, it doesn't know who we are. We're everywhere and nowhere. We don't wear uniforms. We don't have a capital city they can bomb. They don't know if we have a leader, even. They can't negotiate with us. They can't send the army, because we haven't told them where the battlefield's gonna be. Deterrence? Nope. Containment? Mutually assured destruction? Those things might work when you're dealing with another state, but when it comes to dealing with the three of us at this table, they're the wrong implements—like eating soup with a fork. Meantime, they know we have access to stuff that used to be part of their monopoly—chemical, nuclear, biological."

Lucy joined the game. "And have we got it?"

"Doesn't matter. We've got access. Look at all the nuclear material that's been floating around on the black market since the collapse of the Soviet Union. Look at the anthrax lab at the U—suppose I have an angry molecular-biologist friend? The essential technology's all around us, and the government can do very little—frighteningly little—to keep us from getting our hands on it, provided we have the contacts and the moolah. You want more wine in that glass?"

"Please." This time the bottle stayed on the table.

Augie stabbed a chanterelle with his fork and waggled it at Lucy. "Now look at our enemy. He has the resources, the smarts, the manpower, and he's hell-bent on attacking the United States and destroying our system of government, because he believes democracy is a blasphemy against his goddamn god.

"And we'll help him do it. Americans take democracy for granted: they don't stop to think how delicate and fragile it really is. He only needs to create the right set of circumstances, and we'll finish the job for him. We'll do the dismantling and rewrite the laws while he sits at home watching us on CNN, laughing his sorry ass off."

Lucy was struck by the discrepancy between the size of Augie's talk and the size of the man himself. His chair was too big for him, and his white mustache looked as if it had been gummed onto the face of an unhappy boy.

Minna said, "You should see our emergency supplies. We've got a roomful. We've got so much water, and rice, and beans. And . . ." Lucy saw sudden confusion in her eyes.

"More freeze-dried chicken à la king than you'd want to eat in an entire lifetime," Augie said. "We just about filled the utility room."

"My eleven-year-old would approve. She's always lecturing me about earthquake preparedness. A flashlight and some bottles of Evian water is the best I've done so far. I was never any good as a Girl Scout, so I'd make a lousy survivalist."

"You need duct tape," Minna said, "and candles. Would anyone care for dessert?"

When lunch was over, Lucy offered to help load the dishwasher, but Augie led her upstairs to his study. Closing the door, he said, "You mustn't mind Minna. She's been having trouble remembering things lately—we're a little afraid that Dr. Alzheimer may be paying us a call."

Lucy had guessed as much. "I'm sorry."

He looked out through a tall and narrow window. "Osprey," his wan voice said.

From the modern California of downstairs, they'd walked into another century. Of all the weird architectural fantasies on Sunlight Beach Road, this room had to be the strangest—a long, warrenlike affair of molded, fussy-looking arches, nooks, alcoves, floor-to-ceiling bookshelves, and an old-fashioned fireplace, its grate piled with fir cones. And it smelled ages older than the house, a pleasing library scent of glue and must and paper fungus. Lucy had the unsettling, head-swimming sense that she'd been here before. Those arches. That oyster-white color. The small plaster bust on a shelf.

"It reminds me of somewhere," she said.

"It should. It should." The eagerness was back in Augie's face.

Groping for the memory, she said, "It's not . . . Monticello, is it?"

"Bull's-eye! You know, you're the first person to get it? But I guessed you might. Jefferson's library. It's kind of impressionistic. I gave a bunch of pictures to a retired architect here on the island, and he did what he could with the space. I was God's gift to the contractors: we had them in for months, though they seemed to think I was a few sandwiches short of a picnic for wanting it. Tell me, is it *insanely* pretentious?"

"No, it's charming." It was the books that saved it, Lucy thought. They weren't the kind that people bought for show; there wasn't a leather binding to be seen. Wherever she looked, she saw more drab paperbacks, white spines gone yellow, titles in German and in Cyrillic lettering. Even when new they would've been cheap, shabby things; now they gave off a powerful whiff of the old, fallen Communist world in all its threadbare mediocrity. On Jefferson's bookshelves, comically displaced, they gave the room an unexpected human warmth and messiness.

"When were you at Monticello?"

"My dad worked for a federal agency—the Bureau of Land Management. He took me on a business trip to D.C. once, when I was ten. He rented a car, and we spent hours and hours at Monticello. He loved the place. I was the bored kid who hated museums and thought D.C. sucked because there were no rides. I lusted after Disneyland, but I remember the library, and my dad squatting down to read the title of every book, the guard dogging him from shelf to shelf like he was a thief. That was cool to see."

"I used to make weekend pilgrimages to Monticello when we lived in Washington."

"You were teaching there?"

"No, I got a two-year leave from the U to work for the government, like your father. I was with the National Security Council."

From Augie's expression, Lucy gathered that the correct response to this would be to drop dead with admiration.

"In the Old Executive Office Building, on Seventeenth and Pennsylvania. Right next door to the White House. You must have seen it?"

"Well, I guess so, but—"

"Fabulous place. Like the palace of Versailles." Going to his desk, Augie had to step carefully to avoid treading on the litter of new books on the floor around his chair. Most had the word "Jihad" on their jackets. Beside the closed laptop—and Lucy would have dearly liked to find out what was on its hard drive—an old Royal manual typewriter held a sheet of paper with a few lines of jumpy letters, just too far away for her to read them. A partially eaten stick of French bread lay by the typewriter, shedding crumbs.

He handed her a creased tourist postcard of the Old Executive Office Building, which to Lucy looked less like Versailles than a bad-taste Victorian railroad hotel. The picture meant nothing to her, but she said, "Oh, yes, of course. You're right. It *is* fabulous," thinking how strange it was that he should keep the postcard so close to hand, like a talisman. Lots of people liked to keep photos of their families in sight when they worked; what did it say about Augie that he preferred to commune with this hideous-looking government building?

He pointed to an attic window on the far right wing of the building. "My office was just behind there. A cubbyhole, really. I was a humble pen pusher on the East European desk, writing position papers for the higher-ups. But man, that was such a big thing for me. I'd just gotten citizenship, and I had a White House pass. Hey, I even got to meet the president."

"You did?" Lucy was looking through the window beyond Augie's desk: the incoming tide was glassing over the sand flats in the bay, the cloud over Seattle had gone, and there was a clear view southward to Mount Rainier, its snowfields mottled with chocolate patches where the glaciers were receding.

"Kissinger took me to see him. I'd been working on this project about the Sovietization of primary education in the Eastern Bloc. The Russians were putting big money into textbooks for the Czechs, the Poles, the Hungarians, and so forth, and I wrote a memo suggesting that we ought to be doing something similar, like financing textbooks for kids in France, West Germany, Italy, and England to promote the American way of life in the West. Somehow, Kissinger got ahold of my memo and called me to his office in the West Wing. He was seriously interested. Secretly, I disapproved of Henry Kissinger: I thought détente was the worst policy we could be pursuing right then. But to sit in his office, alone with the secretary of state—that was extraordinary. I was nervous as hell, of course, but I made a pretty good job of explaining my memo, and five weeks later, at three-fifteen in the afternoon, he took me to the Oval Office.

"I felt like Henry's puppy—like I'd be whipped if I wet the carpet. The president of the United States! I'd been pulling all-nighters getting ready for this, and I'd overdosed on details. When Kissinger told me to speak, it all came out in a flood. I was telling the president about schools in Poland and Czechoslovakia, and how they were teaching history and civics there, but he wasn't looking at me, or at Kissinger. He was gazing out in space, his face totally blank. I mean, he was *elsewhere.* Don't know where. Might have been back in San Clemente . . . or China. I'd just gotten started on the Baltic states, and he sort of absent-mindedly reaches into a drawer and pulls out a golf ball, which he rolls across his desk to me. It's got the presidential seal on it, and his name. 'Thank you, Mr. President.' I'm so goofy, I go on talking. Couple minutes later, he produces a little blue leather box and pushes that across the desk. I open it, still talking, and it's got cuff links in it. Then Kissinger gets out of his chair, and I realize the interview's over. I never even got to mention my plan for Western Europe."

"What on earth did Kissinger say afterward?"

"He said, 'I'm late—I have to be in Georgetown.' Those are the last words he ever said to me." Laughing, Augie unwrapped the turned-back shirtsleeve on his left forearm and pulled out the cuff link. "There you are. Souvenir of my fifteen minutes with the president."

Lucy took it from him. Nearly all the gold plating had worn to bare metal, and there was little left of the once blue enamel and presidential seal, but the stamped signature on the back, *Richard Nixon,* was still sharp. Quite why Augie should so treasure this token of his own humiliation was hard to figure, and she filed the question in her head for future attention.

"Nixon was a piece of work. For me, it was right place, wrong administration. I'd've given my right arm to work for Ronald Reagan."

Reagan. Lucy had been a sophomore in college at Missoula when he was elected, and she had only to see his face on TV to want to chuck a brick through the screen. His horrible brown suits. The Brylcreemed hairdo that looked as if it should have gone out with giant finned fifties Pontiacs. This was the president who thought ketchup was a vegetable, that cow farts did more damage to the ozone layer than automobile emissions. She'd shuddered at his evil-empire talk, his star wars, his scary, vacant homeyness as he recited ghostwritten platitudes to the camera.

"Yeah, my liberal colleagues at the U used to look at me like that. The cultural elites of this country never did understand Reagan. But regular folks did, and so did the Poles, and the Czechs, and the people in the Gulag. They loved the man. Ask Sakharov, ask Sharansky."

Lucy reminded herself that the business of a journalist was to be a sponge, not a sparring partner. "I'm a knee-jerk Democrat and Reagan freaked me out. I must've missed something, I guess."

"He had this wonderful instinct," Augie said. "He wasn't an intellectual—didn't want to debate ideas. He relied on gut feeling to tell him what to do, and somehow or other it was Reagan's gut feelings that gave him the best grasp of the big issues of anyone then alive. He'd get it right, and right, and right again. Sure, there were stumbles: Iran-*contra,* I'll give you that. But ninety-nine—okay, ninety—percent of the time, he was magic. 'Open this gate, Mr. Gorbachev! Tear down this wall!' He bugged the snot out of the intellectuals, but if you'd been living on the wrong side of that wall you'd have worshipped Ronald Reagan. He was funny, too. Know what he said about détente?

"'Isn't that what the farmer has with his turkey—until Thanksgiving Day?' What a guy. If I had to give you one reason to respect Reagan, it'd be that he never took freedom for granted. Never. And when he saw evil in the world, he wasn't afraid to call it out by name. But I expect you're not much of a believer in evil, being a liberal and all."

Lewis Olson? Lucy thought. Was Olson evil? Sick, yes. Repellent. Oozing with fatuous hypocrisy, trying to make her say the Jesus Prayer with him in jail. But she couldn't quite bring herself to call even Lewis Olson evil. She shrugged and said, "I'm not religious."

"Neither am I, but I know evil when I see it, and so did Ronald Reagan."

Watching as he raised the old-timey Jeffersonian sash window by his desk, Lucy thought he was confusing things. Yes, as a child Augie had faced something for which evil was probably the only word, but when Reagan spoke of evil he was like an actor talking about bad hats in his old movies. Fact and fiction. Surely Augie, of all people, should see the difference?

He reached into his shirt pocket and produced the stub of cigarette he'd been smoking on the beach. "My afternoon gasper," he said, with the conspiratorial wink that Lucy was coming to dislike, as if the two of them were plotting outside Minna's ken. Perched on the window ledge, his feet barely touched the ground. He blew a plume of smoke out over Useless Bay, then ducked his head back inside.

"You make nice to me," he said, "I'll make nice to you."

"What?"

"I sometimes think Americans are just too nice for this world. They assume that other people have the same inherent streak of decency they have themselves. It's bred into the American character to appeal to the other guy's good side—do unto others, and all that crap. But we have to deal with guys who don't have a good side. Never did and never will. You think Stalin had a good side? Hitler? The fanatics who threaten us right now?" He took another suck on his cigarette, then immediately pinched out the burning tip and put the butt back in his pocket.

"D'you always do that? I've never seen anyone make a cigarette last so long."

"I got a one-a-day habit," Augie said. "You know what? I've seen people try to appease *bears*? Minna and me, we used to go camping up in the North Cascades. Fantastic country."

"I've done—"

"Then you know how to haul all your food up to the highest tree branch that you can sling a rope over?"

"Yes," Lucy said, though she'd always locked her food in the trunk of her car and hoped for the best. She and Alida had never encountered a bear.

"There's signs posted all over warning about not leaving food out, but nothing stops dumbasses from making nice to the bears by giving 'em candy and french fries. I've seen it happen. And the quickest way of getting liquidated by a bear is to appeal to his good side. It's taken us a long time to learn that lesson: it's frightening that so many people in this country still don't get it."

Hands stuffed deep in pockets, hunch-shouldered, Augie glowered into his bookshelves. "I guess I'm being naive. What do I know? I'm still a rookie citizen even now. I can get teary just reading the Constitution. So when I see my country under threat, I want to reach for my musket and be a Minuteman."

For a moment, Lucy saw him ridiculously sculpted on a marble plinth, his false teeth and peppery white mustache cast in heroic bronze, and smiled at the thought.

He seized on the smile. "It gets worse. I used to take Minna to see the Mariners. Some leukemia survivor kid's singing 'Oh, say can you see, by the dawn's early light,' and Minna's feeding me Kleenex out of her bag. It totally chokes me up. Then I see the immigrants way up in the bleachers—the Chinese, Koreans, Ukrainians, Afghanis—and they're all sobbing their guts out, you can see their shoulders heaving. They're not crying over the little kid with leukemia, they're crying over the national anthem and what it means to them. Might strike a native-born American as hopelessly sappy, but to someone like me . . ." He was blinking furiously as he spoke. "See, people like you've never known what it's like to not be an American. It gives you a different perspective on things. It teaches you how easy it'd be for America not to be America anymore."

Lucy had edged toward the desk, near enough to read what was written on the typewriter there, but could make out only one word, "Minna"; the rest appeared to be in German. "That's what your book does," she said. "I hadn't thought about it quite like that, but what I loved about it, I think, was that it reminded me of stuff I've always taken for granted."

"Never take it for granted," Augie said. "It's the littlest things. You know, not so long after I got to this country, when I was in grad school, I came across something E. B. White wrote about democracy during World War II. You know E. B. White? I memorized it on the Greyhound bus. We'd be traveling through little no-stoplight towns in the cornfields, and I'd look out the window and see people mowing their lawns, or reading the paper on the porch, or going to the store, or cranking up the car that wouldn't start, and all I'd hear in my head would be E. B. White . . ."

He cleared his throat, threw back his head, closed his eyes, and recited. "'Democracy is the line that forms on the right. It's the don't in "Don't Shove." It's the hole in the stuffed shirt through which the sawdust slowly trickles; it's the dent in the high hat. Democracy is the recurrent suspicion that more than half the people are right more than half of the time. It's the feeling of privacy in voting booths, the feeling of communion in libraries, the feeling of vitality everywhere. Democracy is the score at the beginning of the ninth. It's an idea which hasn't been disproved yet, a song the words of which have not gone bad. It's the mustard on the hot dog and the cream in the rationed coffee.

Democracy is a request from the War Board, in the middle of a morning in the middle of a war, wanting to know what democracy is.'"

"I never read that—it's beautiful," Lucy said, but she'd barely heard
the words, so distracted was she by the fact that Augie had spoken
them in a throaty middle-European accent.

"E. B. White wrote that in New York in '44." He was back to being
an American again. "Know where I was then? Town called Goslar—
picturesque old place, full of steeples and church bells, right on the
edge of the Harz mountains. I was learning to be a good Nazi."

"You flunked."

"Yeah. Got slung out of there for stealing. I was a pretty good thief,
so I must've wanted to get caught, I guess. Goslar was too quiet for
me—no planes, no bombs. I got spooked by the silence at night, and I
was plain bored in the daytime. For me, it was too much like life with
the Widow Douglas. I thought being a Nazi might be kind of fun, but it
was no fun at all. I liked my crooked ways a whole lot better."

A sudden ruckus sounded from beyond the open window—a dozen
or so gulls fighting over some treasure at the tide's edge in a manic
flurry of wings, bursting the bubblelike quiet of the afternoon with
peevish yelps and screeches.

"I think they must've found the gumboot-whatsit," Lucy said.

"Chiton. I do hope not." The look of slack-lipped anxiety on his face
as he peered out the window was absurdly disproportionate to the
occasion. He grabbed the loaf beside the typewriter and pitched it out
toward the distant gulls. For a pint-sized retired professor he had an
amazingly mighty right arm, and as Lucy watched the bread sailing high
over the lawn she almost believed that it would land squarely in the
commotion on the beach; but it fell short, as it must, and came to earth
among the piles of driftwood by the twin kayaks on the berm—just
close enough for a small flight of gulls to peel away from the main
action to investigate. In the dead-still air, she heard their claws scrabbling on wood as they jostled for possession of the bread.

"It's all right, I think. I'm pretty sure I carried the chiton farther
out, so the tide should've covered it by now."

"That bread was conveniently handy."

"Fetish," Augie said. "It's a thing I've always had. Never could work without a loaf of bread close by me. I take one up every morning. It's quite common, so I've read—Jews from the camps often do it. There was a time when I used to hoard them in drawers, but I got over that. Minna used to think it very weird when she kept finding bits of stale bread hidden under my socks." His face clouded as he looked out at the fighting birds. "Gulls are one of the very few predators of chitons. It said that in the book."

The huge bay was almost full now, the unrippled water like a film of Saran Wrap stretched tight from shore to shore. For a short second, Lucy caught a glimpse of rust-red at the epicenter of the gulls' frenzy. She hoped that Augie hadn't seen it, too. To distract him, she said, "I want to write about you, you know—for a m-m-m-m-magazine," deploying her stutter for whatever slight charm it might be worth.

"You have great eyes, Lucille."

EYE ON THE CLOCK, she drove back to the ferry as fast as she dared. Climbing the hill where the accident had happened, she slowed, readying herself for whatever might lie over the brow. Eerily, nothing at all was left of the shambles of a few hours before: no swerving black skid marks on the pavement, no muddy gouges in the roadside grass, no slivers of overlooked wreckage, *nothing*. Every trace of the event had been removed or wiped clean, and for a dizzying moment Lucy found herself wondering if she'd imagined it. So thoroughly had the emergency services done their job that it was as if they'd made the accident unhappen, turning it into a harmless trick of the morning light.

At the terminal, lines of waiting vehicles filled the parking area and there was a two-ferry delay on boarding. Security was out in force, with stone-faced soldiers and state patrol troopers with harnessed sniffer dogs. A red-letter placard at the head of each line warned drivers not to joke with security personnel.

A soldier probed under the Spider with a mirror on a short pole, checking for bombs. Another demanded ID.

She gave him her driver's license.

"National ID?"

"I d-d-d-d-don't have it yet." No one she knew did.

"You know the deadline."

"Yes."

"Get it. Soon."

A third soldier, this one female, said, "Out the car," and brushed Lucy's body head to toe with a metal-detecting wand.

She wasn't tempted to joke with any of these characters, so much less human-seeming than their dogs, who at least showed some interest, even eagerness, as they stuck their heads inside trunks and jumped onto backseats. The handsome yellow lab bitch assigned to the Spider gave the car a thirty-second shakedown and found it innocent. Offering her a biscuit, Lucy thought, would likely get you shot on sight.

Through her flip-flops, the hot tarmac felt like a griddle. She dug her old linen sun hat out of the glove compartment and sat in the open car, torpidly watching the soldiers and dogs going about their business. You could never predict security: sometimes it was nonexistent, and then—usually at the most inconvenient times—it was everywhere around you, obstructive, tedious, intrusive, rude. No explanations were ever given; the authorities seemed to take sadistic pleasure in keeping the public in the dark.

They treat us like children. Whatever was going on, the grown-ups weren't telling. Robbed of information, people childishly filled the vacuum with fantasy and rumor. Some saw the security apparatus as blatant playacting; others took it in deadly earnest. Lucy knew people so spooked that they now refused to fly, enter tall buildings, or cross long bridges for fear of being blown to bits by an enemy they couldn't name—pure self-indulgence, in her view. But she had little more patience with those like Tad, with his oddly cheerful Internet conspiracy theories, his breezy conviction that the whole thing was a gigantic hoax perpetrated by a criminal administration on a clueless electorate. So she oscillated uncomfortably between being somewhat scared and somewhat skeptical, never quite one or the other: an agnostic on this as on so much else, a little envious of the true believers for their easy certitude.

She'd always had a problem with arriving at a confident point of view. In Lucy's experience, almost every case had merit on both sides, and she had an unhappy knack of riling both whenever she incautiously threw in her two cents' worth. Time and again she'd replayed the scene in the Miles City kitchen, her mother yelling, "You know what's wrong with you? You have as much personality as a piece of blotting paper!" And when Lucy considered this accusation, found a speck of merit in it, and replied calmly that since her mother had such a superabundant personality, she'd never felt any great need to cultivate one of her own, she'd nearly been brained by a flying plate.

A ferry came, swallowed half the vehicles on the lot, and went. Lucy called Tad on his cell phone and found him home already: apparently the nuclear catastrophe had been called off early to allow rush-hour traffic through on Route 99. He'd been only slightly injured, he said, and yeah, sure, he could pick up Alida before six from her after-school program.

"So how's Vanags?"

"Oh, he's like, Reagan was the greatest president in history, and I'm like, *Yeah* . . ."

A mile off on the water, the ferry let out a belch of diesel smoke from its funnel, and for a split second Lucy imagined it shuddering from an explosion deep in its guts. How long would it take a ferry to go down?

"That's our Professor Vanags."

Putting the phone back in her bag, Lucy felt a stab of disloyalty to Augie; she'd said that only because it was the sort of thing Tad liked to hear. She needed to get August Vanags down on paper, but in the round, not as Tad's cartoon reactionary. She propped her notebook against the steering wheel and scribbled, "presidential cuff links & presidential library," then "gumboot chiton," then "neediness," then "Slang—*dollars to doughnuts . . . peepers . . . put the kibosh on.*" Looking up from the too-bright dazzle of the page, she saw she'd drawn the attention of a soldier with a glassy, incurious stare. When she made herself smile at him, his eyes drifted lazily, indifferently away.

There was a stir of activity in the lines as a blue Chrysler sedan with B.C. plates was escorted to the far corner of the waiting area, where a bunch of soldiers disemboweled it, pulling out heaps of decent-looking luggage, carpets, papers, headrests, tools, the spare tire. A book was passed from hand to hand, a silver thermos bottle held aloft like a rare trophy and carried to the nearby Humvee. One guardsman weighed in his arms a large cellophane-wrapped teddy bear, as if to price it; another, spread-eagled on his back on a wheeled sled, scooted underneath the chassis, flashlight waving.

The baseball-capped driver, flanked by unamused soldiers, weapons at the ready, was clowning for the crowd. Hopping from foot to foot, he shrugged and showed his palms in a dumb show of astonished innocence, all the time beaming at his audience with a chimpish grin. *Heh, heh, heh! Look what I got into! Just my luck, huh?*

Lucy was with the soldiers on this one. Had she been in charge, she'd have given the guy the works, too. Khaki-skinned, implausibly single, Canadian-plated, he looked like trouble incarnate, and shit-eating fraudulence was written all over that grin. She'd have turned him back at the border—and if he'd crossed at Blaine, why had he taken this devious route through Whidbey Island? She hoped the soldiers would hold him for a good while yet; she didn't want to travel on the same ferry as that joker. Years back, she'd written a "Talk of the Town" piece about the arrest of Ahmed Ressam, the Algerian terrorist who'd planned to blow up LAX, at the ferry terminal in Port Angeles, and this guy looked like Ressam's double.

Then she jolted into reverse. This was stupid "profiling"; no real bomber would so neatly fit the stereotype; and catching stereotypes was the ineffectual best that the army and police could do. Studying the man again, his pathetic jiggling dance, all she saw was bemusement and fear—the natural creaturely terror of someone entangled in the workings of an enormous, incomprehensible military machine. The guy looked like he was peeing his pants—and suddenly Lucy found herself with the ACLU.

He was still under military detention when the next ferry showed, wallowing like a hippo at the dock head. It took an age to empty, then, at last, the lines of cars began to move. As Lucy turned on the Spider's ignition, she saw that the suspect was being allowed to reload his baggage into the Chrysler. Most likely, he'd make this ferry after all. Despite herself, she couldn't help wishing the soldiers had held on to him for just five minutes more.

Climbing the crowded stairwell to the lounge, notebook in hand, she was back to thinking about August Vanags. Out on the gravel, saying good-bye, he'd looked melancholy at losing his captive audience. "Next time you must stay the night—and do bring your little girl. We have acres of space here, and Minna loves to have kids around." It'd be no fun for Alida, but Lucy wasn't above resorting to bribery and main force. Next time she'd bring her cassette recorder, small enough to nestle unnoticed in her bag, to collect Augie's weird speeches on tape. After her *New Yorker* piece on Bill Gates came out, Gates himself had dropped her an e-mail complimenting her on her "great memory." Little did he know.

She was looking around the lounge for a table where she could settle down to making notes when she saw them—the knotted pink silk scarf, the gold chain, the cashmere blazer, the man with his patrician drinker's face, and the frail-looking wife, glossy real-estate brochure spread on the table between them. Lucy's first thought was that by some miracle they'd survived their fatal accident, her second was that her own wits were deranged.

The woman, looking up from the brochure, gave her a faint, querying smile of uncertain recognition, which Lucy fought to return in kind before walking on and putting as great a distance as she could between herself and the couple whose lives she had so confidently terminated earlier in the day.

Well, of course, she thought, as she found a seat out of the wind on the deserted stern deck, *there are a million different kinds of silver cars. They have a silver car, the Infiniti was silver—two and two make five.* It was the sort of mistake anyone in shock might make. Except she wasn't anyone. She'd always prided herself in questioning her own assumptions—how could she have been so fucking dumb? She wanted to weep.

Unpleasantly aware that she was no longer alone, she looked up and saw the man she now thought of as the terrorist. He appeared to be running a fever, or maybe was just trembling as a result of his ordeal. His hollow grin was still in place, as if he were wearing a monkey mask.

He stepped toward her. "Cigarette," he said. "You want?" and held out a pack with an unfamiliar logo, probably Canadian.

"No," Lucy said. Smoking had been forbidden on the ferries for years, though the ashtrays between the seats outside hadn't been removed. She pointed at the NO SMOKING sign. The man looked around the empty deck, then winked at her. Turning away, cupping his hands against the wind, he made his smoker's stink. After officiously shaking his match to kill the flame, he turned back to her. "You go to game?"

She allowed herself a brief sigh of irritation. "No. What game?"

"Blue Jays," he said. "And Seattle Mariners."

"I don't follow baseball," she said with crisp finality.

"Big Blue Jays fan." The pest tapped the front of his cap.

Lucy made a show of setting her notebook on her knees and getting out her pen.

"Writing!" he exclaimed, making it sound a bizarre activity like pigeon racing or numismatics.

"Sorry. I'm busy, can't you see?"

He took two steps back, puffed a gobbet of smoke in Lucy's direction, and said, "Friendly!"

Getting up to go, she decided that she wouldn't greatly care if they carted this guy off in shackles and cuffs to Guantánamo Bay.

3

FOR ALIDA, her homework done, it was a happy surprise to be rescued
from the after-school program by Tad in his ancient sky-blue Beetle.
Alida loved Tad—an uncomplicated equation with no troubling variables. When he showed in the doorway of the classroom looking a bit
lost, eyes swimming behind his rimless specs, sunlight glinting in his
bristles, his denim shirt open to the tangle of gray hair on his chest, the
few remaining kids all looked up. The two eighth-grade boys stopped
their card game; girls suddenly lost interest in their books and work
sheets and just stared at him. It was a knack Tad had: though he wasn't
handsome, he always attracted attention, as if he were somehow bigger,
more alive, than other people.

Alida put this down to his being famous. He wasn't really, really
famous, but he was famous in Seattle. He was Scrooge in *A Christmas
Carol* and he appeared in TV commercials all the time, as Mister Autoglass, George the Plumber saying "Just call George," the crazy chef who
juggled clams for Ivar's restaurants, the MagiGro gardener. He didn't
look or sound like Tad when he was acting: he could change his voice,
shape, face, age, and become a whole different person, so what
strangers saw in Tad wasn't the familiar face of a newsreader or a weatherman but the inner glow of fame itself—something that must come,

Alida guessed, from all the lights, cameras, and clapping audiences he'd faced in his life as an actor.

Whenever Tad appeared in *her* life, questions followed. "Is he your dad?" That was easy to answer—"No, he's Tad with a T, not Dad with a D." But "Is he your mom's boyfriend?" was harder. The thought of old Tad being a boy-anything was pretty funny, and her mom hadn't had a boyfriend for years and years. She didn't want to be disloyal and tell people he was gay, so usually she said, "MYOB," making an enjoyable mystery of it.

In her own mind, though, both questions were a lot more complicated than she would ever let on, and they often teased her during the long strange hours when she couldn't get to sleep and would click the light on her alarm to see midnight and then one or two o'clock in the morning. Because Tad *was* sort of like a dad. He gave her daddish presents, like her iPod, and though her laptop had been a joint birthday present with her mom, she bet Tad had paid for most of it, just as she knew he helped pay for her school fees. Like a dad, he often drove her to parties and sleepovers. If her mom went away to work on a story, she'd stay with Tad in his apartment, in the dark little spare room hung with old framed posters of the plays that he'd been in, in cities as far away as Minneapolis and St. Louis and Houston and Denver. Staying there was always fun. They ate out a lot in restaurants and went to movies and plays, where Tad took her backstage afterward to meet the actors and called her "my date," which was kind of cool. On weekends, she had to make Tad's breakfast for him—half a grapefruit, and eggs over easy on toast done just right. She hardly ever got to cook when her mom was home, and then it was only kid stuff like brownies.

The boyfriend question was an even trickier one: Tad and her mom never slept together or anything, but they did hug and sometimes late at night she heard them arguing like parents. When she tiptoed out of bed and put her ear to the door, she'd hear her own name—because something or other was "good for Alida" or "bad for Alida," as if she were some kind of tender plant in the MagiGro gardener's hothouse. After these arguments Tad sometimes went missing for a day or two, and Alida would have to knock on his door to roust him out. But mostly anyone who didn't know them would think Tad and her mom were just another old married couple.

Loving Tad, Alida worried about him—a lot, and especially when he was out of her sight. But in his presence these worries seemed remote, like a half-remembered nightmare on a sunny morning. A word she'd lately discovered was "hypochondriac," but true hypochondriacs were afraid of disease in themselves; she was a hypochondriac for Tad, and there must be another word for that.

As they walked up the hill outside the school toward the parked Beetle, Alida saw he was hiding a bandaged wrist beneath the cuff of his shirt. "What happened?"

"Oh, nothing, just a scratch. Had a close encounter with a shovel. I was in this stupid play all day—you saw the smoke? That was when the scenery caught on fire."

"A play?"

"*The Comedy of Errors*," Tad said, puffing uphill in the heat, his face even pinker than usual.

You could always see Tad's car from miles away: it was older than anyone else's, and its backside was plastered with an untidy collage of fading stickers. The battered VW, with its rust patches, with the door that had to be wiggled just right to get it open, with the mouthlike gash in the front passenger seat that sprouted tickly stuffing, was named "the heap," and Alida found it hard to understand why he was so proud of it. When his mom died last year, he'd inherited her big white car, which was spooky to ride in because it really belonged to a dead person, but it still smelled new, and Alida luxuriated in its mondo-comfortable seats, the soft red glow of the dials at night, the clock with hands on the dash, and the expensive hush inside even when it prowled through the streets—a silence she'd fill by sliding her Green Day CD into the stereo, which made the whole car shiver deliciously with the thunder of the bass. She'd just decided she could probably get over the car's spookiness when Tad sold it. Asked why, he said that compared with the heap it was a gas-guzzler and got too many caribous to the gallon.

"Think Globally, Act Locally" and "Support Your Local Planet" were two of the bumper stickers on the heap, along with "Just Because You're Paranoid It Doesn't Mean They Aren't Out to Get You," the names of old, forgotten politicians who'd once run for president, and the mystifying "Sack the Cox-Sacker." You could always get Tad going by asking "Who was Jerry Brown?" or "Who was George McGovern?" It seemed like nobody he'd voted for had ever won—something else that Tad took a strange pride in, as if losers were better than winners, and Alida had the feeling that if his hero Ralph Nader had actually become president, it wouldn't have taken Tad any time at all to despise him. He was always saying "He sold out" about some politician, and in Tad's language winning appeared to be the surefire way of selling out.

When Alida herself won—like taking first place in the individual section of the interschool sixth-grade Math Olympiad, which was filmed on community TV—she had to be careful about how she delivered the news to Tad. She didn't want him to think she was a sellout. It probably would've been better to come in third, but Tad seemed happy enough with her first place and bought her the iPod the next day as a reward.

Windows rolled down, the Beetle jounced and rattled into the crawl of traffic on Boren. Alida's seat was unpleasantly, intimately hot. Falling away below them, the city looked as if it were melting: tall buildings trembling in the heat like columns of gas, cars afloat like boats in streets of liquid haze, skinny gold rectangles of water showing in the gaps between the office towers. When Tad turned right into the low sun, Alida caught the sudden blaze through the grimy windshield and covered her face with her hands. "It's kind of like *enervating*," she said, trying the word out aloud for the first time.

"Enervating, right. Be glad you're not a sockeye salmon."

"Why?"

"They were talking about it on the radio this morning. Know what temperature a sockeye gets stressed out with heat exhaustion? Sixty-eight degrees. Last week they measured the temperature of Lake Washington—sixty-nine degrees. It should be like fifty this time of year. By June, when the sockeye come in from the sea, they're saying it could be eighty. Which means that every stupid fish that makes it through the locks is going to die of asphyxiation."

"That's so sad," Alida said, keeping to herself the fact that salmon was her absolute least favorite food.

"Imagine Lake Washington full of angelfish and guppies."

"We did the greenhouse effect. I wrote a lab report about it. We used a heat lamp and soda bottles, black construction paper and water and thermometers and Alka-Seltzer. It was cool."

"Alka-Seltzer?"

"Yeah. It gives off carbon dioxide when it fizzes."

The tang of smoke from the morning fire grew thicker as they drove down over the bridge across the freeway, where the packed miles of cars and trucks were at a growling standstill, toxic gunk spilling into the air from every tailpipe. Alida counted off emissions on the fingers of her left hand: sulfur, carbon, nitrous oxide, ozone. "It's so obvious," she said. "Why can't they just *get* it?"

"All the usual reasons: greed, arrogance, stupidity, blind denial. Lobbyists. President Reagan—he was the one before Bush's dad—said that cow farts did more damage to the atmosphere than the entire automobile industry."

"The *president* said that?"

"I expect some flack for General Motors dreamed that bright thought up for him."

"But the president said *farts*?"

"Maybe he said 'flatulence,' I don't remember. He had it in for trees, too. Very dangerous things, trees. Fouling up the air with their horrible hydrocarbons. Like a Douglas fir is a whole lot worse than a Chevy Suburban or a Ford Expedition, and a whole forest is a frigging ecological disaster." Stopped at a light, Tad was doing his actor thing, assembling his face into a new shape. His cheeks bulged, his upper teeth were exposed in a slightly crooked grin, and when he spoke it was in a solemn, rusty-sounding grandpa voice: "And so, my fellow Americans, today I ask you to join with me in saluting the heroes of the timber industry, the loggers who daily risk their lives to preserve this blessed land, this last and greatest bastion of freedom, from the deadly pollution of trees."

"No he didn't." Tad was a good actor, but his exaggerations could be pretty silly. "He never said that."

"Well, not in so many words, maybe, but he *thought* it."

Which was not, Alida thought, a satisfactory explanation. She didn't like fantasy—had totally hated *The Lord of the Rings*, for instance, which they'd had to read last semester. The trouble with fantasy was that you could always see how everything could just as easily have been otherwise, and Tad's tall stories suffered from the same problem. Like her mom said, though she meant something a little different, Tad's weakness was his tendency to be "unrealistic," and Alida was hungry for realism. Most of her favorite books were nonfiction, like Anne Frank's diary, and Peg Kehret's memoir of the year she had polio as a kid—books where stuff happened because there was no other way for it to happen, however much the author might have wanted it to happen differently.

The Beetle turned the corner onto Adams Street; then Tad wrestled the gear stick into reverse and began to back into a parking spot. "You've got your prosecuting attorney's face on, Ali. What's up?"

"I was just thinking."

"About what?"

Alida unbuckled her seat belt and wound up the window. "Fiction and nonfiction."

Adams Street was where the city lost its fuzziness and noise, swelling into sudden sharp focus like that picture by the famous Dutch artist where everything—housemaids, cobblestones, kids, brooms, chimney pots—was part of a complicated pattern. "It's all in the composition," Mr. McNeil, her art teacher, said, and it was as a composition that Alida saw Adams Street: its chubby pigeons, its yellow fire hydrant, the cracks in the sidewalk, the telephone pole silvered with staples where it wasn't wrapped around with notices of rock concerts and lost cats, the ancient iron manhole cover embossed with the head of an Indian chief, and the rosy purple brick and molded gray terra-cotta of the Acropolis building. She wasn't much good at art, unlike

Gail, who always got A's, but Alida could imagine herself painting Adams Street like—what was the guy's name? Jan something. *Vermeer.*

To Alida, who loved facts, no fact was more reliable than Apt. #701, 420 Adams Street, Seattle, WA 98104, USA, Planet Earth, the Universe. She'd been driven there straight from Swedish Hospital as a one-day-old, and the building held her entire past like a box. Schools and teachers changed, friends were made and lost, people died, but the Acropolis, old as the city, went on being the Acropolis. It always smelled the same, of overbaked cookies and Lysol. She knew every moan and grumble of the narrow elevator that was a tight squash for three. She was comforted by the rusty jungle gym of fire escapes at the back of the building, on which she'd always been strictly forbidden to play. She was strangely proud of the decaying remains of the advertisement that had been painted long ago on the building's west side. Nothing was left of the picture except a few dim flakes of color that clung to the brick. Nowadays, nobody could make out the letters of the message, but when Alida was a little kid, still learning to read, she and her mom had decoded it. It said, or used to say:

COLD OR HOT
SPAM HITS THE SPOT

Recently, Alida had tried it out on Gail, who peered at it for a long time, put on her glasses, peered some more, and shook her head, giving up. Being the knowledgeable guardian of the building's history made Alida feel she was its owner. Then she'd noticed a can of Spam on a supermarket shelf and talked her mom into buying it. The taste was repulsive, like slimy cat food, but she saved the can as evidence and used it as a crayon holder on her homework desk. When the last ghostly letter finally faded from the wall, she'd still see the slogan there: "Cold or Hot, Spam Hits the Spot," as much a part of the character of the Acropolis as the "Semper Excelsior" grandly painted in gold on blue over the arched entrance to her school.

She and Tad were goofing around in his place when her mom

showed up, looking damp and frazzled from the heat. The ferry had been late, she'd got stuck at a roadblock, there'd been an accident . . . Alida knew that voice—the rapid, weary, one-note rat-a-tat-tat that meant her mom was losing it. Tad took charge. Switching character on the instant, he became a cool, soft-spoken ship's captain, or the wise old doctor in the ER. He ordered up food from the Chinese restaurant they liked, told her mom to take a shower, opened a bottle of wine, and asked Alida to set the table in the apartment across the hall.

She'd watched Tad do these split-second makeovers on himself a million times, but was still always a little fazed by how someone she usually thought of as gentle and bumbly could just turn it on, *like that,* as if flicking a hidden switch in his pocket. Big question: did Tad think of what he did as faking, putting on a phoney act, or did he believe that he'd actually become this new masterful-type guy?

Suddenly handsome, with tight lips and squared-back shoulders, he said, "Too hot for candles, but let's do flowers," and scooped up a vase of stinky lilies and carried them through to her and her mom's place. "Root beer for you, kiddo: it's in the fridge."

The lilies helped to mask the smell of smoke in the apartment, whose windows had been left open all day, and Alida, admiring her handiwork, thought the blue cloth, place mats, napkins, glasses, and chopsticks made the table look just like one in a magazine, everything just so, a model of order in an untidy world, like the rooms in Gail's house, which always looked as if they were waiting to be photographed for *Martha Stewart Living* or something. Seeing the table, you'd never guess what a mess the rest of the apartment was.

Her mom showed, smiling, smelling of shampoo, and wearing the splashy muumuu that made her look like a walking flower shop. "You did the table, Rabbit? That's beautiful."

Alida wrinkled her nose and shrugged like it was nothing special, but she was pleased her mom had noticed.

When the food came, Tad tipped the contents of the greasy white-card boxes into bowls. It was only Chinese takeout, but between them Alida and Tad had made the meal into a fancy feast. With the hot city going dark outside, and the lamp by the table throwing the rest of the room into shadow, their dinner had the glowing promise of a lighted stage just before the actors step in to start the play.

Her mom was the first to sit down. "You're such geniuses, you two— thank you. I had the weirdest day." She slopped wine into her glass and passed the bottle to Tad.

Alida, watching the level drop against the side of the label, reckoned that her mom had taken 250 milliliters and Tad barely 150, which was typical. They were drinking zinfandel: 15 percent alcohol, it said, which was a lot. Alida, who'd done her research on the Internet and in the kitchen with a measuring cup, knew that binge drinking for women began at 600 milliliters of wine in one evening, so her mom was almost halfway to a whole binge with one of her big glasses, and maybe even closer with this high-alcohol stuff she was chugging down now. Stored in the Drafts folder of Outlook Express on Alida's laptop was a message to her mom about her drinking, which she'd never quite found the courage to send, even though she'd edited it many times, trying to make it more loving and less stern.

Alida helped herself to four small spoonfuls of rice, lemon chicken, scallops in garlic sauce, and Buddhist Delight vegetables, which she chased around her plate for a while with chopsticks before she gave up, as she always did, and got a fork out of the drawer.

Her mom was saying, "When you knew him, did Augie Vanags have an accent?"

"Augie?" Tad put down his glass. "So we're on pet-name terms now? Sure he did. He talked like a Nazi in a British World War II movie. The kids called him Dr. K."

"He knew Kissinger. He worked for the National Security Council, the dark-arts people. Henry took a brief shine to him, then he messed up with Nixon and Henry dropped him."

Alida switched off, letting her mind address the baffling love life of Jessica King and Steve Kunz, until she heard Tad say, "He used to hit on his students."

"He hit his students?"

"Just an expression," Tad said. "He tried to date them. He—"

Someone started banging on the door. "Land lord!"—two words, not one.

"Don't let him in," Tad said. "He has to give a week's notice, it's state law. Tell him to put it in writing. Jesus, what an hour!"

"Maybe he smelled the food," her mom said. "Rabbit, let him in, will you?" Then, to Tad, in an urgent whisper: "There's no point in needlessly antagonizing the guy."

Alida unlocked the door. The new landlord walked in, beaming, like a celebrity guest on a late-night talk show.

"Hi, how ya doin'? Eatin', huh? Don't mind me. Just checkin' in. Gotta make sure everybody's happy, right? Hey, Mr. MagiGro!" But as he spoke Alida saw his eyes roaming impatiently from wall to wall and floor to ceiling, as if one sidelong glimpse of the people at the table had exhausted his interest in them. He stood frowning in front of the tall bookcases that her mom had built with old wooden Pepsi crates. Without turning his head, he asked, "You got them things fixed to the wall?"

"No."

Alida could hear the defensiveness in her mom's voice.

"Get somebody killed. Next earthquake, them suckers fly all over like goddam ducks. Hit somebody on the head, like little Missy there. Pow!" He reached to an upper shelf, and Alida saw the Pepsi crate wobble ever so slightly under the pressure of his forefinger. "Brain damage," he said, looking disapprovingly at her mom's collection of old novels. He snatched one out—a paperback called *Beloved*—and peered into the space he'd made. "Yeah. What you want is masonry screws. Two-and-a-half-inch. And plugs. You got power drill?"

Tad laughed at the question. Her mom said, "No, I don't."

"I got cordless, heavy duty. You get all them books out, maybe I get that shit fixed on the weekend."

"Well, thank you, Mr. Lee—if you're sure you r-really have the t-t-time." Her mom was blushing, suddenly awkward in the face of the landlord's offer.

"Not a problem." He waved an imaginary drill at the piled crates. "*Vroom, vroom, vroom, vroom, vroom*: take a coupla minutes." He stood back from the shelves, shaking his head. "Wah! You got death trap there."

"I didn't think."

"People don't." He riffled through the pages of *Beloved*, squinting at the blocks of print like a kid with dyslexia. "Story book," he said, and wedged it back into the shelf.

Her mom, wine bottle in hand, said, "Mr. Lee?" But he was at the open window, back turned, hands planted on the sill, looking down into the dark alley that ran along the side of the building. "Riffraff," he said. "Scumbags. Dirt balls."

"Homeless people," Tad said.

The alley had always been off-limits to Alida, and the line of over-flowing Dumpsters, the open-air club of unshaven men with bedrolls and dogs on string leashes, held for her the romantic fascination of for-bidden territory. When she walked past, sometimes men would call out to her—not in a scary way, just sort of saying hi. Schooled by her mother, she'd quicken her step and focus frigidly on the middle dis-tance, making like an automaton. This was what her mom called street smarts: shoulders back, look straight ahead, and walk with purpose, always stay on the outside of the sidewalk, never make eye contact with strangers. Alida usually failed to observe these rules for more than about thirty seconds because street smarts made you look so weird that people would stare like you were some kind of retard.

"*Scumbags,*" the landlord said, turning around to answer Tad. "Low-lifes. They got weapons out there. I could show you. All kind of weapons."

That was another thing. Twice in the last year, Alida had heard the crack of what sounded like gunshots. "Just a car backfiring," her mom said, but so quickly that Alida knew she was lying. One morning, the alley had been cordoned off with yellow tape, and police cars with flashing lights were blocking both ends. Though nobody said anything, Alida guessed there'd been a murder. From her bedroom window, she scrutinized the paving stone for bloodstains, but they'd obviously hosed the alley clean. She hugged this knowledge to herself: what par-ents would let their kids come over to a house on such intimate terms with murder? Yet she was proud of her scary secret. "Yeah, we had a homicide," she'd think, and the thought felt satisfyingly grown-up and sophisticated; it put her in a place where stuff happened that ordinary people only read about in books or saw on TV—though she never told anybody, not even Tad, because she wasn't one hundred percent sure that it was true.

"You got a nice life here," the landlord said, and the sweep of his hand took in the patterned rugs, the stereo, the desktop computer, the pine furniture, everything stripped and varnished by her mom, the big old leather couch on which they'd snuggle up to watch movies on DVD.

For a split second, Alida saw it all as the landlord must see it—its warmth and coziness, its tan and scarlet colors, not just anybody's home, but one that was unique to her and her mom.

"Penthouse apartment. City view, water view. Whole lot of people want what you got here, and you know what? Them scumbags down there hate you for it. They kill for what you got. How often you get break-ins, huh?"

"Never," Tad said with a fierceness that took Alida by surprise.

"Touch wood." Her mom, laughing too loud, made a big show of slapping her palm on the tabletop.

From her window, Alida had often seen Tad talking to the men who slept in the alley. Sometimes he went with food, sometimes with money. So was he like buying protection from them?

"Hey, you guys, I'll show you something. Missy there—you lock me out, okay?"

Alida resented being called Missy but did as she was told, shutting the door on him and hearing the decisive double clunk of the lock spring shut. The moment she was back in her seat, though, the door opened on Mr. Lee, smiling modestly, hands behind his back, tipping his head in a little ceremonial bow to the people at the table.

"No key!" He showed the empty palm of his left hand, then held up a card in his right. "Driver's license." He wriggled it through the air—a quick, falling shimmer of green. "See?"

"Nice trick," Tad said. "I wish I could do that. But I guess they didn't offer Robbery 101 when I was in college." He was using his "gay" voice—nasal, a pitch higher than normal, ending each sentence like it was a question. It was the voice he put on to talk to people he didn't like. Alida saw her mom cast him a warning glance, like he'd better watch it, or else.

The grinning landlord, deaf to Tad's hostility, said, "That's how much security you got. Make you feel real safe, huh? First thing I'm gonna get you locks that lock, not like that chickenshit you got there."

Chickenshit? In Alida's mind, the word "landlord" conjured someone who'd never, ever say "chickenshit," and the more she saw of Mr. Lee, the more he seemed like an imposter. The old landlord—the real landlord—had been an incredibly ancient, fragile bag of bones in a black topcoat and checkered scarf, his mottled scalp shining under a thin fluff of silvery hair, with the voice of a wheezing bird. Every year, just before Christmas, Mr. Winslow would look in for a ten-minute chat, always bringing a wrapped box of candy for Alida. He talked in a roundabout, flowery way, like a character in one of those boring PBS series that her mom liked to watch, where everybody wore costumes and the women had huge fake butts tucked into the backs of their skirts, which was gross. They spent most of their time wandering around gardens speaking in Olde English and never getting anywhere, so far as Alida could make out. Yet she liked Mr. Winslow, even if—or maybe because—he did belong in a wax museum.

Last Christmas he failed to show up, and a few days later they heard that he was dead. Then his kids—a man and a woman who looked almost as old as he did—put the Acropolis building up for sale. The first time Alida had met Mr. Lee, he was standing below her in the stairwell. He looked up, said, "Bang! Bang!" and for one appalled moment she'd thought he was holding a real gun. It turned out to be a laser gun for measuring distances, and the new landlord let her play with it for a minute or two: you pointed it at a wall, clicked the trigger, and the LCD readout showed "008′ 5.75″" or whatever, which was kind of cool. But for that one moment on the stairs, Mr. Lee had looked like her every crazy fear come true.

Now her mom was asking him if he'd like a drink. Mr. Lee shook his head at the bottle of wine but said, "I'll take water," and sat in the empty chair beside Alida. She saw him inspecting each bowl of food on the table like he was giving it a grade—a C for this, a D for that, to judge by his pursed lips and severe eyes.

"Can I get you a plate?" her mom said from the sink, where she was filling his glass. "There's plenty for four."

"I ate already."

He was too young to be a landlord—years and years younger than her mom. His Beatle haircut made him look sort of like George Harrison, if you could imagine a Korean or a Vietnamese George Harrison. He had a pierced ear but no ring in it. His gray suit, riddled through with glittering threads like silver wire, would've fit a much fatter man; its double-breasted jacket, open at the front, sagged over his narrow shoulders and hung in loose folds by his sides. He reeked of perfume, a sharp, waxy, leathery scent that reminded her of Tad's mother's car, and she bet that the label on the bottle said something like Mercedes-Benz.

"Use a fork, huh?" he said suddenly, confidentially, into Alida's ear. "No chopsticks?" He picked up the pair beside her plate, and in his hand they turned into the clacking beak of a fierce bird. She'd never seen chopsticks move so fast and nimbly. They hovered, ospreylike, a foot above her plate, then plunged to snatch a scallop. She thought the landlord was going to put it in his mouth—gross!—but the poor scallop stayed aloft, a single drop of garlic sauce landing on her Buddhist vegetables.

"You want I teach you?"

"It's okay," Alida said.

He let the scallop fall back on the plate and returned the chopsticks to her place mat. "K'why-dzer!" he said.

"What?"

"*Kw-eye . . . dzuh*. Chopsticks."

"Are you from China?"

"Family come from over there." He said *fambly*. "Once. Long time ago." He picked up his water glass, held it beneath his nose, sniffed long and deep, then took a sip, which he swilled around in his mouth exactly as Alida had occasionally seen Tad doing with wine in a restaurant. This strange performance had both Tad and her mom gazing at Mr. Lee and swapping undercover glances. After many seconds of noisy tooth- and cheek-rinsing, the landlord swallowed, and said, "Old pipes."

Tad said, "It's an old building."

"Them Winslow folks, they ever do *any* maintenance?"

"Schuyler Winslow always fixed what needed fixing."

"Wah!" It was not quite a laugh and not quite a sneer. "You better believe it, I'm going to show you a thing or two 'bout what need fixing." *Ting* for *thing*. "I tell you, I got plans you gonna like. Gonna take this neighborhood upscale, clean out all them bums. This ought to be class part of town, but ain't nothing won't happen here without you get them toerags off of the street."

"And what are you planning to use, Mr. Lee? Rat poison? Gas?"

Mr. Lee stared at Tad for a full five seconds, then turned to Alida's mom. "Funny guy," he said. "Why they let this neighborhood go? Downtown so close, it don't make sense. Where's the business? This block, all you got's that old TV store and the antics—and nobody go in there, don't nobody want to buy that crap."

That wasn't fair. When Alida and her mom needed something like a homework desk or a chest for camp, they always went across the street to Mr. Kawasuki's Almost Antiques. Alida had spent hours alone in there, browsing the bookshelves at the back, petting Mr. Kawasuki's two cats, and digging for treasures in the 50¢ and $1.00 boxes. Her jewelry box came from Almost Antiques, and so did most of the jewelry inside it.

"What I see long term?" Mr. Lee was speaking softly, facing her mom but almost talking to himself. "I see you go out the door and you got the restaurant, nice restaurant, right there. You got the grocery store. You got the dry cleaners. And Starbucks. You got to have the Starbucks."

On *Adams Street*?

"You go out a night, and it's real safe, lotta people there, good people. You got the condo blocks, just like in Belltown."

Alida was confused. Adams Street wouldn't be Adams Street, wouldn't be home. For a moment she saw Mr. Kawasuki's store boarded over, wrecking balls swinging through the sky, the street filled with the threatening fog of construction dust. Yet she couldn't help but warm to some of his ideas; she had a particular weakness for iced mocha.

"Like I say, long term. Short term, you got to think security. Way you are now, you come back some afternoon and it ain't gonna be your apartment no more, you know that? You gonna have the riffraff living here, cooking up your food, music on your stereo, shooting up right in your bathroom. Big party, lot of scumbag fun. You show up, they say 'You go!'—and you gonna be looking at thirty-eight automatic pistol. Junkie with the gun, he got the shakes, he don't know *what* his finger do."

Tad said, "I think—"

"I *know*," the landlord said. "I know them low-life assholes, and what they want is what you got. See here!" He was out of his seat and by the door in a single movement that reminded Alida of a hummingbird's mysterious ability to transfer itself invisibly from one space to another. "Okay, you got real lock in here with deadbolt. Now what, huh? What you need? Surveillance. Up here, bell ring—you got visitors. Who down there? You don't know. Oh, sure, you got intercom, but intercom ain't no security. Maybe friend says, 'Is me,' but maybe you got lowlife down there waiting to get in door with friend. Maybe friend don't see lowlife, maybe lowlife hold a gun to friend. How you know what going on down there? Easy, 'cause right here"—he shaped a rectangle with his hands at shoulder height beside the door—"you got TV that show you the street, show everybody who there, fish-eye view!"

"Cool!" Alida said, the word escaping her involuntarily.

"Cool," the landlord echoed. "See? Now you got security. Now you sleep good, not listen all the night for scumbag on stairs." Grinning, he replanted himself in his chair. To Alida, he said, "Hey, maybe I get you a doorman. How you like that, huh?"

Alida tried and failed to imagine a doorman—fitted out in a blue uniform with silver braid—guarding the entrance to the Acropolis. "You're kidding, right?"

"Mr. Lee, uh, do you have other apartment buildings in the city?"

Alida heard the incredulity in Tad's voice, and watched the landlord as he inspected the question from every conceivable angle before he supplied an answer.

"Apartment block? No, first time." He was speaking to her mom again, not Tad. "I got a bunch of parking lots, though. Get one, then two, you know how it goes. Right now I got seven. Downtown, Capitol Hill, Lower Queen Anne, all over. Nearest to you, I got one on Yesler and Second. Excellent Parking—ever go there?"

"Oh, that one," her mom said. "The rates just went way up."

The landlord shuffled his shoulders inside his too-big jacket. "What market will stand, hey?" He laughed, as if this was a kind of joke between him and her mom. "Go to New York City, know what you pay there? Fifteen bucks one hour, what somebody from New York tell me. Like in Seattle, I give you half-price, see?" That laugh again. Never in Alida's hearing had anyone come quite so close to actually going *tee-hee-hee.*

He swung around in his chair to face her. "I'm like you," he said. "Got to go back to school, study up to be land lord. Parking lots I know, apartments whole new ball game, got to learn a lot. You give me feed-back, I see what I can do. Lesson One: got to keep tenant happy, right? So you help me and I help you."

"Okay." That seemed a fair deal to Alida, who was still thinking of how cool it would be to see every visitor on a TV monitor, caught by the camera unawares.

"Hey, I gotta question. Mr. MagiGro!" Arms folded on the tabletop, he leaned forward, grinning at Tad. "I been thinking about the lobby."

"Lobby? The hallway?" Tad sounded distant, disdainful, and Alida wished that the landlord would stop annoying him with the Mr. Magi-Gro thing.

"Need new paint down there. Whole building need new paint. But what I think is to make nice with green, like what I see is palm tree in bucket. Would grow okay in lobby?"

"A palm tree, in a bucket." Tad took off his glasses, wiped the lenses against his shirtfront, and put them back, perching them on the tip of his nose and peering over their tops, exactly as he did in the MagiGro commercials. All traces of irritation were gone from his voice when he looked earnestly at Mr. Lee and said, "You'd be looking at a pygmy Laotian date palm, tolerant of shade."

Alida had no idea that Tad actually knew something about this gardening stuff. She and her mom had two big window boxes of flowers; he had none. True, he often brought cut flowers home, like the lilies, but he'd never shown interest in growing anything at all.

"Loamy soil," he said. "You might want to add a little lime to raise its pH."

Amazing.

"I'd use quite a bit of peat moss. And charcoal. Charcoal's very good for palms."

The landlord was nodding slowly, nodding and blinking, like he understood what Tad was talking about, which Alida was sure he didn't.

"You'd need to keep an eye out for leaf blotch, down there in the . . . lobby. Then you've got to think about winter mulching."

4

"If I was talking about anything at all," Tad said after the landlord left, "I hope I was telling him how to grow orchids or peonies."

"You were making all that up?"

"Pardon my French, kiddo, but one load of bullshit deserves another."

"But why? He was only asking a *question*."

"He just dropped in to terrorize us."

"*Terrorize?*" Alida felt like the floor was giving way beneath her feet, and there was a long, long way to fall. "He was only trying to make us safer."

"Oh, Rabbit . . ." Her mom slid into the landlord's vacated chair and laid her arm across Alida's shoulders, then looked at Tad. "Is he going to triple the rent, do you think? Or turn us into a multistory parking garage?"

"*Parking garage?*"

"Honey, listen. Mr. Lee bought our building. He bought it to make money, and all he talked about, like new plumbing and video systems, costs big money—maybe millions. It was like he was telling us we can't afford to live here. That's what Tad means by 'terrorize.'"

The room swam in and out of focus as Alida fought a humiliating upwelling of tears. "I still don't get it."

"We pay eight-fifty for this apartment."

"Seven for mine," Tad said.

"Which is incredibly cheap. Mr. Winslow never put up the rents, he just let us live here for almost nothing, compared with most places around here. Parking lots! I bet the horrible Mr. Lee makes more money out of one parking space than he does out of our entire apartment."

"That's not true!" Alida recognized home territory when she saw it. "Even if he made five dollars an hour, twenty-four hours in every day, with every single space, that'd be like . . ." She calculated furiously, squinching up her eyes and holding her breath. "Eight-forty. But it's not that much! There's all that Early Bird stuff, and evenings, and weekends, and tons and tons of empty spaces all the time. You have to average it out."

She was shocked by her own arithmetic, having expected the sum to come to much less than it did; for one single lousy parking space, that was, like, *extortionate*. Nevertheless, she tried to put a brave face on the figure. "I bet he'd be lucky to get two hundred a week." She raced over the last few words to minimize their impact, but felt her mom's grip tighten on her shoulder.

"We pay eight-fifty a month, honey, not eight-fifty a week."

Crushed, Alida forced a wobbly grin and dared herself to voice the thought that had just come to mind. "Well, I guess you could get maybe eleven 'Compact Only' spaces into this apartment."

There was an uncertain moment of silence, then her mom and Tad began to laugh, and Alida felt instantly buoyant at being the cause of such appreciative adult laughter.

Strange how by saying the very worst thing you could imagine about almost any situation, you could make it funny—sort of. "So we'll have to live in the Spider and the heap," she said, but a treacherous, wavering hiccup came into her voice on the word "Spider," and Tad reached for her hand, not laughing now, as she had meant him to do, but just smiling, like he wanted to reassure, and to Alida it looked plain scary.

"Ali . . ."

Whatever he was saying was lost in a brain-curdling shivaree that came through the open window—a crazy concatenation of whoops and warbles, yelps and wails, as a parade of emergency vehicles went by a few blocks away. It sounded like they were heading south on Second. Alida picked out the jarring chords of fire trucks and their deep, grunting blasts; the angry *tirra-wirra-wirra-wirra* of the police; the caterwauling ambulances. From the noise they made, you'd think that all hell had broken out somewhere in the city, but lately the sound had grown so familiar that you just had to shut your ears to it. You never discovered where the sirens were going, or why, but most days you'd hear them racing along I-5 or the waterfront, like they were out there for the simple fun of frightening the pants off everybody with their mad music.

Tad got up to pull the window down, which slightly dulled the racket from outside. "Act Three of the exercise, I guess," he said. "They must've needed me for only Acts One and Two."

"When does your lease run out?" her mom said.

"September."

"Ours is December."

Alida said, "Are you sure we . . . I mean, like with his weird English and all, couldn't he maybe just mean . . ." Impatient with herself for sounding so dumb, she bit down on her lip. "Suppose it's all just a big misunderstanding? He didn't *have* to be lying."

"You're right, Rabbit. We're jumping to conclusions. We shouldn't prejudge him like this. Perhaps he really did mean what he said."

But in her mother's face, Alida saw all the signs of grown-up untrustworthiness—the uncertain tremor in her smile, the sidelong glance at Tad that meant *We'll talk about this later.* Everything was impenetrably "ironic," a maddening equation full of minus numbers. Mr. Lee didn't mean what he said, and her mom didn't mean what she said about Mr. Lee. If Mr. Lee was $-x$ and her mom was $-y$ . . .

Another procession of horns and sirens. This one was going west down Jackson Street, its ferocious clamor muffled by the bulk of the buildings in between.

"God, it's like being at a Schoenberg concert tonight," her mom said.

"I was thinking more John Cage."

Adults!

What had Mr. Lee actually *said*? That he didn't want the street people getting in. That he was going to put new locks on the doors. That he was new to being a landlord. That he wanted "feedback." How did you get from such data to the idea that he was going to turn the Acropolis into a parking garage? Surreptitiously, Alida squeezed a zit on her chin. She thought of the landlord installing a video monitor beside the door, of how she'd innocently believed in it, but now she believed nobody—not Mr. Lee, not her mom, not Tad, and herself least of all. She felt lost in the fog of her own stupidity. The zit popped, discharging a little bead of pus onto the tip of her forefinger, which she wiped on the grainy underside of the table.

Tad said, "Don't worry, Ali. You, me, and your mom, we're a team. We'll be fine, whatever happens with the building."

But Alida knew differently. She wasn't on the team. She was sitting out on the bench, wearing cleats and the team jersey, but the coach would never let her play on the field. Blinking back tears, she made herself smile and say "Okay," thinking that this was the first time in her life she had been dishonest with Tad, ever.

BACK IN HIS APARTMENT, alone with mouse and keyboard, Tad Zachary was on his usual late-night prowl through cyberspace. He'd long ago given up on television as a source of news. More recently, he'd canceled his subscription to *The New York Times,* whose reporters he had learned to despise as tame flunkies of the administration. Now he mostly read foreign media to find out what was happening in his own country. His rusty high-school French was just sufficient, and growing steadily better, to skim *Libération*'s accounts of what was going on in La Maison Blanche and Le Bureau Oval. He moused over to Britain, where he read the *Independent* and the *Guardian,* and on to Arabia, where he checked out the *Jordan Times* and *Al-Ahram Weekly.* He visited Al-Jazeera. Then he hit the blogs and forums to keep company with like-minded internal exiles—those lonely late-nighters, as full of rage as he was, tapping out intelligence on the latest mendacities and misdeeds. His face lit by the frigid blue glow of the computer screen, Tad followed these theories and rumors as they swarmed from site to site.

Since Michael's death six years ago, more and more of Tad's time had been spent like this, afloat in the virtual counterworld, a community of people hidden behind pseudonyms who'd never met one another face-to-face. The virtual suited him. Untroubled by libido, he thought of himself now as postsexual, almost disembodied, as if each day brought a measurable lessening of his specific gravity in the actual world. Soon he'd be walking on air.

Playing stepfather to Ali was his last intimate human connection. Described in his will as "the sanest, most thoughtful human being I've ever met," she was Tad's sole heir. Only the attorney who'd witnessed his signature knew this.

He meant to leave her a cool million, not a dollar less; so it was for Ali that he went on working, swallowing both pride and principles to star in the terror shows, to be Mr. Autoglass, the MagiGro gardener, the light relief at hideous convention dinners. He wanted to see his mother's money at last do some real good. In the sleepless small hours, sprawled diagonally across the king bed he'd once shared with Michael, Tad liked to picture Ali at Yale, Ali kitted out in surgeon's scrubs, Ali at the podium in a packed lecture hall, Ali pith-helmeted in Africa— her career and costume changing from night to night. Ali's future was another kind of virtual reality in which Tad found solace. He even relished his own necessary absence from these pictures; the not-being-there was part of their allure, like sitting in a darkened auditorium, magically freed from oneself by the more compelling and luminous life on the stage.

Ali, who could recite the value of π to the thirty-seventh decimal place, but was considerably prouder of her double-jointed elbows.

Ali, who took better care of her mother than her mother took care of her.

Ali, who was his sternest drama critic. "Is he really meant to be *that* much like Scrooge?" she'd asked doubtfully of his Shylock at the first dress rehearsal of *Merchant* at the Rep. She was dead right, and in the nick of time. Hastily but thoroughly de-Scrooged, Shylock got near rapturous notices in the *Times* and the *P-I,* all thanks to Ali.

Ali, the brave but comically graceless in-line skater.

Ali as the Wicked Witch of the West at Halloween. At age eight, she had Margaret Hamilton's voice and delivery to an eerie "t."

Ali.

It wasn't *light of my life, fire of my loins,* but for Tad it headed distinctly, even dangerously, in that direction. He couldn't take his eyes off Ali when she folded her arms across her chest to hide her nascent breasts — so boy, so girl, so girl-boy.

When he thought of Ali and her life to come, Tad had in clear view the threshold on which he himself would have to stand — not now, not yet, but some time sooner rather than later. When Michael went into the hospice three weeks before he died, Tad had seen the whitewashed brick mansion as a Greek house, a fraternity in which each new pledge went through a ritual hazing. As a college freshman, Tad had joined Phi Delta, knocking off the required quart of Jack Daniel's before stripping naked and walking blindfolded on broken glass; thirty-five years later, he could still hear the frat boys' whooping laughter as he trod that bloody path. And so it was with Michael, enduring the relentless, patient smiles of the staff as they put his incredible shrinking body on an IV drip, shot him full of morphine, wrapped and pinned him in diapers.

Death itself didn't scare Tad. All he feared was the indignity of the initiation ceremonies that he'd have to go through to become a member of that enormous, nonexclusive, admirably egalitarian club. He envied people with dicey hearts: one fine day they simply toppled off their perches, on the way to work or in the middle of a story they were telling over dinner. Lucky for them. But Tad was following Michael's lead on the more demanding route.

For now, his medication was doing its job. His T-cell count was still up there in the 220s and 230s. On his last doctor visit, Brian, washing his hands in the sink, had said, "Who knows? I'll probably be pushing up daisies before you are." But Tad knew differently, and he fretted about timing — better that he go at least a year before Ali took her SATs, or held out, somewhat improbably, until after her graduation from college.

Meanwhile, fury sustained in him a disturbing feeling of intense well-being. Hatred of the president and his administration roused him to a kind of dizzy euphoria that he associated with the bizarre love affairs he'd had back in his twenties—first with girls, then with boys. Same sleepless obsessionality. Same sense of being utterly possessed, caught in the grip of something very close to mania. Even the objects of his affections then bore a troubling resemblance to the objects of his hatred now.

Before Michael, Tad had always fallen in love only with impossible people: wrecked young women with raccoon eyes who swallowed bottles of pills and had to be driven to the ER to have their stomachs pumped; waiflike young men, knife-scarred, arms peppered with needle marks, who invariably robbed him. Nancy. Selina. Jane. Ferris. Charlie. Ron. Umberto. Jesus. Thanh . . . and so the list went on. Tad had liked to see himself as a rescuer of birds with broken wings, but his wounded birds had a habit of revealing themselves as monsters. Thanh had gone to jail for attempting to murder Tad, though the attempt was so ridiculously botched that Tad had spoken up for him in court.

Now he was involved with bad guys whose badness took his breath away, as they heedlessly despoiled the planet, killed people on an industrial scale, connived with their cronies over billion-dollar no-bid contracts, and cannily subverted the rapidly unraveling fabric of democracy. Their bland manners reminded him of Jesus, blithely cleaning his handgun over breakfast as if sharpening a pencil or polishing a car. Then, as now, Tad was fascinated by the casual insouciance, the innocence, even, with which bad guys went about their daily work. They gave no sign of knowing they were bad guys: just like Jesus, they prattled on in the language of doing good.

The best thing about hatred as opposed to love was the absence of any feeling on Tad's part that he was here to somehow, against all odds, redeem these people. That illusion, at least, was long gone. He didn't want to rescue the administration from its folly: he wanted to see it blown to atomic dust or drowned in a sack. And he badly wanted to outlive it—to know it had been judged by history before he passed on.

So he surfed the Net, partly to fuel his outrage, partly to probe for symptoms of terminal disease—leaked secrets, crashing poll numbers, the rotten whiff of scandal yet to break. Over the years, the administration had packed the judiciary with yes-men and yes-women to the point where it could now usually operate comfortably above the law, but there were some honest judges left, and lately there'd been an increasing trickle of defectors, whose enthralling tales of government malfeasance gave Tad some hope that even the Department of Justice would have to recognize, however halfheartedly, that at least a measure of justice needed to be done.

That much was sane. What was insane was the giddy excitement that overtook him on these virtual nighttime adventures—the quickening heartbeat, the sweating palms, the acute mental arousal in which he took such involuntary pleasure. This was being in hate, and Tad, when truthful with himself, had to acknowledge that he liked being in hate. A lot. He was aware that if and when this wretched government really did fall, he'd rejoice, of course, but that a part of himself would feel as bereft and purposeless as when Thanh had been led away under a black hood, in police cuffs.

Sometimes he'd pretend that his rage was noble, altruistic, all on Ali's behalf: how dare they fuck over the world into which she was just now beginning to step out? These crookedly elected, braggart thugs in business suits were systematically poisoning the future of Ali's entire generation—and not just of her generation, either, but of every generation yet to come. But if that were truly Tad's concern, his only emotion would be sorrow, and sorrow, strangely, was the least of his feelings. When he saw the browning of Mount Rainier, read of the melting arctic ice cap or the murderous inferno that blazed across the Middle East and South Asia, when the U.S. military practiced besieging American cities with tanks, artillery, and armored checkpoints in the name of "quarantine," when the Supreme Court became the brass-knuckled enforcer of the presidential will and whim, what Tad felt was an adrenaline rush of angry elation. It was like getting off on porn, this secret relish for the wicked drama of it all.

Maybe he'd spent too long working in theater and could no longer distinguish real life from a thrillingly gory production of *Tamburlaine*, whose title role Tad had long dreamed of playing, and whose speeches he'd sometimes used as audition pieces for roles whose directors might doubt his capacity to do butch with suitable conviction:

> *Now hang our bloody colours by Damascus,*
> *Reflexing hues of blood upon their heads,*
> *While they walk quivering on their city-walls,*
> *Half-dead for fear before they feel my wrath.*

Certainly, if you looked for an author of this administration, it'd have to be Marlowe, or possibly Webster. Only an Elizabethan with a strong stomach for Grand Guignol could possibly have written the script for what was going on now.

Tonight the bloggers were off on the trail of laundered money that went straight through the back door of the White House, and the case of the former director of the FBI who'd either jumped or been pushed from the eighteenth floor of a hotel in Baltimore on the eve of his appearance before the grand jury investigating the Vasico affair. The president had made another speech—the usual Tamberlainish stuff about scourging kingdoms with his conquering sword. Great strides were being made in the war of Good against Evil, most of them in secret, the president said, but it would not be long before the American people learned of the noble victories already accomplished in their name. The bloggers were sifting through the text of this speech like soothsayers reading goats' entrails. It was noted that when the president said "Patriotic America knows its strength. To all nations, we say . . ." the initial letters of the first eight words ominously spelled out "PAKISTAN."

Codes, portents, plots, chicanery: Tad was up to speed on them all. Swigging from the bottle of Evian water beside his rainbow mouse pad, he thought of how the ambit of his loathing must now widen to include his new landlord, yet another grinning monkey face in an outsize plumed helmet, as *Le Canard Enchaîné* portrayed the president. Far from being depressed by Charles Lee's blatant threats, he felt hyped by them. Tad Zachary had always enjoyed fights on stage, and he looked forward to this one: a labor of love and hate, whose twin poles he'd increasingly, during the last five years, become unable to tell apart.

LUCY, too tired to sleep, lay in bed watching the news on the postcard-size screen on the TV-clock-radio on her dresser. So that was what all the commotion that evening had been about—they'd evacuated Safeco Field.

A man "of Middle Eastern appearance" had been spotted hurrying out at the start of the seventh-inning stretch. Police had followed him to his car, a blue Chrysler with Canadian plates. When the mobile forensics lab was summoned, "traces of explosive residue" were found in the carpet of the trunk.

It was the clown on the ferry—of course—and Lucy knew exactly what must have happened. Shaking down his car at the terminal, the National Guardsmen, with their ammo-tainted fingers, would have left traces of explosive all over everything. The guy had left in disgust at the performance of his blessed Blue Jays, down five-nothing to the Mariners, the losingest team in the American League.

Now they were still frantically searching the stadium for a bomb, and reporters on the scene were hyperventilating over the capture of a terrorist "believed to have links with Al Qaeda."

For a nanosecond, Lucy thought of dialing 911 and correcting the police's misreading of his flight from the game: he was no more Al Qaeda than she was the Klan. But she'd be on the phone half the night—on hold for ten minutes at a time, asked to spell her name a dozen times over, stuttering wildly, failing to make herself credible to the goon in charge. Let them figure it out in their own sweet time; and it would do that pestering nuisance no great harm to cool his heels for a few hours in the pen.

News just in: *Woman dies of heart attack in Seattle stadium evacuation.*

So he'd actually killed someone. Or rather, they had. "Woman dies of someone else's overheated imagination," more like.

". . . reporting live from Safeco Field, this is Tamara Gold for KIRO 7 Eyewitness News." The tiny screen barely contained the bug-eyed, breathless Tamara, who looked as if she herself were about to go off like the so far undiscovered bomb.

With thirty thousand people summarily pitched into the streets, and with fears of an imminent explosion, there was no other news—no weather, even, and certainly no mention of a fatal car accident on Whidbey Island, which was why Lucy had tuned in.

JOLTED AWAKE from a dream just after midnight, Alida was multitasking: shiny-faced with Clearasil, she was listening to "Wake Me up When September Ends" on her iPod and reading Agatha Christie in the cone of light cast by the hooded halogen bulb on its metal stalk. Insomnia, once a cause of anguish to her, was now a source of pride. While the rest of the building slept, Alida had the world to herself, in the heady company of Jane Marple and Billie Joe Armstrong. With a book propped on the quilted comforter and good music in her ears, she was in charge of her life in these secret watches of the night as she never was during the day.

A pulsing light, now red, now white, played on the thin blue cotton drapes on her bedroom window, as the laser warnings bounced off the low clouds overhead. The lasers were new, put up a few weeks ago to keep airplanes from flying over the city. Alida was still getting used to the spooky quiet of the sky, now empty of the jets that had roared straight over the Acropolis on their approach to SeaTac Airport. But she liked how the lasers fitted their regular flashes to the beat of Green Day's drummer, Tré Cool.

Agatha Christie was her latest literary discovery. Mr. Kawasuki had a whole shelf of her mysteries in his store, nearly all of them battered, grungy paperbacks at 25¢ apiece. Alida loved Agatha Christie more than any other fiction writer because she understood human algebra. It was what the slow fussbudget Miss Marple did all the time—elimination, substitution, intersection. Everything was logical and necessary, however confusing it seemed right up until the moment when

Miss Marple eventually figured out the sum over her knitting, and you realized that of course the pipe-smoking Swede had done it. Alida was sure that if she read enough Agatha Christie books she'd be able to live inside Miss Marple's mind, take over her brilliant mental machinery, and apply it to her own project. At present, she was on her third, *The Mirror Crack'd from Side to Side*, and already could feel stirrings of the latent deductive powers with which she'd astonish her friends in the not-too-distant future.

Her worry was that even Miss Marple, so certain of her ground in St. Mary Mead, England, might be baffled by Seattle. Alida was happy drinking imaginary beer in the Blue Boar pub and doing imaginary shopping at Mr. Baker's grocery. She'd pass the vicarage on the way to visit Colonel and Mrs. Bantry at Gossington Hall, and avoid the cows as she walked across Farmer Giles's fields. There was a kind of logic in this English village that she feared was absent from the city she lived in. Miss Marple, at home in her ancient cottage, Danemead, inhabited a historical world where everything fit together satisfactorily. Like a jigsaw, it would seem an impossible jumble of pieces to begin with, but you knew that the picture was in there, hiding, waiting to be assembled. Seattle was different. America was different. What would Miss Marple make of her mom, or Tad, or Mr. Lee? Logic was logic: it ought to work everywhere, no matter when. But what if you lived in a world where the rules of logic had somehow ceased to apply? Did they work *here* and *now*? Or only in old, logical places like St. Mary Mead?

It was like her granddad's murder in Montana—a horrible accident, with no motive, no mystery, no clues, no logic at all. It just happened out of the blue, like cancer and hurricanes did. To Alida, her grandfather was more a face in framed photographs than a memory, but she was haunted by the flat fact of his murder—a word so scary that neither she nor her mom ever used it in conversation. "When Granddad died," her mom would say. But he hadn't died, he'd been shot to death like a character in an Agatha Christie book, except nothing else about it was Agatha Christie–like. There was no need for Miss Marple in Miles City, since everyone knew from the very beginning that Lewis Olson had done it. The only explanation Alida had ever been given was that he "hated the government," which was a lousy motive since her granddad hadn't been the government. Lewis Olson should have gone to jail for years and years, but they let him out early, and he was still writing letters from Montana that her mom scrunched up unread and threw into the trash. They were easy to spot because they always came in blue envelopes. Alida had fished out a couple and read them secretly— mostly crazy stuff about religion that didn't even mention her granddad or why he'd shot him.

Brain spinning, Alida looked for security in the familiar shadows of her room—the pile of stuffed animals that she'd long outgrown on the chest of drawers, the Avril Lavigne poster that she'd never gotten around to taking down, the cluttered bookshelves where Dr. Seuss and Shel Silverstein and *Winnie the Pooh* kept Helen Keller and Anne Frank and *Go Ask Alice* company. She was reluctant to part with all the relics from when she was little, from dolls to old shoes, not so much out of babyish sentimental attachment but because they were essential data by which she could measure how far and fast she was now traveling. It was like keeping an eye on the speedometer in the Spider, watching her mom's regular infractions of the posted limit. Alida liked going fast, but her mom drove way too fast—one time over seventy in a forty-five zone. Squinting at the dark shapes of flop-eared bunnies and teddy bears on the far side of the room, she wondered if a taste for speed was *genetic* or something.

On the floor, her soccer stuff was packed, ready for tomorrow, in her gym bag. Homework was safe in her backpack. For her alone, as it seemed to Alida, Billie Joe was singing,

> *Welcome to a new kind of tension . . .*
> *Where everything isn't meant to be okay . . .*

She continued to listen for a few minutes more, then closed her book, switched off the iPod, and with the lullaby of "American Idiot" lingering in her ears, fell almost instantly asleep. Her halogen lamp stayed on. On the drapes, the lasers protecting the city flashed red-white, red-white, red-white, like waiting ambulances.

AT ONE A.M., Tad was deep in enemy territory, reading the *Weekly Standard* online. He resented subscriber-only sites because he felt they violated the easygoing democracy of the Internet, but had recently forked out $32 for William Kristol's magazine because it was a source of such rich and alarming intelligence about the thought processes of the administration. Everything Tad hated and feared most—invasions, torture, wiretapping, detention without charge, secret courts—could be counted on to find its champion in the *Weekly Standard*. The president's closest advisers were said to read it, so Tad thought it his duty as a citizen to read it, too.

Tonight he was trying to follow the arguments of a law professor at some university he'd never heard of—an "originalist" interpretation of the Fourth Amendment, based on what he called "a first-clause-dominant" reading of it. Apparently, what the Founders really meant when they wrote of the "right of the people to be secure in their persons, houses, papers, and effects, against unreasonable searches and seizures" was that the federal government could lawfully search and seize, bug and imprison, so long as it deemed such actions "reasonable." The liberal Supreme Court under Earl Warren—always a black name in the *Weekly Standard*—had gotten the whole amendment ass-backwards. The true purpose of the Fourth was to free government from the tiresome, time-consuming business of going to the courts and getting warrants.

Once, Tad would have been incredulous. Now he took stuff like this as just part of the normal weather of the times. In the name of fidelity to the original intentions of the Constitution and the Bill of Rights, the hard-right revisionists were systematically rewriting both documents to bring them into line with administration thinking, brazenly recasting Madison and Jefferson in their own ugly image, turning sentences inside out to reverse their meanings.

There was melancholy satisfaction in the professor's article, so amply did it confirm Tad's sense that a legion of industrious rats was gnawing away at his country's very foundations. Just as he was phrasing this thought to himself, he felt a rippling shudder pass through the seat of his chair, as if a convoy of big trucks were passing by, and the wooden desktop seemed to momentarily squirm under the heel of his palm. He instinctively looked to the doorframe for shelter, but the temblor was already over—a little one, maybe a two-point-something, so slight and brief that at this hour it would be a secret between a few insomniacs and the shivering needles of the seismographs in the geophysics lab at the University of Washington.

The needles were rarely still. Every day brought half a dozen significant tremors to the state, and Seattle, sitting astride its own fault line, with the Juan de Fuca fault close at hand, was built on jittery, uncertain ground. Tad had lost count of the times he'd heard the sound of rock grinding on rock deep below the earth, though to his chagrin he'd been out of town, in a forgettable production of *The Iceman Cometh* in Minneapolis, for the Ash Wednesday quake of 2001, which, had it lasted fifteen seconds longer, would have brought down the Alaskan Way viaduct and wrecked half the older buildings in the city.

Growing up across the Columbia River from the palpitating snowy bulk of Mount St. Helens, Tad learned to relish warning tremors like the one just past. He imagined the great tectonic plates ceaselessly slipping, shifting, rubbing, as if the planet were trying to shrug off the unnatural weight of tar and concrete, brick and steel, that humans had carelessly piled on to it. A native West Coaster, Tad knew the instability of the ground beneath his feet, and when he worked with easterners he was aware of how this knowledge separated them. On the whole, he thought, earthquakes were good for you, and every city ought to be rattled to its foundations every once in a while, to alert its people to their precarious footing in the world.

Cheered by the miniquake, he switched off the computer and went to bed, where he sank almost immediately into a leaden sleep.

THE PRESIDENT and CEO of Excellent Holdings, Inc., slept thinly, hardly grazing the surface of unconsciousness. He was afraid of sleep: whenever he allowed himself to fall into that deep, dream-haunted world, he found himself in the same place, inside the shipping container in which long ago he'd crossed the Pacific from Hong Kong to Seattle—and he always woke up screaming. Nowadays he maintained a vigilant nightly patrol along the dangerous border, forbidding himself to cross into the territory where the barely living and the freshly dead lay in wait for him, tumbled together by the ocean in a floundering, lightless box.

A Delta Airlines blanket he'd saved from a red-eye flight to Atlanta barely covered his body as he lay in his T-shirt, boxer shorts, and socks on the couch in his office. 3040 Occidental Ave. S., Suite #103, Seattle, WA 98134, his home and business HQ, cost him $450 a month: an "executive suite," 150 square feet of white Sheetrock, including restroom, within close earshot of the rumbling shunts, groans, and mournful whistles of the Burlington Northern line. On the black metal table stood phone, fax, laptop, printer, and TV; in the cramped toilet, his clothes hung on the hook behind the door, sheathed in cellophane from the dry cleaner's; a microwave was his kitchen and he didn't bother with dishes, preferring to fork his food straight from the containers. When he made coffee, he heated water in a paper cup in the microwave and added Nescafé and whitener, both collected free from motel rooms that he visited for an hour most Sundays. Parked beyond the single window, whose blinds he always kept drawn, was his new white F250 pickup, a recent acquisition. The owner of a cut-price tow company had tried to get cute with him, so Charles O, as he now thought of himself, had driven his old beater to the guy's home on the East Side, taught him a lesson in elementary business practice, and come away with the new truck, legal title, and a wad of bills that added up to $1,400—a nice evening's work. The F250 was loaded: AC, leather, premium stereo with CD changer, heated seats, the works, and it still put a smile on Charles O's face when he drove it—and never more so than when, caught in a jam in the Battery Street Tunnel, he spotted the tow-company guy at the wheel of his beater, honked, and gave that moron a thumbs-up sign. The guy had stared ahead, rigid as a statue, the veins in his face turning scarlet. What a loser.

The previous tenant of Suite 103 had left behind a four-shelf laminate bookcase, now nearly full, for Charles O loved to read. While the TV played the Cartoon Network on mute, he'd crouch over a Stouffer's Yankee Pot Roast, picked up at the gas station minimart, eating with one hand and holding his book with the other. His lips moved continuously as he sounded out the words, and sometimes he'd speak sentences aloud just for the pleasure of hearing them—especially the ones that ended with exclamation points. "Who learns to adapt in time when he sees changing leads to something *better*!" That was sweet music to him—a tune he found himself singing under his breath at stoplights or on the stairs in his new apartment building.

The titles in the bookcase included *Who Moved My Cheese?*, *The Fred Factor*, *The One Minute Manager*, *Fish!*, *Full Steam Ahead!*, *The Secret*, and *Winning with People*.

For Charles O, buying the Acropolis had been the kind of bold, innovative move that all the books said was the mark of an "elite player." Go the extra mile! they said. Constantly reinvent yourself! Make yourself extraordinary! A lesser man would've stuck with parking lots for their low maintenance and deep, swift revenue stream, much of it in hard, untraceable cash, the many-times-folded ones and fives and tens that he and his team of Mexicans emptied from the boxes around the clock, moving ceaselessly from lot to lot. When he showed up at the bank with his pirate's chest of crumpled green stuff, even the tellers, trained to never show a flicker of surprise, would go bug-eyed at the sight of so much money. Cutting deals with hotels and restaurants for valet parking, jiggling with prices for early birds and event and monthly parkers, he'd grown the business by more than 50 percent on every lot. Having mastered parking, he'd long felt a growing hunger for something more weighty, more intricate, more human.

Now he was going the extra mile, making himself extraordinary.

When he first saw the ancient brick and stucco of the Acropolis, it filled his shallow dreams as nothing and nobody had ever done before. He so craved it that he surprised himself when trying to beat down the owners' attorney on the asking price. He'd believed he was fearless, but at the thought of the Acropolis escaping him, he felt a spasm of fear in his gut, as disabling as an attack of diarrhea, and paid $375,000 more than he'd meant to. That was a recoverable loss, but he was deeply shaken by the discovery of his cowardice.

The building was his great experiment. Its palatial seven stories of rooms and stairwells and fire escapes and hallways were his personal aquarium, and he loved to put his eye close to the glass and study the fish. Tap, tap, tap: how they swam away in fright! He enjoyed the neediness of tenants, their faces big with questions they didn't dare ask, their "Yes, Mr. Lee," and "No, Mr. Lee," as they cast their eyes involuntarily on their unmade beds, their unwashed dishes, their untidy piles of garbage. Tenants always showed you what they most wanted to hide, so he was learning to take in all their secrets at a glance. No parking lot could give him the multitude of pleasures that were available to him in the Acropolis.

For now, he meant to do little except watch. Watch and wait. With the cash flow from the parking business, he could afford to sit tight and study up on how his new world worked. Beyond the Acropolis, he had a hazy, unformed vision of new condos, though it still amounted to little more than an image of cranes maneuvering slowly and deliberatively against the sky. Whenever Charles O saw a crane at work, he liked to stop to watch, in case there was, in this, an omen for his future. But he was in no hurry for condos. Master the Acropolis first, then move on. *Who learns to adapt in time when he sees changing leads to something better!*

Last evening had replanted in his mind the long dormant germ of an idea. The time was coming when he'd need a wife—not for sex, but other things. Sex was an itch to be relieved on Sundays when business was slack, on Aurora Avenue North in a rooms-by-the-hour waterbed motel. At $65 for oral—he disliked the other kind—it was like taking an expensive dump; he was always glad to get back to the truck afterward, and never used the same woman twice. But a wife would be different. The shogun authors of his favorite books all had wives: wives gave substance and background to elite players, making them more 3-D. Wives did accounting and also made food and entertained. Building up his holdings in parking lots, Charles O had treasured the airy lightness of his solitude, the trim and compact life that would fit inside the cab and flatbed of his old truck, let alone his new one. But as owner and ruler of the Acropolis, a landlord, he lacked the ampleness that only a wife could provide.

Of all his tenants, Lucy N. Bengstrom, apartment #701, had interested him the most since the day he first toured the building. Sure, she was old—fifty, maybe even more—but he wasn't prejudiced: on Aurora Avenue, he picked old ones because they worked harder to please and made better noises. Fat, too. That evening, he'd eyed her thick ankles and the rotund swell of her belly under the loose dress that was meant to hide it. He was okay with fat.

But consider her assets:

- She had citizenship. He needed a wife with citizenship.
- She wrote for magazines, so she had good secretarial skills.
- She had the kid. Two for one, a ready-made family. He needed a family, and starting one from scratch took too much time and money. The kid was smart enough, and seemed to like him, a big plus.
- Good homemaker. He liked the bird's-nest coziness of #701: nothing too expensive or fancy, but it felt upmarket. Books, pictures, lot of classy-looking CDs. Everything in the apartment suggested money carefully, economically spent, and he appreciated that. Worst thing in the world was big-spendy women.
- That old car. She'd taken good care of it, not like most American women, who trashed cars in a year or two like they were flashlight batteries or disposable razors. Alfa Romeo—prestige brand, and another testament to the fact that, though poor, she had class.
- Her best asset: an insufficiency that he could smell on her like mold. Why else hang out with that fag actor? A real loser, with his cheap homo sarcasm and funny voices. *Mr. MagiGro* was a prime candidate for an eviction notice. No, to hang out with a half-man like that, a woman must be sick with loneliness, and Charles O could only begin to imagine her pathetic gratitude if

she was to be rescued from this misery by an elite player. She'd be in his debt for the rest of her life. *Thank you, thank you, thank you!* He liked the thought of that a lot.

- What was the kid's name? Mouse? No, Rabbit. He'd have to call her something else, like Nicole, or Meryl, or Marilyn, or Sigourney—a name already stamped with success. When the time came, he'd send her to college: East Coast, Ivy League. She'd need an MBA to help him in the business. "Speak to my PA, my daughter Sigourney . . ." That sounded nice.

The more he thought about her, the sweeter appeared the prospect of life with Lucy N. Bengstrom. Lucy Lee! She was made for the name —it fit just right, like the inevitable destination she'd unknowingly been headed toward all these years. *Lucy Lee. Charles O. and Lucy Lee. Mr. and Mrs. Charles O. Lee. The Lee Residence.* They were fated to be conjoined. It was *meant*. Once upon a time, he'd been full of superstitions— astrologers, feng shui, all that crap. Now, in spite of himself, he needed to find out her birth year. Water-dragon, water-pig would be the best of all combinations, and he had a powerful sense that Lucy N. Bengstrom would turn out to be a water-pig.

Thinking of her had given him a big hard-on, sticking right through the flap of his boxers. Fully awake now, he reached to the box of Kleenex on the floor beside the couch and pictured her pulling the flowery dress over her head . . . nice underwear, not like a hooker's, but lacy, white, high-class intimate apparel from Nordstrom or some place like that. She stood before him in the darkness, strangely luminous, like the Indiglo lighting on his Timex.

"Please, honey, may I take you in my mouth?"

Big-bellied, old, grateful, she went down on him, wet lips busy, making little doggy whimpers of satisfaction as she sucked, cradling his balls in her hands.

Briskly, fastidiously, he jacked off into the waiting tissue. Not a drop spilled.

"God, you taste so good," Lucy said, then faded into black.

He padded into the bathroom, where he flushed the balled-up Kleenex down the toilet and vigorously soaped his limpening cock in the basin. He checked his watch—4:30. By five he'd be out on the prowl in the F250, searching his lots for overnighters who'd failed to pay and display: 5:30 was the hour of the tow truck at Excellent Parking, and his 60/40 deal with the towing companies meant big profits even before the sun began to clear the eastern mountains. On a good morning he'd catch a hundred or so illegals and deport them to places as remote as Kent and Issaquah. What was funny was that the no-goods were almost never clunkers, but late-model Audis and Lexuses and Jaguars; poor people paid for tickets, and the rich tried to cheat him. Just yesterday he'd waved bye-bye to a new red Ferrari, its nose ignominiously hoisted up on the tow truck. Guy would've been legal if he'd paid $6.00, and now it cost him $334 and a $50 cab fare to get his Ferrari Superamerica back. That had made Charles O's morning.

He set a cup of water in the microwave. The breathy, churring noise of the oven mixed with the clank and rumble of a freight train traveling northward through the city. Far ahead, he heard it bellow like a wounded cow as its locomotives trundled into downtown. They'd just about be passing the Acropolis. He wondered if Lucy heard the whistle, too.

Act with decision. The elite player never wavers once his choice is made!

He'd begin at the weekend, with those crates she had for bookshelves. Sipping his scalding Nescafé, he wondered whether along with his cordless drill he should take flowers.

AT A FEW MINUTES before five, the hand set off on its regular morning excursion from under the covers. The terrain was familiar as it snaked in the dark through the thicket of easily upsettable plastic bottles of aspirin, Halcion, St. John's wort, melatonin, and protease inhibitors, then across the spine of the book that splayed facedown on the bedside table, a lurid kiss-and-tell memoir by the latest fugitive from the administration, the former Department of Defense chief of staff.

Eventually the hand found the knurled volume knob of the elderly transistor radio, whose antenna had long ago been replaced by a wire coathanger.

KUOW was still relaying the BBC World Service, a British voice reciting soccer scores, something about the UEFA cup, a cricket match in Australia.

At five o'clock sharp, National Public Radio's *Morning Edition* began with the first news of the day from Washington, D.C., and the sleeper roused himself to listen to the lead headline.

This was how Tad's mornings always began, with the vague, routine apprehension of atrocity. Pacific Standard Time was in part to blame, for the world's most shocking events usually happened while the West Coast was still asleep. By this PST, Cairo, Rome, Madrid, Paris, and London had survived the conventional hours of atrocity, while New York and D.C. were just about to enter them.

Bombs in Baghdad, assassination in Jerusalem . . . the hand embarked on its return journey to the radio. *It*—whatever *it* was, and Tad had only a very hazy notion of what *it* might be—hadn't taken place today, at least so far. He rolled over on his left side and addressed the toilsome job of trying to get back to sleep. But sleep, as ever, was an artful dodger. Oscillating continuously between torpor and electric wakefulness, he chased it, touched it, lost it, caught up with it, only to have it again wriggle from his grasp. Whole hours would pass in its pursuit until, fractious and exhausted by the hunt, he'd haul himself out of bed and into Michael's old sun-emperor silk kimono.

So it had been for Tad since September 2001, which now seemed an epoch ago. The overpunctual reaching of his wayward hand for the radio, reliable as an alarm clock, had grown over the years into a motor reflex. What prompted it wasn't dread, at least not dread alone, but a sick avidity, a hunger for catastrophe. A secret longing for the Big One lurked in his inner core, and its renewed absence each morning must therefore bring it one day closer.

Struggling to sleep, he felt a rankling, rusty stab of shame. *Ali,* he thought. *Think of her now.* But even thoughts of Ali never quite freed him from this perversity. Somewhere out there, sooner than later, the catastrophe lay waiting, along with whatever it was inside him that wanted it to happen.

At 6:40, he gave up, reached for the kimono, and, parting the drapes, peered out into the shadow-ridden half-light. It had begun to rain.

5

RAIN. LUCY, just back from the school run, coffee in hand, watched it from her window. She'd never seen such rain in Seattle. She was soaked from dashing across the street to the Acropolis, and the drive to school had been like a rough ocean-crossing in a small boat, with the Spider up to its axles in water half the time. She'd had to add a fresh set of dry clothes to Alida's gym bag before they set out.

Seattle rain didn't so much fall as precipitate in the air like mist, and you could walk an hour before feeling more than mildly damp. This was something else. From seven stories up, Lucy heard it hitting the streets, sounding like a forest fire and turning every surface on which it landed icing-sugar white. It was what she imagined an Indian monsoon must be like, or Noah's flood—far beyond the wettest, windiest offerings the occasional Pineapple Express would blow through town once or twice a year. The whole city—or the very little she could see of it—appeared to be drowning in this astounding superfluity of water.

She was still watching when the phone rang.

"It's Augie." Just like that, as if they were old friends.

"D'you have this amazing rain, too?" she said.

"Yeah, it's a frog-strangler."

"I'm surprised the lines aren't down."

"No wind."

That was true. It was falling in vertical bolts like densely packed steel bars. "I'm a dry-country Montana girl." She was allowing herself to flirt a little. "I'm never cynical about rain. Even in Seattle I can't separate it from the idea of goodness. Where I come from, every drop's a gift. When people pray in eastern Montana, rain's what they always pray for." She had to raise her voice against the fiery crackle all around her.

"Then maybe some preacher got a tad too zealous on Sunday."

Thinking of his "frog-strangler," Lucy said, "In Montana, we'd call this a gullywasher."

"*Gully*washer. I like that."

She could hear him, up there on the island in Thomas Jefferson's library, adding "gullywasher" to his word hoard like a new postage stamp to a collection.

He'd looked at the forecast, he said, and they were calling for clear skies by tomorrow. "Why don't you and Alida come for the weekend?"

How clever of him to recall her name. But then he was Mr. Memory, of course.

"And if you'd like to bring someone . . ."

A *man*, he meant. "No, it's just Alida and me, and we'd love to." Not quite true: Alida would have to be dragged, but Lucy didn't want to ditch her with Tad again, and in any case he'd mentioned something about a weekend shoot for the MagiGro people.

"Minna will be so pleased. Minna loves children."

He'd said that yesterday. Why be so emphatic about it? Because Minna actually *didn't* like kids? In Lucy's experience, too many positives were usually covering for a negative, and vice versa. "Alida will love meeting you," she said. "She gets out of school at three on Friday, so if you like we could drive straight up to Whidbey then."

"Wonderful. And plan on staying till Sunday. Does Alida like to kayak?"

"Who knows? I don't think she's ever tried it."

"I'd get a kick out of showing her how."

Listening to him on the phone, she could finally hear the ghost of old Europe in his voice—a faint guttural imperfection in his easy vernacular, like a hairline flaw in an otherwise perfect vase.

III

Putting down the phone, she marveled at what a snap this assignment was turning out to be. The prickly recluse was pure pussycat. She saw herself drawing him out, late at night, over wine, after Alida was in bed—and the piece would practically write itself. Remembering her elaborate campaigns to get face time with the likes of Gates and Cobain—the calls to friends of friends, the guileful negotiations with agents and PAs, the endless faxings of her cosmetically enhanced CV, the months-long waits for a reply—she wanted to give thanks for the sheer heaven-sent bounty of this frictionless commission: August Vanags had fallen into her lap, like rain.

The rain outside was getting even louder. Half an hour before, she'd just been able to make out the pale gray liquescent shape of the Smith Tower; now it was completely gone.

As she turned to the first page of *Boy 381,* she heard Tad's trademark two-fingered triple tap on the door. "It's open," she called.

"I just swam to the store. That rain's hot as bathwater."

He looked like Neptune risen from the sea: a rather short and paunchy Neptune, not exactly godlike, but spectacularly dripping.

"You know a motorcyclist drowned out there? Down in Pioneer Square?"

"*Drowned?*"

"All the storm drains are choked, and water's backing up behind the buildings. Apparently the bottom of King Street looks like Snoqualmie Falls. This biker guy—he was on a Harley—hit a submerged curb and fell off. People tried to get to him, but they were sloshing about doing no good at all, and when they finally managed to pull him out, he was dead. He probably wasn't in too great a shape in the first place. He was an old hippie, you know, the white-ponytail faction. Poor sap."

"Hadn't you better get changed?"

"D'you have Lee's number handy? We ought to call him. There's water pooling in the stairwell under the skylight."

She went out to look. It wasn't "pooling," with maybe a dozen large drops on the peeling oxblood linoleum. Tad fussed over trivia. Sometimes dearest Tad could piss the shit out of her.

"It's nothing much," she said. "And he's such an obsessive snoop, he'll discover it for himself soon enough. Do you really want to see him twice in twenty-four hours? I don't."

"I don't know." He looked up to the skylight, where a drip was swelling at the corner; it slowly grew, detached itself from the woodwork, and plopped onto the floor, where a real pool was forming in a perfect circle around Tad's feet. He stood there holding a single forlorn plastic bag, his thick wool overcoat resembling a sopping black sponge.

"Honey, please, just for me, will you go get changed?"

Tad, still gazing upward, conceded. "Okay, I'll find a bucket."

Back with Augie's book, she found it altered since her last reading, the lines of print now infused with his voice, his blue eyes, his military mustache, his prosthetic grin.

Where before she'd heard a boy speaking, in a pure, heart-tugging treble, she now registered a man's dry tenor, and fancied she could tell when he broke for lunch, went to the bathroom, or finished work for the day. This new, slightly embarrassing intimacy between author and reader dampened her pleasure somewhat, but it was authentically *him*.

Here he was in Lodz, in 1943, a pinched and hungry little waif hiding in a bombed-out house with two older girl orphans who'd taken him under their wing. Right across the street, fifth floor to fifth floor, they saw a gang of jackbooted Nazis clearing Jews from a rooming house. One, an elderly man with bad arthritis, couldn't rise from his chair, so the Nazis threw it and him right out the window into the street.

> For a second, the old man remained sitting in his leather armchair, riding on air. Then he fell out of it. We heard two separate thumps in the street: one was the chair, the other the heavy *ker-flup* of a human body landing unevenly on cobbles. None of us could speak. We stayed there, motionless at the window, unable to tear ourselves away from the scene below, too fascinated by what we saw to fear detection by the German soldiers.

He'd written the book in a month, he'd said. It was inconceivable to Lucy how anyone could bear to relive five years, packed solid with such harrowing brutalities, in just four weeks. Wouldn't that drive a normal person to rank insanity? After a couple of days of starvation, rape, torture, and murder, Jews being slung to their deaths from high windows, Lucy would be screaming and ripe for a lobotomy. Yet August Vanags had spent more than sixty years without speaking to anybody of his childhood, rarely even thinking of it, if he was to be believed. What had he said of his book? "A lot of it was news to me." And to have the whole ghastly accumulation of memories of evil pour out of him in a month—how could his brain and heart take it? And to write it down in such a cool, even-toned style? His shockproof composure was beyond her.

She had lunch—a can of chicken noodle soup and a cheese sandwich—at her desk, watching the city reemerge, building by building, as the rain eased.

She'd never lost touch with the exquisite stab of delight she'd felt when she first took in this raptor's view over Seattle, on that late-summer afternoon when Schuyler Winslow's managing agent showed her around the place. Since childhood, Seattle had been Lucy's fabled Emerald City of Oz. It was where Montana people dreamed of going, if there was life after drought. Although Minneapolis was closer to Miles City, everyone she knew instinctively looked to Seattle when they thought of restaurants, theaters, Major League ballgames, all the fantastic, distant pleasures of the metropolis. They were fans of the Seahawks, the SuperSonics, the Mariners. They spoke of dinner at Canlis as if it were the Russian Tea Room or the Four Seasons. When her discontented mother opened her great travel business, Flights of Fancy, on Custer and Main, she put up posters of Paris, London, New York, and Venice, but her hottest tickets, after cattle sale and harvest time in a wet year, were for weekend getaways from Billings to Seattle: two nights at the Mayflower Park, a Seahawks game, lunch atop the Space Needle, a show at the Fifth Avenue Theatre. Returning visitors would be as starry-eyed about their Seattle adventures as if they'd been sung to by Venetian gondoliers and pictured with Beefeaters beside the Bloody Tower.

Lucy bought into the dream. At college in Missoula, she thought as longingly of Seattle as Chekhov's Three Sisters did of Moscow, and when the *Post-Intelligencer* offered her a job as the most junior of reporters, she knew she'd arrived. The view from the top floor of the

Acropolis had set the seal on her big-city success, and now that the impossible new landlord was threatening to take it away, she treasured it even more fiercely.

Yet since 2001 she'd felt increasingly guilty about being here. In February, when the building was rocked by the Ash Wednesday earthquake, she was terrified for Alida, then twelve blocks away from home in her preschool classroom. And after 9/11, dire warnings of earthquakes had been replaced by government-sponsored rumors that Seattle was a prime target for dusky, hook-nosed, towel-headed bogeymen in beards.

Driving back from school this morning, she'd caught the latest news about the Algerian Safeco terrorist on the radio. Still in custody, he claimed that he'd left the game early to spend the night with his brother in Tacoma. An FBI SWAT team had raided the place only to find the brother gone. His American wife had been taken in for questioning, his children put in the care of Child Protective Services, and a nationwide APB had been issued for him and his white Jetta—and all this, Lucy was certain, because the Mariners had lucked out over the Blue Jays. One disillusioned baseball fan and his panicked brother constituted an "active cell," even though no trace of a bomb had been found at the stadium. Again, she thought of calling the police—but why would they have any interest in a one-sided two-minute conversation on a ferry? Much like them, she had no evidence at all. They'd just blow her off, so why bother?

Too often lately, Lucy had felt she owed Alida the true security of the boondocks, instead of the muted daily terrors of Security. Of course Alida would hate the move—and so would she. But was it *responsible* to go on living in a city likely to collapse in an 8.0 temblor and possibly destined to be blown up by a thermonuclear "device," or infected with a germ cloud capable of killing millions? How often did she and Alida go to the Fifth Avenue Theatre? Hardly ever. And they'd never eaten at Canlis. As the dream city became the dangerous city, Lucy was forced to admit that her prized view might be, like smoking, an unjustifiably selfish indulgence.

There was also the question of where to go. Once, she'd've returned to Montana—to Missoula, most likely, or Bozeman, maybe Livingston. But the entire state was tainted now by the presence of Lewis Olson. Even in Seattle, she was frightened of finding him at the door downstairs, piously wheedling, forgiving her her sins. And in Montana he could easily get to her and install himself in her life, ambushing Alida coming home from school, and doing his horrible Jesus stuff to her. No, they couldn't risk Montana, not as long as Lewis—"We have a bond, you and me"—Olson was alive.

From these thoughts, *Boy 381* was a welcome escape. Better to starve in the ragged costumes of faraway history than to think too much about the present. In the pages of the book, a peasant woman writhed and thrashed in her last agonies, strafed by a passing Messerschmitt, while Lucy, quite content now, reached for the peppermints in her bag.

SOME OF HIS STUDENTS were coming to stay for the weekend, so she'd have to air out the sheets in their bedrooms.

Minna Vanags, carrying an empty basket, walked the soggy path through the wide-open reach of waste ground and fenced pasture that backed onto Sunlight Beach Road. These days, she and Augie faced in opposite directions: he looked to the beach and the sea, while she looked instinctively inland. She'd been six when her deckhand uncle Max had drowned when his crab boat went down in a storm up in Alaska. She'd never learned to swim, and the sight of water, rough or calm, roused in her a childish terror of the sea's deep-seated wickedness. It was like being afraid of the dark, and her first thought when she saw the house on Useless Bay was *Too much sea.*

On these daily walks, her favorite moment was when the wind, rustling through the tall grasses and Scotch broom, won out over the sound of waves breaking on sand. From there on in, she was on safe ground, with blackberries and salmonberries, flowering thistles and creeping salal. Names came back to her in a rush from her girlhood, when she would escape alone to the wild ravine of Schmitz Park in West Seattle: willowherb, skunk cabbage, stream violet, foam flower, the piggyback plant.

The path led past a small stand of trees that Minna thought of as her forest, in whose damp shade she foraged happily for mushrooms. She never met another soul on these walks. With no one to disturb the riverlike flow of her daydreaming, she effortlessly reentered that past world, before high-school graduation, before Seafirst Bank, before Augie. Squatting, garden knife in hand, among familiar plants, she'd find herself at the prom, or in the passenger seat of Gerry Dexter's little primrose-yellow Crosley convertible, or hanging out at Zesto's with the gang, or kissing Dennis Lundke in his big old Packard as they watched Bing Crosby and Grace Kelly in *High Society* at the Valley 6 drive-in. Dennis tasted—not at all unpleasantly—of hot pastrami.

Minna had no real friends on the island. Before the move, friends had been as natural a part of her landscape as brambles and firs. She'd had friends from school, from the bank, from the neighborhood, from Augie's college. Now it seemed that she'd shed every last one of them, and gained none to take their place. You'd hardly call Sunlight Beach Road a neighborhood, with its empty houses and migrant weekenders, all too young, too engrossed in their own familiness, to take much notice of oldsters like her and Augie. Or perhaps they were put off by Augie's fame. In her rare encounters with other residents, *Boy 381* always came near the top of the agenda, always spoken of as it were somehow strange and forbidding, something that made her and Augie not quite human. Last summer, one of the young weekenders had said, "Of course we'd love to have you over, but we'd hate to disturb his writing." Minna had said, "Oh, no, he *likes* to be disturbed," but no invitation followed.

The nearest person to a friend she had on the island was Svetlana, the henna-haired Russian who drove over from Langley twice a week to help keep the house tidy. But Svetlana's English was often impossible to understand, she spoke far more than she listened, and she loved to offer Minna her opinions about "Americans." Americans didn't look after their old people; Americans spoiled their children; Americans cared only about money . . . Svetlana had been living in this country for two years, and talked angrily about going back to Russia, where, she said, "they treat me like queen." Minna, of course, was locked out from the conversations she had with Augie in Russian, though she sounded so much gentler and nicer than she did in her hectic, threatening, arm-waving English. Augie made her laugh, and she'd never once laughed with Minna, so she really was his friend, not hers.

Minna stooped on the path to pick a dozen leaves from a clump of wild chard, just enough for supper that night. She looked forward to having company for the weekend. Students had healthy appetites. For dinner on Friday, she'd make a rocket salad with beet, orange, and walnuts, followed by a rack of Whidbey Island lamb. Blackberries she'd canned in September stood waiting in Mason jars on a high shelf in the utility room, and she could give them a nice cobbler for dessert.

FINN WAS UP to something—Alida was sure of it. She watched him in Humanities, paying no attention to the teacher but secretly scribbling. As he glanced down at his binder, a smirk would steal across his face, quick as a squirrel crossing a street in an undulating ripple of gray. Finn's writing was notorious. Nobody wanted him on their team for projects because of his regular B minuses and Cs, and peer-critiquing with Finn was murder: he never got what you were trying to say, and his comments always boiled down to "I think it's stupid." The only thing Finn could write was code.

"Have you *seen* Finn?" Alida asked Gail when they headed for lunch.

"Like, the writing stuff? It's really weird."

"But what *is* it?"

"Well," Gail said, "I think he's writing mash notes. To me."

They had to cling to each other for support as they giggled, and Alida had tears of laughter in her eyes when she said, "Oh my God, that's *so* egregious!"

ON THURSDAY MORNING, Lucy was seated in the austere ceilingless writers' room on the ninth floor of the Central Library, skimming through a toppling pile of World War II memoirs. August Vanags looked down at her from the wall that was hung with black-and-white

photographs of local authors. His white mustache was trimmed to perfect shape like a piece of fresh-clipped topiary, but the bulgy glare in his
eyes made it plain that he'd taken a dislike to the photographer. His
military spruceness set him spectacularly apart from the other authors
with their unkempt hair, their two-day stubble, their air of having tumbled fully clothed from their beds to face the camera.

To put *Boy 381* in context, she'd pulled from the stacks first-person
accounts by refugees, soldiers, civilians, Holocaust survivors. None
were half as riveting as Augie's: where he raced, they plodded; where he
was light and nimble, they tended to a solemn, leaden weightiness. The
more she read of its rivals in the genre, the more certain she became
that *Boy* was a kind of masterpiece. Writing at a sixty-year distance
from the war had given Augie an ironic perspective that no one else
could match, and the extraordinary speed at which he'd written the
book lent to it a dramatic urgency that was missing from these others.
There wasn't a page of *Boy* on which you couldn't feel the author
driving forward under a full head of steam, and that was part of its mes-
meric quality; it infected the reader with what felt like the writer's own
compulsion to find out what was going to happen next.

Less than wholly compelled, she turned the page of Wolfgang
Samuel's *German Boy*:

> We were alone. One wagon, two horses, and five people. The other
> soldiers had left on their motorcycles once the wagon had been
> pulled out of the sand. Below us, flames still flickered in some of the
> village houses. Refugee wagons and several army trucks attempted
> to enter the burning village. As our wagon crested the ridge, the
> horses broke into a trot. With no one in front of us to slow our
> progress, we moved rapidly, and soon saw the last wagon of our
> reconstituted column ahead of us. We were the last one now, but we
> were back with our people. What I had thought was a trap had
> opened and released us. God had answered my prayers and
> rewarded Mutti's faith, I thought. The horses pulled steadily. For
> them, there was no good or bad day; they just did what they were
> told . . .

Samuel was pretty good on the whole, but he wasn't up to Augie's standard—though this wasn't the best place in the world to give any book a fair shake. The writers' room was overlooked from the tenth floor by a metal catwalk serving the glassed-in elevator shafts, and her reading was constantly interrupted by the annoying *poing-poing, poing-poing* of arriving and departing elevators. Fragments of Spanish conversation drifted down to her, and she found herself half unconsciously trying to translate them. People waiting for elevators on the catwalk leaned on the rail, candidly examining her at her workstation. When she looked up and caught their eyes, they stared straight back, as if they were watching an animal in a zoo: *Look,* Homo scriberens! "Throw me a banana," Lucy wanted to call up to them.

So she was glad when her lone tenancy of the room was broken by the arrival of a disheveled-looking, spindle-shouldered older guy in a pink baseball cap that was too young for him. Like most of the authors on the wall, he looked like he needed a long, hot shower. When they traded nods, his face seemed faintly familiar, but she couldn't put a name to it. He sat at a far diagonal away from her and opened a massive, grubby, ring-bound notebook.

Under Augie Vanags' tetchy gaze, she got back to work, methodically scanning pages, but it was impossible not to be distracted by the behavior of the other writer. Though he had a ballpoint pen in his hand, it never touched the paper. Sometimes he leaned back in his chair, cupping his hands behind his head and staring at the black divider that ran between the workstations. Or else, elbows on the desk, he couched his unshaven chin in his palms and frowned intently into the divider as if it were an ebony mirror. An hour passed, then another. So far as Lucy could tell, he didn't write a word. What was he seeing in that black? His furies?

Shortly after noon she got up to go to lunch. Across the street, Tulio's had an okay bar that served hors d'oeuvres and sandwiches.

Seeing her disengaged from her books, the man said, "Isn't this a weird place? It's like living inside one of those trick architectural drawings by M. C. Escher." He had an accent—Australian or British—and he was right about Escher. From the writers' room, Rem Koolhaas' many-angled lozenges of glass and steel looked like an insoluble puzzle of colliding perspectives.

"Yes, isn't it?" she said, looking up, dizzied by the diaphanous zigging and zagging of the library roof.

"I like it here."

She saw that his open notebook contained a few short lines, written in an untidy, spidery scrawl. Poetry? "So what are you w-w-working on?"

"Oh, I'm not exactly *working*. I just like to bring my block up here and look at it. It gets one out of the house."

For a moment it crossed her mind to ask if he wanted to join her at Tulio's, but his aura of gloomy pathos, combined with his unwashed look, made him too unpromising a companion for even a very short lunch. "Well, good luck," she said.

Sitting alone at the bar, she picked at a sandwich and made notes on her morning's reading. When she returned to the writers' room, the guy was gone, having left his chair parked askew, along with a note on top of her book pile. "If you haven't already, you should read *Boy 381* by August Vanags—wonderful book, despite its crass bestsellerdom." No signature, but she couldn't complain. That was what writers were like—compulsive snoopers, shameless readers of other people's letters.

It was getting close to three—and she had to pick up Alida at half-past—when she reached the last book in the pile and began to flip through. *The Pianist,* by Wladyslaw Szpilman. Polanski had made a movie of it, she remembered. "Even by the standards set by Holocaust memoirs, this book is a stunner." So said the *Seattle Weekly*, quoted in the front, but Lucy was unstunned. She was wearying fast of World War II. The glass of pinot grigio she'd had at lunch didn't help, and in the open cage of the writers' room, the passing voices and regular inspections made her feel as if she were in the hospital.

Skimming, she was suddenly arrested by a paragraph on page 80. How very weird: Szpilman, like Augie, had seen Nazis throw an old man out of a window in a chair. It was all different, of course—both the wording and the location, with Augie in Lodz and Szpilman in Warsaw—yet both men had noted the peculiar detail of the body and the chair hitting the street separately and making different sounds.

Surely this was an eerie coincidence, but whatever it was—if anything at all—she had no time to ponder it now. Not trusting the sluggish elevators, she hurried down the stairwells, *The Pianist* in hand, followed by the staccato echo of her own footfalls. Pausing on the third floor to self-check the book out, she flew breathlessly on down to the bowels of the building, where the Spider was parked in the underground garage. When she switched on the ignition, it was already 3:29.

EMPLOYEE THEFT. That was the big downside to the parking business—attendants slipping five bucks here, ten bucks there, into their scumbag pockets. Every day, Charles O watched the revenue line on each of his lots. Over the last six weeks he figured he was short around $2,500, and he knew who'd taken it.

He'd thought his Mexicans were too afraid of him to steal, and he was surprised to find that the thief was Miguel. For the past couple weeks he'd switched the attendants around daily, lot to lot, and whichever lot Miguel was on came up short.

Today the kid was on the Broadway lot on Capitol Hill. Driving up Pike, listening with half an ear to the CD of *Good to Great: Why Some Companies Make the Leap . . . and Others Don't,* Charles O enjoyed the thought of how he was going to teach Miguel a lesson so good he'd run all the way down to Tijuana and never come back. Plus he'd pay back every sorry cent he'd stole, and then some.

At the lot, he saw the kid was in the booth—shambling, and goofy-looking, even for a Mexican. The others treated him like their pet and were always giving him stuff—candy, cigarettes, Pacifico beer.

He lowered his window. "Hey, Miguel!" He could already see the fright in his eyes. "Want to take a ride?"

Stupid kid came straight around to the passenger side and opened the door. He was that goofy.

"Lock up. Put out the sign."

He could hardly work the combination, he was so scared.

"Okay. Now get in. Move your ass."

"*Si*, Mr. Lee?"

Charles O said nothing, just drew away slowly, with the kid beside him and the CD still playing.

"Consider, for example, the buildup-breakthrough flywheel pattern in the evolution of Wal-Mart."

"What you want, Mr. Lee?"

For answer, Charles O reached over and turned up the volume of the stereo.

"People think that Sam Walton just exploded onto the scene with his visionary idea for rural discount retailing, hitting breakthrough almost as a start-up company. But nothing could be further from the truth. . . ."

He turned right, and left, and right again, then found a nice quiet place to park on the street, right beside the reservoir. He killed the ignition. Not looking at the kid, but staring straight ahead through the windshield into the drizzle, he said, "You been thieving."

Big load of silence from the kid.

"Four thousand dollars. That's some chunk of change, Miguel."

"*Noooo* . . ." A moan like a hooting owl in distant trees.

"How much you take?" He let himself sound fierce now, but quiet, his voice holding out the threat of much worse to come.

"*Dos mil cuatrocientos cincuenta*," Miguel whispered.

"English! Say English!"

He was crying, shivering on the seat, and Charles O was afraid he was going to shit up that good new leather.

"English!"

"Two t'ousand . . . four hundert feefty . . ."

"Four thousand!"

"No—I swear of God." He was making the cross sign on his chest.

"Fuckwit."

"I got the money, Mr. Lee."

"Thief!"

"I give you . . ."

"Why you steal from me?"

"*Mi padre*." The kid's face was coming all apart. He looked like a quaking lump of spongy gray tofu.

"What your daddy got to do with my money?"

"Hospital." The word was a whimper.

"What hospital?"

"LA."

"He die?"

"No, he got problem. With heart."

Charles O had to laugh: this kid's dad, going to a hospital in LA? He'd be ruined by the expense. "How much it cost?" he said, interested now.

"T'irty t'ousand, five hundert, forty. T'ree days intensive care."

"How much you gotta pay?"

"Five t'ousand. I got brothers."

Charles O saw the kid's feet down in the footwell—nearly black with ingrained dirt, in flappy plastic sandals. They were five-dollar feet. "The shit you in, Miguel, no way you ever going to get out."

The kid was weeping a fucking river now.

"What do you think I'm gonna do to you? You better *think,* Miguel." He wasn't looking at the kid, who was cowering back in the seat against the window.

"You a piece of garbage, you know that?"

"Yes, Mr. Lee."

"The others. How much they take?"

"Maybe little bit. Sometimes."

"Like Lazaro. Last week, how much?"

"Saturday. Take twenty-five."

"Enrique?"

"Saturday also. He take forty."

"Party time, huh?"

"No—for family. In Mexico. By wire."

"You and me, Miguel, we're gonna do a deal."

"Deal?"

"You be my eyes, my ears. Lazaro takes five bucks, you tell me. I want to know when Enrique took his last crap? You tell me. You tell me every fucking thing I want to know, right? You say one word to them, I tell you this: I make you hate to be alive. You bullshit me, I fuck you up so good you think I am the king of hell." He spoke softly, slowly, making sure the kid got every word. "*Everything.* You tell me *everything.*"

"I do that." He was making the cross sign again.

"You be good boy, I pay for your daddy in the hospital. Twenty-six hundred plus what you stole, asshole."

The broken kid was sobbing out his guts in heaving gasps and grunts.

"Shut the fuck up," Charles O said, starting the engine.

Back at the lot, the kid stumbled, still sniveling, back to the booth.

"Remember: *everything!*"

He was in high good humor as he drove away, having handled it just right. Surprise was the key: surprise yourself, surprise others. That was a mark of the elite player. He switched on *Good to Great.*

"Sam Walton began in 1945 with a single dime store. He didn't open his second store until seven years later. Walton built incrementally, step by step, turn by turn of the flywheel. . . ."

MAYBE IT WAS just that Germans were in the habit of tossing infirm, elderly Jews out of windows in their armchairs.

Nothing else in *The Pianist* chimed directly with *Boy 381.* Lucy had gutted it that evening, cover to cover, carefully reading every page. Both books were set in the same landscape of hunger, wreckage, and brute violence, but aside from that they were as different as could be. Vanags was the better writer: Szpilman, pianist and composer, writing back in 1945, was perhaps a little too close to his terrible material to achieve the sharp focus that was Augie's hallmark. In *Boy 381,* suffering and laughter were constant bedfellows: there were no laughs in *The Pianist.*

Over the weekend, she'd raise the coincidence with Augie—lightly, casually, with tact. He had no reason to embellish his unique experience of the war by lifting a paragraph from someone else's book. Somehow the explanation must lie in the character of the war itself. Yet that one incident—the irregular soft thud of the body, the splintering crash of the chair on cobbles—had thrown the book out of whack for her and become the dominant image in the foreground. Happening on *The Pianist* had made her a bad reader of *Boy 381*, unable to see the forest because of her perverse preoccupation with a single tree. But she was sure that talking with Augie would restore the book to its rightful shape in her mind—well, *almost* sure.

It had been a tough sell, trying to get Alida to buy into the weekend. She'd played the homework card, the date-with-Gail card, the stay-with-Tad card.

"The house is right on the beach. You used to love that beach when you were little. Don't you remember Tom and Maggie Owen?"

"No."

"We'll pack your swimsuit."

"How old are they?"

"Oh, sort of . . . sixtyish."

"Great."

"They have kayaks. Augie wants to take you kayaking."

"Cool," Alida said, making kayaks sound like a second helping of spinach.

The school had recently sent out a booklet, "Understanding Your Child." Alida, at eleven, now exactly fit the profile of "Early Adolescence: Ages 12–14," which advised parents to "resist seeing only the worst in your changing children. Focus on the positive, including their creativity, curiosity, and fresh ideas"—easier said, as Lucy was finding nowadays, than done.

"Anyway, Rabbit, we're going."

"Okay. I really like being a parcel."

Then, when Lucy laughed, Alida abruptly relented. "You know, it's been so *long* since we were at the beach? Not since we went to Hawaii."

And when they were snuggling in Alida's bed at around ten, she'd said, "Mom, I'm really looking forward to going to Useless Bay," but Lucy caught in her voice the unmistakable tone of an adult indulging a child. Perhaps the school had issued a similar booklet to the students: "Understanding Your Parent." What profile, Lucy wondered, did *she* fit?

From under the covers, she clicked on the remote to watch the late-night news. The torrential rain had triggered a massive rockslide near Snoqualmie Pass, closing Interstate 90 in both directions. A murder-suicide in Bellevue: "They seemed like such a normal, happy couple," said a neighbor. More on the Safeco "terrorist," who'd been released and sent back to Canada; but his brother had been found in a Eureka, California, motel, his giveaway Jetta parked outside his cabin, and was now in police custody, charged with immigration violations and tax fraud. Under the new laws, they never arrested anybody who wasn't guilty of something.

As Augie had said, the weather for tomorrow looked good: isolated early morning showers, followed by sunshine in the afternoon. Temperature in the high seventies, rising to the mid to upper eighties on Saturday and Sunday. "For the first week in April that's phenomenal," said the weatherman. "You're talking me into my bikini," replied the forty-ish newscaster in the coy voice that always made Lucy reach for the retch button and switch her off.

Readying herself for sleep, she evicted thoughts of Augie and his book from her mind and returned to the place she so often visited at this time of night—a long, straight, gumbo road riding the oceanic swells of prairie; her dad in the driver's seat, on his rounds; scanty-legged pronghorn antelope leaping barbed-wire fences; the openness, the smell of dust and sage; prairie dog towns by the roadside; seasonal creeks overhung with cottonwoods; cattle on the rangeland; far-apart ranches hiding behind shelter belts of trees. The more remote this world grew from her, the greater the solace Lucy took from it in her most placid and satisfying dreams. So tonight she willed herself back to Custer and Prairie counties, her own patch of Eden before the world went bad. The penalty she paid for these sweet dreams was that occasionally she'd wake up screaming, but only when the dream went into uncontrollable fast forward—a risk that Lucy was prepared to take, for most nights the route in her dreams took her nowhere near where Lewis Olson stood, barring the entrance to his slovenly ranch.

· · ·

ALL VERY WELL for Lucy—the model bourgeois liberal—to tease him about his "paranoia," but Tad wasn't paranoid, he was entirely reasonable.

In the late sixties, in Vietnam demonstrations, he'd seen men in nondescript brown suits—J. Edgar Hoover's ubiquitous spies—taking pictures of the marchers, and with nearly forty years of protest and activism behind him, Tad was certain that somewhere along the way he must have picked up an FBI file. Even though he had drawn a 7 in the lottery, he escaped Vietnam by being "psychologically unfit," their term for being a raving homo—a role he'd played with great conviction for the draft board. And in 1999, he'd gotten into trouble with Equity for marching with Michael, as they jointly held up a banner that proclaimed, SEATTLE ACTORS EQUITY AGAINST NIKE AND GLOBAL EXPLOITATION, during the WTO protests. A stern letter had come from New York threatening him with expulsion from the union after that.

In his time, Tad had demonstrated in favor of women's rights, gay rights, and undocumented migrant workers' rights, and against detention without trial, the sacking of Archibald Cox, the funding of the Contras, the invasion of Grenada, oil drilling in Alaska . . . too many causes to remember. He'd carried placards for Che, Fidel, Huey Newton, and Daniel Ortega, and had recently tried to stage a rally in support of Hugo Chavez, though he'd found too few takers to make it worthwhile. Lucy had said, "Hugo who?"

Of course they were keeping tabs on him. How could they not?

Data mining was Tad's current obsession. Someone, somewhere, was watching as he tramped from site to site in cyberspace. The Patriot Act gave the federal government unlimited power to snoop on private citizens, and a daily visitor to Al-Jazeera must surely have aroused the interest of whoever was monitoring that site. Tapping out e-mail, Tad sensed that his messages were being scanned by an anonymous eavesdropper. Paranoia? Hardly. Internet service providers were required by law to render up complete records of their clients' every digital move if they were sent a "national security letter" by the FBI.

Was he the subject of such a letter? The ISPs were sworn to secrecy on the matter, on penalty of a lengthy jail term, so you'd never know for certain that you'd been watched—until they knocked at your door.

First they'd used the system to catch pedophiles downloading kiddie porn from the web. Now they were trawling for political dissidents, terrorist "sympathizers," which is to say any screwball foolish enough to get up the nose of the administration.

"Lucky your first name's not Ahmad or Osama," Lucy had said, with that annoying laugh of hers. "Don't you think they'd have their hands rather full if they were chasing down every actor with lefty stickers on his car?"

But Lucy didn't understand. They were using a net with a mesh so fine that almost anybody might be caught in it. "Either you are with us or against us." So if you thought it important to read the Arab point of view on the situation in the Mideast, you were a likely traitor to the U.S.—especially if the FBI'd had you in its sights since 1969.

Such thoughts gave spice to Tad's nighttime travels by mouse. Visiting Hizb-ut-Tahrir.org and Khilafah.com, he was making a lone citizen's covert protest from deep in the grassroots against an intolerable and abusive government. Let them knock on his door. In his most expansive fantasies, he imagined Lucy, skeptical no longer, writing about it for *The New Yorker,* and his radical congressman, Jim McDermott, raising his case on the floor of the House. Were he ever to be offered the part of political martyr, he'd give good weight.

Tonight, though, he was doing a little data mining of his own, trawling through cyberspace for the new landlord. According to Google, there were Charles O. Lees living in Wisconsin, Michigan, Mississippi, North Carolina, Tennessee, and Florida, but none in the Seattle area. He moused over to the *Post-Intelligencer* site. Nothing for "Charles O. Lee," so he tried "Charles Lee" and "Charles + Lee."

Mr. Lee had been clever at keeping his name out of the papers, but you'd think a parking lot magnate would've left some kind of public trail. The only name that fit was that of a social worker, Charles Ong Lee of Shoreline, who'd died in a one-car crash on Aurora Avenue in November 1999. The report was very short: Mr. Lee, driving a white

Honda Civic, had spun out on the wet and leafy pavement, hit a utility pole, and died instantly; alcohol was not thought to be involved.

The one detail that gave Tad pause was the man's age—twenty-five, which, had he lived, would make him roughly as old as the landlord was now. Could Mr. Lee conceivably be guilty of identity theft? Probably not, but the possibility, however faint, was so tantalizing that Tad copied the story and e-mailed it to himself as the first item in the file he meant to build on Charles O. Lee. Sometime in the next few days, he'd try chatting up an attendant at one of the Excellent Parking lots. Tad had no doubt that Lee's arrival on the scene meant either eviction or a rent hike so astronomical they'd all have to move. Certainly he was in no position to fork out three grand a month for what he thought of as an attic and Lee would grandly advertise as a "penthouse." He'd been living in the Acropolis for more than twenty years, and it enshrined his and Michael's happiness together. The prospect of being booted out by the insufferable Lee, railing against "scumbags" and "lowlifes" and "toe-rags," was beyond enraging; it called for a manning of the barricades.

He glanced at the Trotsky quote, in Michael's handwriting, on a strip of yellowing paper pasted above the top of his computer screen. "Americans think in terms of continents: it simplifies the study of geography, and, what is most important, provides ample room for robbery."

A LUMINOUS thin haze hung over Elliott Bay as Lucy, at her window, watched what appeared to be a kind of maritime Noh play. Twice, a ferry had steamed into the bay from the direction of Bainbridge Island. Twice, a go-fast cigarette-type boat had approached it, settled along-side, and emitted a rather feeble puff of smoke. Twice, Coast Guard helicopters and patrol vessels had closed in on the supposedly stricken ferry, only to retreat to where they'd come from so the mock attack could begin again. There was something both comical and alarming in the unreality of this exercise, which had "fiction" written all over it. Though it was costing the taxpayers millions, nobody could possibly mistake it for the real thing.

Reality was hard to fake, as Lucy had noticed when she watched

Alida, aged three, master the TV remote. It took her only a split second to recognize and dismiss a talk show, documentary, or news program in her searches for the soaps and sitcoms that held her uncomprehendingly enthralled. Still toddling, Alida knew that fiction was lit differently than fact, and in a single moving image could distinguish one from the other with deadshot accuracy.

The facile imitation of life now in progress on the bay wouldn't fool a six-month-old. "First responders," as they liked to call them, were being trained not for breaking news but for taking part in an episode of *Law and Order* or *Desperate Housewives,* and in the event of real horror they'd turn out to be about as much use as the cast of some crappy sitcom. Come to think of it, Tad and his friends from the Rep and ACT, accustomed as they were to stage emergencies and off-the-cuff improvisations, would almost certainly have done a better job than the Department of Homeland Security.

Tiring of the show, she set about packing their bags for the weekend. Her only real work would be talking with Augie over dinner, which brought up the difficult question of the tape recorder. First she packed it, then she unpacked it. Taping your host in his own home, Lucy decided, would be a serious breach of basic good manners. For this piece, she'd rely on memory and her notebook.

At noon, bags ready for the car, she wandered down to the Bookstore Bar in the Alexis Hotel on First. Even now it felt a little weird going into the Alexis—scene of Alida's strange conception—but she liked the bar, the books, the quiet raised table at the back, where she always ordered a glass of sauvignon blanc, a small Caesar, and the chicken potpie. As ever, she checked out the line of drinkers up at the bar—as silly a superstition as knocking on wood, since she'd be unlikely even to recognize him now, were he to show up, which of course he never did.

For company, she'd brought the bonus double Arts and Leisure sections of the Friday edition of *The New York Times.* She liked reading reviews of plays she'd never see, recitals she'd never hear, exhibits she'd never visit. Lucy was no vicarious culture vulture; it was the language of the reviews themselves that she treasured. After the front-page headlines, body counts, senatorial brawls, and denunciatory op-eds, it was good to loiter in a world where "subtlety" and "restraint" were terms of praise. So, sipping wine, she read about "the innate good taste and nuanced phrasing that informs Mr. Thomas's spectacular, crystal-clear performance" in a dance concert at NYU. *A pity,* Lucy thought, *that Mr. Thomas was unlikely ever to run for president.*

At two, she climbed the hill back to the Acropolis, and by ten to three was outside the school, the top of the Spider down as for a vacation. Alida detached herself, with lingering hugs, from a knot of friends and ambled over, wearing a miniskirt over her jeans—a fashion Lucy thought was ugly, though she'd never dare to say so.

"How was your day, Rabbit?"

"Good."

"What's the homework load?"

"A lot." She groaned.

"They've got a big house, so you'll have a quiet room where you can hole up. I packed your laptop."

"Cool." She'd put on sunglasses and was wiring herself up to her iPod.

Of course it had been sweet of Tad to buy her one, but Lucy couldn't help loathing the little white and silver gadget, which had drawn yet another curtain between her and her disappearing child. By the time they reached the top of the street, Alida was nodding, blank-faced, to the beat in her earphones.

Lucy headed for the interstate. Not long ago they'd sat down together in the living room and listened to the Green Day album on the sumptuous stereo system she'd bought after the Kurt Cobain piece, when Tina Brown had put her on a monthly retainer. She was surprised by how much she liked them, their unexpectedly complex melodies reminding her sharply of the Beatles. But the words! She had to work hard to figure out the lyrics and was shocked by their bleakness once she decoded them.

"What's your favorite track?" she'd asked.

"'Give Me Novocaine,'" Alida said, as Lucy herself at the same age might've voted for "All You Need Is Love."

Give me novocaine—at eleven? Green Day had about as much optimism as Noam Chomsky, and about as much humor, in Lucy's view. But they were *the* band for Alida and her friends, for whom tuneful despair was apparently the going thing. At least Alida liked—or pretended to like—the Beatles, too.

There were long lines at the I-5 checkpoint, where Lucy was again lectured about not having a National ID card, and a two-ferry wait at Mukilteo. Shortly after six, she drove onto Whidbey Island.

In the buttery evening light, the rinsed green of pasture and woodland looked like another, blessedly peaceful world. Not wanting to pass the scene of Monday's accident, Lucy took a maze of little back roads, with Alida map-reading.

"In about half a mile, the road will turn to the left. You want to take a right immediately after the bend. . . ." Her map skills were of motor-rally standard now. Last summer, she'd navigated them down to LA on the coastal roads and back to Seattle via the Mojave Desert and the Sierras without a single wrong direction. Along the route they'd talked and talked, about everything. But that was before the fucking iPod, which she continued to wear as she read aloud from the map, nodding away to some suicidal song that Lucy couldn't hear.

"Look at how green it all is after the rain," Lucy called out, as if to someone far off in the fields.

After a long pause, Alida said, "Cool."

"Oh, Rabbit."

Nod. Nod. Nod. Who gives a rat's ass about greenery when history's coming to an end and all you want is to be numbed with novocaine?

"Sunlight Beach Road is the next left, coming up in a bit less than a mile. You said they had kayaks, right?"

"Yes, Augie said he'd teach you if you wanted."

"That'd be cool."

"Like *cool*-cool, not like okay-and-what-else-cool?"

"Yeah, cool."

As she swung the car onto the raked and virgin gravel of 2041, Augie Vanags came out the door to greet them.

He bowed to Alida and held out his hand. "Alida, hi! I've been so much looking forward to meeting you."

"Me too." Alida was reliably polite with strangers.

"Lot of questions I want to ask you."

They were exactly the same height—Augie nattily tricked out in black turtleneck, white duck pants, and blue suede loafers, Alida in her weird skirt-over-jeans outfit. To Lucy they looked alarmingly like some May-November couple. God, those sunglasses: they turned her into a nymphet. Still, the just-visible sprays of zits on her forehead and around her chin helped to detract from the effect, which was something.

"Lucy."

So she was Lucille no more: he must have looked her up on the Internet.

Squiring Alida by the elbow, Augie led them into the house, and Lucy remembered Tad saying that he used to hit on his students.

TAD, shopping at Trader Joe's, mostly for wine, was waiting in the checkout line. The guy ahead of him, fortyish, with specs and an Abe Lincoln beard, looked familiar, though Tad couldn't place him. The guy's basket was bare: ground beef under cellophane wrap, a single can of tomatoes, three netted onions, a small box of mushrooms, a pack of cheap American-made spaghetti. Tad watched him pay with a mixture of food stamps and ones and quarters. Then he remembered.

"Mr. Quigley!"

The guy turned, blinked for a moment, and said, "Mr. Autoglass?"

"Alida—Alida Bengstrom—was in your class last year."

"Yes, Alida. Smart kid, and kind, too, which counts for a straight A in my book. It was fun teaching her." He looked forlorn at the memory.

"I'm sort of like her godfather."

"Cash back?" the clerk said.

"No thanks." Tad clicked Enter on the $143.04 he was charging to his debit card.

"How's she liking sixth grade?"

"She's doing great, but she still misses your class. You were the best teacher she's ever had, you know that? You turned her on to so many things. Like that world population and income distribution project—with the kids on the desks and the M & M's? She's never going to forget that. I was pretty turned on by it, too."

"Not too many M & M's for Africa," Mr. Quigley said. Not too many M & M's for Mr. Quigley, either, by the looks of it. He appeared wrung out of everything except for that stubborn trace of schoolteacherly wryness, the ingrained habit of his trade.

"How've you been holding up?" Tad asked.

"Well, I've learned a lot about the bus routes, going to interviews. And biking." Tad had noticed that the cuffs of his pants were tucked into his socks.

Tad was involved in a complicated bit of stage business: trying to scratch off the $18 price tag from the most expensive bottle he'd bought, shielding this from Mr. Quigley while keeping him engaged in conversation. The wine—a 2001 Château Gigault—wasn't anything to write home about, but it would have to do.

"Nice meeting you," Mr. Quigley said wanly, turning to head out into the street and get on his bike.

"No, wait—Mr. Quigley? Alida wants to be remembered to you. It's a thank-you note from her. It ought to go okay with spaghetti Bolognese."

"Thanks—thank Alida for me." He took the bottle, but looked utterly humiliated by the transaction, and clearly couldn't wait to escape Tad's *de haut en bas* solicitude.

As he scuttled from the store with his string bag, pant-legs flapping free of his socks, Tad thought, *Fuck! How the fuck could I have been so stupid?*

It was just the sort of actorish gesture he despised, landing poor Quigley on the receiving end of such paltry, self-aggrandizing largesse. He should have found out his address and sent him a crate of the stuff with a covering note from Alida, who would have instinctively known how to handle it gracefully. Tad carried his two paper sacks, bottles clanking, out to the VW, cursing himself under his breath.

Hating himself, he felt a resurgence of hatred for the conniving band of mothers who'd brought Quigley down, and for the supine weakness of the school's principal, who'd let him go. It had been politics, of course. Quigley had polluted his fifth-grade classroom with "left-wing opinions." That was the festering complaint of the suburban moms, especially those from the East Side. But when Quigley made fun of "intelligent design," the mothers saw their chance and sprang. They were technically outnumbered by the secular, liberal group of parents from the city, led by Lucy, but they had the big guns, including control of the PTA and a vociferous moral indignation that the liberals couldn't match. Their precious beliefs were being contemptuously mocked by a dangerous atheist, a man grossly unfit to take charge of their too-easily-impressionable darlings, and when they confronted the principal, she put up about as much resistance as a sponge. When Lucy's army tried to counterattack, the principal went into tearful meltdown: oh, of course she was on their side, really, but what could one do when the Jesus freaks were on the warpath? So she sacked him.

The worst thing was that the arch-freak, Elizabeth Tuttle, chair of the school board and a "homemaker" married to a venture capitalist, was the mother of Ali's best friend. At the time it had felt to Tad, staying up till all hours talking with Lucy, advising her on strategy, like the War between the States.

They'd debated as to whether to remove Ali from the school in protest. But Ali was happy and settled there and hardly deserved to be a pawn in this grown-up feud.

Lucy had heard that Mr. Quigley's wife had taken wing soon after his dismissal, and that he was now an every-other-weekend parent to their two kids. Perhaps the miserable-looking spaghetti Bolognese was meant for them. That Tad had so empty-headedly added to the luckless Mr. Quigley's indignities made him take it out on the Beetle. Wrestling the car angrily into reverse, he came within an inch of slamming into a harmless elderly couple jointly maneuvering their shopping cart across the lot.

"Well," Augie was saying over dinner, "I suppose you'd be for the Equal Rights Amendment? Gay marriage? A woman's right to choose?"

"Guilty on all counts," Lucy said, digging into her pink and tender rack of lamb.

"Which is exactly why we have to fight the war on terror, don't you see?"

"*Animal* rights?" Alida looked up from her untouched chop, though she was cleaning the plate of the vegetables around it.

"Sure, animal rights. We're talking all rights here. Rights I happen to believe in, along with a whole bunch of rights I don't. It's what living in a democracy is all about. You have certain rights, you want others, you argue people around to your way of thinking, you vote—well, you'll be able to vote quite soon. You make the laws—you and all the millions of other Americans who exercise their democratic freedoms. And that's why we're fighting now, against people who want to take away our freedoms, like our freedom to lobby for animal rights. Here, let me get you a fresh Pepsi."

Alida, fork in the air, was looking grave. Still at the age when adults tended to talk to her in voices they used exclusively on children and dogs, she'd warmed to Augie's grown-up-to-grown-up earnestness.

"I'm so sorry about the lamb, Alida," Minna said. "I used to be a vegetarian once, so I totally understand. If there's anything else . . . like eggs?"

"It's okay. I really liked the potatoes and beans and carrots, thank you."

Lucy said, "It may be short-sighted of me, but . . . Like if I could see grand ayatollahs in the governor's mansion and the White House, if I could imagine the spread of sharia law across the state of Washington, and Pike Place Market filled with American women in burkas, I'd sign up for the National Guard tomorrow morning. Me and my AK-47. But I guess I'm misunderestimating the power of the enemy."

Augie treated Lucy to a momentary, sardonic flash of cracked-china blue, and turned to Alida. "What do you think?"

"Well . . ." Alida said. "(A) . . ."

This (A) and (B) business was a new ploy she'd been practicing a lot lately on Lucy and Tad, and meant to stake out in advance a broad acreage of conversational space.

"(A) I think we're too freaked out by the terrorists. I mean, like just about every country in the world has got terrorists blowing up stuff. You know, like it *happens.* Like airplanes crash, and tsunamis, and earthquakes—stuff like that. Like what if I was a kid in Africa or India? But in America all we act scared of is the terrorists—and it's not *true!* And (B) I think the president spends all his time thinking about terrorists when he ought to be thinking about so much other stuff, like *emissions.* I'm really, really scared about emissions. We did this project once—but America won't even sign the Kyoto proto-thing. It's like we don't care about the world at all, we just want to fight a bunch of stupid terrorists. It just doesn't *compute* to me. It's like two plus two equals five."

Lucy had never heard Alida talk like this before. Did it come from Tad? From Bill Quigley's class? Surely it didn't come from her, though she found herself rooting for her daughter's argument, holding her own against Augie Vanags, even as she felt an unsettling pang, half loss, half pride, at seeing Alida as this articulate stranger on the far side of the dinner table—someone whom Lucy ruefully thought she'd be glad to get to know.

"I take your point," Augie said. "Or points, rather. But—"

To Lucy, Minna said, "It's not too rare for you?"

"No, it's perfect. I'm going to grab Alida's, too, if that's okay."

Minna laughed, the first laugh Lucy had ever seen from her. "I'll tell you my secret recipe for rack of lamb. If Julia Child ever caught me doing it, I'd probably get sent to cookery jail. But what I like to do is turn the oven to Self-clean, then I put the rack of lamb in, and when smoke comes out the oven door I know it's done."

"That's the kind of recipe I can follow."

"I like to cook," Minna said. "I don't know why. My mom used to hate it—she always thought everything tasted best if it came out of a can. I was in high school when they invented frozen TV dinners. Mother *loved* those. Sliced turkey, cornbread dressing, peas, sweet potatoes, and gravy. We'd have that four, five nights in a row."

"What did your dad do?"

"He was an engineer. At Boeing."

They were still talking politics at the other end of the table. Lucy heard Alida say, "This like scenario . . ." *Scenario?*

"That totally makes sense to me," Lucy said. "You're a gourmet cook because your mom cooked out of cans. I'm a lousy cook because my mom was so into haute cuisine—she had whole shelves of French cookbooks—but never had the time to do anything properly. She'd come in with this casserole and say in her two-packs-a-day-of-Tareytons contralto, 'It's just a simple *daube de boeuf provençale*—and it was *horrible*, like chunks of saddle leather floating in a lake of grease and vegetables. But it was from France, not Montana, so we had to sit down and say how brilliant she was to have found the recipe. God, we had so much cassoulet, and carbonnade, and noisettes of this and noisettes of that, that I'd've died for one of your frozen turkey TV dinners."

It was fun to make Minna smile. Her face lost its usual mistiness and came into sudden focus, again putting Lucy in mind of Marilyn Monroe. In her teens, she must've been like flypaper to the boys, and even now it was hard to credit that she must be only a couple of years younger than Lucy's mother. Thinking of her mom, turtle-faced, peering short-sightedly from behind the chained door of the Coral Gables condo, Lucy said, "I only have to get near the stove to start feeling I'll mutate into her and produce something utterly inedible with a fancy French name."

Augie was saying, "That's just not a biggie for me. The way I see it, the gut issue—"

"Politics!" Minna said. "You know we lived once in Washington, D.C.? Augie loved it, of course, but I just couldn't wait to get back to the Pacific Northwest. That awful climate. Summer in D.C.—it's like a sauna! And the people there, they're so different from Seattle people, they didn't hardly seem real to me."

Lucy tried to imagine Minna hanging out with National Security Council types and their wives in the age of Nixon and Kissinger.

"Martians!" Minna said with a conspiratorial giggle.

She'd've been—what, in her early thirties?—in those chauvinist days, and a prime piece of cocktail-party prey. "You had to fight them off—the men, I mean?"

"Oh, yeah, I got to be a champion wrestler in D.C. And in Seattle, too, back then. You know how it is. I bet you've slapped a few faces in your time."

Lucy heard Alida say, "Like when I was at preschool, I used to think Hitler lived on Bainbridge Island. . . ." What was *this* about?

Minna leaned toward Lucy. "Had to slap Augie's once. Right around the back of the bank. He was getting fresh before we even got inside the car."

Augie was saying, "Nah, that dog won't hunt, Alida."

Minna said, "That old Ford of his, it was a wreck. His students used to laugh at him for driving it. But he had such a way with words."

"Hey, what are you two yakking about down there?"

"Mind your own beeswax," Minna said; then she and Lucy cleared the plates from the table.

There was blackberry cobbler for dessert, wolfed down by Alida. "Yummy!" she said to Minna, suddenly a child again.

"At CollierParnell," Lucy said, "did you work closely with an editor?"

"Oh, yeah—Charlie Shaw. Good man. He made me empty my box of commas. Come to think of it, he just about eviscerated my entire system of punctuation. He was big on what he called 'sentence speed,' and thought my grammar was too fussy and academic."

"But the text itself? Did he ask for revisions or like suggest incidents that were needed here and there?"

"No, he hardly changed a word. He just pulled out all the punctuation."

At least the issue had been broached, and Augie seemed to take it in stride. When Alida left the table to go to the bathroom, Augie looked at Lucy and shook his head from side to side. "She's a delight."

Waking early Saturday morning to the first slivers of gray light between the blinds, Lucy heard the irregular chatter of typewriter keys coming from Jefferson's library across the hall. What was he writing now? A sequel to his blockbuster, a Horatio Alger story of a poor European boy making good in rich and generous America, or one of his dry-as-dust polemics for *Foreign Policy* magazine? Whatever . . . Listening to the pleasant, distant *clackety-clack-clack* of Augie at work in the gloaming, she fell asleep again, only to wake up, almost immediately it seemed, but actually two hours later, to the sound of a piano down below: over and over again, the same sequence of notes, though never twice in exactly the same rhythm. Then came a deep, resonant chord struck first hesitantly, experimentally, then again with confident force.

She took a shower, giving a wide berth to the hostile scale on the bathroom floor. Her weight had begun to frighten her lately, a problem she dealt with by hiding it under muumuus and shunning those escalating red digital numbers. She dressed to the accompaniment of Augie exercising his democratic freedoms at his Steinway grand, then poked her head into Alida's room next door. The bed was empty, and it looked as if she'd upended her bag and shaken out every piece of clothing in a tumbled heap.

Downstairs, Augie was alone, sitting at the piano.

"Poor old Schubert. What did he ever do to deserve the way I murder him? Alida went off to the beach, Minna likes to sleep in on weekends, there's coffee over there."

From the squared-off kitchen area, Lucy called, "Do you want some?"

"No, I've been tanking up on caffeine since five-thirty."

"Do go on playing. I like it—even if the piano's better than the pianist. How long have you been learning?"

"Three months. From scratch. I couldn't read a note of music when I started." He tinkled out a few bars.

"Sounds like you're doing great."

"If I could learn to play just this one sonata semi-fluently before I die . . ." He went back to practicing a wobbly arpeggio, not at all embarrassed by Lucy's presence.

She found it pleasant to sit on their cruddy old sofa, sipping at her coffee and listening to Augie hacking away, banana-fingered, at the keys. During a pause, she said, "Is that in A major?"

"B flat. Number Twenty-one. His last."

Behind Augie's halting notes, she was beginning to hear the ghost of a performance on disk that she was sure she had at home. There was something more than mildly megalomaniacal, she thought, about an absolute beginner tackling a work so obviously difficult and emotionally lavish. But that was Augie, and being Augie he'd most likely crack the sonata before his deadline. Still, it was strange that a man so ambitious and doggedly competent should have failed to make full professor at UW—or was it that only in retirement, in his new life on Whidbey, that he'd uncovered in himself this ferocious willingness to beat the odds?

His practice was interrupted by a string of thin electronic beeps. Augie shut off the alarm on his watch and closed the piano lid. "Two hours," he said. "My daily stint."

"You've read *The Pianist?*" Lucy said offhandedly, looking at the piano rather than at him.

"Oh, didn't they turn that into a movie? No, I haven't read it. Ironically, as a historian I'm not that big a fan of memoirs. Of course they have their uses, but their narrators are chronically unreliable."

"You might like this one, just for the bits about music."

"I'll have to check it out," Augie said, his tone of voice suggesting that this wouldn't happen anytime soon.

"The odd thing is that Sp—Spuzz—Szpilman saw almost the exact same thing as you did. Like when you were in Lodz . . . is that how you say it?"

Augie laughed. "You mean *Wootsh?*"

"Wootsh?"

"L, O, D, Z. Wootsh."

"Wow."

"Poles are tricky that way. Lot of others, too. Yeah, Wootsh?"

"Well, when you were in . . . Wootsh . . . with those two other kids, and you saw the Nazis throwing an old Jewish guy with arthritis out of a window in his armchair? The guy who wrote *The Pianist*—however you say *his* name—he described pretty much the same thing: Nazis throwing an old man in an armchair out of a high window in the ghetto in . . . is it Warsaw?"

"Funnily enough, Warszawa's pronounced pretty much like Warsaw. Polish inconsistency, you see."

"I was struck by the coincidence."

"Why?"

"Well, these two old guys in armchairs, both hurled out of windows . . . it all seemed so shockingly particular that I was kind of amazed to read of it happening in two different places. Warsaw, and Wootsh, you know?"

"No surprise to me. Face it, Lucy, in war brutality gets to be fun, and like every other kind of fun, like football or checkers, brutality develops its own rules. It gets conventionalized. Remember the pictures that came out of Abu Ghraib? They were of jocks having fun, playing games by the rules. All those human pyramids of naked prisoners? Naked guys on all fours being led around on a leash by a grinning woman? Hooded guys with electrodes attached to their testicles, strung up like carcasses in a butcher's? It was ritualized play, like a frat-house hazing. The players weren't making up that stuff as they went along, they were going by the rulebook, playing the torture and humiliation game.

"The Nazis were like that. It was a game for them to empty out the tenement buildings of the cities they invaded, especially in the ghettos. Architecture had a lot to do with it: think tall sash windows, with sills just a foot or two above the floor. You raise the sash, you create a space just right for a person in a chair. If some old guy can't get up when you break into his apartment, it's out the window with him. Do that once, you electrify the entire goddamn ghetto, and you've got a new move. Word gets around: here's a trick *pour encourager les autres!*"

He laughed, an arid little chuckle. "When we saw what we saw in

Lodz, it looked like they were doing it for the hundredth time. It had that practiced air. Makes me think of the Ik. You know the Ik?"

"I don't think so."

"Tribe in Africa—Uganda, Sudan, somewhere up there. The Ik lost their hunting grounds; then they had a go at being farmers, which they were no damn good at *at* all. When they hit starvation point, they figured the only way to save the economy was to get rid of their old people. It's a tough assignment in any language to kill off your own close kinfolks, so the Ik had to ritualize it, turn it into a kind of elaborate game. They pushed their grannies off the top of cliffs like it was some Olympic event, you know, Tossing the Granny.

"Two years plus into the war—by the end of '41, beginning of '42— the Nazis were behaving pretty much like the Ik, like a barbarized people. They could do the unconscionable because they'd worked it up into a whole series of rituals. Oh, hey there! How ya doin'?"

Alida had stepped into the room. Barefoot, hair a blond tangle, in shorts and baggy T, she was carrying a plastic bag and looked more eight than eleven.

"Oh my God," she said, "I've got so many sand dollars it's obscene."

To Lucy, Augie said, "I need sand dollars for my research, so I commissioned Alida. We had a deal: a dollar per dollar, if that's okay with you."

"Sure."

"So what's the score, Alida?"

"Forty-seven."

"Lay 'em out on the floor there. Let's count them."

Alida unpacked her trove of sandy skeletons. Augie, down on his knees, was talking nature study as if the Nazis had never existed, explaining cilia and pores and tube feet. "That one's got a nick in it. Doesn't qualify. Let's break it open. See those little hard white pieces inside? Sand-dollar teeth."

"Cool."

"What do you think it eats?"

"I don't know. Plankton?"

"Right. Juicy little plankters. Uses its tube feet to shovel its food into its mouth here, then sifts it through its teeth."

Three sand dollars were rejected as unfit for research purposes, so Augie got out his wallet and paid off his assistant with $44.00. Alida stowed away the loot in the buttoned back pocket of her shorts. Grinning at her mother like the cat that got the cream, she said, "I think the tide's coming in quite fast now."

Augie looked at his watch. "Mid-tide should be about eleven-fifty, then we can think about getting the kayaks out."

"Have you had breakfast yet, Rabbit?"

"Yes, Augie cooked me scrambled eggs."

"With some expert assistance. She's a better cook than I am, I'm afraid."

"You'd better put that money away before you go kayaking," Lucy said, hearing in her voice the annoying note of the parent trying to repossess her child.

At nine Minna showed up, looking particularly busty and skinny-legged this morning, dressed as if for a picnic in a knee-length skirt and a tight white angora sweater—hardly the same person as the faded woman in a housecoat who'd met Lucy at the door earlier in the week.

Alone with Lucy in the kitchen, she said, "I have to go into Langley to pick up some things." Clearly an invitation.

"Can I drive you there?"

"Oh, in your sports car? That'd be such a treat. Driving our Corolla's a drag."

So *that* was what lay hidden behind the doors of the three-car garage. Lucy had expected something grander.

"We can have some girl talk," Minna said over the gruff snarl of the coffee grinder.

"I THINK I'm going to throw up into the fucking aspidistra."

"Asphodel, Tad, asphodel."

"Whatever. 'It's my allergies, you know, honey.'"

"Just swallow it, and we'll break after this take, okay? Silence on set!"

"Rolling."

"MagiGro 9, take 7."

"Now is the season . . ." Tad sometimes bought free-range eggs from an old man with a little truck farm on the Snoqualmie River, and it was his voice—an old-West tobacco-chawing burr—that Tad borrowed for the MagiGro commercials. "Now is the season when all our thoughts turn to planting out our prettiest summer annuals . . ."

He *hated* these MagiGro things.

SETTLING HERSELF into the crimson leather of the top-down Spider, Minna said, "This is nice. It reminds me."

"Of what, Minna?"

"Oh, you know . . . just memories."

Driving coast to coast across the narrow island took only a few minutes. As she crossed the central highway, Lucy looked right, up the hill to where the accident had happened, half expecting to see again the play of red, white, and blue lights among the firs. Safely past that hurdle, she relaxed, enjoying the twisty road that snaked through fields and clumps of woodland. Accelerating hard out of a bend, she said, "Sorry, is this too fast for you?"

"I like fast," Minna said.

But in the store at Langley, she was one of the slowest shoppers Lucy had ever seen. Expertly, fastidiously, she sniffed and fingered her way through the produce department. Spinach was rejected as tired, apples as old, celery as spent. She paused for a while over a box of early, expensive Mexican peaches and held one up to Lucy's nose. "They don't smell peachy yet to me."

"Me neither."

A mango narrowly passed muster; a papaya failed the test. Getting into Minna's shopping basket was like Harvard entrance for fruits and vegetables: many were called but few were chosen. When Minna, trailed by Lucy, at last reached the checkout with her scanty haul, they were patronized by the boy behind the till.

"Find everything you want, ladies?" Lucy saw that she and Minna were perfectly invisible to him—two old bats on whom to give his charms the lightest of workouts. "Are we enjoying the nice weather?"

Disappointingly, Minna swallowed the bait, explaining that Lucy and her daughter were visiting and that her husband was taking Alida kayaking, that . . .

"Oh, cool!" the boy said, in Alida's not-listening tone. To his "Have a nice day, ladies!" Lucy wanted to steal Joan Didion's riposte and say "I have other plans."

Crossing the parking lot, Minna said, "I do like the people at the Star Store—they're all so friendly."

Poor Minna: was it for the boy at the checkout that she'd dressed to kill?

Knowing the answer to the question, Lucy asked, "Do you know many people on the island?"

"Oh, no, hardly a soul. There's another retired professor and his wife, but they live in Coupeville and neither of us like to drive at night, so we don't see too much of them. Augie calls him the Liberal Revisionist: they're not really friends."

They left Langley on a different road, with Minna giving directions. As they passed the county fairgrounds, Lucy said, "When you first knew Augie, did he talk much about his past?"

"Oh, yes. He talked a lot about Ann Arbor, where he'd been in grad school, and Binghamton, where he was in college. And Schenectady—he was in high school in Schenectady. We were always talking then."

"But Europe and everything that happened to him there—did he talk about that?"

"Not really. Of course, I knew his mom and dad had passed. I got the idea they must have been killed in the camps over there, but it wasn't something he ever spoke about directly. After all he'd been through, I think he just wanted to forget, and talking about it would've brought it back. I remember him telling me about the day he arrived in New York City—he was nine then—and being amazed by the skyscrapers, and the lady from Latvia who took him to Macy's, and this fountain they had in the store. It was like his whole memory began that day, and everything that happened before was kind of dead to him. I'd see stuff on the news about Berlin and say 'You've been there, Augie,' and he'd nod and say yeah—and that was all he ever said. *Yeah*. He was bottling it up inside himself and wasn't saying nothing to nobody."

"I wonder how it was when you took him home to meet your parents? He must have struck them as quite an odd bird."

"Oh, they got on really well. My dad called him 'the prof,' of course, but then he saw how good Augie was with his hands. They'd spend hours out in the yard together, working on Dad's Hudson. Augie tuned it right up, even though my dad was the engineer. Augie could fix anything back then, which was how he kept that old Ford of his going, and my dad looked up to him for that. He called himself a 'shade-tree mechanic'—an expression he'd picked up someplace, and he used it a lot.

"I think we were the first real ordinary family he'd ever known, and he kind of glommed on to us: not just me, but Mom and Dad, too. We'd go on weekend outings together in the Hudson—it was a Hornet—me and Augie in the backseat, Dad and Mom in front. It was a funny way to go dating, I guess, but we'd drive up in the mountains, and Augie was always in charge of the campfire. He had a knack for that, could make just anything burn."

When Lucy glanced over, Minna's whole face was a smile. But the island was too narrow to contain her memories; they were almost back at Useless Bay when she said, "Dad and Augie used to go steelhead fishing in the spring . . ." and her voice trailed off as the house came into view. Lucy resolved to entice her into the Spider again later in the weekend.

The moment they walked through the front door, Lucy knew that Alida and Augie were gone: the house was no better than a Holiday Inn at holding the imprint of the human, and she could smell its vacancy. Minna, out of habit, called "Augie?" but the name came back on echo.

The sands were glazing over under the incoming tide. The two kayaks looked like one—a jerky water boatman, scuffing along the surface with its feet. Squinting at the glare, Lucy made out Augie ahead, Alida just behind him: identical in size, they looked married in their oblivious preoccupation with their own small world. She picked up the birdwatching binoculars from the patio table and had a hard time bringing the swimming image into sharp focus. The kayakers went from fuzzy to more fuzzy, then turned crisp. Both were wearing puffy orange life vests, she was glad to see. Augie's paddles sliced the water as cleanly as knives; Alida's splashed. She was saying something, and Augie turned his head. In close-up, they were a couple no longer, but grandfather and granddaughter—and no sooner had Lucy voiced that thought in her head than she wished it gone.

"She'll be quite safe with him."

She hadn't realized that Minna was standing at her elbow. "Oh, I wasn't—"

"Augie loves children," Minna said, with exactly the same stress that he'd put on the same words.

ON THE SEVENTH FLOOR there was no sign of the fag actor or Lucy Bengstrom. Charles O let himself into 701, dumped his tools on the floor and his bunch of tulips on the table, then stepped into the bathroom and turned the lock.

The close, female stink of the place made him catch his breath. Both the windowsill along the edge of the bath and the glass shelf below the medicine cabinet were so crammed with lotions, scents, shampoos, gels, paints, creams, and ointments that a dozen women might be living in the apartment. He unscrewed the top of a perfume vial and held it gingerly to his nose. *Wah!* You could kill a horse with that one.

Two toothbrushes: good. Then he spotted a pink razor on the windowsill. He had to reach for it carefully with forefinger and thumb to avoid knocking over a whole bunch of little bottles with colored stuff in them. The razor looked as if it hadn't been used for a long time; a cracked rime of old soap whitened its twin blades, and speckles of rust showed through the rime. Looking more closely, he found some short hairs embedded in the muck on the blades, too fine for beard stubble. He set the razor back exactly where he'd found it.

American women had hairy legs, like American men had hair on their backs. Passing construction sites in summer, Charles O was offended by their monkeylike hairiness. So American women shaved, and you'd find a razor in any woman's bathroom. Get a wife with citizenship, you'd get the hairy legs thrown in. He was okay with that. He'd *want* her to shave.

He checked the inside of the medicine cabinet—nothing there but cold cures and Kotex, and some prescription pills that had expired back in 1999.

From the bathroom door, he listened for a moment before going into her bedroom, where he rummaged expertly through the closet. Women's shirts, women's dresses, women's pants, as he expected, but he'd needed to make sure. He pulled back the blue comforter on the bed to expose white pillows still dented by the weight of her head. He bent down and sniffed their thick, musky American Woman odor, like old cheese. Lucy Bengstrom.

Lucy. He tried saying the name aloud, softly, to a pillow. "Lu Si." Sounded good. "Lu Si."

Happy with the results of his research, Charles O went back to the living room and began to pull books from the pile of old boxes she used as shelves.

FULL OF HER TRIP, Alida babbled on. They'd seen an osprey diving for fish, and she spoke of it with hardly less wonder than if they'd spotted a flock of African parrots out there on the bay.

"Like we watched it—*watched* it, right?—and then these two seals came up right beside us. They were *so* cute. Augie called them Lewis and Clark. They kept on swimming ahead of us and looking back to see if we were following. Lewis had this sort of sad, whiskery face, but Clark always had a big grin. They stayed with us for *ages.* Augie said I was getting to be a real hotshot at paddling, that I was like a natural."

Augie said was her refrain. Lucy had never seen Alida so instantly smitten by an adult, and found herself having to stifle the resentment that rose in her as she listened to her daughter's copious rave review of August Vanags.

"All humanity is united in its hatred of a headwind."

"What?"

"Augie said that all humanity is united in its hatred of a headwind."

"You need some lunch inside you," Lucy said, thinking that somewhere she'd read or heard that epigram before. "Did Augie make that up, or was he quoting somebody else?"

"I think he made it up."

Twenty minutes later, sitting down to lunch, Lucy said to Augie, "Alida tells me that all humanity is united in its hatred of a headwind."

"Isn't that good? Know who said it? John McPhee, in *The Survival of the Bark Canoe*—great little book, especially if you like paddling as much as I do."

"Oh, that's where it's from—I think I read it when it was excerpted in *The New Yorker.*"

"Punch with the paddle, don't sweep it," Alida said. "I'd really, really like to go kayaking again this afternoon."

"Rabbit, Augie's a busy man. You have to think about *his* schedule."

"Schedule? What schedule? We're on island time here." Augie looked at his watch. "I think we could fit in another hour after lunch before we lose the tide."

So Lucy was left behind on the patio, watching the two figures, plumped out like puffins in matching PFDs, as they dragged their kayaks to the water's edge. True, she thought, kayaking wasn't for her; she'd be too afraid of capsizing, but it would have been nice to be asked. For a few moments she allowed her feeling of exclusion to rankle, rather pleasantly, before she was joined by Minna, carrying an enormous shaggy creation of mud-brown yarn that looked as if she was trying to knit herself a grizzly bear.

"It's nice for Augie to have someone to go kayaking with," Minna said, over the fast, regular ticking of her needles. After a long pause, she added, "I'm not much of a sea person." Then, after an even longer pause, "I lost my uncle to the sea."

"Really?"

Tick, tick, tick, tick, tick. "Which reminds me. Does Alida eat crab?"

"Yes, she does. She doesn't have too many fads—lamb's the exception, not the rule. Her favorite soft toy was a lamb. She just hates the thought of eating Larry."

"There's a place up near Ebey's Landing that sells live Dungeness crabs out of a pen. I thought tomorrow morning, we might go get some for lunch—if you felt like driving."

"I'd love that."

Minna smiled her shy, winsome, Monroe smile and returned to her knitting. Companionable silence was what she seemed to want, so Lucy turned her gaze to the bay, where Alida, paddling ahead of Augie this time, was confidently setting her own course out to sea.

The windless water was as still and as viscous-looking as a pool of mercury, and the two kayakers shimmered and dwindled like mirages in the haze. Lucy thought of how moments like this had lately become the pattern of life with her daughter: Alida lost to her soccer game, Alida lost to a writing project Lucy was no longer permitted to read, Alida lost to her iPod, and now Alida lost to this aquatic adventure. The sight of the two of them out there roused the familiar pang, half pride, half pain; loss, love, and wonder all balled up together.

She reached for the birdwatching binoculars, then let them be. Better to learn, like Minna, how to keep her place ashore. Yet she couldn't help wishing that she trusted August Vanags a bit more. Of all the marine life on view at Useless Bay, Augie was the slipperiest fish by far.

BEFORE WALKING the hundred yards to the studio, Tad had left the car at the Excellent Parking lot just off Broadway on Capitol Hill. Now, starting back to the Beetle, he sorted through his meager stock of bare-bones Spanish. Three months of living with Jesus and his Saturday-night special had set him up with the elementary basics of the language, and regular winter breaks with Michael in easygoing, gay-friendly Puerto Vallarta, where Tad appointed himself translator, had brought him to the brink of fluency. His grammar was atrocious, his vocabulary sparse, but his knack for accents sometimes got him mistaken for a native speaker—a half-witted, illiterate native, probably, but better that than a dumb Yanqui tourist.

"*Muchas gracias y muy buenas tardes,*" Tad said aloud on the street. "*Por favor, más despacio.*" A passing woman gave him a wide berth.

The kid manning the booth was dark-skinned, an *indígeno.* Chatting the boy up as he paid and collected his keys, Tad learned that he came from Oaxaca, had lived in L.A., had been in Seattle for one year. But the conversation was like pulling teeth; the boy's vagrant eyes looked everywhere except at Tad's face, as if scanning the lot for a route of escape. Still, Tad persevered.

"*Charles Lee es la dueño de Excellent Parking, ¿sí?*"

"*Sí, el Sr. Lee es el dueño.*" The boy's voice was sullen.

"*Escucho que es difícil para trabajar por él. El gentes dicen eso.*"

With sudden, unexpected force, the boy said, "*¡No! ¡No es verdad! El Sr. Lee es un buen jefe: es amable, considerado, muy honesto y siempre nos paga a tiempo. El Sr. Lee nos cae bien. ¿Qué quiere saber del Sr. Lee?*"

He looked freaked.

"*Okay, muchas gracias. Buenas tardes.*"

Back in the car, Tad reached to adjust the rearview mirror and was appalled to see the face of the MagiGro gardener leering back at him. He'd forgotten to wash off his makeup: his forehead was thickly powdered, the bags under his eyes caked in pale blush foundation, his cheeks as red and cheery as those of a department store Santa. Poor kid—he must have thought he was being propositioned by some hideous old queen.

PUNCH, don't sweep. While Augie put names to the birds overhead, Alida had eyes only for the limpid submarine world below. Augie called the water shallow, but to Alida it appeared miles deep. Each paddle stroke sent refracted sunbeams racing across the sandy sea floor and through the waving meadows of spinach-green eelgrass. The beams lit on bright purple sea stars and the gross sea cucumbers that littered the bottom. A hurrying crab skedaddled along the sand and a fish flashed like the wink of a silver spoon.

Augie had shown her these things in the morning; now she was making them her own. She'd never felt more grown-up, more satisfyingly in charge, than now, scooting the kayak through the water with her paddle. She couldn't stop smiling. The one thing missing from her happiness was Tad's presence in the picture. She wished he were standing on shore now, watching her captain her own boat at sea.

"Hey! See the little shark there! He's coming your way!"

Alida thought Augie was joking, then saw the mottled brown elongated shape glide right beneath her kayak like a winged cigar, so close that she could've touched it with her paddle. *Little?* It was huge—easily as long as she was tall. "*Shark?*" She heard the hiccup of panic in her voice.

"Dogfish. Spiny dogfish. It's a member of the shark family, like the great white's baby cousin."

"Shark! Oh my God, you mean it could *attack* you?"

"Oh, no. A dogfish is pretty harmless—unless you threaten him, in which case he might give you a nasty bite."

For Alida, the whole character of the sea had changed on the instant. She was afraid of looking down now, for fear of seeing another gliding monster.

And Augie made it worse. "It's kind of odd to see one out on his own. That's why they're called dogfish—they hunt in packs. See one, you usually see a hundred."

Packs!

"They can live for fifty years, maybe even a hundred, which is a helluva great age for a fish. Hey, there's another! I thought so."

She didn't dare look.

"Scavengers of the sea, they're called, and they do a fine job of cleaning up."

Shakily, she said, "Can we go back now?"

"Sure, but we still have a good half hour left. We could follow the sharks."

Terrified of losing her balance, Alida turned her kayak toward the beach and began to paddle fast and splashily, sweeping not punching, through water squirming with hungry hundred-year-old sharks, their bald, underslung jaws opening and shutting to bare repulsive yellowed fangs.

"Alida!"

She was far ahead of Augie now.

"Alida, it's okay! Really, it's okay! They're just dogfish. There's nothing—"

But she was deaf to anything he might say: she was paddling for her life.

6

"Poor kid—she thought she was in *Jaws 4,* and it was all my stupid fault." Augie was making martinis. Alida, who'd come back white-faced, lower lip trembling, had taken herself up to her room to do her math homework. Minna, refusing Lucy's offer to help, was in the kitchen doing something complicated and French for dinner.

"I like mine dry," Augie called from within the house.

"So do I. My dad used to say that one bottle of vermouth should last a decade, if not two."

"Man after my own heart. Olive? Twist? Both?"

"I'd like a twist, thanks."

He was quite the bartender, buttling the martinis out to the patio on a silver tray.

"I'm so sorry about Alida."

Lucy laughed, trying to put his mind at rest. "It's a good lesson to learn, that there are sharks in the sea."

"Before we saw the dogfish, she was happy as a clam."

"How is it that clams got their reputation for proverbial happiness?"

"I don't know—all that squirting, maybe? That looks pretty much like fun." Augie peered into the depths of the house for a moment, found a half-smoked cigarette in his shirt pocket, and lit up.

The thought crossed Lucy's mind that this smoking business was a bad-boy act staged expressly for her benefit. Beyond the labyrinth of drying sand flats, the sea was turning copper in the late afternoon sun. "Would it be okay to ask what you're working on now?"

"You may not like the answer. It's a salvo in the war you don't believe in. Wearing my last remaining academic hat, as an adjunct fellow in international affairs at the Council on Foreign Relations, I'm doing something for them about how to combat anti-Americanism abroad, especially in the Muslim world."

"Sounds like you have your work cut out for you."

"I don't want to seem a lard ass, Lucy, but I love this country, and it breaks my heart to see it turned into the most hated nation on earth."

"I'll drink to that."

"We share a premise!"

"Oh, I think we share quite a few."

Gusting smoke, Augie said, "The way I see it, every poor sap living under a dictatorship, when he dreams of being free he dreams of being an American. Most probably he doesn't even know that himself. But it's our freedoms he's dreaming of, and in his heart of hearts he wants to be here on this patio, drinking martinis, talking like we're talking now. He wants his press to be like our press, his elections to be like our elections. He wants our movies, our TV, our music, our automobiles, our standard of living. Syrian, Egyptian, Saudi, Indonesian—doesn't matter what his nationality is—he dreams of being *us,* and if we can only waken him to that knowledge we can roll back this terrible tide of anti-Americanism that's sweeping around the world.

"We got to invest, and invest big, in secular education in countries like Saudi Arabia and Pakistan. We need a whole lot more scholarship programs in this country. But most of all, we got to open that guy's eyes to what he's really feeling. I'd like to believe that inside every would-be jihadi in a madrasa there's a frustrated democrat trying to get out—and our job is to liberate that weak, uncertain little voice inside of him that talks of freedom and show it for what it is."

So *that* was what the morning clatter of the typewriter was all about. "A pity we don't set a better example, isn't it?"

"What do you mean?" He was burying his cigarette stub deep in the watered earth of a potted hibiscus.

"I mean we go yakking on about human rights, then we torture them in their own jails. We talk up freedom of the press, then close their papers down, or bribe them to print feel-good stories *about* us, written *by* us. If I were your poor sap living under a dictatorship, I think I'd more likely see America as a hypocritical tyranny than as the land of the free."

"Oh, abuses happen. Just because you're a democracy doesn't mean you're perfect. Some commander in the field makes a wrong call. A department head in Langley, Virginia, okays something that he shouldn't. Of course it happens. But because we're a democracy we get to hear about it, and that's the difference. If you read *The New York Times*—not my favorite paper—you'd think that's all that ever happens, abuse after abuse after abuse, and that's part of democracy, too. Sure we make mistakes, but we make them in public, and correct them in public. Trouble is, with an open society like ours, outsiders looking in think, *Hell, if they're putting all this bad stuff in the papers, what else is going on that doesn't make it onto the news?* What they don't understand about America is that what you see is pretty much what you get, and that in their countries *The New York Times* would have been closed down long ago for sedition and treason."

"So what is your favorite newspaper?"

"I think *The Wall Street Journal* has pretty balanced coverage on the whole. But I wouldn't want to lay a finger on *The New York Times*, any more than I'd want to lay a finger on Fox News. It's the spectrum I care about, liberal and conservative—I want the whole nine yards. Don't get me wrong. I'm a First Amendment nut, and I've lived under a regime where the only newspaper was called *Truth*. Sometimes, when I hear liberals talk, I have a dream: I'd like the ghost of Stalin to come back and rule the U.S. for, let's say, three days, and after that we'd pick up the conversation where it had left off. Boy, you'd see those guys change their tune. 'Tyranny,' you say. Lucy, I can tell you in all sincerity that you don't have the faintest inkling of what tyranny is."

He was the host, she the guest. She twirled her martini glass around and around between fingers and thumbs. To the receding sea in the far distance she said, "You're right, of course. I don't. But I still find it very hard to stomach a lot of what my country is doing in the world right now."

"I know. It's partly a matter of age, I think. I envy you being still young enough to be so intolerant of imperfection. Me, I've hit that stage of geezerdom when you recognize that everybody and everything has its flaws. Deep flaws. I think of Thomas Jefferson. 'All men are created equal and independent'—when he wrote that, if he looked down from his window up there at Monticello, he'd've seen his own slaves working out in the fields. Hypocrisy? And what about Sally Hemings? Or how viciously he trashed his rivals, like Hamilton and Burr, with lies and spin? He was a master of the dirty-tricks campaign, could've taught the Watergate burglars or Lee Atwater a thing or two. It's only by a whisker that Jefferson comes out on the side of the angels, and he's still my great American hero. He's *huge*. You've read Montaigne?"

"No."

"Good. He's a writer best discovered when you're old. Give yourself his essays on your sixty-fifth birthday, or your seventieth, and you'll see what I mean. Anyway, Montaigne said that there is no man so good that if he placed all his thoughts and actions under the scrutiny of the laws he wouldn't deserve hanging ten times over. Jefferson—even Jefferson—deserved to hang. Every president we've ever had deserved to hang."

"Some more than others."

"True, but when you judge this president, remember Jefferson. I believe this war we're fighting is a just war, a necessary war, but just like in every other war we've made mistakes, some of 'em terrible ones. We're only human. The president's only human. Even on the most exalted throne in the world, we're only sitting on our own bottom."

"Montaigne again?"

"You got it."

"But your war still seems so disproportionate to me. I mean, America against who, exactly? All I see is a bunch of mad criminals who obviously ought to be in jail for life without parole—and heaven knows we've lived with criminals long enough without trying to fight a world war against them."

"Yeah, well, in 1941 you'd have been with Lindbergh, a fascist fellow traveler. Millions were. It was Lindbergh who sneered at FDR for trying to spread freedom and democracy by force of arms throughout the world. Sound familiar? Most everything I read in *The New York Times* these days sounds a helluva lot like goddamn Lucky Lindy. That's something else that's wrong with liberals—they've lost their memories."

"You think Roosevelt would've backed the war on terror?" She meant it as a sarcasm, but Augie took it as a straight question.

"Sure he would. No doubt about it. We're fighting the vilest movement on the face of the planet and the greatest threat to western civilization since the Nazis and the Soviets. They're not 'criminals'— they're soldiers in an international army without a uniform, and they're uniquely dangerous. I'll tell you what Roosevelt would've said—exactly what he did say in a Fireside Chat in '42 . . ." He peered at the sky, apparently searching for inspiration, then shrugged and began to recite. "'Those Americans who believed that we could live under the illusion of isolationism wanted the American eagle to imitate the tactics of the ostrich. Now, many of those same people, afraid that we may be sticking our necks out, want our national bird to be turned into a turtle. But we prefer to retain the eagle as it is—flying high and striking hard.' Sorry about the eagle: there's usually one up there, but we seem to be out of luck tonight. Care for another martini, or shall we go on to wine?"

The sea had disappeared completely. No wonder they'd called the place Useless Bay—low tide revealed it as all sand. The magnified sun stood right over the jagged, deckle-edged Olympics; it was going to be one of those butcher-shop sunsets.

"Wine would be nice—red, if you have it."

Getting up from his chair to take her empty martini glass, Augie said, "There's no conversation more boring than the one where everyone agrees."

Emboldened by gin, Lucy said, "Montaigne."

"Oh, smart-ass," Augie said and walked chuckling into the house.

. . .

RATHER TOO MUCH deliberation had gone into the choice of books that filled the small bookshelf on the dresser in Lucy's room: Emerson's *Self-Reliance and Other Essays,* Mencken's *Prejudices, The Devil's Dictionary* by Ambrose Bierce. Looking over the titles, Lucy thought they looked less like bedtime reading than a bedtime reading list. Augie's politics were signaled by George F. Will, the only living author on the shelf.

Everyone except Lucy had gone to bed early. At ten, as they parted company on the landing, Augie had said to her, "'Good night, America . . . and to all the ships at sea'"—another of his compulsive quotations, though she couldn't fathom why Walter Winchell had to be dragged into it.

She considered going downstairs to fetch herself another glass of wine, but even in this millionaire mansion, the walls were thin and every sound carried; she'd heard the murmur of voices from Minna and Augie's room, and didn't want to be fingered as a solitary late-night drinker.

Thinking of Augie's quotes made her remember that one of her dad's favorites was from Ambrose Bierce: "War is God's way of teaching Americans geography." She pulled out *The Devil's Dictionary* and looked it up. Disappointingly, the long entry under "War" didn't have those words or any that remotely resembled them, nor did "Geography." She was certain that he'd attributed them to Bierce, so he must have written them someplace else.

In the pink armchair by the window, she scribbled a few lines into her ring-bound notebook, memory prompts like "Hudson Hornet," "Good with his hands," "Lindbergh," "FDR eagle." The sea had come back and filled the bay to the brim; a hazed three-quarter moon silvered the tarry water, which lay as still and silent as a mountain lake, not the smallest ripple breaking on the sand. Distracted by the view, Lucy abandoned her note-taking and turned out the lamp to better enjoy the play of moonshine on the sea. Quietly as a burglar, she released the window catch and raised the sash to freshen the air of the room, which was rank with the smell of lavender Febreze.

From behind the Sheetrock wall, she heard a yip-yip-yip-yipping sound like the muffled barking of a puppy, becoming less muffled by the moment, then a sobbing cry: "Au-gie!"

Strange. Minna's apron, from which she was rarely separated, said that kissing don't last, cooking do. Not true for Minna, apparently: lucky her. Pushing seventy, she was still coming like a twenty-year-old, which was a very great deal more than Lucy could say of herself.

Maybe it was the stimulus of having strangers in the house. Or maybe — but the idea of Augie being turned on by Alida in her Lolita sunglasses did not bear thinking about. She switched on the lamp and forced herself to plow through Ambrose Bierce, beginning at the beginning.

ABASEMENT, *n.*, A decent and customary attitude in the presence of wealth or power . . .

AUGIE BROKE OFF his excruciating piano-playing to say, "Would you like to take another shot at kayaking later on this morning?"

"Well," Alida said, "I'd really like to, but I've got this really big load of homework."

She'd slept badly, haunted by the image of the enormous brown dogfish stealing beneath her, triangular fins outspread, a predator on the hunt for warm flesh. She'd read, she'd listened to music, then she'd dozed, only to be woken by what she thought was a scream in the unfamiliar country darkness outside. Body tensed, she'd dared herself to listen to murder, but heard nothing more. She told herself that the scream must have happened in a nightmare already forgotten, and reached for her iPod again, drowning her racing thoughts with the sound of Good Charlotte singing "Lifestyles of the Rich and Famous," "Emotionless," and "My Bloody Valentine." It had been nearly two A.M. before she'd finally dropped off.

It was cowardly of her to be so weirded out by the dogfish. She badly wanted to recover her pleasure in paddling the kayak, the blissful feeling of command and control, and it was truly feeble to allow a stupid fish to spoil what had been just yesterday a revelation and a joy.

She said, "*You* can go."

What she really meant was that if she saw Augie putting on his life-jacket and dragging his kayak down to the water, she might be unable to resist joining him. Impossible to explain that to him, but she hoped against hope that he'd somehow get it by osmosis or something.

He didn't. "Well, maybe I ought to follow your example and do some homework of my own. What's yours?"

Crestfallen, she said, "Oh, we've got this project for Humanities."

"What's the project?"

"It's on heroes. We have to pick a hero and write about them. It's not that big a deal, and it's not due till Friday." Maybe he'd pick up that cue.

"So who's your hero?"

This wasn't going at all as she'd planned. She shrugged and said, "Anne Frank," trying to make it sound like the most boring topic on Planet Earth.

"Anne Frank!" He swung around on his piano stool. "Yeah, she's a fine hero. You've read the diary, right? You remember where she writes, 'My first wish after the war is that I may become Dutch'?"

"Kind of."

"That really interested me—Anne's impatience with her own Jewishness, her longing to be just Dutch. Lot of people have tried to gloss over that part, but I think it's important. What's your take on it?"

"I dunno." She didn't have a "take." She wanted Augie to take her kayaking.

"Remember Mr. Dussel, the dentist? Praying all the time in yarmulke and shawl? That really turned Anne off. She didn't want to be Jewish, she wanted to be Dutch."

"I guess so." Alida was more interested in stuff like Anne having her first period, and her boyfriend Peter, than in this Dutch-versus-Jewish business, which she hadn't even noticed in the book.

"What I admire so much about Anne Frank? She thought for herself. She always had her own point of view, and could be kind of spiky, which gets up the nose of all the people who've tried to sweetie-pie her into the classic Jewish victim. I think she was a bit like you."

Alida blushed. In a recurrent fantasy, she liked to believe that she *was* Anne Frank, and that the seventh floor of the Acropolis was the secret annex at Prinsengracht 263 in Amsterdam. It was amazingly discerning of Augie to have spotted the resemblance. She said, "You're kidding, right?"

"Alida, I wouldn't dare to kid around with you."

She was trembling on the edge of admitting that she'd like to go kayaking, but Augie had to be the one to take the initiative. "Well, I guess I'd better go upstairs and do my homework. . . ."

"You gotta do what you gotta do. Hey, I'd love to read what you write about Anne Frank, if you feel like showing me."

So Alida went up to her room, raging at herself for her own sucky chicken-heartedness. Those stupid dogfish: she really, really, *really* hated them—especially in daylight, with the sun on the water, where she should have been.

"OH, MY MOTHER WAS—she *is*!—the bane of my life." Lucy was driving Minna to Ebey's Landing. "She lives in Florida now, Coral Gables, two blocks from the Miracle Theatre. She's a big theater freak. When we lived in Montana, she started this amateur company, the Miles City Players, so she could play all the plum parts. She used to rent the high school auditorium and strut her stuff as Antigone, Hedda Gabler, Cleopatra, Blanche DuBois, and God knows who else. 'Someone has to bring culture to the West' was how she put it. She was born in England, and though she left when she was three, she's always liked to pretend she's a Brit. Nobody much ever came to her plays, except for family members, and we'd sit in that vast auditorium, listening to my mom roar out her lines to a nearly empty house. I doubt if anybody else in the West did more to put people off culture for good. If you saw her play Hedda Gabler, you'd want to go off and strangle Ibsen at birth. Of course I just saw it as my own humiliation, and I'd sit there beside my dad trying to make myself invisible."

"You sound awfully hard on your mom," Minna said.

"Oh, I am—and how. She was a lesson in how to be a bad mother. I was just about Alida's age when she told me I had a personality like blotting paper. Can you imagine? I think of myself saying something like that to Alida, and I have to laugh."

"Parents were different then."

"None was more different than my mom. She gave my dad a hell of a time, too, for dragging her out to the sticks—which he didn't. She was on a big nature kick when they moved, reading too much Thoreau and Gene Stratton-Porter, and by the time I was in junior high he and I were in a sort of defensive alliance against her. But I still visit with her once a year. Nowadays she creeps Alida out. She's the original Wicked Witch of the East."

"But she is your mother."

"Yes, and you can see how I take after her, too. Tirading on like this, I sound exactly like her."

Minna laughed. "I sometimes like to have a good tirade myself."

"Who do you tirade about?"

"Well, it used to be the branch manager at the bank, but now it's Augie, mostly. Poor Augie. You know how marriage is."

"Actually, I don't. I've never been married."

"Oh, I thought—"

"No, Alida just sort of happened. All by herself—almost."

"But she still sees her dad?"

"No. They never . . . got acquainted, you could say."

"That must have been brave of you."

"Or just plain selfish. Like I told you, I take after my mom."

Minna patted her leg. "I think anybody who has a baby by herself is brave."

"Thank you, Minna." It was the wind in the open cockpit, surely, that caused the momentary prickle of tears in Lucy's eyes. She blinked, dropped into second, and accelerated hard out of the bend. "My one big sorrow is that my dad isn't around to see her now."

At the crab pen—a makeshift pond sheltered by a tent of flappy plastic sheeting—Minna was as choosy as she'd been in the produce department. In the crowded shallow water, Dungeness crabs were clambering on one another's backs and clawing fretfully at the air with their pincers. Guiding the crabber with his net, Minna pointed—this one, no *that* one, or the one over *there*. Lucy tried and failed to figure out her principle of selection; crabs were crabs to her, though Minna clearly knew otherwise.

They came away with four, two to a bag, and even with the engine turned on, Lucy heard the dry scrabbling of claws in the trunk. Could crustaceans—in darkness, out of their element, destined for the vat of boiling water—feel terror? She was glad to get the car in gear, step on the gas, and drown the noise.

Minna said, "Do you want to talk about your dad passing?"

"Yes. Yes, I think I do. The guy who shot him was crazy. He was being treated for schizophrenia but was off his medication. He had this lousy little twelve-section ranch, a mess of rusted-up old farm machinery. He'd come back from hunting when my dad drove up, was just taking his gun out of the gun rack in his pickup. I think my dad was invisible to him. All he saw was the Bureau of Land Management Jeep, the federal government, and foreclosure. That's what he pulled the trigger on—I'm certain of it.

"But what hurt, almost as much as losing Dad, was the trial. They held it in Billings instead of Miles City where everybody knew my dad. They started out talking murder in the first degree, then whittled the charge down to involuntary manslaughter on grounds of diminished capacity.

"Okay, I could've accepted that. He was crazier than a hoot owl. But it was the jury that got to me—they were on his side. If the judge had let them acquit, they'd have acquitted. It was like to them my dad was a fair target, and Lewis Olson was this folk hero for standing up to the federal government—which is how a lot of people in Montana think. My dad wasn't my dad: he was Washington, D.C., a federal agent, and Olson was Robin Hood.

"They gave him four years, and he was out in two. I broke down when I heard the sentence. My dad was the kindest man. He loved the ranchers, loved the land, and it was just unimaginable to me how much those strangers hated him."

"I think, if it had been my dad," Minna said, "I'd've wanted to see him go to the electric chair."

"Or just locked up for life. But it gets worse. I went to see him in the jail—I had this stupid idea it might bring 'closure.' I was even going to write a piece about it, you know, a daughter reconciles herself with her father's killer: I was like, 'This is my therapy, and *The New Yorker* will pay ten grand for it.'

"He'd gotten religion in the penitentiary. He had this mad seraphic smile and sort of vacant eyes, like he was some kind of goddamn *saint*. He tried to make me go down on my knees with him, in the fucking visitors' room, and say the Jesus Prayer with him: 'Lord Jesus Christ, Son of God, have mercy on me, a sinner.' I mean, not just once, but over and over and over. He'd murdered my dad, and here he was, telling me to confess *my* sins to *him*. That's when I would've happily pulled the switch on the electric chair."

"Funny how really bad people—the most horrible people—always think they're good people at heart. And they do, too. I've seen that."

"He told me that if I came over to Jesus, I'd meet my dad in heaven. Like it was going to be him and me and my dad, sitting around some celestial campfire, reminiscing about old times on the prairie."

"You've told Alida all this?"

"No. She knows her granddad was murdered, but not about the Jesus stuff. She doesn't know Lewis Olson keeps on writing to me—just to warn me that if I don't repent I'll never see my dad again. Then he brings me up to date with his stupid news, like he and I are family. Blue envelopes and block capitals. The sight of a blue envelope in the mail makes me want to vomit. I have a Google Alert on his name, hoping to see his death notice in the *Billings Gazette* or whatever. But you'd be amazed how many Lewis Olsons there are. Mostly I get the latest dope on some New Zealand glass artist."

Again, the island was too small for the conversation; again, Sunlight Beach Road came too quickly into view. But even though—or, rather, because—Lucy had done all the talking, she'd found out one thing crucial to the *GQ* piece: why Augie married Minna.

ON SUNDAY AFTERNOON in the Dew Drop Inn on Aurora, Charles O was waiting for his girl to come out of the bathroom.

She was good and old, this one—as old as Lucy Bengstrom, maybe even older. "Hi, I'm Estelle," she'd said when she stepped into his pickup. It was a made-up name. Last week's girl had called herself Dolores.

"I'm Don," Charles O had said.

"Hi, Don," she'd said, hitching her skirt up to show her thigh. He saw her appraising the leather upholstery, the premium stereo, the power seats, the AC.

She sure took her time in the bathroom: lot of water running and the toilet flushing. Still fully clothed, he sat on the edge of the waterbed, lightly bouncing, waiting for his date.

At last she came out, in her underwear—red bra, red panties, black stockings and a lot of hooks and elastic to hold them up. She turned around, cocked her fat ass up at him, big meaty buttocks bulging out from the lacy stuff that barely filled her crack, looked over her shoulder, and said, "How you like me, Don?"

"Lookin' good, Estelle."

"I like Asian men. They keep themselves clean, not like Americans. I'm big on personal hygiene. I mean, what with all the DSTs nowadays, you gotta be clean, right?" She perched herself on his knees, arm around his neck, then reached for his pants. "Hey, your little elvis, he's got *wood.*"

She unzipped him, easing his pants down to his knees. He liked the motherliness of her as she swabbed his dick and balls with a Wet One.

"What a *big* elvis he's getting to be."

Charles O knew the drill. He handed her the condom that he'd taken from its wrapper when she was in the bathroom. Gently, skillfully, she unrolled the latex sheath down his dick, as if she was hanging wallpaper. Then she put her lips to the teat of the condom, teasing him.

"Does little elvis want to come in my mouth?"

This was what the old ones were good at. They liked to play around, to pretend. Charles O liked that.

"Is he going to be a good little elvis today, then?"

It was like his entire being had gone into his dick now: he was his dick. "Yeah," he grunted. "Yeah."

She had him all in her mouth now, licking, sucking, squeezing, as if she had a whole bunch of baby chipmunks working overtime inside there.

As she labored on him, he thought of Lucy Bengstrom. Lucy, Lucy, Lucy, Lucy, Lucy, *Lucy*!

"Oh, you're a quick one, aren't you, honey? Was that nice? I like a quick man."

He went to the bathroom to rid himself of the Trojan and wash up. When he came back, Estelle said, "I only go hoing for my little daughter. Sharon's ten. You'd like her. She's doing great at school."

"Where she at now?"

"I got an aunt looks after her on weekends. In Shoreline. That's a nice neighborhood. You know Shoreline?"

She was chatty, this one. He shrugged. "Yeah, I been all around there."

"I gotta go to the little girls' room," she said. "You wait there. Turn on the TV. We could watch TV together."

Impatient to settle up with her and get back on the road, he paced the room, wondering why she trusted him to stay. Then he saw her watching him through the just-open bathroom door—her eyes on his every move as she pulled up her skirt and tucked her shirt into it. She had him covered.

When she came out, she was smiling. He hadn't noticed her bad teeth before. She said, "I got an idea, Don. I'm really hungry. I thought, you and me, we could go out to lunch someplace, somewhere fancy, like with a cocktail lounge, you know? Like we were on a date date. Then after, maybe I could do your little elvis again—wouldn't cost you no more, 'cept for the lunch, and you could give me like a *gratuity*?"

He was sufficiently tempted to check the time on his watch. "Nah.

Too much business I got to see to." He handed her three twenties, as agreed.

They parted company at the door, Charles O to his truck, Estelle to the street. She was almost at the corner of the motel when she turned around and called, "Don?"

"Yeah?"

"And fuck you too, *honey.*"

He was laughing as he switched on the ignition. What a ho—drive two stoplights down Aurora and she'd be gone forever from his mind. Yet the good blow job had only further imprinted the beckoning thought of Lucy Bengstrom. He didn't want hos no more, he wanted her. *Lucy!* Just thinking her name made his dick begin to twitch again.

He turned on the stereo.

"Next, when you attain deep understanding about the three circles of your Hedgehog Concept and begin to push in a direction consistent with that understanding, you hit breakthrough momentum and accelerate with key accelerators . . ."

The deep, confident, moneyed voice filled the cab. *Breakthrough momentum*—that was where he was at, and Lucy Bengstrom was part of it. Half listening, half dreaming, he was struck by an idea so new to him that it took several blocks to recognize it for what it was, or what he presumed it must be. Love, never an item on his agenda, and a term so far outside his usual vocabulary that he classed it along with such other dim abstractions as "amortization" and "fee simple," had at last caught up with him in the shape of the tenant of #701 in that big flowery dress of hers. Crossing the Aurora Bridge, Charles O felt suddenly, mysteriously gifted.

LUCY WAS GLAD that Alida had been upstairs in her room when the live crabs had been slid, claws flailing, into the massive pan of raging water, each letting out a desolate whistling sigh as it met its death. At lunch, Alida was engrossed in managing the novel implements—the hinged crackers in the shape of claws, the slender two-pronged forks for teasing the flesh out of the shells.

"So how goes the homework?" Augie said.

Alida looked up from her splitting and crunching. "Oh, I finished it. It was pretty easy. I found the part where Anne says she wants to be Dutch, and put that in."

Lucy didn't know what she was talking about. "Who's this, Rabbit?"

"Anne Frank."

"We were talking about her earlier," Augie said.

Alida never discussed her homework with Lucy.

"It's an interesting question," Augie said. "Was Anne Frank an emblem of the human spirit in general, or was she the archetypal Jewish victim? Her father, Otto, always claimed her as the first. This guy Meyer Levin tried to turn her into the second. There's been a big battle over the possession of her memory, so by now there are two different Anne Franks—maybe more."

This was Alida's homework—multiple Anne Franks? "I thought you didn't like memoirs," Lucy said.

"And here's why. Otto Frank's Anne is one person, Meyer Levin's is another. You read her diary through Otto's eyes, then through Levin's, and they're two different books entirely. One's about the trials of humanity, the other's about the suffering of the Jews. Memoirs are always tricky that way."

"Augie, I was thinking . . ."

"What were you thinking, Alida?"

"Well, like if we could go kayaking after lunch?"

"Oh, Rabbit, there's no time. There'll be long lines at the ferry, particularly in this weather. You've got school tomorrow. We have to get away in less than an hour. I'm sorry."

Alida's face went pinkly limp with disappointment.

"Hey, talk your mother into coming next weekend, we can go then."

"Oh, Mom, can we? Please?"

Lucy was aware of a whole battery of alarms going off inside her head. August Vanags was her subject, her paycheck; he was food and rent. She needed distance to get him in perspective, to hold him coolly at arm's length and not get drowned in this warm tide of hospitality—a tide, she feared, that issued from his and Minna's loneliness. In the case of Bill Gates, she'd won two one-hour sessions, three weeks apart, and that was about right. In the case of August Vanags, it felt as if she and Alida were moving in. Her piece was in danger; she must get her priorities straight.

"Rabbit—"

"Oh, yes, we'd love to have you over," Minna said.

"Of course we'd love to come, but . . . can we talk about it later, on the phone?"

"Take your time," Augie said. "No urgency about it. We're on island time here."

It was the second time he'd said that, and Lucy always found the phrase faintly annoying. Even people who lived on Bainbridge used it, smugly, to insinuate that the most technical of insularities was some kind of moral virtue to be paraded over mere mainlanders.

They left the house at 2:30. At 2:31, Alida began campaigning for a return to Useless Bay on Friday.

"Oh, maybe, Rabbit, maybe . . . But it's difficult."

"Why is it difficult?"

"It just is."

In response, Alida wired herself to her iPod and turned the volume up so loud that Lucy could hear the thin, tinny dribble of teenage nihilism coming from the earphones.

"Sorry! I know that's a lousy answer!"

Tinka-tinka-tinka-tinka-tinka-novocaine.

"Alida?"

But there was no reaching her. She might as well have been in Idaho, lips twitching to the lyrics, eyes half focused on the middle distance, left foot tapping in the footwell. She was gone.

There was a three-ferry wait at the terminal, where Alida tried to make overtures to a sniffer dog and was repulsed by its handler. Lucy made notes. "Memoirs are always tricky that way." Talking of Anne Frank, had he really been speaking of himself and of multiple August Vanagses? She saw no obvious connection, but it was too hot to properly think. Ferry came and ferry went. The low-tide reek of drying bladder wrack grew steadily stronger as the water sank around the harbor pilings. The waiting cars kept their engines running for the air conditioning, filling the dead air with their fumes. At last the line began to move, and aboard the ferry there was blessed cool.

They sat by a window in the passenger lounge, next to a bulkhead. Alida—still wired—pointed approvingly to a framed notice that boasted, THIS FERRY IS POWERED BY SOYBEANS—BIODIESEL FUEL IN USE. Lucy responded with a thumbs-up sign and went on making notes. Maybe she'd have to learn sign language if she was to keep in meaningful communication with her daughter.

Halfway across Discovery Passage, she noticed for the second time the man in the Hawaiian shirt, jeans, and tightly buttoned poplin summer jacket. His tourist getup was at odds with his purposeful stride down the rows, eyes swiveling from passenger to passenger. On the instant that he registered Lucy and Alida, he appeared to cancel them from his attention. Then she saw the bulge in the jacket under his left armpit: a holstered sidearm.

An undercover marshal. Until now, she'd believed these guys were figments of Tad's paranoid imagination. He claimed he'd seen them everywhere—on buses, ferries, and "all over" Pike Place Market. Sometimes he called them Stasi, sometimes just the secret police. *Yeah, Tad. Go, Tad, go.* She'd paid no attention. Now that she'd seen one for herself, she felt rebuked, like a doubting Thomas. Over her shoulder, she watched the man on his unrewarding beat. Whom was he hoping to catch? Bin Laden, returning from his weekend hideaway on Whidbey Island? Or perhaps his whole point, in his loud vacation gear, was not to observe but be observed, the watcher watched, as she was watching now.

"It happens slowly," Tad had said, "so slowly you don't see it happening. You think you're living in a democracy, then one morning you wake up and realize it's a fascist police state, and it's been that way for years."

But that was Tad, speaking from inside his world of dark "intel" and crazy theories garnered from the Internet. On the day Ronald Reagan died, he'd said matter-of-factly that of course Reagan had been dead for months, if not years, and that they'd been keeping his corpse on ice in readiness for a political emergency. They'd chosen to announce his death on that particular day in order to divert attention from some pickle that the president had gotten himself into over in Europe. All this Tad said as flatly as if he were reporting the weather forecast, which had made Lucy wonder for a moment if he might be clinically insane.

Whenever Tad got going on the federal government, Lucy bristled with unease. It was too damn close to Lewis Olson, his knee-jerk conviction that everyone in Washington, D.C., was conspiring to subvert the Constitution and enslave the American people. It was cheap and dangerous thinking, and she couldn't count the hours she'd spent railing back at Tad, telling him he was no better than the Montana Militia with their kooky crap about black helicopters and the New World Order. "You and John Trochmann," she said, "you're like Tom Sawyer and Huck Finn."

The guy in the Hawaiian shirt had taken a seat on the far side of the passenger lounge. Tiring of his search for terrorists, he was staring, or pretending to stare, at the crisscross wakes of pleasure boats as they stormed around the glassy sea. If they had undercover marshals on planes—which Lucy thought was okay, even reassuring—why shouldn't they put them on the ferries? Just because you saw the occasional plainclothesman with a concealed gun didn't mean the country was turning into a police state. The trouble with Tad was he had no sense of proportion. Michael had been the one with common sense, and after he died poor Tad, more often out of work than in, had tried to lose himself in cyberspace, where he was natural prey to all the psychos out there with their hot little secrets and spurious insider dirt.

On I-5, traffic was backed up from the checkpoint for the best part of a mile. Stewing in gridlock, Lucy was reminded of another of Tad's unlikely stories, expounded over dinner as if it were gospel. There was a huge program to renew reflective lane markers on highways, ostensibly the baby of the Department of Transportation but known by Tad to have originated in the National Security Agency. These weren't just any old lane markers; they were clandestine—you might say clairvoyant—lane markers that would track the number, make, and color of your car as it went by. When the system was complete, they'd be able to track the exact movements of every vehicle in the U.S. It was, Tad said, all done by microchips and wireless technology.

"Microchips? How could microchips do that?"

Tad, wearing the lofty smile of the privileged initiate, said, "You'd better ask the NSA that question."

The uniformed boys at the checkpoint, faces red with sunburn, were surprisingly polite, considering the tormenting weather. One asked Alida what she was listening to.

Alida removed an earphone to say, "Good Charlotte. 'Young and Hopeless.'"

"Cool. Okay, ma'am. Drive safe."

Definitely not the manners of a police state.

She took the Union Street exit and drove into the muggy haze of downtown.

"Temperature inversion," Alida said, at last breaking the long silence of the ride.

"What?"

"When warm air gets trapped by even warmer air in the upper atmosphere, so it can't rise and all the pollution has nowhere to go. You know that just living in Seattle's like smoking twelve cigarettes a day? I bet today it's like smoking thirty. Yuck!"

"I never heard the cigarette thing."

"We did it in Science. It's really, really scary."

"I'm afraid science is scary now. It never used to be. When I was in junior high in Miles City, it was always about exploring the wonders of the world. It's so different for you guys—exploring all the terrors."

"Thirty cigarettes a *day*. It's the particulates in the air. You know what?"

"What, Rabbit?"

"Tonight, can we get pizza?"

ENTERING THE APARTMENT, Lucy was immediately aware of something odd and wrong, though what that something was she couldn't place. Then she saw that her wilted lilies in the vase on the table had been replaced by fresh tulips. That would be the ever-thoughtful Tad, who had a key to 701 as she had a key to 704. But it wasn't just the tulips. She scanned the living room and fixed on the bookshelves: her small library was all out of order, with many of the books stuffed in backward, spine first. It looked like some ham-fisted ape had been at work, wrecking her careful alphabetizing, with Kathy Acker where Virginia Woolf should be. Outraged and bewildered by this weird invasion—violation—of her territory, she cast helplessly around for an explanation until she remembered the landlord's promise to attach her shelves to the wall.

She pulled out an armful of books and saw the new screws, neatly countersunk into the wood of the Pepsi crates. How could anyone go to such trouble, yet show such blatant contempt for her books? It would take hours and hours to put them back in order.

He had no right . . .

Yet anger with the landlord contended with a wary lightening of the heart, for if he was really bent on eviction, why on earth would he bother to anchor his tenant's possessions so securely to the building? Each crate was now attached to the wall by four big silver screws. Stolen night by night from outside the grocery store in Missoula, lightly sandpapered, and brushed with four coats of Varathane, the Pepsi crates had traveled with her since her sophomore year of college.

"Rabbit, what are four eighteens?"

"Seventy-two," Alida called back from her room.

How long would that have taken him? More time than it was worth, surely. One screw per crate, two at most, would have done the job, but he'd created a structure of such rigidity and permanence that it would take the total collapse of the Acropolis to shake these shelves from the wall. If that was any indication of how her tenancy stood in his eyes, she ought to be delighted with his work, despite the shambles he'd made of her books.

"Are you busy, Rabbit? I'd love for you to come and help me in here if you can."

"Oh my God, what *happened*?" Alida said when she saw the bookshelves.

"Our helpful landlord."

"Oh, right—I remember, like earthquake retrofitting. He said he'd do it over the weekend."

"I'd forgotten all about it."

Admiring the exposed screw-heads, Alida said, "Cool."

"You know what? I don't think we're going to have to live in the Spider. I think it's a good sign. But he's made one hell of a mess."

Together they set to work, emptying the shelves and putting books back in order. The landlord's indecent haste was everywhere in view: paperbacks with their covers creased back, torn dust jackets, here and there a broken spine. Filing Marge Piercy's *Braided Lives* alongside Eleanor Pierce's *All You Need to Know About Living Abroad,* Alida complained of the promiscuous mingling of fiction and nonfiction.

"You ought to use the Dewey decimal system."

"What? All those numbers . . . 943-point-blah-blah-blah? You have to be kidding."

"It's really logical. The thing about Dewey is like there's a special space for every book that's ever going to be written, and for subjects that nobody's even dreamed up yet. It's *über.* The Dewey system reaches to infinity."

"Where did you learn all this, Rabbit?"

"Mrs. Markowitz, she's the school librarian. What you have to remember about the Dewey decimal system is it always goes from the general to the particular."

"Which is the exact opposite of how my mind works."

"My favorites are the 500s and the 900s. Like 943 whatever? I know that's history—the history of somewhere. Europe, maybe—I dunno."

"The things you teach me."

"It's never too late to learn." Alida's voice was pure schoolmarm as, standing on a stool, she slotted *Dr. Atkins' Diet Revolution* next to the now doubly unfortunate Ms. Acker.

Every book was back in place, and Alida on the phone to the pizza joint, when Tad made his one-two-three rap on the door. "I saw the car," he said. "Don't tell me—you had the weekend from hell."

"Actually, no. We—"

"Tad!" Then, into the phone, "Wait!" then to Tad, "Goat Cheese Primo?" then back to the phone, "Can you make that a three-way large—with Original, Brooklyn Bridge, and Goat Cheese Primo?" In the last few weeks Alida had taken command of all telephone orders: she now dispatched them with the alarming authority of a career waitress hollering to a short-order cook.

"Oh, dear," Tad said to Lucy. "I'd so hoped we could *share*. My weekend has been such a *succession* of humiliations, I can't tell you. I've been spending all today in the time-out corner."

"Why the gay voice?" Alida said as she went to hug him.

Tad laughed. "Because I'm being a self-hating old fag is why. How was it, Ali? You have an okay time?"

"It was good."

"Alida went kayaking," Lucy said.

"You fall in? The only time I went kayaking, I spent the entire time falling in."

"No, but I got really freaked out by the sharks."

"Oh yeah, those famous Puget Sound sharks."

"No, *really*. This shark—it was *this* big." She stretched her arms out as far as they'd go. "It went right under my kayak. Augie saw another. He said there were usually *hundreds* of them. They're called dogfish, but they're really sharks, and cousins of the Great White. They hunt in packs, like wild dogs, and they can give you a real bad bite."

Tad flashed Lucy a *What the fuck?* look, then said, "How far out was this?"

"Oh, not far."

"And he told you there were hundreds to a pack, and they'd attack you?"

"He said if they felt threatened."

To Lucy, Tad said, "You weren't there?"

"No, I was back at the house, but—"

"He was messing with your head, Ali."

Lucy heard this as the exposed tip of an iceberg of anger, but luckily

Alida didn't seem to catch it. She said, "The one I saw, it was like this brown color, and it was *so* close. I mean, I could have like touched it with my paddle."

"Dogfish," Tad said, "are totally harmless. They'd no more attack you than a guppy or a goldfish would."

"But Augie's like this big expert on nature."

Tad let the subject drop, but the sharks cast a long inhibiting shadow over dinner.

Alida excused herself early from the table, which was unusual for evenings when Tad was there, asking if she could watch *The Incredibles* on the DVD player.

"Sometimes I hate journalism," Lucy said. "Especially profiles. The more friendly you get with a subject, the more you feel like a spook."

"We're all spooks now. Look at the way people Google prospective dates. Everybody's trying to spy on everybody else. At least you know you're a spook, which is something. Most people are in denial." He stared gloomily at his untouched glass of white wine. "You ever played with Google Earth? I zoomed in on the Acropolis and you could see everything—the chimneys, the water tank, the skylight in the hall, the place where the tar paper's ripped on the roof, both our cars in the street, the guys in the alley, the manhole covers . . . everything. What this means? You're thinking of dating a guy, you enter his address on Google Earth, and you can check out his house, how he keeps his yard, whether he should take out a loan to redo his roof. You can practically see into his bedroom and go through his underwear drawer. *Everybody does it*. And if we can do that, just think what the boys in Yakima can do."

"Yakima?"

"Yakima's the western headquarters of the NSA, the No Such Agency. I've seen the NSA setup there, at least the domes and dishes. It looks like a farm of humongous white mushrooms. It's the ECHE-LON system. You send an e-mail, you make a phone call, ECHELON's looking out for keywords. They use a program called Dictionary, a global search engine that does continuous roving wiretaps, going through millions of messages at a time. If you're buying fertilizer in bulk, or want to take flying lessons for jetliners, you can count on your message landing up on somebody's desk in Yakima. And if you say 'jihad,' they'll be right inside your room before you can hang up the phone."

Alida froze the picture on the screen to go to the bathroom. Tad said, "Look . . ." then stopped himself. "Let's leave it till later."

Lucy, thinking of the bored marshal on the ferry, said, "I think you overrate their competence. I mean, if their technology were that clever, wouldn't you expect them to be a little better at their job? Read the 9/11 Report—it's not about masters of espionage, it's about a bunch of doofuses chasing one another's tails."

Alida, returning, said, "What are you talking about?"

"Doofuses and mushroom farming," Lucy said, pouring herself a third glass.

"Cool." Alida clicked the remote to liberate *The Incredibles.*

"We used to spy on the Russians, on their military and politicians, but now we've turned all that equipment—plus a whole lot more—on ourselves, on ordinary American civilians. You realize what we're looking at here? This is the machinery of tyranny."

That word again. "Oh, Tad, we've got an army. Armies are machines of tyranny. So are police forces. It's not the machinery that makes tyranny, it's how it's used and who's using it. Look, if your mushroom things can detect a terrorist attack before it happens, which I have to say they don't seem too hot at, then I'm all for them. I mean it's not as if the mushrooms belong to Joseph Stalin."

"No? I wouldn't bet the farm on that."

"I wish I could get you in the same room as August Vanags. You'd make a great double act."

"Vanags!" Tad glanced across at Alida, who was lost in her movie. "He's just like all those Euro-types, like Kissinger and Brzezinski. They come over here from the old country, then they try running things like they were scheming away back home in rat-ridden Vienna, or wherever."

"Actually, I think he's the most American American I've ever met."

"Actually," Tad lowered his voice to a confidential mutter, "I think he's what our charming landlord would call a scumbag son-of-a-bitch."

"Which reminds me," Lucy said in as airy a tone as she could muster. "I forgot to thank you for the tulips."

AS SOON AS *The Incredibles* ended, Alida was sent to bed. Her mom came in for a snuggle, but Alida pretended to be asleep. She now stood at the door in her baggy Hotel Honolulu T-shirt, ear pressed to the wood, though there was hardly any need for that since the voices on the other side were rising steadily in pitch.

"I was there," her mom was saying.

"Maybe I see it more clearly than you do because I wasn't there."

"It wasn't like that."

"You heard what she said. It's not something you can argue about—it's plain as daylight. All that bullshit about sharks? The guy's a raving sadist."

"Oh, Tad, you're making your usual goddamn mountain out of your usual goddamn molehill. I mean, why the hell would he want to do that?"

"I don't know. Because he's a power freak? Because of something in his fouled-up European pathology? Because frightening kids is the nearest he can get to fucking them? You tell me. You're his new friend."

"They went kayaking. They saw a dogfish. End of story."

"You're totally deluding yourself. He took her out there for one reason: to scare her shitless."

"It's not true!" Alida flung the door open and stormed into the living room. "It's not true!" Her whole body shaking with fury, she stood her ground, glaring at Tad. "He so did *not*." She felt her lower lip trembling, out of her control. "I love Augie."

In helpless tears now, she found herself in Tad's arms, gagging on her sobs like she was throwing up.

"Ali, Ali, Ali." He was stroking her hair.

"It's not true."

"Okay, okay, so I was wrong."

But she didn't believe him: Tad was saying that just to humor her, he didn't sound like he really believed that he was wrong, and even in his arms she felt the nub of anger still burning inside her. She had the sudden sense that in the last minute she'd arrived at some new place in her life—somewhere colder, grayer, more inhospitable than anywhere she'd ever been before.

Hands gripping her shoulders, Tad held her at a distance, but she couldn't meet his eyes. She was staring straight ahead, into his white shirtfront, now all mussed up by the imprint of her face, a blurry mask of snot, tears, and flesh-tinted Clearasil.

7

STORIES. For years, Lucy had been telling stories about the absent father in Alida's life. She had sworn to herself that she would always try to tell the truth, but she allowed herself to ration, stretch, and gloss that truth as circumstance dictated.

Turning three, Alida had asked, "Do I have a dad?"

This, Lucy decided, was really two questions. The answer to the first, about a biological father, would obviously have to be yes. But a dad was something different. Dads read bedtime stories, took out the garbage, dabbed shaving foam on their kids' cheeks. In this sense, she reasoned, Alida obviously didn't have a dad, so the answer was a firm negative.

"No, honey, there's just you and me."

Alida seemed content with the idea of her immaculate conception until one day, riding home from preschool, she said that they'd been discussing dads in the Rainbow Room. "I said my dad was dead," she said, sounding rather pleased with herself, and went on to talk about the kites they'd made. Good solution, Lucy thought, and there was no further mention of Alida's paternity for several months.

Then it was, "Who was my dad?"

Tricky, this one, but Lucy was grateful for Alida's use of the past tense.

"Well," Lucy said, playing for time. "I really, *really* wanted to have a baby. I wanted to have *you*. But I needed someone to help me, so I found this guy."

"Like a doctor?"

"Yes. Exactly like a doctor. And he helped me to have you."

"Did you have to pay him money?"

"No, he did it for free," Lucy said, remembering the bar tab, the Painted Table dinner, the nightcaps from the minibar in his suite. Alida's conception must have cost him—or rather, his law firm—a couple hundred bucks at least.

"Did it take long?"

"Oh, no, just a few seconds. Like getting a shot."

"I hate shots," Alida said, and moved on.

Another year passed before she asked the hardest question so far: "Where is my dad?" which moved him firmly out of the past and into the present and gave him a potential location in actual space. Lucy had to avoid saying "I don't know," which would encourage Alida to imagine a mystery that might be solved by a quest, so she said, "He just flew in and out; he was only in Seattle for two days."

She'd flubbed on that one, but Alida's curiosity was so shallow and fleeting that almost any response, so long as it wasn't "He's in Tucson, Arizona," would've allowed her to change the subject, which she did. Whatever dad-shaped hole there might have been in Alida's world was filled so amply, so lovingly, by Tad that recent years had passed without a single question. When Father's Day came around, Tad got the cards, the lopsided bits of pottery, the clumsily sewn hearts filled with pot-pourri. The accident of his name helped: he was so very nearly *Dad* in every sense.

Yet Lucy remained on guard, ready if necessary to field two danger-ous questions so far unasked: "What's my dad's name?" and "Does he know I exist?" They would be hell to handle, but Lucy dreamed that when Alida was nineteen, twenty, twenty-one, they'd be able to share the true story of her conception, woman to woman, fondly and without embarrassment. It wasn't a story Lucy was the least bit ashamed about, and when Alida was grown up she ought to be able to prize it, laugh over it, tell it to her own lovers as a gift. But it had to be kept secret from her until she was of an age to understand.

It had begun with the Spanish Inquisition of fact-checking at *The New Yorker*. For eleven days, Lucy had undergone torture at the hands of two humorless peremptory inquisitors, Rosemary and Maureen. Usually the magazine assigned only one fact-checker to each case, but fear of Bill Gates' phalanx of lawyers had led it in this instance to double the usual allocation of womanpower to the spiked chair, the iron maiden, the rack and the screw. She dreaded the phone ringing. "A couple of people here have read the piece and . . ." Or, "You mention traveling south on Elm. It's one-way, going southeast." Not a sentence of Lucy's piece was left untouched. She had described visiting the Microsoft campus in heavy rain; a local TV meteorologist had been consulted, and the phrase emended to "steady drizzle." She had written that talking with Gates had put her in mind of speaking with an autistic, given how he rocked in his chair and evaded eye contact; that passage had been struck out on the advice of a child psychologist, who had sternly opined that "the evidence supplied entirely fails to support the allegation." Talking to people who'd known Gates in the past, she'd sometimes used a notebook rather than a tape recorder. Called by Rosemary or Maureen, they invariably denied every word they'd said, and, unless it was preserved verbatim on tape, out it went. For "legal reasons," adjectives and adverbs fell from the piece like leaves from a tree in an October gale. Day by day the piece grew thinner, blander, less her own. She dreaded the ringing of the phone, the "just a couple of details," the pitiless guillotining of every sentence she was proud of.

But even the Spanish Inquisition came to its eventual end, and, late on a Friday afternoon, her editor called to say that the issue had gone to press and her ordeal was over. "Everyone here likes the piece a lot." Having come to hate it as a result of Rosemary and Maureen's brutal ministrations, Lucy said, "I can't think why—I just wish it could be published under a pseudonym. Why don't the fact-checkers put *their* names on it?"

Yet putting the phone down, she was giddy with relief. She had to celebrate. She called Ron, then Jeff, then David, then Alice, but got only their voice mails. She'd try them from her cell later; in the meantime, she meant to down a large and richly deserved martini at the Bookstore Bar in the Alexis.

Hoisting herself onto a stool, she noticed that the man two stools away was reading the "Talk of the Town" section of that week's *New Yorker.* He said, she said, he said, she said (entirely free of the stutter that usually afflicted her when talking to strangers), and within minutes of getting her martini she'd told him she sometimes wrote for the magazine on retainer. He had the grace to claim that he remembered one or two of her pieces—even brought up, with no prompt from Lucy, her epic Kurt Cobain interview-epitaph. "I'm way too old for grunge rock, but you made him real to me. I found it very touching."

His name was Edward; if he told her his last name, she'd forgotten it that very instant. When her cell phone rang in her bag, she reached inside to switch it off. By the time they agreed to have dinner together, she knew that he was an attorney, that his specialty was intellectual property rights, that he was in Seattle for a conference on copyright and the new media, that he'd gone to college at Williams, then on to Yale for law school. His manner was light, quizzical, self-deprecating. She liked his rather-too-big nose and not-too-preppy haircut.

Once they'd been served their first course—Dabob Bay oysters on the half shell—she knew that he had a wife and young son in Westchester County, but that he lived in an apartment in the East Village, traveling most weekends to Mount Kisco to keep in touch with the boy, Asher.

"We have to do something about it soon," he said. "But as a lawyer I'm more afraid of the mechanics of divorce than most people. I'm like the dentist who neglects his own teeth for fear of the drill."

For her part, Lucy spun the tale of Maureen and Rosemary into bright comedy, casting herself in the part of dupe. Edward probed her for details. He wanted to know the reason for every cut and change.

"Total bullshit," he said, producing legal arguments that validated nearly all of Lucy's original phrasings, elegantly wiping the floor with Rosemary and Maureen.

"God," she said, "I wish I'd had you standing at my elbow for the last two weeks."

"Honestly, there's no place on Earth I'd rather have been." He made the remark easily, with a smile, showing those glamorous metropolitan manners that surely reflected the enviable milieu in which he must move in Manhattan.

This was just after the halibut arrived.

Never once did he put the moves on her. The progression from dessert to nightcaps and coffee in his suite to the bedroom was a safe and relaxed glide, with much laughter along the route. From the moment she stepped into the elevator, she knew that he knew that she was going to spend the night, and that neither of them was going to make a fuss of it beforehand or after.

As they helped each other undress, Lucy pointed to her thighs. "Cellulite," she said.

"You're perfect, Lucy. I hate those bony sylphs."

"Is your wife a bony sylph?"

"Bony, yes. Sylph, no."

In sex, too, he was a paragon of good manners, both teasing and patient, waiting to come until after she did, which was surprisingly quickly and strongly. Still on East Coast time—midnight for her, three A.M. for him—he was asleep in minutes, with her snuggled up behind him, her arm crooked around his waist, her open palm on his very slightly paunchy stomach.

She woke before six, with no hangover, no bewilderment as to her whereabouts, no regrets. He was giving a paper that morning, and she had a hair appointment at 8:45. As she separated herself from him, limb by cautious limb, a phrase came into her head: "the tenderness of the one-night stand." He stirred for an instant, then rolled back and began to snore.

She picked her clothes up from the floor and went into the living room to dress. She came back to the bedroom with a stub of old lipstick from the bottom of her bag, to write a message on his dressing-table mirror. *That was so sweet . . . thank you. Talk well today. Must go (Dr.'s appt.) Fondly, Lucy.* Then she wrote her phone numbers, landline and cell, in unmissably bold numerals. Before leaving, she rested her hand on his sleeping haunch through the bed linen. Snore, snore. She was glad he was sleeping in.

That afternoon, still in a buoyant mood, she traded in her old rust-bucket Honda for the Spider—a car she'd fancied, in its various incarnations and remodels, ever since she watched Dustin Hoffman drive one in *The Graduate,* a movie already ten years old by the time she saw a TV rerun in Missoula. Gingerly maneuvering the new car back to the Acropolis, she looked forward to showing it off to Edward. Perhaps they could go Dutch tonight at Ray's Boathouse, which would give her an excuse to put the Spider through its paces.

He didn't call. She told herself that it was perhaps best to leave things exactly as they were, a warm memory, unalloyed by complications. Having gone through one bicoastal romance, she'd sworn never to try another. So farewell, Edward, nice to have known you. Or so she tried to feel.

Three weeks later, she was four days late. The Rosemary/Maureen nightmare had probably fucked up her cycle. The night with Edward must have been at least three days before she started ovulating, but sperm have tenacious survival skills. She bought a test from Bartell's, peed onto the stick thing, and saw lines in both windows. A blood test at the doctor's the next day confirmed it. She was pregnant.

She was shaken by her own delight. At thirty-eight, with forty looming fast, she took the news as a pure, undeserved gift from gods in whose existence she had no belief at all. Of course she'd have the baby. How could she not?

But then there was the question of Edward. It would take five minutes to locate him. No need to snoop through the Alexis guest register; all she had to do was get the list of speakers at his conference. But in the last three weeks, Edward had rather dwindled in her estimation. It wasn't that he hadn't phoned, more that in retrospect his charming, ironic manners had come to seem a bit too easy, too practiced, too ostentatiously East Coast. It was as if all he was was manners. When she thought about him, she realized that she didn't know a person so much as Williams College, Yale Law School, Westchester, and the

Village. If she were to tell him this news, she didn't have an inkling as to how he might respond. Horror, as likely as not, and a gentlemanly offer to arrange for an abortion.

As the slogan said, it was the woman's right to choose. And faced with this most personal, impulsive, and daring decision—the biggest decision of her life—Lucy thought that the last person she wanted to consult was a lawyer, especially one as quick-minded and fluently logical as Edward had shown himself to be at dinner. She was frightened that Yale Law School might be horribly adept at talking her out of it, even though she held out a distant hope that Greenwich Village might be more understanding of her need to have the baby.

She forced herself not to find out Edward's last name. There had been times in the last few years when the thought did cross her mind that a New York lawyer dealing in intellectual property rights, the hottest specialty in the Internet age, must be unbelievably rich, and that she might sort of owe it to Alida to make her existence known to this legal tycoon. But each time the thought came into view, she quashed it: to follow up on it now would put her own behavior back then in a very bad light indeed.

Lucy was glad Alida had inherited Edward's hair and height, and much relieved she hadn't got his nose.

TAD WAS ANGRY. He was angry with himself, angry with the presidency, angry with the nation, angry with the century. That much was rational, justifiable. In his view, only the ignorant, the hopelessly self-preoccupied, the Halliburton fat cats, and the mad Christian zealots were in any position not to be angry. Decent people now were angry people, and what America needed at this low moment in its history was more anger, not less.

But lately his own anger had been metastasizing at such speed, and in all directions, that it frightened him. It felt *terminal*.

He was angry with the landlord, that smarmy shyster Chinese bully so obviously bent on robbing him, Alida, and everyone else of their rightful homes. He hated the man's ill-fitting double-breasted suit, his droopy eyelids, his real estate jargon, his vile *heh-heh-heh!* laugh. His ownership of the Acropolis was a prime symbol of how the world had lately fallen into the hands of grifters, liars, and cheats.

He was angry with Lucy, so willfully deaf and blind to the reality of what was happening, with her smug little sarcasms, her tolerant smiles. *Aren't you overreacting?* That drove Tad wild.

He was angry with total strangers. One day last week, two women yakking in a supermarket and blocking his passage with their carts had managed to rouse in Tad his inner murderer. When he saw moms on the school run driving Hummers, he wanted to fling bricks through their tinted fucking windows. A knot of lawyers in Armani suits and tasseled loafers, talking outside the Rainier Club after a long and evidently profitable lunch, made him want to reach for his thought machine-gun.

Such anger was alien to him. As a lifelong student of Stanislavski, Tad had always taken pride in losing himself inside a character. He believed that a certain capacity for self-abnegation was an essential part of the actor's job. He'd gone to Zen workshops, to meditate himself nearly out of existence. Through dire professional disappointments, like the part he'd so nearly won in the New York premiere of Albee's *The Play About the Baby,* as through grief after Michael's death, he'd been able to find in himself a quiet, deep-breathing place from where he could contemplate the worst with something not too far from equanimity.

No more. Now he found himself raging like the most psychotic of the poor bastards down in the alley, waving his bottle and howling imprecations at blank windows.

Until Sunday, he'd been unaware of just how dangerously far his disease had spread. It felt closer to demonic possession than he could have conceived when he found his anger boiling up against Alida. He was astonished and terrified by himself.

Unthinkable. Yet the too-familiar shivering, the stiffening of muscles in his cheeks, the seismic disturbance in his foundations, were out of his control. The mad interloper standing in Tad's shoes was raging internally at Alida the way it raged at the moms in the Hummers. *It,* not *him.* It was a thing, not a person—a cancer doing what cancers must.

He'd lain awake all night, pressing his fists into his eyes to stop the tears. It was futile and cowardly of him to blame his anger on the times, which were no excuse for his wanton fury with Alida. He wished he could pray, for redemption and absolution, but he despised sky-god religions; there was nobody up there to pray to. He ached for Michael, the most understanding and level-headed of confessors. At four he clambered out of bed to rummage through his narrow shelf of Buddha books, unopened for years.

Anger. One of the great obstacles to Nirvana, a delusion, a belief in a false I and a false object. "Holding on to anger is like grasping a hot coal with the intent of throwing it at someone else; you are the one who gets burned," said the Buddha. "You will not be punished for your anger, you will be punished by your anger." And here was the Dalai Lama:

> If we examine how anger or hateful thoughts arise in us, we will find that, generally speaking, they arise when we feel hurt, when we feel that we have been unfairly treated by someone against our expecta-tions. If in that instant we examine carefully the way anger arises, there is a sense that it comes as a protector, comes as a friend that would help our battle or in taking revenge against the person who has inflicted harm on us. So the anger or hateful thought that arises appears to come as a shield or a protector. But in reality that is an illusion. It is a very delusory state of mind.

Anger the false friend: yes, for the last few years Tad had found com-panionship in his anger. How often had he soothed himself to sleep by plotting the destruction of his enemies, from the president of the United States to the new artistic director at the Rep? Time and again he'd reached out gratefully to his anger as a buddy and a bedfellow; yet on Sunday night with Alida, he'd found himself to be his anger's slave.

Now, he read, he must learn to feel "compassion" for his anger. But he could no more feel compassion for it than he could turn himself inside-out like a sock. That he was too angry with his anger was the problem: he wanted to get his hands around its neck and throttle it to death, which was, as they said in the Buddha books, incurably bad karma. By 4:30, Tad was getting angry at the Dalai Lama. At five, he turned on the radio to listen to the news: suicide bomber kills thirty-six, White House defends new measures to combat terrorism . . .

Fuckers! Tad thought. Those guys *are* the fucking terrorists.

RELUCTANT as Lucy was to go back to Useless Bay for the weekend, she had to accept Augie's invitation because Tad had forced her hand. Not to go would give the appearance of caving in to his ridiculous out-burst on Sunday night. He hated Augie because he'd refused to demon-strate with his students against the war in Vietnam—so far as Lucy could see, that was the long and short of it, and his paranoid tirade about Augie's "sadism" was just an attempt to settle an ancient political score. Either that or he was being babyishly jealous of Alida's fondness for Augie. Whatever—they now *had* to go to Useless Bay. To do other-wise would be bad for Tad's character.

Yet she was concerned. Tad's increasingly odd behavior over the last few weeks was truly frightening. She looked anxiously for signs of weight loss, but on his inhibitors and whatnots he was deceptively pink, portly, and Pickwickian. When he came back with his wrist band-aged after the TOPOFF exercise, Lucy's first appalled thought was *Kaposi's sarcoma—he's hiding a lesion.* Tad had always been chattily informative about things like his T-cell count and the changes in his cocktail of medications, but lately he'd brushed off her inquiries with *I'm fine* and *My doc threatens to predecease me.* What was really going on?

She was terrified by the thought of him dying, and not just on Alida's behalf. Tad could be maddening, but he was her best and closest friend, the only person besides Alida whom she loved. She'd often thought wistfully that if only he weren't gay, the best place to settle their absurd political disagreements would be in bed, where she could take him in her arms and exorcize his black fantasies with kisses. These fantasies arose, she was certain, from the loneliness of his life without Michael: Tad was someone made to need a partner to cherish him, a role that Lucy, had things been differently constructed, would have volunteered for at the drop of a hat.

The sight of his bandaged wrist had panicked her, but when the bandage was off the following day, what it concealed was exactly what Tad had said, a nasty scratch inflicted by an amateur actor with a shovel. Though she hadn't said a word about it, the relief that swept through her was immense.

She loved him dearly, but he could not be allowed to get away with the outrageous performance he'd put on last night. So she called the Vanagses' number and got Minna.

Augie was out birdwatching. "He'll be so pleased—he likes to talk to you," Minna said, her faint Mittel-Europa accent sounding more pronounced over the phone.

"What can we bring?"

"Yourselves only. Everything on the island's so much fresher than in the city."

"Wine?"

"You see Augie's cellar? We are *drowning* in wine."

After Minna's openheartedness, it was with a feeling of unpleasant disloyalty that Lucy sat down to her assigned task for the morning, which was to read a truly false memoir of World War II—Binjamin Wilkomirski's *Fragments*. No ordinary fraud, Mr. Wilkomirski, having persuaded himself that his childhood lay in the Nazi extermination camps, had produced a work of fiction that, before it was exposed by a Swiss journalist, had won prizes and international attention as a work of harrowing documentary fact. Could you tell just by reading the book, Lucy wondered, by studying the way the words fell on the page, that it was untrue? If so, could *Boy 381* stand up to the same test?

Most reviewers had been taken in by *Fragments,* comparing Wilkomirski to Primo Levi and Anne Frank, though one or two had raised cautious doubts as to its authenticity. Then the Swiss journalist, Daniel Ganzfried, had come along, with the shocking news that Wilkomirski "knows Auschwitz and Majdanek only as a tourist." The last thing that Lucy wanted or expected was to be Augie's Ganzfried. In fact, she hoped very much that reading Wilkomirski would put her mind finally at rest about Vanags.

No doubt about it: there was something thin, stagy, melodramatic, unreal in the opening chapter of *Fragments,* where Wilkomirski's father was killed on the third page.

> No sound comes out of his mouth, but a big stream of something black shoots out of his neck as the transport squashes him with a big crack against the house.

She didn't buy it—but might she have, had Ganzfried not blown a hole in Wilkomirski's story? Was the alloy ring in the words themselves, or was it just the wisdom of hindsight that made them sound so readily disbelievable? The childish voice felt contrived to her, as Augie's never did. Surely no child, watching his father, would see him as so deliberately childish a stick figure? The falsity was right there in the words, she was sure of it.

She read on:

> There's a station in my memory. We have to go through a barrier, papers are shown and looked at—maybe false ones.
>
> Sighs of relief and we're standing on a platform and it's sunny—

"Land lord!"

That imperious knock: him again. Letting Mr. Lee into the apartment, she did her best to make nice, lavishly thanking him for his work on the shelves.

"No problem, no problem. Got new lock for you today. Security!" He held out a chunky piece of machinery, somewhat scratched, that had obviously led a previous life in another building.

"Mr. Lee, was it you who brought the t-tulips?"

"Tertelips?"

She pointed at the vase.

"Oh, flowers, yeah. Old ones all dead and crackly."

"Well, how kind."

"No problem." He trailed an orange cable across the carpet and laid out a filthy sheet beneath the door.

"Can I get you coffee? W-w-water? Tea?"

"You make coffee, Lucy. That be great. Cream, no sugar." He waved his power drill at the kitchen area, as if to dispatch her there.

It was astonishing that the replacement of a lock could make such a racket, and the electric tools whizzed and screamed as if a complete remodeling of the apartment was under way. When she took the coffee to him, he waved at her from behind a churring saw. She tried to return to *Fragments,* but the din made it impossible to read a line. In a momentary pause he called, "Good coffee, Lucy. How I like it—strong."

"I'd better remember that," she said.

"Don't drink tea," he said over the whine of a bared screwdriver.

It took him the best part of an hour to finish the job; then he made her try the lock.

"Terrific," she said. "Fantastic." What could one say about locks? "Very solid."

"Keep you safe."

"Thank you."

He made no move to clean up his stuff and go, but just sat down on one of the chairs around the dining table. "So you a rider, Lucy. What kind of riding you do?"

"Oh . . . articles, mostly, for newspapers and magazines. I'm working on one now. Against a tight d-d-deadline, so I'm afraid—"

"Whaddaya write about?"

"People, places."

"What people?"

"Sometimes celebrities, sometimes p-people nobody's ever heard of."

"I like to read. How 'bout you give me something to read what you wrote?"

Desperate to get rid of him and back to Wilkomirski, she scanned the heaps of old magazines in the corner, where all her published stuff was filed, though nothing there could make much sense to a Chinese parking-lot tycoon. She said, "I wrote a piece about Bill Gates once, a long time ago."

"Bill Gates, huh? Lemme see."

She rummaged through a toppling stack and pulled out the old *New*

Yorker from very near the bottom. She stuck a Post-It on the page where her piece began, and handed him the magazine. "There you are. Now—"

But he remained sitting and started to read, scowling at the mass of small print, his lips moving. The piece, even in its eviscerated state, ran to nearly seven thousand words; at this rate, he'd be sitting there forever.

"Wah!" he said, half shout, half whistle. "It say here, 'Gates told me that . . .' You *meet* Bill Gates?"

"Well, yes, twice. I always meet my subjects."

"Bill *Gates*! You mean you talk to Bill Gates like you talk to me?"

"I spent an hour with him in his office. Then another time he showed me his house."

"What tips he give you?"

"Tips?"

"Like business tips."

"We weren't really talking business. It was more like personal."

The landlord shook his head slowly in reproach. She'd evidently missed her great opportunity. "How much they pay you to write this?"

"Not enough," Lucy said in what she hoped was a briskly deterrent tone.

"Like they pay by the hour?"

"No. By the p-p-piece."

"No benefits?"

"I wish."

"You ought to read some books." Now he sounded severe.

"I do." She gestured at the shelves he'd fastened to the wall.

"Nah. Not storybooks. Good books. You ever read *Who Moved My Cheese?* That's a good book. Kind of like a storybook, but different. Lot of tips. Maybe I give you it sometime."

"That would be nice. Now, please, Mr. Lee . . ."

At last she succeeded in budging him from his perch. He folded his dirty sheet, gathered his tools into their canvas bag, picked up the *New Yorker,* and at the door tapped the new lock. "You're safe now, Lucy."

"Thank you for taking all this trouble, Mr. Lee."

"No trouble. Enjoy." Smiling weirdly, tools in one hand, magazine in the other, he made a stiff little bow, and left.

Fast running out of time, Lucy lunched on a yogurt that was past its sell-by date and returned to the seemingly unconscious fraudster Binjamin Wilkomirski, finding the book increasingly irksome as she plowed through his disordered ragbag of false memories. She was at the point of giving up on it altogether when, in Chapter 12, an odd passage caught her eye. The boy Wilkomirski, now supposedly in a concentration camp, saw a "mountain" of naked women's corpses. One appeared to have a bit of life in it: a sudden twitchy movement of the stomach.

Now I can see the whole belly. There's a big wound on one side, with something moving in it. I get to my feet, so that I can see better. I poke my head forward, and at this very moment the wound springs open, the wall of the stomach lifts back, and a huge, blood-smeared, shining rat darts down the mound of corpses. Other rats run startled out of the confusion of bodies, heading for open ground.

I saw it, I saw it! The dead women are giving birth to rats!

The author, who'd spent years in psychotherapy, was clearly on overly familiar terms with Freud, and Lucy saw his disgusting rat story, or rat dream, as evidence only of his distinct talent for morbid fantasy. Yet the passage immediately recalled a bit in Augie's book. Of course, everything was different: no mountain of bodies, just one male body, naked except for a woolly hat and one sock, sprawled face-down in a German street after a night raid by RAF bombers. Augie wrote that he'd seen a small, wet rat wriggling out of the cleft in the man's buttocks like an agile four-legged turd.

Where there was war, there were bodies; where there were bodies, there were rats. It was no more than that. Lucy was just new to its ghastly everyday vernacular.

· · ·

IN MATH CLASS, all Alida could think of was how wrong her algebra was—her human algebra. She'd had little sleep, whiling away the long dark hours first with Agatha Christie, then with *The Secret Diary of Adrian Mole, Aged 13¾*, unable to lose herself in either. The equation involving her, Tad, and her mom had suddenly, terrifyingly, come apart. *Isolate the variable*: the variable, the big x, was obviously Augie, though Alida couldn't begin to figure why. *Get every term containing the variable on one side of the equation; then get any term that doesn't contain the variable on the other side of the equation.* Which was a lot easier said than done, because somehow Tad was tied to x, and so were she and her mom. The obvious solution was to eliminate x, but she couldn't do that because her mom was writing an article about him, and it looked like x would be in their lives for weeks and weeks. She eventually maddened herself to sleep with fruitless variations on this theme, and woke up with a, b, c, and x still jostling furiously in her mind.

Looking across the room she saw her own perplexity reflected in the face of Finn, who was scowling, frowning, scribbling, then wildly staring into space. Finn could be a math genius when he bothered, so he surely wasn't fazed by the problems set by Mr. Tennyson, which were easy: Alida had worked out all three in less than five minutes. She knew "poor Finn" had his own difficulties with human algebra, so maybe he was working on a baffling equation parallel to her own. Whatever it was, he seemed to be in a state of mental torture, and for the first time ever she found herself actually sympathizing with Finn. Then he caught her eye and pulled his Tasmanian-devil face at her. Boys!

8

WALKING THE FIVE BLOCKS from the Acropolis to the King County Adminstrative Building on Fourth Avenue, Tad assured himself that he was simply doing what any sensible citizen would do, which was to check out the facts. Besides, he envisioned the Office of Vital Statistics—obviously named by someone with either a good sense of humor or none at all—as a Dickensian warren of musty files and papers, the dead stacked in their hundreds of thousands, maybe millions, organized, alphabetized, at rest. Tad felt he could do with their company for a while—an act of self-mortification that might be good for his soul.

The office was a disappointment, not Dickensian at all, just the usual motley of computer terminals, copiers, microfilm viewers. The dead—at least, the recently dead—had gone digital and couldn't lend Tad the solace of their society.

He filled in the form, stating his Reason for Inquiry as "genealogical research." He wrote in the name of Charles Ong Lee, his date and place of death (November 25, 1999, in Seattle), paid $17.50 in cash, and ten minutes later was in possession of a copy of the certificate. Here was the unlucky social worker. "Cause of Death: blunt trauma to head and torso incurred in single-vehicle automobile incident." He hadn't gone far in his life, this Mr. Lee. Born in Tacoma on February 13, 1974, he'd traveled about forty-five miles north to Shoreline, then met his death on the road between the two.

Tad folded the certificate and put it in his wallet. Heading back to the apartment, he resolved to take his time before making his next move, which would need more rehearsal and stagecraft than he could possibly manage on this gray, penitential morning. As he walked, he muttered to himself, "Eliminate the sins and hindrances that I have accumulated by disparaging the Dharma since the beginningless past. Eliminate the sins and hindrances. Eliminate the sins and hindrances. . . ." It sort of seemed to work.

THE PILATES STUDIO on South Main looked to Lucy like a dominatrix's well-appointed dungeon. Walled on three sides by floor-to-ceiling mirrors, it was furnished with gruesome implements—the Reformer, the Half-Trapeze Bed, the Ladder Barrel, the Tower, the Ped-a-Pul. Huffing and groaning, half a dozen other clients, male and female, were being punished by trainers in spa pants and black hoodies.

The first check from *GQ,* for preliminary research and expenses on the Vanags piece, had come through. Lucy was spending $280 on a month's worth of weekly Pilates classes to try to get herself in shape. She nearly backed out of the deal when she saw the bodies in the studio, most of whom would've looked good on the frieze around a Grecian urn. Wearing her old sweats, she felt painfully self-conscious, a dandelion among the orchids, but took comfort from the sight of a sturdy red-faced woman in her fifties who was being tortured on the Reformer by a gay-looking Adonis. If she could go through with it, surely Lucy could.

"Find your abdominals," said Lindsay, Lucy's trainer. "Suck them in as if you're pulling them out through your back."

All very well for Lindsay to issue this impossible command: she was a dancer, sore at having just lost her job in the corps at Pacific Northwest Ballet. Lucy wasn't sure she even had abdominals anymore, and though she sucked and sucked, all she achieved was a very modest diminution of the intractable mound that was her stomach.

"This is like cellular. Your body feels things even if your mind refuses."

I don't do woo-woo, Lucy thought, spouting air like a breaching whale.

"But it was turning into a really hostile work environment for me," Lindsay said. "They brought in this new woman as ballet master—Martha Slater, a control freak and a total bitch. Okay, now we'll do circles."

Circles meant Lucy opening her legs and waving them round and round, exposing her crotch to the world.

"Wider!"

Wider still and wider, Lucy felt as if she was posing for beaver shots. She stared resolutely at the ceiling to avoid catching her reflection in the mirrors.

"But after like six years at PNB, to get canned like that was such a bummer I could've offed myself when I heard."

"I know," Lucy gasped. "It's awful. It's happening to everyone. The d-d-d-downturn in the economy . . ."

"Anchor—don't *arch*—your sit bones!"

Wearily, Lucy rearranged herself.

"Knees in tabletop!"

At least she could now keep her legs together.

"Your sit bones make you focus on your core. Now you have to say to yourself, 'My core is strong and solid.'"

And *that,* Lucy thought, was her abiding problem. It was her mother's perennial accusation that she had no core, that she was an insipid sopper-up of other people's feelings and opinions, by which she meant in the first instance that Lucy spent far too much time listening to her dad. Though she fought her mother fiercely, Lucy had always been depressingly conscious that she might have a point. On down days, she wondered if perhaps it was her lack of core that had led her into journalism—a trade where a good listener, a human sponge, could hide her secret corelessness behind a bold-type byline. Every opinion she held was provisional, and a smart remark by someone else could alter it in a heartbeat. She was instinctively reluctant to "commit"—to men, to salaried jobs, to causes, to ideas. To remain not entirely sure of where she stood had become a lifelong habit, almost a principle. As to this *core* business, if *core* meant some unique and irreducible essence of self, Lucy was as unsure of that as she was of most things. But she was absolutely certain that if she did have a core, she wouldn't find it in a Pilates studio with her fucking "sit bones."

So they talked about the ballet company, Lucy drawing Lindsay out. By the end of the hour, after the agonizing "hundreds," Lucy could've written a feature on the tribulations of being a dancer in the corps—her pay, her many diets, her smoking to stay thin, her tendonitis, her shallow hip sockets, her hamstrings, her cheating boyfriends, her shrinking dream of making it to principal. At twenty-four, Lindsay was as grimly experience-hardened as a forty-year-old. Did she really say to herself, and mean it, "My core is strong and solid"? Maybe so—and, if so, lucky her. Not sure of what the form was here, Lucy tipped her twenty bucks at the end of the session, which Lindsay, looking grateful but furtive, tucked inside her sports bra for safekeeping.

ALIDA TAPPED on Tad's door.

"Ali!" Sag-shouldered, puffy-eyed, Tad looked less like Tad than some character he was acting in a play, a man crushed by sudden bad news.

Frightened, Alida held out her arms for a hug, thinking that the hug would say more than the words she'd prepared. She clung to him for a moment: $a + b$, and a million miles from x.

"Ali."

"You know what? The dogfish stuff? I got scared, but he didn't mean to scare me, he was just telling me the truth, and I was being stupid and I scared myself, it wasn't him, it was all me, he's not like *bad* or anything, he's . . ." Alida felt she wasn't saying this right. It had sounded much better when she'd rehearsed it in her head.

"Oh, Ali. Right, and right, and right again. I got mad over nothing—nothing. I'm so sorry. It's a lousy fact of life that sometimes people do get mad for no good reason at all. I had a sort of brain fart."

"I had a brain fart today. I got really mad at Gail."

"What about?"

"Nothing."

"Weird, isn't it, that *nothing* makes so many things happen? It's so important it really ought to have a different name."

Alida thought for a moment, then said, "Factor Zero?"

"I love you, Ali."

"I love you, too."

"Factor Zero. Now I have the word for it. I'll always call it Factor Zero."

"I have this idea," Alida said, revealing her project to the world for the first time, "that everything is really algebra."

"And you know what? I was always terrible at math in school."

"Will you come to dinner tonight?"

"I'd love to come to dinner, but I promised Gilda—you remember Gilda?"

"Yeah, she's the actress, right? She was with you in that play."

"I have to take her out to a fancy meal in a restaurant. She's going through a rough time. A lot of people are going through a rough time right now. It's Factor Zero at work again."

Leaving Tad's apartment, Alida was reminded of kayaking—the giddy elation of being afloat and in control. She'd taken charge, she'd used her paddle right, her boat had skimmed safely over the yawning deeps below.

"I DON'T want to go."

It was 9:30, and Lucy and Alida were snuggling in Alida's narrow bed.

"Why, Rabbit?"

"I don't know, I just don't."

"But yesterday you wanted to go so badly."

"Yeah, but that was yesterday."

Watching the troubled face beside her on the pillow, Lucy cast about for irresistible inducements. The whole weekend would be thrown out of balance if Alida stayed home. The invitation had been provoked by Alida's eagerness to go kayaking again, not because Lucy had wanted more face time with her subject. It was essential that Alida come along. It didn't help Lucy's mental clarity that every muscle in her body ached from the Pilates class. She said, "You were getting so great at kayaking . . ."

"You can go. I can stay with Tad."

Tad! Damn him! Alida had gone to his apartment after school and come back with an ambiguous Gioconda smile, saying nothing of what had transpired between them. Evidently they'd made a pact—Tad and Alida versus the Vanagses, like the Allies against the Axis powers.

But Lucy had to hide her anger. "Rabbit, it's really important to me that we go together."

"I don't want to."

"Try and tell me why."

In a small voice, Alida said, "It's because like . . . I think it might hurt Tad's feelings."

"Is that what he said?"

"No. It doesn't have anything to do with what Tad said. It's just how I feel."

"Oh, Rabbit." There was candid misery in Alida's face now. "I promise you it won't hurt Tad. Would it help if I talked to him?"

"No."

"This is a you-and-me thing. We just can't back out now." Cradling her daughter, she remembered how, at her age, she'd felt physically torn apart in the intermittent Cold War between her parents. Her great ambition had always been to protect Alida from anything like that, and now Alida was suffering exactly as she had done.

"Is it really super-important?"

"Yes, but . . ." That *but* was the crucial word. Lucy realized that Alida had somehow, just recently, gained the power, the right, of refusal; it wasn't that Lucy wouldn't force her on this, it was that she couldn't.

Alida suddenly smiled—exactly as she had when she returned from Tad's apartment. "Okay, then. I'll come."

"Thank you, my darling."

"I really do want to go kayaking again."

Five minutes later, she was asleep. By ten, Lucy was back at the computer, continuing the research she'd begun earlier in the evening and plowing through the reader reviews of *Boy 381* on Amazon.com. There were more than seven hundred of them, and it was dull, repetitive work. The book had an unblemished five stars, and the readers all said the same thing: they'd cried, they'd laughed, they'd stayed up all night to finish it, they'd missed their subway stops in their engrossment, Augie had changed their entire view of the world, they'd felt his pain, and so on, and on, and on. It seemed to be part of the house rules at Amazon that to praise a book you had to manifest an exaggerated physiological response—laughing till you cried, cracking up, weeping buckets, or, as a woman from Akron, Ohio, claimed, wetting yourself, choking for breath, depriving yourself of sleep, as if readers were competing for some emotional dysfunction award. Growing impatient with these displays of I-felt-it-more-deeply-than-anyone-else-did, Lucy clicked Next, and Next, and Next on each batch of ten reviews until boredom sent her over to Amazon.co.uk. Maybe the Brits had a different take on it.

Four stars over there, and there were only ninety-something reviews. She scrolled through them, not knowing what she was searching for until she found it: a review headed FRAUD by "A Reader from Thetford (*See more about me*)," written very shortly after the book came out back in 2005.

"I knew 'August Vanags' during the war years," it began. "He was an orphan and a refugee, but spent most of the war living on my parents' farm in Norfolk. I possess a copy of the very same photograph that is shown on the cover of his so-called 'memoir.' He is not in a refugee camp—he is standing in front of the part of the farm that my father fenced off in 1940 in order to raise chickens, as many people had to do after Lord Woolton was made minister of food. He was a very thin child because he suffered from coeliac, a wasting disease. He was always in and out of the Jenny Lind children's hospital in Norwich, where he was treated for this condition. He was nowhere near Poland or Germany or any of the other countries described in his 'book.'"

Lucy reached for the quote-unquote book and checked the inside back flap for the provenance of the picture. It said, "Jacket photograph of August Vanags (1945): Philip Cahan"—the name of the U.S. Army sergeant who'd rescued Augie in Germany at the war's end.

The Reader from Thetford was inexorable: the review ran for at least a thousand indignant words, detailing the family farm, how the boy had been taken in, and his ingratitude after the war, when a Latvian aid society had found him a permanent foster home in Braintree, Essex, and he'd never responded to the many affectionate postcards sent to him by the reviewer's family.

If true, this was the Wilkomirski story all over again. Lucy forced her mind into a state of numb agnostic cool as she clicked back through the later reviews to see if anyone had picked up on these revelations, if they were revelations. Nobody had. The preponderance of comments echoed the American ones, though many had that sniffy old-boy air of self-important judiciousness. She then went back to Reader from Thetford and clicked on *See more about me*.

Marjorie Tillman of Thetford, Norfolk: she liked books on history and travel, and her Favourites list included *A Short Walk in the Hindu Kush* and *Mountbatten: A Biography*. Lucy dialed Qwest for international directory assistance and got the number for an M. Tillman, 3, The Broadwalk, Thetford. It was midnight, eight in the morning in England, and too early to roust Ms. Tillman from her bed with a call out of the blue. Lucy made coffee to keep herself awake for another hour.

If true. She had to see that photograph. As a piece of writing, the Amazon.co.uk review was itself suspect—its rankling, aggrieved tone sometimes verged on the crazy. People's obsessions with the famous led them into all sorts of delusions, and this woman might turn out to be on a par with the cranks who sighted Elvis in their local supermarket. Interesting, too, that no one had followed up her accusations; maybe habitués of the British site knew her to be a nutcase. Lucy checked out a dozen of her other reviews, which were all peevish but not noticeably insane. On travel books, she sounded like a *New Yorker* fact-checker, forever putting people to rights on trifling mistakes, so presumably she had money to spend on globe-trotting.

By the light of the architect's halogen lamp on her desk, Lucy pored over the book jacket. Until this moment the picture had said "refugee camp" in stark, unambiguous terms: the skeletal boy with his feet in grass, the closely spaced lines of barbed wire, the bare dirt beyond. Now that she was reading it as "chicken farm," it made equal but unsatisfactory sense, for there were no other clues—no human figures, and no chickens, either. It could as easily be a refugee farm or a chicken camp.

At 1:03 A.M. Lucy dialed the fourteen-digit number in after-breakfast England.

"Hello?"

For a millisecond, Lucy thought she'd accidentally got her mother on the line, for the voice was hers—or rather, it was the voice her mother liked to affect when she was feeling grand, one often heard on PBS but never, in Lucy's experience, in real life. She asked if she was talking to Marjorie Tillman, and the voice said, half bray, half bark, "Yarse?"

Stating her business, Lucy talked up the reputation of *GQ,* though she doubted if it would mean much in Thetford, Norfolk. But the woman, far from treating her as a rude intruder on her morning, sounded as if she'd been waiting for years for Lucy to call her, though she was practically shouting, as if conveying her voice across an ocean and a continent via satellite required an extraordinary effort of the lungs.

"But of course I remember. I was ten when the war ended, four when it started, so the whole period's very vivid to me! He was rather a dim, moony sort of child, always wandering round the garden picking *flarze.* We had to take him in. Either one took in refugee children or one got billeted with evacuees!"

These, Lucy gathered, were an even lower form of life than refugees.

"I mean, it was the shock, you see—seeing that picture on the cover. I have to say I'm glad my mother's not alive. It would've killed her, the sheer ingratitude! And he never wrote back, not once. Then this . . . atrocity! We had to drive him to the hospital in Norwich." *Norritch.* "Week after week, with petrol desperately short in those days. For his ruddy *coeliac.* And this is what we get for thanks, these barefaced lies about having survived the war in concentration camps and God knows what. Poland, my foot! Thetford was where he was, two miles outside Thetford. We used to have a hundred and fifty acres there."

It didn't sound like much to Lucy. Even the wretched Lewis Olson had twelve sections at 640 acres to a section, but of course English farmland was exceptionally wet and rich, so perhaps such a negligible acreage might go with Marjorie Tillman's very upstairs accent.

"He had to be fed on bananas, you know? Bananas were *incredibly* scarce during the war, but they were one of the few things that child could keep down. They were specially flown in, in RAF transports, for the likes of him."

"But you have the same photograph as the one on the b-b-b-book jacket?"

"I'm looking at it right now! It's in a frame, on the Welsh dresser, on the knickknack shelf, where my mother used to keep her mementos. Even though he never wrote, she kept his picture to remind herself of the war years. 'Our little refugee' was what Mummy used to call him. I can't tell you how this ridiculous book would have hurt her. It would've cut her to the core."

"And you're sure it's the same one?"

"I'm not blind!" That shout again. "Of course the printers have done things to the one on the book, touched it up and so forth. But it's him, all right, by the old chicken run."

Frantic to see Augie publicly exposed as an ingrate and a liar, Marjorie Tillman was Lucy's eager collaborator. She checked her local phone book for the nearest Federal Express office, which turned out to be in "Norritch," agreed to have the picture copied later that morning, and wrote down Lucy's FedEx account number and her address at the Acropolis.

"And you're going to show him up in your magazine? In America?"

"If it really is the same p-p-picture."

"There's no *if* about it. You'll see—and I hope your magazine has an *extremely* large circulation. It's about time someone put a stop to that man's dreadful nonsense."

As Lucy was thanking her for her help and about to say good-bye,

Marjorie Tillman said, "Of course he didn't call himself August Vanags then; he called himself Juris Abeltins."

"Could you spell that?" Lucy said.

UP LATE after dinner with Gilda Hahn—at which she'd spent the dessert course, followed by two Courvoisiers, in tears—Tad was web surfing the world's news. He read a long glum article in the *Guardian,* by an English jurist who was cataloging the erosion of civil liberties in the UK since the London bombings in July 2005. The Brits were playing Simon Says, slavishly following every move dictated by the U.S. administration—imprisoning people without trial, battening down on free speech, giving the police and secret services unprecedented powers to mine private data and tap phones of legislators, to harass and arrest citizens, to deport aliens . . . the usual story. Apparently in Britain there were even more spy cameras than here, with motorists followed around the country by the hidden eyes of government. According to this guy, the Brits—with no written constitution—were pretty much screwed. Canada was beginning to look like the last place in the English-speaking world where civil liberties were still relatively unscathed. It was always at the back of Tad's mind that one day the time would come when he, Lucy, and Alida might have to cross the 49th parallel as political refugees—if the Canadians would let them in, which was a big *if,* for half of Canada's neighbors to the south must be harboring similar thoughts. And of course Lucy would have to be dragged up there by her hair. Until the undercover agents were actually at her door, she'd go on living in her bubble of delusion that all was for the best in the best of all possible worlds.

The worm of anger was beginning to work in him again. He fought it back and went over to the BBC site.

Police in Wolverhampton raid terror suspects' home . . .

Strangely, for there was usually no advertising on the BBC, a pop-up appeared, a very amateur-looking pop-up saying he'd "won £100!!!" Tad clicked on the close-window X button on its top right-hand corner, realizing he'd done the wrong thing when an unfamiliar web page appeared, succeeded by his Outlook Express address book. Then blood-colored letters from some paint program began to slowly write themselves across the screen. F . . . R . . . E . . . FREAKED!!!

He took the cursor to the Start button to close down Windows, but it was immobilized. The hourglass symbol appeared next to the traveling arrow. The computer was frozen solid. He had to turn off the power strip.

His first major virus. He'd never opened a suspicious attachment and was protected by a Norton firewall. The experience of watching the familiar screen turn suddenly, mockingly hostile on him was more unsettling than he could've imagined. It was like a spookily successful exercise in black magic—like seeing a domestic cat transformed into a toad. Five minutes later, hoping this was some momentary cyber aberration, he switched the power on again. The computer started up normally, then told him he was truly

FREAKED!!!

ON TUESDAY MORNING, Lucy dropped Alida off at school with just seconds to spare before the eight o'clock bell. When she switched on the NPR news, the lead story was about a Trojan horse named Freak, which had spread overnight through America, Europe, and Asia, burgling people's address books and forwarding itself to unsuspecting millions. Sites like Amazon and eBay were temporarily down. A spokesman from Microsoft, who promised a patch within two hours, described Freak as "a malicious act of cyber terrorism," which Lucy thought wildly overblown. Vandalism, certainly. Terrorism? Surely not. The cant word of the last few years was graying from repetition, decaying in a process of inevitable entropy—which, come to think of it, was another cant word from an earlier decade. Entropy itself had fallen victim to entropy.

The Microsoft man explained the virus in breezy technobabble. It was, he said, a "WMF exploit" by a hacker who'd uncovered a "Day

Zero vulnerability" in the Internet Explorer system, blah, blah, blah. The important thing was that his geeks had been on the case since midnight, and a solution was imminent.

Senate committee hearings had begun on the appointment of another judge to the Supreme Court—a born-again guy whose views on *Roe v. Wade* were characterized by liberal Democrats as "beyond Neanderthal." A threatened subway strike in New York, more bloody news from the Middle East . . . She switched off the radio to concentrate on her own, more pressing news from Thetford, Norfolk.

She neither believed nor disbelieved Marjorie Tillman, whose story was full of oddities that fit together badly. Lucy found it hard to imagine that Augie Vanags had ever been a "dim" or "moony" child. The boy in his book was instantly recognizable in Augie the man, while the boy of Marjorie's memory was a total stranger. There was the business of the printers "touching up" the supposedly identical photo, which surely meant the two were not identical. The FedEx package should arrive tomorrow or the day after, by Friday at the latest, and until then any speculation about the pictures would be pointless.

What about the two names? If August Vanags had once been Juris Abeltins, why, reinventing himself in America, had he chosen another Latvian name? Had Lucy been called Juris Abeltins, then emigrated to the States, she would've gone for a more American-sounding moniker. Juris could have turned himself into Lowell Cabot, so why choose August Vanags? When the Freak virus was safely patched, she'd try Googling this Mr. Abeltins to see if he was leading a separate existence somewhere; there couldn't be that many Juris Abeltinses in the world, and if she could locate one in England, the whole fabric of Marjorie's tale would unravel.

Plus there was Marjorie's voice. During their conversation, Lucy hadn't warmed at all to her vengeful tone and absurdly snobby accent— though perhaps that was because Marjorie was so irresistibly reminiscent of Lucy's mother at her worst, and "picking *flarze*" was exactly how her mom would say it.

For all these reasons, Marjorie Tillman was someone Lucy was inclined to take with a large pinch of salt, at least until the photograph arrived. If it really showed Augie on an English chicken farm, the *GQ* piece would raise a storm, not just in America but around the world. For a journalist, that would be an incredible windfall, yet even as Lucy allowed herself to savor this thought for a moment, she felt a wrench of alarm and pity for Minna. If Marjorie turned out to be right, she'd be destroyed. Augie, much as Lucy had learned to like him now, could be said to deserve whatever might be coming to him, but Minna was innocent, defenseless, and trusting, and no more deserved the hurricane in which she'd be engulfed than she deserved hanging, regardless of what Montaigne might have to say on the subject.

Lucy was impatient for Microsoft to sound the all-clear. Despite herself, she badly wanted to find an English Juris Abeltins.

TAD'S SECOND-TO-LAST rent check, returned to him with his most recent statement, was stamped on the back:

PAY TO THE ORDER OF
UNITED SAVINGS & LOAN BANK
SEATTLE, WA 98104
FOR DEPOSIT ONLY
EXCELLENT HOLDINGS, INC.
125004587

The bank, on South Jackson, had a line of customers waiting for the four available tellers, which was fine by Tad as he scoped the place out. Most of the bank's staff were Asian-looking, with Chinese names, but he spotted two Caucasians, one with the name tag *Amy* on her chest, the other—fortunately—a man. He'd do "Jeff," though because the guy was in his twenties, the voice would be tricky: easy to play old, much harder to play young.

When Tad's turn came, he cashed $100 on his Visa card to make himself a legit customer, then went to the courtesy phone. If that number, or the bank's name, showed up on Lee's cell phone, he'd have no cause for suspicion.

He was nervous as he always was when waiting in the wings for his cue. He checked the other Charles O. Lee's Social Security number on the slip of paper in his hand, then dialed the landlord's cell. One ring, and it was picked up.

"Yeah?"

"Hi, this is Jeff from United Savings and Loan, South Jackson branch." Tad lifted his pitch to a height just short of falsetto, and tempered it with a butch Seahawks-fan accent. "I'm looking for Charles Lee."

"Yeah, is me." There was no hesitation in the voice at the other end.

"We got a minor problem here, nothing serious—this Freak virus hit us, I sure hope it didn't hit you, Charles. Dang thing seems to have messed up some of our records. Just wanted to check your SSN. The number we have for you is 015-48- . . ."

"7816," Lee said.

"Right—that's what we've got. Thanks for your time. Have a great day!"

Bingo! Walking away from the bank, Tad trod on air. It was the law of averages, of course. He'd been wrong, and wrong, and wrong again—he had to turn out to be right sometime.

What he'd found would be his secret. He meant to tell no one, not even Lucy, at least not yet. That he could now prove the odious Lee was an illegal with a stolen ID was, Tad thought with giddy self-satisfaction, his nuclear option.

9

The brouhaha over the Freak virus was over by lunchtime, when Lucy applied the patch and went onto the disinfected Internet. Googling Juris Abeltins, she found just one—a Latvian socialist politician, "dzimis 1947." From the context, she guessed that "dzimis" must mean "born," but just to make sure she Googled "dzimis + born," and there, beside the name of some entrant in the Eurovision Song Contest, was "Dzimis Latvija (Born in Latvia)." A Latvian baby boomer clearly couldn't be the same person as Marjorie Tillman's wartime refugee. This was a setback, but by no means conclusive. There were still billions of people too obscure to show up on Google, and a dim and moony child might well have grown up to be one of them. Marjorie's Juris could easily be working as somebody's gardener, growing flowers now, not picking them, beyond the reach of any search engine.

When Lucy drove up to the school at 3:30, Alida ditched her friends with wholly uncharacteristic speed and came racing over to the Spider, her face pink and bulging with excitement.

"Oh my God! You won't believe it!" she said, opening the car door. "You so won't believe it!"

"What is it, Rabbit!"

"You won't believe it."

"Cool your jets! Won't believe what?"

"Finn! It's Finn!"

"Finn what?"

"Finn's been arrested—by the *FBI*! We're all getting counseling! It's *amazing*!"

Lucy switched off the engine. "I'm lost. Can you just remember to breathe, please?"

"He wrote the virus! He was always signing himself 'Freak' in e-mails. Four FBI men came, in two cars. They caught his mom first and brought her to the school. They weren't wearing uniforms or anything; they were in *suits*. Then the principal came and called Finn out of Humanities—this was this morning—and in the lunchroom there were these eighth-graders talking and they said Finn was going to get seven *years*. In *jail*! He wrote the virus! Finn wrote the virus!"

Holy shit! Lucy thought, but said, "Can I just say one thing?"

"Yeah, sure."

"He won't get seven years in jail."

"He told me and Gail he was into horses. He meant *Trojan* horses! He wrote this Trojan horse thing and it did billions and billions of dollars of damage! The FBI came to our school!"

"How did they manage to find him so quickly?"

"The eighth-graders said he didn't cover his tracks at all—because he *wanted* to get caught!"

"Why would he want to do that?"

"For the attention. Like, Finn's famous. I mean, not famous like Tad's famous—he's *famous* famous! He's so *über*-famous it's unreal! *Finn!* I think his mom's in jail, too."

Lucy knew Finn's mom slightly—a pallid blonde named Beth who worked for some online outfit but had once been a journalist. Despite that connection, they'd had an annoying conversation at the sixth-grade picnic in September and had barely spoken since.

"Rabbit, honestly, I wouldn't worry too much about Finn. He won't go to jail. They don't jail eleven-year-olds for stuff like that. They'll give him the fright of his life, confiscate his computer, and send him back to school. Either that or they'll hire him as a consultant on cyber crime.

But I don't believe for one second that he'll see the inside of a prison—him, or his mom."

"Finn wrote the virus." Alida's face gave new meaning to the word *boggle*: there was no other term for it, her eyes were *boggled*.

"Holy moly." Lucy switched on the ignition and pulled out of the parking space. "Jesus, what a day for you. I don't suppose you managed to get any actual work done?"

"No, we had counseling. And there's no homework."

"So what did the counselor say?"

"Oh, you know. Stuff. I *knew* Finn was doing something. He's always weird, but these last few days he's been weirder than weird."

"Funny—looking at him, I'd never have guessed he was smart enough to do something like this."

"Finn's a genius. He's *awesome*."

"Rabbit—you mustn't think of him as some kind of hero. . . . He's just a nerdy, fat, unhappy kid who wrote some code, and what he did was just plain wrong. It wasn't cool."

"You sound like the counselor."

"'Poor Finn' is what I'm thinking. I wonder what drove him to it."

"I think he misses his dad—I saw him writing an e-mail once. But now he's *famous*."

"So you said. Now, I thought for dinner I'd make some really special macaroni and cheese."

"Cool."

At five o'clock sharp, Alida, never normally a newshound, asked to watch the news. Finn was indeed famous, though not by name. He was "an eleven-year-old Seattle boy," and the school, thankfully, wasn't mentioned. Experts talked about the mechanics of the "vulnerability." Then came the child psychologists.

Do you know what your child is doing on the Internet? Etc., etc. A solemn fellow in a bow tie advised parents to ensure that their kid's computer was permanently located in a "family room," where they could constantly "monitor" the screen.

"Parents today often fail to understand the growing computer literacy of the upcoming generation. Children as young as seven and eight are now performing complex operations far beyond the comprehension of moms and dads. Parents have a great deal of catching up to do. You have to ask yourself, 'Do I understand what Junior's doing here?' And if you don't, get Junior to explain it to you. If you're not immediately satisfied with the explanation, you need to seek outside help. Do you have a tech-savvy friend? Who's the IT teacher at your child's school? This Freak virus is a wake-up call to parents everywhere."

Pernicious nonsense, in Lucy's view. Whenever she went into Alida's room, Alida automatically closed the laptop on which she was instant-messaging with her friends, and Lucy respected that: just because she was a kid didn't mean she had no right to privacy. What a lousy example to set, to snoop on your own child's every move. Finn Janeway's astonishing escapade was being used as an excuse for universal parental paranoia. And as for Mr. Bow Tie's talk of "Junior," that showed how hopelessly out of touch *he* was.

"Right," she said. "Rabbit—laptop into the family room, screen facing me. And when you're I.M.-ing, I need you to read me every word."

Alida sniggered.

"Can you and Gail write HTML?"

"Nah, we leave all that stuff to Finn. Even the twelfth-graders go to Finn. You have to pay him with muffins."

"I have a feeling Finn's seen his last muffin, which won't do him any harm at all. Better by a long shot than seven years in the pokey."

"You really think he won't go to jail?"

"I'm positive, Rabbit. He won't be allowed near a computer, he'll have to go muffinless, but he won't go to jail. It was just a kid's prank that went too far—way, way too far. And if I ever catch you writing a virus I'll kill you with my bare hands."

"I'm cool with that," Alida said, idly watching the weatherman gesture at his map.

"Now I need some help with dinner."

The recipe, cut from a newspaper, had grown yellow but untried on the fridge door, where it shared a magnet with a sheaf of cards from take-out delivery joints. It began with the intimidating injunction to

"Make a *roux*" and called for chopped ham, chopped green peppers, grated nutmeg, jalapeños, skinned and deseeded tomatoes, ricotta, and cheddar. It promised "tender elbows of pasta nestling in a complex and colorful cheese sauce." Minna Vanags would no doubt have found it as easy as boiling an egg, but to Lucy it looked like the Everest of haute cuisine.

She set Alida to grating cheese. After the hysteria of the Finn affair, she needed to be returned to Earth. Alida babbled as she grated, while Lucy feigned a wise and airy cool about the whole business, though the pretense grew increasingly hard to maintain as her own hysteria about the recipe mounted. With every move she made, she foresaw the threat of Chinese takeout in the offing. Congealed lumps appeared in the *roux*; she fiercely mashed them out with a wooden spoon. Deseeding tomatoes was beyond her, so she substituted canned. Jalapeños, she thought, might be more than Alida's palate could take, so she sprinkled the now-bubbling mixture with a dusting of cayenne instead. The water for the pasta—she had straight macaroni, not "elbows"—refused to come to a boil on time. The kitchen counter turned into a slovenly chaos of spilled tomato juice, nutmeg, pepper cores, seeds, and cheese that Alida had managed to grate almost everywhere except on the designated plate. Lucy scalded a knuckle when she tried to take a taste, said "Fuck!" then "Excuse me!" then "Fuck!" again when the wooden spoon slid unaided from the counter to the floor.

Alida was still going on about Finn and his famous Trojan horse, but Lucy had ceased to listen. She thought wistfully of all the varieties of macaroni and cheese that came frozen in containers, to which all you needed to do was prick the cellophane top and shove them in the microwave. With such drama around the stovetop, who needed news? Most of all, Lucy feared duplicating one of her mother's culinary atrocities, and swore she'd stick to Stouffer's in the future.

Eventually, the whole pinkish, greenish slumgullion made it into a casserole dish, was sprinkled with more cheese, and was placed under the broiler, with the timer set for fifteen minutes. Lucy rewarded herself with an extra-large glass of Oregon pinot noir.

The knock on the door came just when the timer started beeping.

"Oh, Jesus—Alida! Get the door, will you?"

It was the landlord. Bowing, smiling, he had a tape measure in one hand and a book in the other. Lucy, hair in her eyes, holding the heavy casserole in burned and greasy oven gloves, grimaced at him.

"Home cooking!" Mr. Lee said.

"S-S-S-Sorry, we're just about to eat."

"Came to measure up." He pointed back at the door. "Video monitor."

"What?"

"Like I told you—video monitor for security."

"Oh, that." She put the casserole on a mat on the table.

"Bring you the book." He placed it beside the casserole. It was a small book, grown fat and soggy with rereading: *Who Moved My Cheese?*

"That's funny. I was just making m-m-macaroni and cheese."

"Lots of good tips—you'll see."

"Well . . . thank you." She wished he'd get on with his measuring, though the last thing she wanted was a video monitor. The landlord appeared to be using her as a guinea pig for his projects: the lock on Tad's door had remained unchanged. Why was her apartment being singled out for these experiments? And why did he always have to show up at such inconvenient hours? "Mr. Lee, do you mind if we just g-g-get on and eat?"

"No, no—smells good!" He didn't budge from the table, just stood there, smiling expectantly.

Lucy gave up. "Alida? You'd better set another place for Mr. Lee."

Alida was happy to welcome the landlord to the table, treating him as a fresh pair of ears to which she could tell her astounding news. She'd been deeply disappointed to find that Tad wasn't home when they'd returned to the Acropolis, and now she had the captive audience she craved.

"You heard about the Freak virus?"

"Oh, yeah. My bank got hit—call me this morning."

"You know who started it? It was a boy in *my class*! Finn—"

"Alida, I don't think—"

"Finn Janeway! The FBI came to our school! He got *arrested*! They took him away, in two cars."

"Janeway? *Finn?*" Mr. Lee's overslung eyelids seemed for a moment to be working overtime. "He do all this with his home computer?"

"I think so—or maybe from the computer lab at school."

"Big mistake," the landlord said. "He shoulda gone to library or someplace. Kid smart enough to do that stuff, he should know better. Do it from his house . . . that's crazy. Why he do that?"

"I think he like wanted to get caught."

The landlord frowned and shook his head disbelievingly. "Like I say, this kid crazy."

Lucy, annoyed by the landlord's too-ready adoption of the criminal point of view—surely not the way to talk to Alida—said, "Do help yourself, Mr. Lee."

He did so, generously. The golden crust on top made the dish look almost professionally respectable: Lucy thought it a pity that the landlord's uninvited presence so detracted from what should have been her pride and pleasure in having successfully carried off the recipe.

Still, he praised the food lavishly. "Good cook, Lucy!"

"Thank you, Mr. Lee. Alida?"

"Yummy."

Looking around the room, the landlord said, "You keep things nice. Real homey."

"We like to think so."

He quizzed Alida about her school, then said, "You think about college?"

"Sometimes I do. I want to be a math major."

"Math, huh?"

"It's hard to think seven years ahead when you're eleven," Lucy said. "People change. By the time you get to twelfth grade, who knows what you'll want to major in? It might be math, it might be astrophysics, it might be anthropology."

"Lot of good colleges in the U.S.," Mr. Lee said. "What college you want to go to?"

"I don't know. I haven't like thought about it."

"Harvard College. That's good one. You heard of Harvard College?"

"Yeah," Alida said, carefully forking the green bits out of her macaroni and cheese.

"You want an A-one education, you go to Harvard College."

Alida shrugged. "Maybe."

"You need big bucks to pay for Harvard College. Tuition!" He was speaking to Lucy now. "Costs a fortune."

"So, you have children, Mr. Lee?"

"Me? No. No wife, no kids. Single man!" He reached for the casserole to give himself a second helping. He munched rather noisily for a while, then said, "Been reading what you wrote. Good writing, Lucy! Bill Gates, he knows what it takes to go from good to great. Can learn a lot from a guy like him." To Alida, he said, "Bill Gates went to Harvard College."

"He dropped out," Lucy told him.

"What do you mean?" Alida said.

"He didn't finish. He never got to graduate. He quit in his junior year there."

"Like me." The landlord eyed the casserole for the third time. "Never got to graduate from college!"

"So where were you, Mr. Lee?"

"Seattle Central Community College. Took class there once, Business Studies. Shoulda gone to Harvard." He laughed. "But I was poor man then. Couldn't pony up no tuition."

The notion of him as a Harvard student was so absurd that Lucy giggled out loud.

"Is true!" Mr. Lee said, grinning. "Hey, I live like dirt once. Work my way up, right from the bottom. Not like Bill Gates. More like Sam Walton." He turned to Alida. "Wal-Mart guy. When Sam a kid back in Depression time, his family didn't have but just one cow. Every morning, five o'clock, this kid be out there milkin' the cow. Then he bottle that milk and sell it all over Oklahoma on his bike. That how he got started. Know Wal-Mart's turnover right now? Two hundred, eighty-five *billion* dollars!"

After a longish pause, Alida was gracious enough to mumble, "Cool."

It took the landlord an age to leave. Then Lucy realized he'd never gotten around to taking measurements for the damn video monitor.

FINN'S EMPTY CHAIR was the focal point in Social Studies. They were meant to be doing this new project about George Vancouver and the Northwest Indians, but no one was paying attention. His absence from the room only made the cyberterrorist more present in everybody's mind. In the minutes before the eight o'clock bell, all the talk was of Finn's scarifying future. Most thought he'd spend years—behind bars!—in a juvenile detention center. Alida tried to say roughly what her mom had told her, but that wasn't nearly exciting enough for the other kids.

"If he doesn't talk, they'll probably torture him," Alex said in a matter-of-fact voice.

"He'll go to trial."

"He'll be *incarcerated.*"

"He'll have to spend the entire rest of his life paying for what he did. They'll take it off his salary every month. He'll never even have a *car!*"

"He'll have to work on road gangs, wearing a yellow jacket with *Prisoner* on it. He'll be picking up litter."

"Can you imagine Finn like really, really thin?"

In class, Mrs. Milliband was saying, "Then Lieutenant Peter Puget and his men rowed ashore, and that was their very first meeting with the people we now call the Coast Salish Indians."

Who *cared*?

MIRACULOUSLY, the FedEx package arrived mid-morning. Given the time difference, Marjorie Tillman must have moved like greased lightning to copy the photo and deliver it to the Norwich FedEx office. Lucy tore the flap of the package twice in her haste to get it open.

Two sheets of stiff cardboard enclosed a dust jacket of Augie's book, a print of Mrs. Tillman's original photograph, and four pages of small, old-fashioned, scrolly, blue-ink handwriting. Lucy grabbed the photo and immediately saw that it wasn't—quite—identical to the one on the book, but could easily have been the next picture on the roll: boy, barbed wire, grass in the foreground, dirt in the background. The light had changed between the two shots, though. In Marjorie's version, the boy—who sure *looked* like Augie—was squinting into the sun, and his shock of pale hair had changed shape a little, probably because of the wind.

She went to Alida's room to dig out the magnifying glass that had been Alida's constant companion when she was eight and deeply into *Harriet the Spy*. She found it in the third drawer down in the homework desk: Alida, the neat freak, always kept her drawers in perfect order.

It was hard to be sure, but under the glass she thought she saw discrepancies. Marjorie's copy was nearly as good as an original, but both had clearly been taken with a Box Brownie's crappy little lens. Even fresh from the processors more than sixty years ago, their resolution would have been smudgy. The dust jacket version wasn't helped by its multitude of creases—creases that both served to authenticate its age, and now made it infuriatingly more difficult to read. But, look, wasn't that barbed wire more widely spaced, and somehow spikier, in the photo on the book than it was in the copy?

And the boy himself: on the book his features were relatively sharp, but in the other they were almost whited-out from overexposure. The rule in those days—reverently observed by Lucy's dad long afterward—was that the photographer had to keep the sun over his left shoulder to get the best picture, so a smidge too much sunlight could reduce a human face to a cipher. The boy—if it *was* the same boy—had obviously moved. In the first, his feet were hidden in the grass; in the second, Lucy could see the tops of a pair of sandals.

Suppose, now, that she were looking at two Latvian boys, both the same age, both Oxfam starvation cases. Substitute Chinese or African-American for Latvian, and would she expect to be able to securely tell them apart? How do you tell one munchkin from another?

It was the setting that was so damning. But then again, weren't dirt and barbed wire part of the basic vocabulary of wartime, like Augie's and Wilkomirski's rats? A single fencepost would've helped confirm that the fence was the same fence, but in both shots there was only wire.

Maddening, since Lucy had expected the new photo to either convict or acquit at a glance. Her feeling was that both pictures were of Augie, taken a few minutes apart, but there were just enough differences to allow—no, to enforce—a wedge-shaped sliver of doubt.

She thought of showing them to Tad, who was interested in photography and might know more than she did about boys, but of course he'd confidently place Augie on the chicken farm and delight in seeing his book trashed by the world.

She turned to the letter. Marjorie's notepaper was embossed with a letterhead printed in red—*Mrs. Peregrine Tillman, 3, The Broadwalk,* followed by her phone number and e-mail address, where, rather surprisingly, she was informally *marjiet@* somewhere or other. Peregrine, how quaint! Peregrine must have died, though, since everything about Mrs. Tillman suggested a widow with too much time on her hands.

"Dear Miss Bengstrom," it began, the women's movement having apparently bypassed Thetford, Norfolk. The neat lines of immaculately legible writing ran on and on, peppered with words like "liar," "ungrateful," "deceitful," and "cad." Mrs. Tillman's sea-blue fountain-penmanship uncannily conveyed her speaking voice—precise, imperial, and loud. She appeared to have the memory of an elephant: sentences would start "In early April 1944 . . ." and "Sometime around the 15th of February 1945 . . ." Perhaps she'd worked from her schoolgirl diaries. Lucy didn't doubt her facts, but whether they were facts about Juris Abeltins or August Vanags she simply couldn't tell. She learned more than she'd ever wanted to know about the symptoms of coeliac, and was in a position to draw a detailed map of Major Vickers'—Mrs. Tillman's father's—farm in all its hundred and fifty superior acres. The tone of the letter was of one conspirator to another: Marjie T. and Lucy B. had the author of *Boy 381* pinned squarely to the ground. All that remained was to disembowel him in public.

The letter ended:

I am most grateful for your assistance in this matter, and will be happy to supply you with further information as required. Please do not hesitate to phone or write. When your magazine article appears, I would much appreciate it if you could send me a dozen copies at the above address, preferably by your "Federal Express" service. This nonsense has gone on for *far* too long.

Yours very sincerely,

Marjie Tillman

"SEIZE THE DAY!" was a phrase he'd glommed onto from his audio books. Seize the day!

All morning, Charles O had ridden around town in his pickup, practicing his lines. Driving from parking lot to parking lot, he felt a mounting certainty and masterfulness. Today was the day to seize; if he left it till tomorrow, his confidence in his own power might falter.

Banking $3,461 in cash at United Savings and Loan on Jackson, he said to the teller, "You beat the virus, huh?"

The teller, looking puzzled, said, "Yes, I had the flu a couple of weeks ago."

"Never mind," he said, stuffing the receipt in his wallet.

He climbed into the truck and drove on to the Acropolis. Each time he saw the building, he liked it more: spend $50,000 on minor refurbishments and it would be a palace. Repoint the bricks, freshen up the stucco. A gang of Mexicans could work wonders in a week. Possession of the big, old, stately building had mysteriously enlarged Charles O's own character; its air of permanence in the world was now his. Just looking at it made him feel bigger, older, grander. After parking across the street, he spent five minutes sitting in the truck, window down, drinking in the sight. Swollen with feelings he found impossible to name, he walked over and took the creaky elevator to the seventh floor.

Lucy was in. Dressed in tight jeans and a black silk blouse, she looked flustered.

"Look, Mr. Lee—about the video thing, I've been thinking, and—"

He held up his hand commandingly and said, "No video! Must ask you something!"

She crossed the room, sat down at her desk—a litter of papers, books, and pictures. "Yes?"

He remained standing. He needed the advantage of height.

"Maybe this come as big surprise but—"

"If it's our l-l-l-lease—"

"No!" She mustn't interrupt, or he'd lose his thread. "First time I see you in this apartment, I know you're smart. You a writer—good writer. I read what you write about Bill, you got him all figured out. You a born American—know stuff I don't. So I gotta ask you."

"Yes?"

"Washington is community property state. You know community property?"

"Precious little, I'm afraid."

"I got book about it. Means all assets and property acquired after marriage belong to man and wife, fifty-fifty. Book say that. Like I get married, make a million dollars, spouse get five hundred K. I buy parking lot, apartment building, spouse own half. Big money!"

He had her attention now. She was interested, smiling.

"Spouse get rich—assets and property *commingled*! Word in book, I looked it up. 'Commingled.'"

"I can see how that might be a problem."

"No problem! See, guy like me, guy with property, need spouse. Time to marry! Need good homemaker. Like entertaining, I got business associates, dinner party, reception, all kinda stuff. See? I need wife. Look at Bill—him and Melinda. Sam and Helen. Time is come. Lucky this is community property state, huh?"

"Well, depending on how you look at it, I suppose."

"I think lucky."

"That's very generous of you."

She was really smiling now. She'd got his drift. No more fluster, she was listening keenly.

"Not generous. Make good sense. Spouse be nice to big guy from like New York, D.C., whatever—more money in bank! Fifty-fifty, like I said."

"So who are you planning to marry, Mr. Lee?"

"Lucy, moment I see you, voice inside me say 'She the one.'"

"Mr. Lee! Please! D-D-D-D-Don't—"

"Stop! I *finish*!" He shouted her down. She sat tensely on her chair, smile frozen on her face, staring. "You old—no problem. You little big—no problem. You got Alida—great. Smart kid like that, I pay for Harvard College. Fifty-fifty, Lucy. Commingled."

"Mr. Lee!" Her voice was a shriek.

"Come like shock, huh? Big decisions I always sleep on like overnight. Time to think, right? I give you time to think. Lucy?"

Her hand was at her mouth, her shoulders shaking. She was overcome with emotion—of course she would be, hearing it for the first time like that. Charles O knew from movies what to do. He stepped across to her, was about to put his hands on her shoulders and draw her close, when he saw she wasn't crying. She was laughing.

10

"OH GOD," Lucy said to Tad in his apartment, five minutes later. "It was word for word out of that scene in *Pride and Prejudice* when the ghastly Reverend Collins proposes to Elizabeth Bennett."

"Or Titania and Bottom, except the other way around, if you see what I mean. Remember my Bottom, at the Rep?"

"I was in hysterics. It was like, oh Jesus! we're really fucked now—at least Alida and me. The guy's *Chinese*. I swear I read somewhere that to laugh at a Chinese man is practically punishable by death. I couldn't have insulted the poor bastard more. He slammed the door so hard I thought he'd ripped it off the hinges. Then running down the stairs like a fucking avalanche. Fuck! Fuck! Fuck! My stupid fucking fault. I just couldn't control myself."

Tad had his arms around her. "Everybody corpses sometimes. And it's always the worst time. Love scenes and death scenes are the ones that bring it on. I corpsed once in the middle of Juliet talking sweet nothings about Romeo—I was the nurse, in drag. Just couldn't help myself. It was *terrible*: I was in purdah for weeks."

"Why did he have to pick me? I must be nearly twice his fucking age!"

"Well, along with all your other charms, he wants your citizenship."

"What d'you mean?"

He told her about the Office of Vital Statistics, the call from the bank, the stolen Social Security number.

"Well, aren't *you* the clever gumshoe? What are you going to do, then, turn him over to the INS?"

"Have you ever *seen* the INS jail down by Union Station? They've got hundreds of Hispanics locked up in there. You see them standing at the bars like animals in cages, crying, yelling out messages to friends and relatives. Every time I go past, my blood ices up. I hate the INS. I hate the INS more than I hate Lee, even more than I hate the fucking FBI. For pure, cold, bureaucratic cruelty, I'd give the INS a perfect ten. So no, not yet, not now, and if and when I do, I'll hate myself even more than I hate the INS."

"I don't see the use of knowing he's an illegal unless we can get him deported."

"Try thinking like your new pal Kissinger. Lee's got the bomb and we've got the bomb: mutual deterrence, mutually assured destruction. *Détente.* I kind of like the idea of playing Henry—Iago with a funny accent."

Later, he told her, "I copied everything and put the papers in my bank, so you'll know where they are. Just in case."

She said, "I don't see how we can go on living here, not after what happened."

"So maybe we move out. But if we move, we move on our terms, not his."

When she said *we* she meant Alida and herself; when he said *we* he meant the three of them—the family. Lucy was surprised by the comfort she took from that.

FINN, back in school, looked strangely older, paler, and even, Alida thought, a little thinner, though his smirk was permanently in place. His home PC had been confiscated, and he was forbidden access to the computer lab. The boys mobbed him with questions.

"The FBI don't do juveniles," Finn said, in the new vocabulary he'd acquired over the last two days. "It's like federal law. They're gonna send my papers to the state prosecutor. Guy'll read 'em and see if he's got a case." He saw Alida on the outskirts of the group. "Who you staring at, dude?"

Even the teachers seemed in awe of his fame. There was no "Wake up, Finn!" or "Let's hear from Finn—just this once." Alida's mom had shown her a whole article about Finn—again, he was disappointingly unnamed—in *The New York Times* that began right at the top of the front page: "11-Year-Old Hacker Has Experts Puzzled." At morning assembly, the principal had warned the entire student body not to speak to reporters. Two policemen now stood outside to shoo away the TV vans that had tried to merge with the parents' SUVs as they waited in line to drop kids off.

By the afternoon, Finn mania had begun to subside, and even Social Studies was interesting. Peter Puget had mapped exactly where he was on the Earth's surface by using a sextant—Mrs. Milliband had brought one into the classroom—to measure the angle of the sun from where he stood on the Olympic Peninsula. He'd used a tray of reflective mercury as an "artificial horizon." Alida couldn't wait to get her hands on the sextant, which looked way cool with its swinging arm, its hinged mirrors, its protractor and micrometer. Listening to Mrs. Milliband talk, she thought navigation might turn out to be right up there with algebra.

"My husband's a big sailor. One of the first things he taught me when we went sailing—this was back in the 1960s—was how to use a sextant."

Which meant that Mrs. Milliband must be over sixty years old. Maybe seventy, even. Cripes! As old as Augie, or almost.

AT USELESS BAY, the weather—light showers and heavy overcast—was almost suspiciously normal for mid-April, coming as it did after the succession of heat waves and floods. It was how Lucy remembered springtime in the 1990s. She even liked keeping the top up on the Spider. A dose of normality was what she craved, and badly needed in order to handle this trickiest of weekends with Augie.

At dinner—a rich and winey *boeuf à la bourguignonne* that nicely fit the fifty-degree temperature outside—it was Augie who brought up the Freak virus.

"This kid—"

"He's in my class, and his name's Finn."

"Really? Wow. So you're on first-name terms with the infamous terrorist?"

Lucy said, "I think 'terrorist'—"

"It goes back to what we were saying about infrastructure a couple of weeks ago."

"Imagine, eleven!" Minna said to Lucy.

"Your friend Finn, it's just a hop and a skip from doing what he did to crippling the country's entire financial infrastructure. A sixth-grader! No offense, Alida, but if a sixth-grader can manage that, imagine what a bunch of determined Islamists could do. They've got college degrees from our own universities—Ph.D.s, a lot of them. They're biochemists, physicists, computer engineers, you name it. They're not peasants from the desert, but well-off professionals in their fields. They've got all Finn's considerable skills and a whole lot more."

"What are Islamists?"

"It's a long story that I'll tell you when we're kayaking, if you like. For now, just think of them as men made mad by weird beliefs in a warrior god. Fanatics who hate America."

"Okay."

Lucy thought this rather less than okay, and had no desire to see Alida return from her kayaking trip converted to Augie's peculiar brand of neoconservatism.

"Fact is, Finn deserves a medal for exposing how open to attack we are. I just pray we're capable of learning our lesson from this, though I wouldn't put a five-spot on that one. You think Internet Explorer's vulnerable? You better think about the water supply, the electrical grid, the railroad system. And all I see is a lot of people who ought to know better blowing smoke up our collective hiney."

"Augie!" Minna made a face at him across the table.

"My educated guess is that Alida's perfectly familiar with the word 'hiney.'"

Alida laughed. "I never heard that one, though, about blowing smoke up it."

"It's not a bad expression to learn. Most of politics consists of blowing smoke up people's hineys."

Over dessert—a chocolate and orange mousse, for which Augie brought out a bottle of Muscat de Beaumes de Venise—Lucy steered the talk around to *Boy 381,* the movie.

"They say it's still in preproduction, whatever that means. I take no interest in it: my attitude to that deal was to grab the moolah and run straight to the bank. They bought it, so it's their story now. They can turn it into fiction, which is all the movie'll ever be. I'll read a junk thriller on a plane once in a while, but I've never really cared for fiction."

"You mean they're turning your book into like a *Hollywood* movie?"

"You have to read it, Rabbit. It's a bit like Anne Frank's diary, about Augie as a boy, growing up in World War II. As soon as I'm done with my piece, I'll lend it to you."

"Steven Spielberg called him up on the phone," Minna said.

"Once. A single, solitary phone call. They wanted me to be a consultant on the film, but I wasn't having any of it. They can make up their own details. Besides, I have an irrational prejudice against southern California in general and Los Angeles in particular."

Minna giggled. "He applied for a job at UCLA a long time ago and didn't get it," she told Lucy in a whisper meant to be heard by her husband.

"Like I said, the prejudice is irrational. How's that piece coming, anyway?"

"Oh, I haven't started writing yet," Lucy said. "It's odd—I find writing profiles harder and harder as I get older. It's that conclusive tone they tend to have, as if the journalist has gotten to the bottom of the subject's soul in a one-hour interview, and the piece is like the last word."

"Woe to those who conclude!" Augie said.

"Montaigne?"

"Close, but no cigar. You got the language right, at least. Flaubert."

"I thought you had no time for fiction."

"It's his letters that I like. They're great. I've done little more than flip through *Madame Bovary.*"

"I prefer nonfiction too." Alida was practically licking the last of the mousse from her plate.

"Like your mom said, you might try my book. It's about a kid a good bit younger than you are now."

"Okay, cool. And it's your *true* story?"

"Sure, it's everything I remember from being three to around nine."

"Did you *meet* Adolf Hitler?" Evidently Alida believed that a person who got phone calls from Steven Spielberg must habitually have moved in high circles.

"Not personally, no. But I was in Germany when he was in charge."

"Cool!"

"No, it was just about as uncool as you could imagine. Read the book, you'll see."

As Lucy and Minna were loading the dishwasher, Minna said, "You know, I haven't seen Augie as happy as this in years. You're such fun to have around, you and Alida. For me, too."

Lucy felt like Judas.

Alida usually slept in on Saturdays, but this morning she'd set the alarm for six-fifteen to catch the tide. Muffled in two heavy sweaters and her yellow anorak, she had to breathe in deeply to fasten the clips on her life vest. Augie, too, looked like the Pillsbury Doughboy.

They set off in a dank, gray, windless chill, the sound of each paddle stroke uncannily amplified by the dawn silence. In the days following her last outing, Alida seemed to have unconsciously absorbed the new skill; she paddled, as Augie said admiringly, "like a pro."

They went farther out this time, letting the houses that rimmed the bay shrink behind them. Alida told Augie about Peter Puget and navigation by sextant.

"Yeah," he said. "George Vancouver was a stiff, uptight guy. You wouldn't want to get on his bad side, which was about the only side he ever showed. But Puget was quite different—a real people person. He got fascinated by the Indians, bartered with them, tried to learn their language and understand their customs, all that. He'd be a good guy to share a yarn with. I sometimes wonder what he'd say if he could see Puget Sound today. Okay, so obviously his eyes'd be bugging out on strings, but would he feel proud, or sad, or what, do you think?"

"I dunno. A little sad, I guess. Like we drove the Indians out and gave them bad diseases and stuff. Look! Dogfish!"

"Right. Just very, very junior members of the shark family. There's nothing—nothing at all—to be frightened of."

But she felt no fear. There were at least a dozen circling right beneath the kayaks in a fishy spiral. The light was insufficient to give them any color; they were dark shadows, each three or four feet long, up to their own business in a submarine world that wasn't hers. She found herself watching them with detached wonder—just as a scientist might, she thought.

"See how they chase one another's tails? Dogfish have the IQ of a medium-sized pumpkin."

As the spiral moved, they quietly shifted their kayaks on the water to keep them in view. At some invisible signal, the shadows suddenly scattered and were gone.

"Wow!" Alida said.

"I love to watch critters in the wild—they keep one in mind of one's own critterliness. IQ or no IQ, we're not so different from the dogfish, really. Time to go back, or we'll have to drag the kayaks way too far up the beach."

LUCY WOKE violently from a bad dream. She'd stepped from the elevator to hear an explosion of noise from her apartment. When she walked in, she found it had been taken over by a weird crew of bums who were playing deafening rock music on boom boxes and snorting lines of devil's dandruff from dollar bills. They'd torn down her pictures and covered the walls with lewd graffiti. When she told them to go, they laughed and sneered. She went to the phone to call 911, but the line was dead; they'd cut it off. A grinning bum with missing front teeth shook a broken bottle in her face. She screamed and came awake in the scented bedroom of the Vanagses' house, fearing she'd woken her hosts. Or was it just a dream scream that hadn't found an actual voice?

The dream seemed to her at once infuriatingly familiar and totally obscure. Then she remembered it was exactly the scenario promised by the landlord when he'd first talked about changing her lock. Now Charles O. Lee, comical and horrible in equal parts, had wormed his way into her dream life—an intolerable violation, fuck him. *She the one!* Absurd, of course, but when she recalled the landlord's phrase, she felt like the victim of an attempted murder. *She the one!* No wonder he was visiting her in nightmares.

She quickly fell asleep again, and reawoke just past nine. Given Augie's rigorous schedule, surely he ought to be practicing his Schubert now, but the house was quiet: no typewriter keys, no fumbled chords from the piano. In pajamas and bathrobe, she went barefoot downstairs to get coffee and bring it up to her room, but there Augie was on his piano stool, nodding his head as he listened to an iPod. *Alida's?* She never lent her iPod to anybody except Gail.

"Hi!" He removed the earphones. "Alida's out on the beach—I seem to go through a lotta sand dollars in the course of my research. I've been listening to her favorite band."

"Oh, right, Green Day."

"No, not Green Day, Fall Out Boy."

Lucy had never heard of them. "Yes, of course. Green Day was like last month's craze. So yesterday now. What d'you make of Fall Out Boy?"

"They're . . . cool, I suppose."

"If you say so."

"We were out in the kayaks and saw a pack of dogfish. Not a peep of fright from Alida. She enjoyed watching them."

"She's at that age when they change so fast from week to week that you can't begin to keep up with them."

"She was paddling like a pro today. We had a fine time on the water."

Lucy's inner eleven-year-old stirred in her once again. Why did he never ask her to go kayaking? Well, he was smart enough to know she really didn't want to—that was why.

Augie turned to assassinating Schubert, so Lucy, coffee in hand, went up to get dressed. She was sitting by the window scribbling Augieisms in her notebook when Alida came into the room, holding a book.

"Look what Augie gave me."

It was a hardback copy—first edition, she saw—of *Boy 381*. A collector's item, for it had gone through umpteen printings.

"See what he wrote in it for me?"

On the title page, he'd inscribed: *"To my cool friend, Alida Bengstrom, with admiration, from your uncool friend, Augie Vanags."* Then *"Useless Bay"* and the date.

"Rabbit, you're going to have to take extra special care of this. It's valuable."

"Valuable?"

"It'll be worth several hundred dollars, at least. Especially after the movie comes out. We'd better buy a paperback for you to actually read. You should keep this in a safe place in your room."

"I'm going to read it now." Her tone of voice refused contradiction.

"What about homework?"

"We don't have much this weekend, just some math. And I really, really want to read Augie's book."

When Alida left, Lucy gazed at her notebook, her mind devoid of every thought except the certainty that she shouldn't have allowed things to turn out like this. The rats' nest of work all tangled up with friendship had placed her in a hopelessly compromised position. Whatever she wrote after this weekend was bound to be untrue. She tried to accuse herself of having too many scruples, but decided that the opposite was closer to the mark: she had too few.

She stared blankly out the window, and the fast-receding sea looked as glum and gray as she was feeling now.

MINNA WAS on her regular daily path through the grasses and Scotch broom, her basket filling with greenstuffs for a lunch salad. She'd looked forward to having Lucy's company, but Lucy was up in her room and Minna was shy of disturbing her. So she walked alone, letting her mind drift in whatever direction it chose.

This weekend took her back to the days when she and Augie were first married, and he used to invite his students back to their little rental house for end-of-semester parties. Minna loved these student parties, though she dreaded faculty ones, where the faculty wives were always asking her, "Where were you?" meaning "Were you at Bennington? Or OSU? Or Stanford?" Then she'd have to say she'd worked at Seafirst Bank. Then they'd ask what she did there, already looking for an excuse to walk away.

With students it was different—like it was with Lucy and Alida. But how they drank and smoked in those days! She had to fumigate the house after each party, but still was eager to throw the next one, where students introduced her to Ray Charles, Peter, Paul and Mary, the Beatles, the Rolling Stones, Dusty Springfield, the Beach Boys, and Bob Dylan, confided their love lives to her, and taught her to smoke pot. Augie never smoked any, but she loved how warm, colorful, and friendly the world seemed when she was high.

She and Augie used to go to the students' own, even wilder, parties, on falling-to-pieces old houseboats and in joss-stick-smelling walk-up flats, and always the invites came directly to her, though of course Augie was asked to come along, too. She could still recall the students' names—La Verne Geiger, Byford Starling, Melvin Kolar, Ron Schnowske, Betty Frailey, Kermit James, Arlo Fruin, Janet Bane . . . Strange how last week was hard to remember, when things so long ago were crystal clear.

Lucy and Alida somehow triggered these memories. Not that they were like students, but they'd brought with them into the house on Useless Bay some happy vestige of that mood. Minna wondered if Lucy liked Bob Dylan, then remembered her LPs wouldn't play on Augie's new stereo system. Minutes later, she recalled they'd got rid of them when they moved out here from Seattle. She'd wanted to hold a yard sale, but Augie had called in a charity for the blind to haul all their old junk away.

In the small stand of trees by the stream, she found three clumps of moist, honey-colored chanterelles. They'd go great tonight with the remainder of the beef burgundy. As she picked, she listened in her head to "Ballad of a Thin Man," Dylan singing, "Something is happening but you don't know what it is. Do you, Mr. Jones?"

It was when Mr. Johnson was president, she remembered, and the students were burning their draft cards, that all the parties stopped.

AFTER LUNCH they were up in the Jeffersonian study. Lucy surreptitiously scanned the shelves for novels and war memoirs, but didn't see a single one. Augie had been talking about his first days in America, first in New York, and then in Schenectady, where he'd "bached with" a Latvian-American widow.

"And the photo of you on the dust jacket—the one taken by Sergeant Cahan—you carried that with you wherever you went?"

"I didn't have too many papers—you can imagine. The Latvian aid people in New York got together what they could, including that picture. I still have the old brown envelope. There isn't much in it."

"I'd love to see it."

"Sure. I'll dig it out for you. Remind me."

"I don't suppose the name Thetford means anything to you, does it?"

"*Thetford* . . . Only Thetford I know is a town in England. I think it's in the Midlands—no, East Anglia. Minna and I, we vacationed over there once—I had to do some research, not on sand dollars, at the British Museum Library and the Bodleian in Oxford. We drove around

the country as much as we could, and spent one night in Norwich."
He said *Norwitch*. "They've got a castle there, and a cathedral that
Cromwell knocked around a bit. Thetford's near Norwich, I believe.
Seems like we drove through it but didn't stop. Why do you ask?"

"Because an odd woman from Thetford sent me this." She got the
photograph from her bag. "She thinks it could be you."

"Yeah, looks like me. Though it's difficult to make out the face." He
took it over to the window, tilting it to catch the diffuse sunlight.
"Why'd she send it to you?"

"Oh, you know. I've been trying to do some not-on-sand-dollars
research."

"Hey, what's that? And there's another, I think." He pulled open the
drawer of his desk and found a magnifying glass. "Look," he said, point-
ing at the dirt in the background, holding the glass over it. "Doesn't
that look to you like a chicken?"

Preoccupied with the boy and the barbed wire, she hadn't properly
attended to the dirt. There was a distinct but out-of-focus chicken
shape there, the same nearly black color as the earth.

"And there's the other one."

"You're absolutely right."

Augie laughed. "Couldn't be me. If I'd been that close to chickens in
those days, I wouldn't have been lallygagging by that fence. I'd be
wringing those critters' necks."

His tone was light, open, guileless. Lucy, certain now that she was
looking at a picture of Juris Abeltins, no relation to August Vanags, felt
giddy with relief. She said, "But isn't it a weird coincidence—that boy,
the wire, and all?"

"He looks like he's living in the land of plenty. So why's he all skin
and bone?"

"He had a disease called coeliac. His name was Juris Abeltins."

He corrected her pronunciation and said, "Latvian, like me." He
checked his watch. "Gotta go—date out on the water at four o'clock
sharp."

Looking out the window, she saw the sea was back. On the sand berm at the end of the lawn, Alida, in T-shirt and jeans, was buckling herself into a life vest. "Have a great paddle, or whatever one says."

She preceded him down the stairs. At the bottom, he said, "Juris Abeltins! Well, whaddaya know!"

He moved to join Alida on the berm, while Lucy went in search of Minna.

FOR AS LONG NOW as it seemed he could remember, he'd spent nearly all his time brooding in his office suite. It was torture to him to drag himself on his rounds through the city on necessary business; he got through it as fast as he could, then drove back to Occidental Avenue to tend his wounds. He wasn't awake and he wasn't asleep—at once fully conscious and in the grip of a terrible dream. No distraction worked. When he tried to read, the words were foreign symbols on the page. The cartoons he watched were meaningless colored drawings on a screen. He noticed neither darkness nor light outside. He ate, pissed, and shat—the only punctuations of his unending, unendurable days. Nothing could divert him from the memory of the scene in #701, at which his whole being went rigid with fury and shame.

One thing he knew: he was through with people business. Parking lots were clean, uncomplicated by comparison, generating a revenue stream as pure and untainted as a river gushing from a mountain crag, while the people business was as contaminated as a pipe of swirling sewage, drenching him in filth from head to foot.

Strange to think that only days before he'd looked on the Acropolis with love and pride. Now he wanted it gone—obliterated, wiped off the face of the city. His sole slow-dawning satisfaction lay in the thought of a giant wrecking ball smashing into the building, *Pow!* and *Pow!* again, reducing it to a heap of splinters and brick dust.

He'd show those fuckers—all of them, and especially the bitch in #701. They could live in the street along with the rest of the scumbags, making fires in buckets, digging in Dumpsters, begging for quarters, crying, fighting, sucking on their stupid bottles. The street was where garbage in human form belonged. They could scavenge in the alley beside the smoking red-dirt mountain that would be all that was left of the Acropolis.

Where the building had stood, he'd gouge a massive underground garage, multistory, deep as he could go, then lease the space above to some big commercial interest—supermarket, maybe, or bank. Let them build. He wanted only to destroy, right down to the infected foundations of the apartment block.

Pow! He saw the wrecking ball arc slowly through the air, the collapsing walls, the explosion into dust. For the first time since his excruciating humiliation, Charles O caught a distant glimmer of what it might be like to be himself again.

LUCY HAD GROWN to anticipate with pleasure Minna's regular graces before meals. The meals deserved them, and in her mouth the words "for health and food, for love and friends" sounded just right.

As soon as they sat down, Alida began asking Augie about his book. She was already ninety pages into it, and before dinner had told Lucy that it was "Good—*really* good."

"And you were really there? Everything really happened to *you?*"

"Oh, yes, but of course it was all a long, long time ago."

"If even some of that stuff happened to me, I would've turned out totally freaked and weird."

"You don't think I'm weird? I sure am—at least, if you ask some people. Your mother, for instance. She thinks I'm a fabulist and an exaggerator, that I make it up as I go along."

Aghast, reddening, Lucy said, "Augie! That's *not* true!"

He ignored her. Chuckling to Alida, he said, "You only have to see her face when I'm talking about the Islamist threat. She thinks I'm some nutty right-wing hyena. Oh, yes you do! Don't deny it! Alida, can you pass your mom the wine? She spends far too much of her time reading *The New York Times*—either that, or I really am the madman she believes me to be." To Lucy he said, "Don't think I haven't considered the possibility that my views may have been warped by my crazy childhood—yeah, it's possible, but of course I hold them to be entirely rational."

"To be honest," she said, "I sort of envy you your views. The trouble with me is I'm an agnostic about everything."

"I'm a believer. I've gotten to the age when it's smart to buy into Pascal's wager, but it's not God I believe in. You know what I believe in."

They ate in silence for a minute, then Augie said, "What Montaigne said about it? 'The old believe everything, the middle-aged suspect everything, and the young know everything'—though of course that old geezer never got the opportunity to meet Alida, which was his loss."

To beat the traffic, they set off late on Sunday morning after a light brunch, Alida doubly preoccupied in the passenger seat with her iPod and Augie's book. It was like driving alone, and for once Lucy was content to be left in solitude with her thoughts, which began to tumble from her mind as soon as they'd made the right turn at the end of Sunlight Beach Road.

Magically, the piece she'd thought unwritable was unfolding itself inside her head. *Woe to those who conclude!* as Augie had said. Which was what was wrong with most feature journalism, her own included. Profilists were no better than the hacks who went on a week's freebie in some five-star hotel in Venice, then came back to regale a credulous world with "their" Italy. The conceit of it! The idea that you could "capture" a city, a country, or a man in twenty-odd paragraphs; you might as well say you'd captured Seattle with a digital photo of the Space Needle, or, as Augie tiresomely insisted on calling it, the Space Noodle. The judicious tone, the summing up, the obituary-like placing of a terminal period at the end of your subject's "life"—all flummery and hokum, the smoke-and-mirrors of the journalist's trade. When she looked back on it, Lucy realized she'd tried to bury everyone she'd ever written about—Gates, Cobain, Jeff Bezos, everybody. Each piece had aimed at the finality of a tombstone. *Here lies the body of . . .* in five thousand words.

Well, not this piece. She imagined it rather as she expected a postmodern New York loft might look—all the beams and pipes of its construction, its artifice, would be not only exposed but highlighted. They, as much as August Vanags, would be its subject. It would be full of tourist snapshots of Augie on the patio, on the beach, lecturing a dinner table, up in his study quoting Montaigne and E. B. White, or out kayaking with Alida, who had to be in the picture, too. Augie with Minna, Augie trying to learn his Schubert sonata, Augie the European, Augie the American, Augie the neocon, Augie the nature-lover . . . But they would be just that—snapshots, nothing more, disjointed one from another like the capricious jumble of images that every camera-toting traveler brings back from a trip, some more in focus than others. They wouldn't add up, wouldn't form a narrative, because the narrative of this piece would lie elsewhere. The *GQ* guy had spoken of a "unicorn hunt." She'd catch a multitude of glimpses of the elusive unicorn, but the piece would be about the comic intricacies of the chase, and its ultimate futility.

They were on the ferry now, but Lucy didn't even remember parking on board, and there was no temptation to leave the car for the passenger lounge. Alida was as lost in her own thoughts as she was in hers.

She'd write about the journalist on the job: the phone call from the editor—the pen-in-hand race through the book—the rushed and skimpy library work—the routine Googling—the meeting with the subject—the leaps to judgment on the subject's "character"—the amateur espionage—the rapid shifts of mood and mind—the gathering suspicions—the trespassing back and forth across the border between reporting and friendship—all that and more. Lucy saw, but would not write, herself in the third person, as a harassed, untidy, inept figure, floundering out of her depth yet always puffed up by her habitual old illusion that there must be something to be gotten to the bottom of.

There'd be no bottom to this piece, no key to the "real" Augie, no problems solved, no pseudo-urbane assembly of Augie in legible and transparent form on the page. Rather, readers would find themselves in the same position as the writer—perplexed, fascinated, engaged, and sometimes repelled by August Vanags—just as aware of their own shortcomings as she was of hers, aware that facets and surfaces were just facets and surfaces, and that, like the writer, they must not conclude.

For these inconclusive times, it would be a topically inconclusive piece, and the most ambitious thing Lucy had ever tried to write. Augie wouldn't be hurt by it; she'd make him laugh at himself when he wasn't laughing at her. The visits and kayaking lessons would continue—maybe even through the writing of the piece—and their growing friendship would not be damaged. Yet she'd tell the truth. Most of all, she'd tell the truth about journalism, which was that ninety percent of the time there was no real truth to tell.

When the Union Street exit came up, Lucy was out of breath with her windfall cascade of ideas. She wanted to get a rough outline of the article down on paper before it slipped from the present and became something she had to ransack her bad memory for. Entering the apartment, she ignored the red flashes on her answering machine and went straight to her desk, notebook in hand. She'd never felt more certain of what needed to be done.

11

"MOM'S WRITING," Ali said.

"Ah, one of *those* days."

Ali was full of her trip, and Tad was happy to listen. Elementary Buddhism helped him suppress every niggle of what might otherwise have been his irritation at Ali's wide-eyed wonder at the marvels of this reactionary old coot. When she showed him the inscription in the book, he said, "Fantastic—cool how he calls himself uncool, huh?"

"He's pretty cool. We saw dogfish again when we were kayaking, and I wasn't scared at *all.*"

"You get your homework done?"

"Nah, it's just some math that'll only take half an hour."

"Bring it here. If your mom's so busy writing, I guess I can take care of dinner. I've got strawberries and cream, and pasta, and some pesto sauce that I made fresh. We can all feast on that."

"Great," Ali said. "Minna, that's his wife, she's like a gourmet cook."

Tad needed a few more grams of Buddhism for that.

Over Tad's pasta and pesto and ten-dollar wine, Lucy was in a state of silent distraction, hair all over the place like Struwwelpeter's. Declining the wine, she asked for water, a sure symptom of major mental disturbance. Every so often she'd rouse herself, or try to.

"Did *he* come here over the weekend?"

"I don't think so. He's probably sulking in his tent."

"Whose tent?" Ali said.

"Achilles' tent. The landlord's tent. We're talking about Mr. Lee."

"He's got a tent?"

"It's just an expression," Lucy said. "Achilles was this ancient Greek who spent a lot of time sulking in his tent." Which was about as near as she came to sociability during the course of the entire meal. When she left, after eating three strawberries, she said, "Tad—God, I'm sorry I'm so elsewhere. But thank you. It was lovely."

"Go enjoy your elsewhere." Tad kissed her, cheek to cheek. "It's not as if we're not used to it, honey. We just wish you were on medication."

Tad and Ali washed the dishes, then played chess.

Ali took Tad's last bishop with her knight. "Check . . . *mate!*"

"The king is dead," Tad said.

BY TEN O'CLOCK, Lucy had covered twenty-five pages of her notebook with scrawled notes. To bring off what she wanted to do, in seven thousand words or less, would take extraordinary craft and guile. There was material here for a full-length book about the relationship between journalist and subject, and the prospect of the sheer labor involved in boiling it down to an article made her feel defeated before she'd even begun. But in the morning it would all look different. She needed the fresh eye that she'd bring back from the school run.

Dog-tired, she checked her messages. There were three of them, all from Mrs. Tillman, each more testy than the last, demanding to know whether the package had arrived. It was too early to call England now, and Lucy was damned if she'd stay up till after midnight. More than anything, she craved sleep.

At five A.M. she was punished by the insistent trilling of the phone. She groggily reached for the receiver in the dark.

"Marjie Tillman—I've been trying to reach you since Friday."

"I'm sorry, we were away for the weekend. . . . just got back. When I got your messages, it was still too early to call you. But thank you, yes, it did come. Excuse me, I'm not too c-c-c-c-c-coherent right now, you see it's five in the morning here and I was—"

"Five? It's surely eight!"

Mrs. Tillman was accusing her of self-serving deception. "No, no—it's eight on the East Coast, like in New York, but we're three hours behind out here. It's only five."

"Well, in that case, perhaps you—"

"No, honestly, I'm awake now, we can t-t-talk—" Better to deal with this call straightaway than to wake again at seven with it still hanging over her head. To get to her piece, she needed to be done with this peremptory and deluded pest. "But thanks so much for getting the picture to me so fast—it must've wrecked your day. I'm hugely grateful to you."

"So now you see."

"Sorry?"

"It's *him*."

Speaking gently, trying as best she could not to offend, Lucy explained the differences between the two photos—the change in lighting, the overexposure of Juris Abeltins' face, exactly how the two sets of barbed wire looked not quite the same. She said, "And then there are the chickens. If you look carefully at the picture of J-J-J-Juris you can see chickens pecking in the background. That's obviously taken on your farm. But there isn't a single chicken in the V-V-Vanags one."

"Well, of course not!" She spoke as if Lucy were a total half-wit. "They use airbrushes and things!"

Lucy remembered the brown envelope of papers that had accompanied Augie all the way from Germany to Useless Bay. He'd asked her to remind him to dig it out for her, and, maddeningly, in the happy conviviality of Saturday's dinner, when she'd gotten more than a little drunk, she had neglected to do so. The contents of that envelope would prove everything.

"Marjie, August Vanags has papers to prove his identity. He's not your Juris Abeltins."

"Papers? What papers?"

"Well . . ." For inspiration, she rummaged in her memory for the background reading she'd undertaken more than two weeks ago. She had to somehow rid herself of this madwoman at the far end of the line. "There's a sort of temporary passport issued by . . ." Who would it be issued by, the embassy? Did they even have an embassy there then? "By the American authorities in Berlin. Then there's . . . a l-l-l-letter from his sponsors, a group of Latvians in New York. There's another letter from Sergeant C-C-Cahan, the soldier who took care of him for a while. Oh, and there's another one from someone in UNNRA, an Englishwoman, like you. She was in charge of displaced children at the c-c-c-c-camp. . . ." Surely that would do. "And of course there's the ph-ph-ph-ph-photograph on the book."

"What's the date on this so-called passport?"

"I'm not sure. I think . . . August or S-S-September in 1945?"

"You can't place it more exactly than that?"

"No."

"And you've seen all these 'papers'?"

Lucy paused fractionally before saying yes. That she hadn't seen them was, after all, her own silly fault. And if they weren't precisely as she'd described them, they must be very similar. There was no doubt in her mind as to the existence of the brown envelope.

Thousands of miles away in Thetford, Norfolk, there was silence. Evidently Mrs. Tillman was taking time to adjust to the fact that she'd been wrong from the start. At last, her voice came back on the line. "Miss Bengstrom?"

"Yes?"

"*If* these 'papers' exist—which I have to say, with all due respect, I rather doubt—they're forgeries."

A click at the other end, and then the dial tone.

IT *HAD* BEEN FIVE in the morning, after all—a time when anyone could be forgiven for being, as Augie liked to say, a few sandwiches short of a picnic. Besides, Marjorie Tillman was both unbelievably rude and downright crazy, possessed by her unshakable but totally bogus idée fixe. If she really had anything on Augie, as opposed to Juris

Abeltins, she'd have said so in her letter, which Lucy pulled out and read carefully again. It was simply a long, tedious complaint about the immense inconvenience to which her family had been put by harboring the boy. There were rambling, digressive paragraphs about ration books, the coeliac stuff, the Jenny Lind Hospital, and something they'd had to eat, apparently called snoek, if Lucy was reading the word right; rants about a politician named Herbert Morrison, the bananas that had to be specially flown in, about the indignities of being forced to raise chickens; scattered admiration for "Winnie," whom Lucy took to mean Churchill; but otherwise only ingratitude—how could the child be so ungrateful to his benefactors? There was nothing *whatsoever* to connect Juris Abeltins with August Vanags. No wonder the poor kid had never written back to the Vickers family, who appeared to have treated him like Oliver Twist in the workhouse.

Yes, she'd lied, but not only was it five in the morning, she'd lied in the service of the truth, trying to rid this unpleasant woman of a vengeful fiction that had its entire basis in a chance glimpse of a dust jacket in a bookstore. For what else was there? And Mrs. Tillman hadn't caught her in her lie; she was merely desperate to evade the truth, which was that she was living in Fantasyland. It was written all over her letter, and palpable in her every pronouncement: the bitch was a fucking psycho.

Yet against all reason her adamantine certainty still shook Lucy, *They're forgeries!* continuing to ring in her head, a measure of the power of even psychotic certainty to sway one's feelings in spite of one's better judgment. Spend enough time with the mad and you'll catch their madness, because sanity is a fragile, feeble, defenseless thing when battered by the intractable, lunatic conviction exemplified by Mrs. Tillman. It was weak of Lucy to feel so shaken.

She badly wanted to drive back to Useless Bay and get Augie to show her the papers in that envelope. She thought of phoning him now; he could make photocopies in Langley, FedEx them over, and she'd have them in hand tomorrow. That'd stop Tillman's toxic shit. But then, of course, having described them in such probably inaccurate detail, Lucy could hardly send copies to Thetford, because now they'd really look like forgeries.

Last night, she'd so looked forward to this morning, to reading through her notes and seeing how she could pull this story off elegantly, economically, in a space that *GQ* could print without cutting. But that phone call had blighted the day. She'd never gotten to sleep again and had squandered the next two hours rearranging the pillows to find a cool surface on which to rest her hot head. She felt jangled and hungover, though she hadn't had so much as a sip of wine on Sunday.

She read over what she'd written yesterday. Here and there it was hard to decode her own handwriting, so fast and excitedly had she been scribbling. But overnight all excitement had leaked out of the words. What was she trying to do—reinvent New Journalism? Surely Janet Malcolm had already done this in . . . what was it called, *The Journalist and the Murderer*? Not quite this exactly, but uncomfortably close. In her twenty-five pages, she found only four or five that still seemed workable, and they were all Augie-specific and indistinguishable from how she might have written about any other subject. She told herself she was too tired, too rattled by the madwoman, to fairly judge what she was reading, but that tomorrow she might perhaps be able to recapture the elation and ambition that yesterday had her so firmly in their grip.

Gazing dispiritedly at her notebook, Lucy thought that had Mrs. Tillman been anywhere in the vicinity, she'd willingly have slit her throat.

FINN'S VALUE seemed to have shrunk over the weekend from ten to zero. He was just another boy now, doing such Finn-ish things as covertly picking his boogers and scowling lumpishly into space. Alida, having zoomed through the page of math problems, alternated between spying on him and doodling on the piece of scrap paper covered with her calculations.

First, she drew kayaks. She was really bad at art, and Gail's pictures put hers to shame. But her kayaks, slicing through the water, looked real enough to feed her daydreaming. Then she tried the dogfish, which were a lot more difficult, though their mean jaws, set low and far behind their long blunt noses, were easy enough; those, and their piggy little eyes. It was the rest of them that was the problem, and Alida's dogfish repeatedly turned into ferocious goldfish. When dogfish swam close to the surface, she wondered, did their dorsal fins stick out like other sharks'?

She longed for the bell. Humanities was next, and she needed to catch Mr. Tonelli early to ask if she could do her book report on *Boy 381*.

She'd brought the book to school, wrapped in a plastic bag, and carefully placed atop all the other stuff in her backpack. She wanted to show Gail—and maybe Emma—the inscription.

ACT WELL, and you'd live; act ill, and you'd soon die. This was Tad's one medical theory, to which he tried scrupulously to adhere. On visits to Brian, his doctor, he sat in the waiting room taking deep breaths, preparing to go onstage. When called, he gamboled into the examination room, not quite like a spring lamb, but at least like a man of, say, forty-five, who wasn't HIV . . . His handshake was firm, his smile wide and confident, and his cheeks bore only slight, nearly invisible traces of cosmetic color to convey the impression of someone in a state of ruddy, impregnable good health.

He and Brian went through the routine: weight, blood pressure, chest and back, blood sample.

Brian went to the sink, took off his latex gloves, and washed his hands. "Stools?" he said.

"The usual. Not too light and not too dark."

Before Michael got sick, they used to sometimes see Brian in a gay bar, now long closed, on Capitol Hill. They'd socialized a little, the three of them, talking work and politics and gossip while sizing up newcomers. Brian had a roving eye, especially for young black men. Michael had been first to go to Brian as a doctor; Tad had followed, shortly after his death. Their relationship now was mostly guarded and professional, doc and patient, though sometimes Brian still let his mask slip and became, momentarily, a friend.

Tad couldn't quite put his finger on it, but this morning it seemed to him that Brian, too, was acting. His voice was just a little too detached, too professional, his examination a shade too perfunctory. Tad was out of the doctor's office within fifteen minutes, armed with Brian's usual reassurances, yet less than usually reassured by them.

Stepping onto the sidewalk, he first felt fear. Brian was holding out on him, knew something he wasn't telling—bad news he couldn't bring himself to deliver on this sunny but cold April morning, with the wind blowing unseasonably out of the mountains to the east. Then it occurred to him that what Brian was holding back was something about himself. Last time, he'd said cheerily, as Tad thought then, "I'll be pushing up daisies before you do."

What was it, cancer? Tad thought, then felt a rush of sympathy and pity. It would be even worse for a doctor; unlike Tad, Brian couldn't believe that he might act his way out of the disease, and would review the biopsies with the same clinical absence of illusion he directed to those of his patients.

Tad next reverted to his first thought. It wasn't Brian's condition, but his own. He was trying to shield him from the death sentence, and perhaps would call him up later, inviting himself to a drink at Tad's apartment in order to break the dire news to him there. He was dreading Brian's anticipated call when he switched tack again, back to worrying about the illness Brian was so bravely trying to hide from Tad.

He wished he'd spoken up in the office. They knew each other well enough, surely, for Tad to say, "Come on, Brian, come clean with me." But he'd been so busy maintaining his own character that any such line would've broken the vaudeville rules of their established double act. Now he was stuck with the worst of both worlds, fearing for both himself and Brian without knowing who, or what, or why.

Crossing Second, he ran into traffic stalled by a shoal of Humvees clad in camo netting, with troops around the Scoop Jackson Federal Building, arms at the ready. Streets were blocked off with tape and cops. Far up on Second, somebody was barking something through a megaphone, but Tad couldn't make out the words. Just one more scare to be ignored.

Puffing up Adams Street, pausing for breath midway between intersections, he thought, *It's me,* then *No, it's Brian,* then *Maybe I was just imagining the whole thing.* Down by the federal building, the emergency vehicles, honking and wailing about what would almost certainly turn out to be nothing, were sending him a personal message.

SEATED AT HIS LAPTOP, he clicked on Word, and when the blank page came up he selected from the control panel first 150%, then Arial Black, then 48-point type, then Bold, then Underline. Prodding at the keys with his forefingers, he typed:

<u>NOTICE OF DEMOLITION</u>

Looked good. He thought the dense, black, official appearance of his handiwork would scare the living shit out of the fuckers when they found it in their mailboxes.

He reset the controls and with his old *Webster's New World Pocket Dictionary*—its pages now held together with a fat rubber band—at his elbow, began to compose the letter to his tenants:

Sir or Madam:

AFTER A LUNCH that included a cautious glass of chardonnay, Lucy's spirits rose a little, and when she went back to her desk she felt ready to write the first of what she thought of as her "snapshots." She chose this one at random: Augie at the piano, his thick and blunt "shade-tree mechanic's" fingers splayed awkwardly across the keys, white mustache bristling as he squinted intently at the score on the stand.

For help, she went over to the stereo and put on Stephen Kovacevich's recording of Schubert's last piano sonata—as she'd thought, an insanely ambitious piece for a raw beginner. The first movement, molto moderato, wasn't moderate at all. It began with a deceptively simple, plangent tune, but within moments one began to hear darkness in the ominous rumble of the bass; then the music rushed and slowed, rushed and slowed, continually dissolving from gentle, elegiac lyricism into crash and clangor. As the notes that came with the CD said, it was "as if the grim reaper himself were present, forbidding any touch of solace, let alone *Gemütlichkeit.*" The emotional swings—sweetness to fear, threat to anger—followed so fast on one another that Lucy could hardly keep up with them. Bipolar Schubert, with his alternating bursts of mania and depression, seemed to be in the room with her as she listened. He'd died at thirty-one, dogged by failures in love and his musical career, and riddled with syphilis, according to Grove's great musical dictionary.

Augie himself would surely die long before he could play just this first movement with anything remotely like Kovacevich's sureness of touch and feeling.

First she tried writing in the past tense, then changed to the present. *Vanags*—no, *Augie—sits at his brand-new Steinway grand. . . .* The paragraph was brief, mainly about his haphazard fingering. By 3:25, when she had to go pick up Alida from school, she had three paragraphs she could live with: Augie murdering Schubert, Augie discovering the gumboot chiton, and Augie displaying his presidential cuff links. Not bad for half an afternoon, considering.

Though the sun was out, it was still too cold to drop the Spider's top. And driving to school, she found herself beset by the question she'd been fighting off all day: why was Mrs. Tillman so keen to know the exact date of the temporary passport that Lucy had invented for him?

RICH ON her sand-dollar money, Alida wanted to catch Mr. Kawasuki's Almost Antiques before he closed the store at six.

"You finished your homework already?" Her mom didn't even look up from her writing.

"Yeah, it wasn't much."

"Don't be too long, Rabbit—and watch out crossing the street."

12

RATHER THAN TRUST the slow and temperamental elevator, Alida ran down the stairwell and, in the foyer, saw Mr. Lee stuffing letters into the bank of mailboxes.

"Hi," she said, but he didn't turn or even make a grunt of recognition. It was like talking to a deaf person. Too weird. Once past him, she pushed through the double doors onto the sidewalk and looked both ways, but there was no traffic.

Alida had taken two steps from the sidewalk when suddenly she felt wobbly—almost, but not quite, falling-down wobbly—and had to plant both feet wide to steady herself.

Her first thought was that she'd been hit by a lightning strike of stomach flu; then she heard the car alarms, hundreds of them, coming from all across the city. On the far side of the street she saw the water bowl that Mr. Kawasuki always kept full. It stood under a notice saying "For Our Four-Legged Friends," as if dogs could read. Now water was slopping out of it, rocking west to east and east to west, and as she watched the level in the bowl sank by more than an inch.

She heard the foundations of the buildings grinding, deep down, against rock, like they were being gnawed by a tribe of giant rats.

Four feet from Mr. Kawasuki's dog bowl, a hairline crack showed in the sidewalk, then came snaking across the pavement toward her, made an abrupt swerve, and headed off in the direction of downtown. The crack widened, became a rift and then an open trench. Alida had never guessed how much went on below the surface of Adams Street—the bundled cables of different colors, the rows of pipes. It was like seeing a massive wound open in the body of the city, exposing all its internal organs, its intestines and ganglia and stuff. Augie's word "infrastructure" came back to her. So this was what infrastructure looked like. She caught the stink of shit from a sewer pipe; then the trench started to fill with a firehose-stream of water from a burst main.

She'd been a little kid during the last big earthquake, which happened one morning when she was in preschool. Teacher Ellen had told everybody to hide under the tables, which was kind of fun at the time, and they'd stayed there, huddled together, giggling, long after the temblor was over, with their teacher yelling hysterically about "aftershocks."

No tables to hide under here. Too many bricks and tiles and things were falling onto the sidewalk for her to lurch back to the steps of the Acropolis. Looking for shelter, she saw the Spider, parked in front of Mr. Kawasuki's shop, but just then a falling piece of masonry dropped right through the top, leaving a mouthlike gash in the tan vinyl. God, how her mom would hate that gash.

Tad's heap was parked maybe fifty yards away—too far, she thought—and then was gone, as the front wall of the old spice warehouse detached itself from the rest of the building, wavered for several moments, and collapsed sluggishly onto the street, burying the car under a hill of smoking bricks. She bet that when they eventually dug the VW out of the rubble it would still work. Tad's old car was like immortal, and he wouldn't care about the dents—he'd be proud of them.

Alida thought it was best to stay on the pavement, as near to the middle as she could. She managed three steps, tottering as she went, and then sat down on the asphalt, hugging her knees.

It was odd how very slowly things were falling—thirty-two feet per second was the usual rule, but gravity didn't seem to be working normally this evening. A tile would float down like it was suspended on a parachute or something, with Alida following its every movement during its casual, leisurely descent.

Below the overflowing trench, Adams Street had become a shallow river, trickling down to Elliott Bay, where Alida saw the strangest thing yet: the sea had disappeared and a ferry was stranded, leaning halfway over, on a bank of exposed mud, showing its rust-colored bottom, as if some crazy, drunken captain had been in charge.

She wished someone could put a stop to all those car alarms, whose noise was so *distracting*.

Looking up, she saw the Acropolis bulge outward as if it were being pumped up like a balloon from within. Then a narrow, zigzag crack ran helter-skelter down the brickwork from the top story to the bottom. But the building held. It looked like a big old cypress tree, shaken but not toppled by a violent wind.

Alida wasn't afraid. She felt as she had the day before, watching the dogfish—she in her world, they in theirs, with a sort of protective glassy film dividing them. Comfortable, now that she was sitting down, she concentrated on making observations, like she was going to have to write an essay on the earthquake. The last one—they'd done a project on it—had been a 6.8, and Seattle had been miles north of its epicenter in Nisqually. This one felt bigger. Much bigger. Alida figured it might even be an 8.0. The Richter Scale was like *exponential*: a 7.0 was ten times stronger than a 6.0, so an 8.0 would be really, really big.

All of downtown was *shivering*: the Smith Tower, the office skyscrapers, every building in sight had got the shakes. When she hadn't been looking, the witch's-hat top of the Smith Tower had disappeared—hatless, it looked funny, like it was naked. Glass was falling all around her, and every window was flexing in its frame—but how weirdly pliable and stretchy glass turned out to be! Then they reached the breaking point, crazed over, and came floating down into the street in a zillion little pieces, making a sound like churning surf. Several windows were gone from the Acropolis, and in the empty spaces Alida could see people's stuff—books, bottles, ornaments, CDs, plates and dishes—sailing lazily in air.

Down below ground, the grinding noises were getting louder, the rats really getting their teeth into the job.

From somewhere, she couldn't tell where, came the long, tumbling thunder of what must be a building coming down. But from where she sat, all she could see was a trembling city, still more or less intact, shivering on the brink of she knew not what. It seemed like not just Seattle but the whole country must be like this, caught in the grip of a delirious rippling and shuddering that wouldn't stop.

The dog bowl was almost empty now, the sidewalks steadily heaping up with smashed stucco, smashed bricks, smashed tiles, smashed glass. But in the middle of the street it was okay, at least so far, though when Alida felt the ground beneath her moving like it had muscles, it made her think of horseback riding: she was riding the quake, saddle joggling underneath her, holding on.

Amazing that the bottom of Elliott Bay was bared. With the sea gone so far out, how and when would it return?

It came to her, as she saw the Smith Tower go into a kind of slow corkscrew motion, twisting impossibly, defying whatever law of physics ought to govern steel frames, wood, and terra-cotta, that never ever had she been so piercingly conscious of her own singular existence in the world.

A cat—one of Mr. Kawasuki's—bolted across the road, a yowling streak of stand-on-end orange fur, and its terror roused her from her dreamy detachment. Where was Tad? Had her mom taken shelter safely? This temblor was going on *forever*. For the first time since the quake began, Alida felt fear, a wrenching twist of ice in her bowels. The chorus of car alarms was joined by a mad band of sirens and whistles, and, from somewhere close by, a thin and lonely cry, like a sheet being torn down the middle, that Alida was shocked to realize was her own.

MINNA, sitting on the patio, was puzzled. She was certain Augie had said the tide was coming in and that's why he'd be going out in his kayak before dinner. Yet she could see the water withdrawing from the bay, retreating to the cold deeps of Puget Sound. One by one, new turtle-backed sandbanks were surfacing. Either she or Augie must have got it wrong. It was probably her mistake; she got so muddled nowadays, and had never understood the mystery of the tides. Augie had tried more than once to explain the phases of the moon and the force of gravity, but she hadn't listened properly. Now, watching the sea draining from the land, she felt a little safer in herself, as she always did at low tide; she just wished it would stay that way. She was glad that Augie wouldn't be kayaking this evening. They could have an early supper of clams in a sauce of shallots, parsley, cream, and cheese, and Minna thought that in a few minutes she'd better start preparing the sauce.

She heard the sudden clatter of Augie's footsteps coming down the uncarpeted stairs.

"Minna? Minna? *Minna!*"

Jiminy crickets! What did he want now?

A NOTE ABOUT THE TYPE

The Hoefler Text and Hoefler Titling families of typefaces, designed by Jonathan Hoefler, were designed to celebrate some favorite aspects of two beloved Old Style typefaces: Janson and Garamond No. 3. Unwittingly, the names Janson and Garamond both honor men unconnected with these designs: Janson is named for Dutch printer Anton Janson, but based on types cut by Hungarian punchcutter Nicholas Kis; Garamond is a revival of types thought to have originated with Claude Garamond in the sixteenth century, but in fact made a century later by Swiss typefounder Jean Jannon. Hoefler Text and Hoefler Titling are published by the digital typefoundry Hoefler & Frere-Jones.

Composed by Stratford Publishing Services, Brattleboro, Vermont
Printed and bound by Berryville Graphics, Berryville, Virginia
Designed by Robert C. Olsson